Timeless Treasure

MaryLu TYNDALL

Timeless Treasure
by MaryLu Tyndall

Library of Congress Cataloging-in-Publication Data is on file at the Library of Congress, Washington, DC.

ISBN-13 978-1-7344420-4-5
E-Version ISBN: 978-1-7344420-3-8

Cover Design by Ravv at raven.com
Editor: Louise M. Gouge

RANS☉M
PRESS

Dedication
***To all who have wandered away from the only true path
to life***

*There is a way that seems right to a man and appears
straight before him, but at the end of it is the way of death.
Proverbs 16:25*

.

If you wish to see character pictures and scenes from the book
while you're reading, visit my Pinterest page at

https://www.pinterest.com/mltyndall/timeless-treasure/

CHAPTER ONE

Lexington, Virginia, Present Day

Lexie Cain was completely and utterly alone in the world. Glancing over the cluttered attic, she drew a deep breath and watched as specks of dust turned to glitter in the sunlight spearing through the window. If only the dust of her life would transform into diamonds as well. But that was not to be. Not with her mother now six feet under.

The only person who loved her. The only person who cared.

Now what? She pursed her lips, searching for the small antique chest filled with God knew what...family photos? Birth certificates? Deeds? No, not deeds. No one in her family had ever owned any property. No one in her family had anything to brag about except how many times they had eluded the law. There would be no family holiday photos filled with smiling faces, warm embraces, and elaborate feasts. No letters filled with wisdom handed down from generations long since passed, no family heirlooms or trinkets or medals to make a person proud. Then why had her mother made Lexie promise to find the chest and keep it safe?

Skirting a stack of boxes taller than her 5'5" frame, Lexie tripped over an old golf bag stuffed with rusty clubs, then stubbed her toe on the foot of a broken-down desk blanketed in dust.

"Ouch!" She bent down to rub it when the ladder to the attic creaked, and the one face she hoped never to see again popped up through the hatch.

"I thought you had all your stuff." George Bennet rose like a sea monster from the deep, lips in a pinch and nose wrinkling as he took in the dusty attic. "You better not be taking anything of mine." Hunched over to avoid striking his head on the low beams, he brushed imaginary dirt from the sleeves of the expensive tailor-made suit he'd worn to the funeral.

"Why would I want anything of yours?" Lexie spat out as she stepped over pails of emergency food, hoping if she ignored her stepfather, he'd go away.

No such luck.

He snorted. "You had no trouble taking my money all these years."

Her stomach clenched, and she closed her eyes for a moment. *I will not let him get to me. I will not. Not today.*

"Who bailed you out of Juvie when you were sixteen? Who put a roof over your head and food in your stomach these past five years? Hmm?"

Brushing away a cobweb, Lexie skirted an old bicycle and flipped on her flashlight. Why the man was asking questions they both knew the answers to was beyond her. She shone the light in a dark corner. There. What looked like an old chest sat buried beneath boxes.

"Who paid for your college the past two years?" He uttered that annoying loud sigh that rang with disappointment and disdain. "Then you just quit anyway. But what did I expect?"

That did it.

Spinning around, Lexie faced him, gulping down a slew of nasty names she longed to call him. "I quit school because Mom got can…"—she could hardly bring herself to even say the word—"cancer, and you refused to help take care of her."

Hands on his hips, he stared at her with the same look he'd always directed toward her, like she was a nuisance he longed to be rid of. "I offered to pay for a home nurse."

"She needed family, *George*." She knew he hated it when she used his first name. The subsequent twitch of his eye gave her some small satisfaction. He wasn't family. He'd never been family. Her mother had married him merely so he could help Lexie. She knew that now. George was a powerful lawyer who had freed Lexie from prison to do community service instead of time. Then with his money, he'd lifted her and her mom out of poverty, given them a nice home and Lexie a good education.

But it had come at a great cost.

"Would you have allowed her to die in a stranger's arms?" she continued. No, her mother had died in Lexie's arms, breathed her last in painful agony. Tears filled Lexie's eyes, but she blinked them back. Not in front of this man. Not when she had not seen him shed a single tear.

A waft of his expensive aftershave stung her nose. "That's been your problem all along, Lex. You don't appreciate anything. You're spoiled rotten. You expect handouts just like your mother."

"Don't!" Her shout startled even her. Dust sprinkled from above as the pitter-patter of little feet made her cringe. "Don't speak of her. Not today. Not ever."

Shaking his head, he flattened his lips. "I want you out of my house today."

"As you made quite clear. I'm taking my mom's old family chest, and then you'll never see me again."

"Be quick about it. I'll be downstairs to make sure you don't take anything else." He turned to start down the ladder. "*And* to get your key."

Anger fired every nerve until she felt she would burst. Still, she offered no response. It wouldn't do any good. The man was a heartless fiend. And she was now homeless. Homeless and penniless.

"Oh, Mom." Forcing back tears yet again, she made her way to the chest, moved the stack of boxes from the top, and knelt to examine the lock. "I miss you. What am I supposed to do now? And why did you care so much about this old chest?"

There was no lock. Just a latch, which Lexie flipped open, then raised the lid. The musty scent of age and mold blasted over her as she shined the flashlight over the contents.

Notebooks, papers, an old photo album, a few small jewelry boxes, and a large scrapbook.

Picking up the photo album, she brushed off the dirt and examined it. She should just close the chest and take it to her car. But if she took her time, sifted through the belongings, it would irritate George, keep him from the office and his *very important* work that always took precedence over everything else. And oh, how she loved to irritate George.

The first picture was of her mother when she was young, probably Lexie's age, standing arm in arm with a handsome man. Drawing the flashlight closer, Lexie squinted. Her father? It had to be. He had the same light blond hair she did, the same green eyes, both of which she had not inherited from her mother. They looked happy. In love. She'd never really seen her mother happy before. The picture blurred beneath tears she could no longer hold back. He left them six months after Lexie was born. She'd never met him, but her mom said he was in prison somewhere. Armed robbery.

Her emotions far too raw, she swiped the tears from her face and closed the album, unable to look at any more pictures. Setting it aside, she picked up a stained cloth. No, a blanket. Baby blanket? Hers? Drawing it to her nose, she took a deep breath, but all she smelled was mold and decay. Just like her life. Beneath it, she shoved through what looked like her school papers and report cards, surprised and touched her mother had kept them. Then from the bottom of the chest she drew out what appeared to be an old leather scrapbook. Holding the flashlight up, she opened it and sifted through the contents. Nothing but a dozen or so antique papers preserved within sealed plastic sleeves. Odd. The writing was an elaborate cursive and difficult to read, but she could make out the signature at the bottom of the first letter—Stede Bonnet.

The name filtered through her mind, pricking her memory. Hadn't her mother mentioned this man long ago? Wasn't he a distant relative of theirs? And a *pirate*, if she remembered. She *did* remember that fact because it had shamed her, along with everything else about her family history. And she had not wanted to know any more. Her mother had never mentioned it again.

Slamming the scrapbook shut, Lexie picked up a jewelry box. Maybe her mother had kept something of value Lexie

MaryLu Tyndall

could use to support herself until she got a job. She pried it open and found an aged gold coin inside. Picking it up, she rubbed her finger over etchings, trying to make out the words. It was remarkably heavy, which meant it was probably solid gold. A four-leaf clover was etched in the center with what looked like scepters piercing the sides. In the middle of the clover was a four-sided cross, while Spanish words circled the outside of the coin. She flipped it over. A crown and a shield, along with more Spanish words, were engraved on the back. Wait. There was something out of place. R-T-10-7 had been carved into the coin. Some kind of code? She held the flashlight closer to the year. 1718? Was she reading it right? Whoa. Over three hundred years ago. This thing must be worth a fortune!

She allowed herself a shred of hope. Didn't pirates hide treasure? Maybe that's what these old letters were about, clues to buried treasure. And this coin was just a sample. Picking up the first letter, she noted it had been sent to some woman in Charles Town, Carolina. Could that be Charleston, South Carolina? Only one way to find out.

"Thank you, Mom." Pocketing the coin, Lexie closed the chest and hauled it across the attic and down the ladder, feeling more optimistic about her future than she had in a long while.

CHAPTER TWO

November 2, 1716, Barbados, Caribbean

Stede Bonnet knelt before the tiny grave and placed a bouquet of begonias near the marker. He still could not bring himself to read the engraving on the stone, though he well knew what it said.

In Memory of
Allamby Bonnet, Beloved Son
Born May 15, 1712
Departed this life, November 2, 1712

Why he could not recover from the loss of this precious boy, his firstborn, was a question Bonnet asked himself every day. He'd since had other children, two boys, in fact, and another child soon to be born. He owned a massive estate, possessed great wealth, a wife, a liberal education, and was a gentleman of good reputation—everything anyone could want. But the loss of his precious Allamby still haunted him.

In truth, it tormented him.

The dark clouds that had stolen the sunlight early that morning now hovered heavy and low above him. Thunder rumbled in the distance, and the light *pitter-pat* of rain sounded on the leaves of the palm and calabash trees surrounding the family grave site. Fitting weather for such a dismal scene. Fitting for the darkness that enveloped his heart.

The snap of a twig, followed by a light footfall, alerted Bonnet, and he rose to his full height and glanced around. It couldn't be his wife, Mary. She'd never mourned Allamby more than a week. After the funeral, she had yet to come to his grave and pay her respects. Not even on the date of his death.

Leaves rustled, and Bonnet gripped the pommel of the blade hanging at his side but instantly released it when the one face he longed to see emerged from the greenery.

Melody. Dear, sweet, Melody.

Dashing for her, he took her hands in his and brought them to his lips for a kiss. "You came."

"Of course, my love." Sapphire blue eyes stared up at him, naught but love pouring from within them.

Releasing her hands, he drew her close, pressing her head against his chest and inhaling the sweet scent that was uniquely hers—a mixture of jasmine and rose *and* Melody.

She embraced him tightly. And for the next few precious moments, there was naught in the world but her. No grave, no death, no obligations or responsibilities, no ground beneath them or storm above. 'Twas just them, two hearts melding into one.

Finally, reluctantly, he nudged her from him, his eyes roving over her, soaking in her beauty like a man denied water for days. Wisps of alabaster hair peeked from within the hood of her cloak, fluttering over the creamy skin of her elegant cheekbones. Pink, plump lips, a spry little nose, and a grove of dark lashes surrounding her eyes completed the exceptional beauty of his Melody.

Yet 'twas not her beauty that attracted him, but her heart, the beauty of which would never fade. He ran a thumb over her cheek. "I've missed you."

"And I you." She glanced at Allamby's grave. "I knew you'd be here. On this day. How could I stay away?"

Bonnet smiled. "It pleases me greatly you did not."

Thunder moaned above them as if angry with the proceedings below.

Retreating, she hugged herself, a sudden sorrow tainting her glistening eyes. The *pitter* of rain transformed into plops, dripping from leaves and striking the ground.

"What is it?" He reached for her, but she looked away.

"I am to leave Barbados."

Bonnet's heart felt as though it sank into a grave beside his son. "What madness is this?"

She swallowed as her eyes grew misty. "My father is moving us to Charles Town, a city in the colony of Carolina."

Wind swept over them, bringing the scent of the sea and the sting of rain.

Bonnet took a step toward her, his mind and heart reeling. "For what purpose?"

"He feels he has served God's will here and wishes to preach to the barbarians who inhabit the American Colonies." She pulled her hood further over her head against the rain. "Word comes to him that Charles Town is full of brigands, pirates, and heathens."

Bonnet stared at his son's grave, watching the rain create tiny craters of mud in the dirt. "I cannot lose you…too."

"My dear Stede." Her pleading tone brought his gaze back to her. "We must face the truth that I am not yours to lose. You chose another and are now wed. And with *three* children." She glanced toward the plantation house on the hill.

"I wanted you. You know I wanted you as my wife." Withholding a curse, Bonnet lifted the collar of his coat against the rain.

"But you would not defy your guardian, Mrs. Whetstone's, final wishes." She lowered her chin.

A mistake Bonnet paid for every day. "'Twas my father's wishes enforced from the grave through her." His father had not thought the daughter of a poor parson a worthy bride for a landed aristocrat.

"I beg you, Stede. Give Mary the love she deserves."

"She is a shrew," he hissed.

"You mustn't."

"I cannot deny the truth. Her constant nagging and bickering would drive a priest to pirate."

Melody approached and touched his arm. "I pray 'tis not me who has put a wedge between you."

"Nay, my love." He took her hand in his. "'Tis true my heart belongs to you and no other. Yet I would accept my marriage. I would make an effort to be a good husband if only she were...."

"Me?" She gave a sad smile.

"Nay. No one could come close to you."

Lightning stabbed the dark sky, mimicking the pain in his heart, as the raindrops grew larger.

Melody fumbled with her hood but finally gave up and swept it behind her, unleashing a cascade of ivory curls. "I merely wish for your happiness, Stede."

"How can I be happy when I shan't ever see you again?" He gently wiped raindrops from her face. "At least here on Barbados, I might catch a glimpse of you in the market, at soirees, and at church. And, of course, speak with you, touch you, hold you in my arms at secret meetings such as these. 'Tis all I live for."

She stood there gazing at him with such love and sorrow, he could no longer resist. Clutching her arm, he drew her close and pressed his lips to hers. She responded and folded against him, allowing his kiss to deepen, to express all the love he had stored up for her. He ran fingers through her hair, pressed his chest against her curves, drew in the scent of her, the taste of her, until he was near mad with desire and love.

She pushed from him and backed away, leaving him breathless and cold. "We mustn't, Stede." She glanced toward his home in the distance once again. "You must find a way to be happy with Mary."

Lord knew he had tried. He had done his best to accept his marriage, to love Mary and be a good husband and father. Everything the good book said. But his wife had only grown worse. And he had only grown emptier.

Rain soaked through his doublet, sending a shiver down his back.

"I'm building a sloop of war."

Her pert little nose wrinkled. "Whatever for? Are you mad?"

"Quite possibly."

"What need have you of a ship?" She swiped the moisture from her face and brushed a damp curl aside. Gadzooks, she was lovely! Even wet, with her skin and hair glistening with rain.

Reaching in the pocket of his doublet, he pulled out a gold doubloon. "There are thousands of these for the taking on these seas."

"Thievery? What are you saying? You have no need of wealth."

"Come with me, Melody." He took her hands once again. "When the sloop is finished. I beg you, sail away with me. We can settle in a sweet haven where no one will find us."

"Egad, sir, you speak foolishness." She tried to smile, but it faltered on her lips. Instead, she retrieved her hand and stroked his jaw, fear in her eyes. "I could never do such a thing to your wife and children. Tell me you have not gone mad, as they are saying."

"*Who* is saying?" He'd heard the rumors, saw the way people looked at him and whispered behind raised hands.

"People in town. They say your mind is not right."

He heaved a sigh. "In truth, I quite agree. My mind, my spirit, my *very* soul is not right. And I fear should you leave me, they will only grow worse."

She backed away and drew her wet cloak tighter around her neck. "I have no choice, my love. You must forget me."

"Never."

"Then what do you intend to do?"

Thunder bellowed in the distance and the rain suddenly stopped, leaving the ground muddy and water dripping from leaves. "I intend to become a pirate."

CHAPTER THREE

*L*exie withdrew a wad of bills from her wallet, dumped the contents of her purse on the bed, then separated the coins from the rest of her things. Tossing the purse aside, she began counting. $1,333.22. That's all she had left to her name. She drew a deep breath and glanced around the one-room studio apartment she rented a week ago for $700 a month in Charleston. If she didn't find a job soon, she'd only be able to pay for one more month. The rest would have to go for food and utilities.

Plopping onto the bed, she forced back tears. She'd never been so afraid. *And* so alone. She'd never been responsible for her own bills, her own survival. Mom had always been there, an anchor of love and security in an otherwise stormy world. She didn't even really know how to find a job. Sure, she'd worked at a couple of fast-food restaurants as a teenager, but then she'd gone right to college after high school. Who wanted to hire someone with little-to-no experience and a worthless two-year associates degree in English? Not many, she had discovered. She'd spent the past week applying for every job opening she could find—waitress, store clerk, barista, even landscape assistant.

A Harley thundered by the apartment complex, shaking the windows. It wasn't the nicest place to live. Cracked and peeling paint covered the walls, and the carpet looked as though it hadn't been professionally cleaned in years. Perhaps it was her imagination, but it felt greasy beneath her bare feet. Hence the constant need for socks. But she had a bed, a couch, coffee table, flat screen, a small kitchenette, and a bathroom. What else did a person need?

A job.

She fingered the tiny gold loop earring her mother had given her for her 21st birthday, then grabbed a hair tie from the bed and gathered her long hair atop her head into a loose bun.

She wasn't on the street yet. One thing her mother had taught her was to never give up. In fact, her mother had many important things to say to Lexie during the last years of her life when she'd gotten all religious. Lots of things about God. But Lexie wasn't interested in a God who had so little concern for her life or the life of her family. Nope. She was all alone, and she'd better quit feeling sorry for herself.

Rising from the bed, she put her hands on her hips and glanced over the room. Her gaze fixed upon her mother's chest perched in a corner—the reason she was in this city in the first place. She chuckled. She'd come to find buried pirate treasure. How foolhardy was that? What she *should* do was take that gold coin to an appraiser and sell it. Along with all those old letters. Maybe some historian would pay her a decent price. She'd been so busy looking for work, she'd only had time to read the first one. Not that reading them would help her situation. If her ancestor really had been a pirate, it only confirmed that her family was nothing but a bunch of losers and had been for over three hundred years. Pirate treasure. What a joke.

Her cell phone chirped. Plucking it from her bed, she pressed the green button. "Hello."

"Is this Lexie Cain?"

"It is."

"This is Mrs. Anderson from The Old Exchange Museum."

Lexie allowed a spark of hope to rise. "Yes."

"I've looked over your application for store clerk and was wondering if you'd be interested in another position here at the Exchange?"

"Mrs. Anderson, I'd be interested in any position you have available."

"Even a night janitor?"

Janitor? How low could Lexie go? "Yes." Apparently pretty low.

"Great. Can you come down for an interview now?"

It took Lexie twenty minutes in rush hour traffic to get to the Exchange from her apartment. Finding parking was another problem, but soon she mounted the steps of the museum, drew a deep breath, and entered the building.

The interview went as well as could be expected. Good grief, how much experience did a janitor need? Mrs. Anderson, a woman in her fifties with graying hair styled short and curly, black-rimmed glasses, and a modest, loose-fitting business dress, methodically went down a list of questions in a computerized, monotone voice, hardly ever glancing up.

Yes, Lexie knew how to hold a broom, how to mop, dust, clean fragile and delicate artifacts and statues. No, Lexie had no experience as a janitor. Yes, she had two years of college.

Mrs. Anderson finally glanced at Lexie above the rim of her glasses. "Why would you accept a position you are clearly overqualified for?"

"I need a job, Mrs. Anderson. True, I have some college, but it's not enough to land me a position in my field." Field? Who was she kidding? She had studied English only because it seemed the fastest way to get a degree.

"We've had quite the turn around with janitors. How do I know you won't leave us as soon as something better comes along?" Her nose pinched, slightly lifting her glasses.

"I have no plans to look for other work."

Mrs. Anderson's lips pursed. "Can you work nights?"

"I do my best work at night." Lexie smiled, hoping her joke would lighten the woman's mood, but she only stared at her curiously.

"Very well. If the pay of $12 an hour is acceptable, you are hired."

"It is. Thank you, Mrs. Anderson."

The woman pulled out several forms that Lexie quickly signed.

"You will begin tomorrow night. Be here by 9:00 p.m. for an hour of training before you start."

"Yes, ma'am."

"Now, I'll give you a brief tour if you like before you leave."

"That would be great."

Lexie had never been interested in history. She had troubles enough in the present without worrying about the past, but she had to admit the Exchange was full of fascinating artifacts and interesting stories about the history of Charleston. As Mrs. Anderson explained the various exhibits, she transformed from a dour, uptight woman to a lady of passion and delight.

"Here in 1788, South Carolina leaders ratified the U.S. Constitution." She pointed to a copy of the Constitution hanging on the wall, complete with signatures, before leading Lexie into a large white room with two huge fireplaces.

"George Washington came here once as well," the lady continued, "entertained by Charleston's leaders and elite."

The pride in her tone was unmistakable, and even Lexie was in awe that she might be walking in the very spot where Washington once walked.

The tour continued with various paintings, flags, swords, plaques, and statues, including many fascinating stories of Charleston heroes.

Finally, they descended a flight of stairs into the dungeon area, lit by lights made to look like antique lanterns. Several small alcoves extended into the distance, each with thick brick walls that curved upward, forming arched ceilings above. The smell of the sea, mold, dust, and antiquity tickled her nose as Mrs. Anderson told her that several famous patriots were imprisoned here during the British occupation of Charleston in the American Revolution. They moved to stand before one of the prison cells made up to look like it might have centuries before. Lifelike wax figures dressed as pirates were displayed inside in various poses, each looking so real that Lexie could only stare. She was only half listening to Mrs. Anderson prattle on about the history when one word echoed through the dungeon, jarring Lexie's mind.

She faced Mrs. Anderson. "Stede Bonnet?"

"Yes, he was one of the most famous pirates to be imprisoned here. Are you familiar with his story?"

"Not really. But I think I may have some old letters of his."

The woman snorted and wrinkled her nose, as if such a thing could never be possible. "Really?"

Lexie cleared her throat. "Of course they are probably not real. Um, but would you know someone who could authenticate them?"

"Hmm." Mrs. Anderson led the way back up the stairs to the main museum. "I believe there's a professor at Charleston Southern University. Johnson is his name. Barret Johnson. Yes, that's it. He's writing a book on Stede Bonnet. At least that's what he told me the last time he was here."

Thanking Mrs. Anderson, Lexie left the museum. This Barret Johnson was just the person she needed to see.

Barret Johnson's head hurt. He'd been grading freshmen essays on the historical significance of the Lords Proprietors of Carolina for hours, and he'd yet to see a decent composition on the topic. Some, in fact, had been downright ludicrous. If this was the next generation of historians, the world was in deep trouble.

Tossing down his pen, he leaned back in his chair and glanced out the window onto the green lawn that extended across the center of campus. Morning sunlight angled through dirty panes before draping his favorite antique Victorian chair and spearing across the flat-woven Turkish rug centering his office. Perched against the walls, wooden bookcases circled his desk like the embrace of an old friend, filled with every history book imaginable. Yes, they *were* his friends…had been his friends for years.

A painting of his great-grandfather, Edwin Johnson, stared at him from between two of the cases. He wondered what the man would think of him. Would he be proud? But why wouldn't he?

Lacing his hands together behind his head, Barret leaned back and smiled. It was still hard to believe that he'd finally made it. After eight hard years of study at Harvard, he graduated top of his class with a PhD in history at the young age of twenty-five. Soon after returning home, he procured a prestigious position teaching South Carolina history here at Charleston Southern University. When he wasn't teaching, he worked on his latest project, a book on the pirates of Charleston, which he was sure would win him recognition from the American Historical Association. Everything was going according to plan. God had truly blessed him.

Leaning forward, he grabbed his cup of espresso and took a sip. Cold. Of course. He'd been so engrossed in grading papers he'd forgotten about it. No problem. He'd finish the last few essays and then make a run to Pete's down the street.

Picking up his pen, he sighed and flipped to the next paper when a *tap, tap, tap* sounded on his door. One look at his watch told him it was only 9:00 a.m. and not student visiting hours yet. Ignoring the knock, he started reading the paper.

Rap, Rap, Rap. Louder this time.

Barret growled and continued reading. Surely whoever it was would go away.

Knock, knock, knock. The door suddenly swung open, and he heard a student march inside.

Of all the… "Visiting hours aren't for another hour." Barret tossed down his pen and looked up.

No, not a student at all. At least not one he had ever seen. Gaping, fringed holes dotted jeans that seemed glued to her thin frame. A black t-shirt with the word *Metallica* scrolled across it was tucked in at her waist. Three earrings pierced one ear. The other held a small gold loop. She gripped a folder in one hand while a worn purse hung over her shoulder. Light hair the color of cream was pinned up behind her in a haphazard bun from which strands stuck out in all directions. But it was her eyes that captured him, emerald green and as hard as the gemstone itself, directed straight at him.

"Are you Barret Johnson?" she asked as if she were the one in charge.

"Professor Barret Johnson," he returned. "And as I said, visiting hours—"

"I'm not one your students, *Professor*."

"I can see that."

"I need your help."

"Well, miss." Barret rose from his chair. "You have a fine way of asking for it."

"Listen, I'm sorry to barge in, but I only have an hour on the car meter and no more change. I promise to only take a moment of your time."

Barret glanced around her toward the open door. "How did you get past my assis—"

"I have some old things I found in my mom's belongings that I need you to look at."

"Listen I…"

Ignoring him and further stirring his anger, she walked to his desk and opened her folder across the top, revealing what looked like an antique letter cased in a plastic sleeve.

"I need to know if this is authentic."

"Miss, you need to take that to—"

"It's part of a group of letters from a pirate named Stede Bonnet. Mrs. Anderson from the Exchange sent me to you." She lifted her brows and offered him a tiny smile that he was sure would work with any red-blooded male—except for him.

But she had him at the name Stede Bonnet. Bonnet was one of the pirates he'd been researching for his book. Surely this slip of a girl wouldn't be in possession of…

Circling his desk, he picked up the paper and brought it close. The signature at the bottom certainly looked authentic, the writing was definitely in the flowing cursive style of the time period, and the paper was definitely vellum. Against his reason, excitement raced through him. If this was what it appeared to be…No, he wouldn't allow himself to get carried away. Not until he examined it further. However, if it was the real thing, Barret was surprised at the good condition, especially if it had been handed down for three hundred years and only kept within this plastic sleeve.

"Where did you get this? How many do you have?"

"I told you. My mother had it tucked away in a chest. There are at least eighteen of them." The woman glanced around the office, clearly uncomfortable in her surroundings. "She said our family was related to this guy."

"Stede Bonnet?" Barret couldn't help but laugh.

She frowned. "Listen, *Professor*, I didn't come to be laughed at. Is it real or not?"

"I don't know yet. I have to take it to the lab for testing."

She only stared at him.

He arched his brows. "If you leave it with me, I can test it and get back to you in a week."

Mistrust flooded her narrowed eyes. "Why should I trust you?"

"You brought it to me, remember? I'm a history professor. I'm hardly going to steal it from you." He glanced back at the document, his pulse ratcheting as he noticed the lack of punctuation, another sign of the time period. "Give me your info, some way to reach you."

Hesitating, she bit her bottom lip, studying him as if she could assess his truthfulness. Finally, she approached his desk again, grabbed a pen and paper, and scribbled something down.

Only then did he notice a small tattoo on the back of her neck—an eagle.

"I'm staying at the Land's End, Apartment 33. Here's my cell number." Then closing the folder, she picked it up and nodded toward him. "A week?"

"Yes."

And just as quickly as this enigma of a girl entered, she turned and left, leaving a trace of vanilla perfume in the air.

Slowly sinking into his cushioned Victorian chair, Barret began to read the letter.

CHAPTER FOUR

July 1718 Gardiner's Island, Off the Coast of New York

Postmaster
Charles Town, Carolina
Attention: Miss Melody Rogers

My most precious Melody,
Though it has been but eight months since I last saw you, it seems an eternity. I do not know when this letter will reach you, or even if it will reach you. However, I find writing to you good for my soul, for it enables me to feel close to you. I pray for you every day, my dearest, and hope this missive finds you in good health and happiness. I have much to tell you, and I hope you do not think less of me for the events in my life which have recently transpired.
You see, my dear I became a pirate as I said I would. I am captain of a sixty-ton sloop with ten cannons which I named Revenge. Why revenge? For the life which was dealt to me, the loss of the two most precious things in the world, you and my son...

A knock rapped on his door, and Captain Stede Bonnet looked up from his letter as his first mate entered the captain's cabin, followed by the quartermaster. Setting down his pen, he rose, angry that the crew refused to treat him with the respect his station deserved.

"What is it, Carter? I told you not to enter until I give the word."

The man, who looked more rat than human with his long pointy nose and tiny dark eyes, continued chewing his tobacco and staring at Bonnet. "The men are askin' to go ashore and do some lootin', Cap'n."

"Looting?" Bonnet adjusted his silk cravat and circled the desk, his gaze wandering to Mullet, his quartermaster, who, though lacking in education, oft seemed of sounder mind than most of the crew.

"We be needin' supplies." Mullet answered Bonnet's unvoiced question as he shifted bare feet across the deck. Several dark greasy strands had escaped the man's queue and fell across a red, silk-embroidered doublet he'd pilfered from their last conquest.

Bonnet had been both surprised and repulsed at the slovenly attire, continual filth, and uncouth manners of the sailors he'd recruited to man his sloop. But he supposed 'twas the case with most pirates.

He glanced back at Carter. "Then I shall give you money to purchase what we need."

At this, his first mate guffawed and slapped the knee of his stained breeches. Mullet smiled.

Bonnet gave a frustrated sigh as the stink of body odor blew over him. Did these men never bathe? In truth, during the past four months, Bonnet's senses had been constantly assailed with the most obnoxious odors.

Carter recovered. "Yer serious?"

"I am."

"We're pirates." Mullet complained. "We don't buy wha' we need." His confused expression contorted as if the thought were ludicrous.

"We are good pirates, are we not? Under my leadership, we have captured five prizes in the past four months." Bonnet waved his hand through the air. "There is no need to rob innocents and cause unnecessary death when we have the money to purchase what we need."

Carter scratched the back of his neck.

"The *Anne* and *Young* from Scotland, the *Endeavor* from England, and the *Turbet* from Barbados." Bonnet reminded the men of their most successful raids. All easy conquests, for they took one look at Bonnet's cannons and the Jolly Roger he hoisted, and they gave up without a fight. His only regret had been that the crew of the *Turbet* recognized him from Barbados. Hence, he'd been forced to burn their ship and keep them prisoner. Though he imagined news of his piratical adventures would eventually reach home, he didn't relish the shock and disdain he would receive from friends and family— the prelude of which he had already endured from the captain and crew of the *Turbet*.

"Then, of course, there was the sloop we recently took as prize off New York. Gentlemen, have we not acquired enough prizes thus far? What need have we of more violence?"

Carter chomped on his tobacco, staring at Bonnet as if he spoke a foreign language. "I can try to purchase goods, Cap'n, but the men are itchin' fer a fight."

Stretching his neck to appear as tall as he could, Bonnet affected his most authoritative voice. "Tell them to scratch their itches elsewhere, or I will leave them here and find other crew. Do I not pay you sufficiently?"

Mullet's lips slanted. "Aye, by Davy Jones, ye do, Cap'n."

Returning to his desk, Bonnet opened a drawer, retrieved a key from his pocket, and opened a lock box. He withdrew more than enough for necessary supplies and handed it to Carter. "Then do as I say."

With scowls on their faces, Carter and Mullet spun about and stormed away, leaving Bonnet's door ajar.

After a few moments, he followed them down the companionway and up the ladder onto the main deck. He would finish his letter to Melody later. For now, he needed to ensure his crew were behaving themselves. A gust of briny sea air fluttered the lace of his cuffs as he fisted hands at his waist and glanced over the deck with his fiercest look. If he had learned one thing these past four months, 'twas that he must command respect through fear. These men were not his friends, would never be his friends. According to the pirate code, they could vote him out as captain any time they wished.

Saint's blood, 'twas a foreign concept for Bonnet. He had been a major in the British army. He owned a massive sugar plantation with dozens of servants and slaves. Never had his authority been questioned. Never had those beneath him dared to even look at him with the disrespect with which some of these men looked at him now. There were seventy pirates in all, most of whom crowded the deck of the *Revenge* at the moment. Some whittled away at wood carvings, others cleaned their pistols, some mended ropes, while others played cards. A sordid ballad rose from a group near the bow as they passed around bottles of wine they'd stolen from the *Endeavor*. All of them were attired in pieces of lavish attire *liberated* from passengers on board the ships they'd taken as prizes. All of them were as filthy and malodorous as pigs in a sty.

Mullet and Carter didn't once glance his way as they commanded the crew to lower the cockboat for their trip ashore. In the distance, Gardiner Island rose from the sea like a green turtle, lush with trees and encircled by sandy beaches.

His frustration boiling, Bonnet marched to the larboard railing, away from most of the men. Aye, he'd gotten seasick, terribly seasick, during their first month at sea. No doubt that was the cause of some of the crew's insolence. But he had recovered. His sea legs stood firm and steady on the deck that even now rolled over incoming waves. Gadzooks! He barely noticed any movement beneath his feet anymore. In addition to the prizes he'd won them, he paid them a handsome salary and provided his own sloop on which they could pilfer the sea of all her treasure.

Ungrateful miscreants!

Closing his eyes, Bonnet gripped the railing and drew in a deep breath, relishing the scent of salty air, moist wood, and tar. Wind tossed his dark hair behind him as he stared over the churning sea toward the eternal horizon. Such beauty, adventure, and freedom! Nay, he could never return to his former life—one of responsibility, emptiness, and the constant nagging of his wife. One where he had to live by the dictates and mores of a society in which he no longer felt he belonged. Saint's blood! He'd even tossed his periwig overboard, happy to be rid of the oppressively hot thing. Now, as the wind danced through his hair, he wondered why he had waited so long.

Behind him, the cockboat splashed into the water, and Carter issued orders for the men who were going ashore to climb aboard and cast off.

Not once did his first mate approach Bonnet for his orders. Not that Bonnet had much experience with such things. 'Twas true he relied on Carter and Mullet for their expertise, but Bonnet was a quick learner, and he would soon understand the workings of the sloop as well as any seasoned sailor.

Mayhap then he could win the respect of the crew.

Pushing from the railing, he turned to see the boat rowing toward shore. Good. He would go below and finish his letter to Melody before they returned.

Back in his cabin, he picked up his pen and began where he left off. He informed Melody of his seasickness and the exploits and successes of his crew, of his misgivings of their loyalty, and his assurance that he would soon become a captain they could respect and follow.

My precious love, I hope you do not think less of me for these exploits. I am kind to my crew. I pay them well, and we do no harm to those we capture. Perhaps this does not make up for my crimes, but please know I do this for you. For us. I left all I had in Barbados, all my wealth and land, enough to support Mary and my children the rest of their lives. Thus, I have embarked on this venture with nary a shilling to my name. Once I have procured enough fortune for us to live comfortably the rest of our days, I will come for you. I can only hope and pray now that I am free of my obligations, you are willing to sail away with me to live out our days in loving bliss.

I long to see you. My heart aches for but a glimpse of your sweet face. Indeed, 'tis my plan to sail to Charles Town on the morrow. Look for me in a week, for I shall see if I can find a way to come ashore in secret.

Until then... you own my heart.

*Forever your beloved
Stede*

Barret set the letter down on the table beside his chair, carefully... reverently, his hands quivering in shock. Either this letter was the real deal, or it was one of the best forgeries he'd ever seen. Not only did every detail—the writing style, punctuation, the archaic words used, and the paper—indicate its authenticity, but the content as well! The events relayed by the writer fit the history of Bonnet perfectly.

Rubbing the back of his neck, Barret rose, wishing he had asked the strange young lady more questions. Regardless, he should get this letter down to the antiquities' science lab immediately. The sooner he knew the truth, the better.

There wasn't a single spot on Lexie's body that did not ache. And she was only twenty-two! She had to admit that thus far in her short life, she had not known what hard work was. Not even working at a fast-food restaurant was as grueling as the past week of cleaning the entire Provost Museum by herself. How one place could get so dirty every day was beyond her. But it did. The worst part? Random pieces of still-moist gum stuck on displays and under tables. *Ugh.* She shivered even now at the thought as she swerved her car into a spot at her apartment complex and shut off the engine. She really should look for more prestigious work, but there was something about the museum…the dungeon in particular, that drew her. Maybe she was related to this pirate, after all, for on her breaks, she'd stand before his cell and stare at his wax figure, wondering about him, sensing him drawing her into his story. She should read the remainder of his letters, but she wanted to hear from Professor Johnson first. The last thing she needed right now was to get involved in a story that was mere fabrication.

Besides, it would be better *not* to get involved at all. If the letters and the coin did not lead her to Bonnet's buried treasure, she planned on selling them to the highest bidder. Leaning her head against the headrest, her thoughts drifted to the arrogant professor. She'd been expecting a gray-haired man with bifocals, a paunch, and ink stains on his white dress shirt. She hadn't been expecting a six-foot-one hunk with jet-black hair and piercing eyes the color of mahogany. What brainiac was as thickly muscled as a hockey player while also looking as though he could grace the cover of *GQ*? No. More like Pirates-R-Us with his hair slightly longer than his collar and that dark stubble on his jaw. She would have swooned if she was the swooning type.

But then he'd opened his mouth.

Pretentious haughty snob. He had looked at her as if she were an irritating gnat, someone he could swat away and be rid of. Until, of course, he saw the letters. She would have walked out if she'd had anyone else to consult. As it was, it had been a week and no word. She would call him after she slept, after her temper cooled.

Gathering her purse and bags, she stepped from her car and glanced toward the east where the sun had just risen to begin the day. Or *end* it for her. All she wanted was a hot bath and a warm bed. She'd managed to train herself to sleep with earplugs during the day, despite the noise that went on around her. But first things first.

Weaving through the sea of cars, she made her way to apartment 111 and knocked. She had no doubt Tracy would be up since she had told Lexie many times that Ellie always woke her up at dawn. Sure enough, the door opened, and Tracy smiled, despite her haphazard appearance. Brown hair askew, still in her bathrobe, the young mother, who was close to Lexie's age, always seemed happy to see her.

"Come in. I was just getting breakfast for Ellie."

"No, I can't. I'm exhausted and in need of my bed. But I brought you something." Lexie held out the bag.

Brows pinching, Tracy took the bag and peeked inside just as three-year-old Ellie appeared beside her, holding a doll.

"Milk! You got me milk and a loaf of bread!" You would think it was a hoard of cash the way Tracy reacted.

"I told you I would help when I could. I know it's not much—"

"It's everything! Thank you so much." Tracy leaned in to hug her while Ellie tugged on Lexie's t-shirt.

"Present for me?" Blond curls framed a cherub face, and Lexie hoisted her into her arms. "Would I forget my favorite girl?"

Tracy looked back in the bag. "It's a book, Ell, a book about pirates. And a tiny pirate ship!" She withdrew both and showed Ellie, who glowed from ear to ear.

Lexie shrugged. "Sorry, that's all they had for kids at the museum."

"Thank you, Lexie!" Ellie took the items, and Lexie lowered her to run off and play.

"You shouldn't be spending your hard-earned money on us."

"Of course I should." Lexie smiled. Tracy and Ellie reminded Lexie of her and her mom, moving from place to place, struggling to survive, living off odd jobs and food stamps. She had vowed back then that when she got older, she'd help single mothers as much as she could.

Tracy's eyes filled with tears. "You're a godsend."

Clearing her throat, Lexie turned to leave. "Have a great day."

"We will now!" Tracy's sweet voice followed her as she mounted the two flights to her apartment. A godsend? No. God had not sent her. Why? Because she and the Almighty had not been on speaking terms for quite some time.

Turning a corner, she withdrew her keys from her pocket and approached her door.

It was open.

Heart leaping into her throat, she crept closer, eased the door further ajar, and glanced inside.

Bedsheets and blankets had been torn from her bed, stuffing flowed from split-open cushioned chairs, clothing spilled from drawers, and broken dishes littered the small kitchenette.

CHAPTER FIVE

*B*arret pulled into the Land's End Apartment complex, parked, and rubbed his eyes. He had not been able to sleep for two nights. Not since the antiquities lab had confirmed that, after a chemical analysis of the paper and ink, the letter the young lady had given him originated in the early eighteenth century. Precisely the time in which Bonnet had been alive! And this Lexie Cain woman—which was the name she wrote above her phone and address—had said she was in possession of at least fourteen more. He had called her right away, but either her phone was turned off or she'd given him a bogus number. But why would she do that?

Exiting his BMW, he glanced around at the neglected neighborhood and the dilapidated apartment building and clicked the alarm button on his key fob. Why would a woman who lived in such a place be in possession of something so valuable? This was the motherlode he'd been searching for! Letters from the pirate Stede Bonnet himself. Original letters which, from the contents of the first one, had never surfaced before…letters that would provide new and important information for Barret's book. And quite possibly win him a prestigious AHA award with a grant or fellowship to continue his research.

Plucking the piece of paper from his pants pocket, he looked at the address. Apartment 33. He located a set of stairs and proceeded across the parking lot, only then noticing a police car parked behind the building. "Great neighborhood," he huffed under his breath as he mounted the two flights without difficulty and started down the walkway. The sound of a police radio blared from one of the apartments. The door was open. Apartment 33?

For a brief moment, alarm fired through his veins at the thought something had happened to the other letters. Then he saw the woman sitting on a bed, shock and fear written on her face and her eyes swollen from tears, and he chastised himself for his selfishness. A lady police officer knelt before her, consoling her, while another officer examined the room, jotting notes on a small notepad.

Ms. Cain glanced up at him and blinked in recognition but then continued to answer the lady officer's questions. The other officer whose back was to him spun around.

"Barret!" Adam Wright, Barret's good friend since high school, approached, looking confused. "What are you doing here?"

"Um." Barret thumbed toward Ms. Cain, who was now hugging herself as the lady officer rose. "I came to see her. What's going on?"

"Break in," Adam said. "She came home from work to find her door busted open and her things tossed around. Oh." He turned to the police lady who was walking toward them. "My partner, Cheryl Gade."

"Nice to meet you, Cheryl." Barret nodded to her as she eased by him onto the walkway.

"You as well." She dipped her head at him then shot a glance at Adam. "I'll meet you at the car."

Adam slipped his pad back into his shirt pocket, then turned to face Lexie. "Miss Cain, I'll file a report and request that a patrol car canvas your neighborhood more frequently. But since nothing was stolen, I doubt whoever broke in will return. Most likely drug addicts looking for a fix or some loose change. And have your super fix the door lock and use the chain lock when you are home."

Nodding, Ms. Cain stood. "Thank you, officer."

Adam drew Barret out onto the walkway. "Friend of yours?"

"I barely know her. We're…um…collaborating on something."

At that, Adam's brow raised above a sly grin.

"Not *that* kind of collaborating. You know me. It's about old documents she has."

Adam smiled. "Whatever it is, she could use some comforting." He stretched his back. "But I gotta run to another call." He started away. "And she's pretty too!" he added over his shoulder.

Barret had already noticed that fact, though now as he reentered the apartment, she appeared worn, her expression flat, as if all her hopes had been run over by a steam roller.

"Professor Johnson, what are you doing here? Why didn't you call me?" She wiped her hands on her faded jeans as if trying to rid them of something.

"Please sit. You've had a shock." Taking her elbow, he led her back to the bed, then took a seat in a chair across from her.

"I'm okay." She rubbed her arms and let out a sigh that sent a tremble through her. Raising shaky hands, she fingered one of her earrings. "I just don't know why anyone would do this. I have nothing of value. Isn't it obvious from where I live?" Rising yet again, she moved to the front window and looked out. Glistening like cream in the morning sun, her blond hair stuck out from a bun in every direction. A stained white t-shirt and skin-tight jeans left little to the imagination, including the outline of a phone in her left back pocket and a large round object in her right.

"But that's not *your* problem." When she turned around, all fear had vacated her expression as if she had flipped a switch, a much-used switch, and it fled into hiding somewhere deep within her.

"Maybe not, but I still don't enjoy seeing anyone's place broken into."

"Did you have the document analyzed?"

"I did." Barret stood and smiled. "And I'm happy to tell you it's authentic."

A tiny spark crossed her eyes, and her breathing heightened. "Whoa," was all she said.

"Do you have the rest?" Barret looked around at the mess the thieves had made, and his heart squeezed. "They weren't—"

"No. I had them and the coin in my car. I never took them out after we spoke."

Thank God. He followed her gaze to a small open chest in the corner, an old blanket, photos, and trinkets scattered in front of it. "What coin?"

"Why didn't you call?"

"I tried. Several times. No answer, and no phone mail."

Looking confused, Lexie pulled out her phone and tapped it a few times. "Nope. No calls."

"540-555-5773" Barret retrieved the paper to make sure he remembered correctly.

She shook her head. "No, the last number is an 8."

"This is clearly a 3." He held up the note and pointed, his annoyance growing.

She gave him a sharp stare as if *she* were the one annoyed.

Barret rubbed the back of his neck. "Okay, it doesn't matter. I'm here now." Oh, how he wanted to get his hands on those other letters! "You've had a scare, and I can see you're tired. Maybe I could come back another time?"

"For what? You've told me what I need to know."

Barret's entire body froze, waiting for her to start laughing at her joke. But instead, she gestured toward the door with her head.

"Thank you for authenticating it." She opened her hand, palm up. "May I have it back?"

Barret closed his eyes for a moment, attempting to gather his rising temper. "You can't seriously expect to keep these letters to yourself, Ms. Cain. They are of great historical significance and should be shared with the world."

Her eyes narrowed. "Listen, *Professor*. I will gladly pay you for the work you did on this, but those letters belong to my family, and I intend to keep them. Now, if you'll return the one I gave you, I need to go to bed. I've been working all night."

Barret crossed arms over his chest, still not believing this foolish girl. "I don't have it with me." He'd kept it locked in a drawer in his office for fear it would get damaged from the air and sunlight. And at the moment, he was glad he'd done so.

Her pert little nose wrinkled as if she smelled something foul. "Should I call the cops back here to force you to return what is mine?"

"Listen, miss, I don't think you fully understand what—"

"Yes, I do fully understand. I understand now that I have something of value *you* want, you are treating me with some level of respect." She still had her phone in hand, her jaw tight as if she would follow through with her threat.

Barret made his way to the door, confused and shocked. He'd never been treated so badly, nor tossed out of a place like a piece of trash. In fact, he'd never encountered such an infuriating woman! He stopped in the doorway. "I'm sorry Ms. Cain. I promise to return your letter."

"Good. Then bring it here tomorrow. Same time."

The last thing he saw was the chipped paint of her closed door.

⚓

Infuriating, presumptuous man! Lexie would growl if she didn't think he could hear her through the door. Yes, he was still standing there. She heard him breathing—puffing hard like a rhino about to charge. Then finally he walked away.

Looping the chain through the catch, she looked around at the mess—clothes, books, soap, shampoo bottles, broken glass and plastic cups scattered across the apartment. She should clean it up, but she was so very tired. She hoped the policeman was right, and whoever broke in was just looking for drugs and wouldn't be back. Still, an hour later, after a hot bath and dressed in her pj's, she couldn't sleep.

Maybe reading one of Bonnet's letters would help. Now that she knew they were real and could lead to treasure, she was excited to find out what they contained. Dashing to her car, she popped the trunk and grabbed her folder, then ran up and jumped in bed.

Picking up the second letter, she studied the flowery cursive writing, then ran her fingers over the plastic sleeve. To think that her ancestor wrote this, that he really was a pirate.

Her thoughts drifted to the wax figure of Bonnet in the museum, and she wondered if it bore any likeness to him. More importantly, did he give clues to his buried treasure within these letters?

For if there's one thing she needed right now, it was money.

CHAPTER SIX

Nassau, Bahamas, September 1717

My precious Melody, my greatest hope and prayer is that this letter finds you in good health and filled with happiness. As for myself, I find it difficult to rejoice in my present circumstances, for I am both bereft of my health and the health of my sloop. At present, my crew has deserted me for the taverns and brothels of Nassau, the pirate haven in which I have been forced to lay anchor. I do not wish to grieve you, dearest, but suffice it to say we had the misfortune to engage a Spanish ship of war and did not emerge unscathed.

Allow me to go back in time a mere month and tell you of my adventures in Charles Town and how my every attempt to come ashore to see you was thwarted. We arrived at your city in early August, where we laid becalmed, hidden between O'Sullivan's Island and Morris Island, waiting for merchantmen to sail by unaware. 'Twas during this time that I determined to row ashore under the cover of night to make my way into the city and would have done so despite the protests of my crew, save that we sighted a brigantine from Boston heading straight for us.

Tomas Porter, the captain, a man of fine stature and bearing, upon sighting my Jolly Roger immediately hove to and lowered his sails. I do suppose my reputation preceded me, *for he and his crew surrendered quickly. However 'twas to my misfortune and the crew's immense disappointment that their ship bore no valuable cargo. To hear the grumbling and complaining of these ruffians, dear, along with such coarse and ignorant language is difficult to bear, but I suppose 'tis the lot of most sailors. I do find myself longing for more refined company and hope to rectify that soon.*

Nevertheless, we kept Porter and his brigantine prisoner lest they sail to Charles Town and warn the authorities of your fine city. My next attempt to see you was also thwarted when a sloop was sighted coming from the south...

"A sail, a sail!" The shout came from above and Bonnet raised his spyglass to his eye. A single sail came into focus, stark white against the blue horizon, the owners yet unaware of the danger awaiting them.

"How stands she?" Bonnet shouted, finally becoming accustomed to the right commands to issue.

"A single masted merchantman, four guns, sittin' low in the water!" came the quick reply.

Bonnet faced his crew. "Lay aloft and loose all sails!"

His first mate Carter took up the charge and began issuing further orders. "Loose topsail, course and main! Man tacks and sheets! Clear away the jib!"

Sails dropped and flapped impotently, before the wind caught them in a loud snap, and the *Revenge* jerked to starboard, picking up speed through the churning waters.

Stumbling over the heaving deck, Bonnet took a position at the bow of the sloop, hands on his hips. Wind whipped his hair behind him as the ship bucked over a wave, showering him with salty spray. He'd come to love the chase, the stiff breeze, the leaping deck, the power…the freedom!

"Raise my ensign, run out the guns!" Bonnet shouted and was once again dismayed to find that most of his men made no haste to do his bidding but rather shifted their gazes to Carter for his affirmation.

The first mate nodded and then added a few of his own commands. "Sheet home to lee! Haul out the top bowline!"

Two pirates hoisted the Jolly Roger on the head of the mainmast.

Saint's blood! 'Twas Bonnet who paid these ingrates and provided this sloop for their thievery. The least they could do was obey his orders forthwith. This insubordination was not to be borne, and he intended to inflict stricter punishments in the future. But for now…he shifted his gaze back to their prey.

Sailors scrambled across the deck of the poor merchantman in an attempt to adjust sails to veer away from the oncoming menace.

They think to escape, eh? "Fire a warning shot!" Bonnet shouted over his shoulder.

Robbins, his gunner, brayed a series of orders and the gun crew gathered around one of the guns with powder, a shot, and a burning wick. Within minutes a thunderous boom reverberated through the sloop and echoed across the sky. The sea exploded in a mighty splash just yards off the port bow of the merchantman. To their credit, the sailors understood the danger which faced them, for soon, they lowered their sails and raised a white flag.

Smiling, Bonnet turned about to order his own sails lowered, but Carter was already shouting to the crew, sending them up the shrouds. Several minutes passed as the ships maneuvered keel to keel, minutes in which Bonnet kept his gaze on the man he assumed was the captain. Finally, when they were close enough, he raised a speaking cone to his lips and shouted, "The pirate ship, *Revenge*, welcomes you, gentlemen. Good quarter will be given if you lay down your arms and prepare to be boarded."

Their captain offered a sarcastic salute in reply, but there was something familiar about him. Bonnet continued to stare as the sloop slipped closer and closer. "Of all the..." He growled and spun around, taking up a pace across the deck, his thoughts in such a whirlwind, he could not bring himself to shout further orders.

No matter. When the vessels were close enough, Mullet ordered grapnels tossed. The huge hooks gouged the deck of the merchantman, and the pirates tugged on the ropes, drawing the sloops together until their hulls collided in a jarring crunch.

Sweat trickled down Bonnet's back, whether from the hot sun or nerves, he could not say. Finally, he faced the captured crew as his men lifted cutlasses and pistols in the air and fired curses and threats at them like grapeshot.

"They have surrendered. There will be no killing," Bonnet reminded them, though he began to wonder if they'd obey.

Carter leveled a look of disgust his way before the first mate issued the order to board. *Without* Bonnet's permission. He should draw his cutlass and lead his men onto their prize, but he couldn't bring himself to do it. Not out of fear, but out of shame. Hence, he remained on the *Revenge* as the pirates swarmed onto the merchantman like rats before a flood. A plank was laid and secured between the ships, and their captain was urged forward onto the *Revenge* by the press of a flintlock on his back.

He stood before Bonnet, studying him as if he'd grown a tail and become a mermaid. "By all that is holy, Bonnet! What are you...what madness is this?"

Most of the pirates were busy rounding up the merchantman's crew or dropping below her decks to hoist up the cargo, but those around them stopped to stare.

"Joseph Palmer, a pleasure, sir," Bonnet replied in as haughty a tone as he could manage. "Is it not obvious? I have become a pirate."

At this, Joseph began to laugh, glancing over the deck of the *Revenge* as if he expected the real captain to emerge from below. Slowly his laughter abated, and a rather strange look overcame his expression.

He snorted, removed his hat, and rubbed his chin. "I see the stories are true."

"What stories are those?"

"That you have lost your mind."

Bonnet smiled. "I prefer to think I found it." He turned to Carter, who had assembled the merchantman's crew on the main deck. "Lock the prisoners below and"—he glanced toward Palmer's sloop and found the pirates had already brought up several crates and barrels from the hold. "Hoist all the cargo onto our deck."

With a nod, Carter turned, his shrill orders echoing over the ship as Bonnet faced Captain Palmer. Around five and thirty years of age, older than Bonnet, the man stood at least an inch shorter, but the width of him hinted at a sturdy, muscled frame.

Shame washed over Bonnet at the man's incriminating gaze. "This is most unfortunate, my dear friend."

"Indeed, for I find that I've been robbed by a friend and a gentleman."

"'Tis *fortunate* that 'tis me who captured your sloop, for my fellow pirates would gladly gut you and your crew and toss your carcasses overboard."

The man didn't flinch. Bonnet glanced at his sloop. "However, I cannot have you sailing back to Barbados with news of my...um, *madness*. Hence, I will keep you and your men prisoner and burn your ship."

Captain Palmer heaved an impatient sigh. "I wait with the hope that this is all some sort of prank, Bonnet. Tell me it is."

"I fear I am quite serious. As you will soon discover."

A pirate named Henry approached Bonnet. "He's got slaves too, Cap'n. What d'ye want done wit' them."

"Put them below with the prisoners."

Both vessels eased over a swell as wind flapped their loose sails.

Withdrawing a handkerchief, Bonnet dabbed the sweat from his brow. "You have my assurance, Captain Palmer, that I will treat you as a gentleman deserves. Do I have your word you will comply?"

For a moment, the man stared at Bonnet as one would a pesky rodent, but then he forced a smile. "I am most grateful, Captain Bonnet."

"'Tis Captain Edwards for now."

Palmer raised a brow. "Ah, disguising your name did no service to you in this case."

Bonnet shrugged and then turned to Carter. "When you are finished plundering the sloop, release the grapnels and burn it.

"But Cap'n." Carter frowned, sheathing his cutlass and spitting to the side. "We can make use o' it.'

"And how is that?"

"We're in need of a good careening, Cap'n, and it will 'elp to 'ave two ships to 'aul the *Revenge* over."

Bonnet sighed. 'Twas a good point and one he should have known, for his first mate had explained careening to him a week ago and said the *Revenge* was overdue.

"Very well, send a small crew over to man her and we'll head north to Cape Fear."

When all was finished and the prisoners, including Captain Palmer, were locked below, along with the booty of rum, sugar, and slaves they'd confiscated, Bonnet gave the order for the ships to set sail.

Now, standing at the larboard railing, he stared over the passing landscape. The sun dipped just below the treetops, transforming them into shadowy giants and painting a rainbow of colors in the gray sky above. The *Revenge* rolled over a wave, and he glanced down at the foam clawing up the hull, then sinking back into the sea. Just like his heart, all hopes of seeing Melody crushed.

A sliver of a moon appeared in the darkening sky. "Ah, my sweet Melody, so close that my heart surges with your presence, yet so far outside my reach, you might as well be on the moon."

He gripped the railing and drew a deep breath of sea air.

He would return to Charles Town. Perhaps the next time 'twould be with all the fortune he needed to escape with Melody and start over far away where no one would ever find them.

"I'm coming, my love… I'm coming."

Hence, my dearest, we set sail for Cape Fear River with Captain Porter and Captain Joseph Palmer aboard and their vessels in tow. Once in the shallows of the river we used the captured ships to both house our crew and goods and also to tip the Revenge so we could scrape her of barnacles. You must know, my precious one, that after the careening was completed, I burned Palmer's sloop and set him and his crew aboard Porter's brigantine, stripped them of their sails, and sent them both back to Charles Town. Do seek out Palmer when he arrives, for I have given him some letters for you. I hope he gives you a good report of me, despite my capturing his sloop.

I hesitate to inform you of the next event for it will do me no credit in your eyes. Remember my love that I am new to the trade and hence must rely on the expertise of my first mate and crew. Unfortunately, 'tis not how things work with these barbarians. I have discovered that a pirate captain only maintains command out of fear and intimidation. In addition, he must exhibit exemplary skills, courage, and a keen wit in battle or the crew may mutiny. Thus was the situation in which I found myself as the Revenge sailed toward the Florida straits. The crew began to outwardly voice their disapproval of my heretofore performance, citing that my conquests had been in spite of and not due to my skill and that I lacked a competence in maritime knowledge.

Mewling muckrakes! 'Tis I who supply their ship and salaries. I admit to leaning on my first mate and quartermaster for direction, but I am a quick study and have learned much. Nevertheless, as we rounded the tip of Florida, I found myself forced to enact certain harsh punishments, even for the slightest infractions, to keep order. Punishments I will not relay to you, my dear, for I do not wish to upset your sensitive nature.

This, however, only caused the men to glare at me all the more with insolent sneers...

Prowling about the quarterdeck, Bonnet halted at the railing and rubbed his eyes. He'd not slept in two days, fearful his crew would murder him in his bed. To make matters worse, he'd overheard the only two men he trusted—Carter and Mullet—cursing him to the crew. He was alone on a ship of fools, *murderous* fools. Only one thing remained to save him, another prize, but only one loaded with pearls, silver, and doubloons. Surely that would cause the men to follow him again, mayhap even earn their respect.

Wind whipped through his dark hair, cooling the sweat on his back. In the heat, he'd cast off his embroidered doublet and wore only breeches and a white holland shirt. He felt naked, though he had to admit, the lack of elegant attire brought a certain freedom he'd never experienced. It mattered not one's education and status upon these turbulent seas. It only mattered one's skill and bravado. Both of which he intended to acquire.

"Sail to starboard!" The shout came from the bowsprit, and Bonnet plucked the spyglass from his belt and raised it to his eye.

"Make all sail, three points to starboard!" he commanded. Perhaps this was the prize he was looking for.

"She flies the flag of Spain!" one pirate yelled, igniting the others in an excited frenzy.

Bonnet smiled. A Spanish merchantman would no doubt be carrying a vast treasure. He turned to Carter to issue orders, but the man had already taken charge and was bellowing commands across the deck.

That would change soon enough. He'd put the insolent first mate in his place and win this prize for his crew. Or he would die trying.

Yet the foolish Spanish ship wasn't tacking about to attempt an escape. Instead she headed straight for the *Revenge*, within yards of firing range. "Run out the guns!" he shouted to the gunner. Surely that would scare these Spanish papists into surrendering as it had all the other ships Bonnet had encountered.

The Spanish vessel replied by running out her own guns—twenty, Bonnet counted, on the starboard side as they closed in. Which meant forty guns to just ten of his.

"She's a man-of-war!" one pirate exclaimed, and before Bonnet could shout an order, the helmsman turned the wheel hard to port to make a run for it.

"Nay! Nay! I command you to stay the course!" Bonnet yelled at the man, then marched onto the main deck and glanced over the crew. "We attack! We can take them and win ourselves a worthy prize!"

Instead of cheering in agreement as he'd seen them do so often, their expressions fell as they glanced at one another with a fear so seldom seen on their faces.

Don't attack. Sail away. The words rang through Bonnet's soul, clear, strong, and commanding. But from whom? No doubt merely his inner fears—fears he must ignore if he was ever to earn his crew's respect, ever to gather the wealth he needed.

Carter approached, loathing and disgust firing from his eyes. "We don't stand a chance, Cap'n."

Bonnet balanced on the leaping deck. "Don't be a coward, Carter."

Other pirates began to mutter. "Yer gonna kills us all!"

"We can't take on a man-o-war. They'll sink us fer sure."

Hot sun speared Bonnet's back as he glared at his men, hiding his fear that they would charge and toss him overboard. "What are you, pirates or women? We fight, I say! We fight!" This was his moment—his "do or die" moment, and he knew it. He would either captain this ship to victory, or he'd forfeit his life to these bloody cullions. "Full speed ahead, Hewet! That's an order! Bring our starboard guns to bear!"

Terror streaking across their faces, the pirates dashed across the deck, some grabbing lines, others leaping into the shrouds. Bonnet breathed a sigh of relief. The *Revenge* veered to larboard, and with all canvas billowing, sliced a foamy trail through the turquoise sea, her timbers creaking and groaning with the strain. The deck tilted, and Bonnet gripped the railing, shaking off the salty spray and allowing the exhilaration of the chase to consume him, embolden him to become the captain he knew he could be.

Still the warship came, her bow lifting and plunging into the sea, her fully armed crew with their black corselets and high-crested helmets standing on the deck, glaring their way. Suddenly she veered to starboard and presented her larboard guns. The gaping holes of twenty dark muzzles stared at Bonnet, daring him to resist. He turned to order his crew to do the same, but Carter must have anticipated the move for he'd already ordered the *Revenge* on a tack that would bring the two ships broadside to broadside.

"Fire!" Bonnet shouted, but the only reply that came was the repetitive Boom! Boom! Boom! of several distant cannons. The *Revenge* exploded in a hail of splinters and fire.

CHAPTER SEVEN

*M*usic crept through the cobwebs of Lexie's mind—Evanescence's "The End of the Dream"—one of her favorite songs. No… no, not yet! She wanted to sleep, *needed* to sleep. Groping for her phone on her nightstand, she brought it to her face.

7:00 p.m.

"Ugh." She tapped off the alarm and closed her eyes. Just another minute. No, she couldn't. She had to get up. As she struggled to sit, the letter she'd been reading slid off her lap, and she gently picked it up. *Bonnet's letter.* Good thing she was a sound sleeper, or she might have rolled on it and caused damage. Tossing off her covers, she flung her feet over the edge of the bed and carefully slid the plastic sleeve back into the folder.

She'd been so enthralled with Bonnet's story she was surprised she'd fallen asleep. The last thing she remembered was him being attacked by a Spanish man-of-war. Poor guy. He had a rough time adjusting to piracy. She longed to read the rest of the story, but she had to get ready for work and grab a bite to eat. Slogging toward the kitchenette, she put on a pot of coffee and headed toward the shower.

An hour later, all clean, with a cup of joe in her stomach, and dressed in her work jeans and a fresh black t-shirt, she stood before the mirror and pinned up her damp hair. Mom had always urged her to either cut her hair or learn how to style it better, but Lexie preferred to sweep up her long tresses in a haphazard bun and allow strands to fall any which way they wanted. It suited her personality *and* her lifestyle. And it kept the more refined men away—the ones who felt they were better than her.

Men like Professor Johnson. *Barret.* Who names their son Barret, anyway?

Satisfied with her hair, Lexie reached for the jeans she wore yesterday and pulled the coin out from the back pocket—the gold Spanish coin that surely must have belonged to Bonnet. She stuffed it in the pocket of her new jeans, then grabbed her phone and backpack and headed for the door.

Wait. She glanced back at Bonnet's letters. Best not to leave them here, especially since the lock was busted. Grabbing the folder, she left and closed her door, making a mental note to call the super from work to have it fixed.

After parking and grabbing a burger from Five Guys on King Street, Lexie made her way down Broad Street to the Exchange Museum. Even at night the city was alive with tourists, workers, and citizens filling the streets. Scents of fish, fried delicacies, sweet pastries, horseflesh, and the sea all combined into a unique Charleston smell. A horse-drawn carriage *clip-clopped* by, making her smile. She'd come to love the Historic downtown of Charleston with its old buildings and unique architecture, especially St. Michael's church, coming up on her right. Streetlamps gleamed on the white columns positioned along the front, and she stopped to gaze upward at the massive white steeple stretching into the black sky.

Something, a sense… a feeling, made her turn around.

A man instantly stopped and stared into the window of a building. Except it wasn't a store, but a large brick warehouse. Strange. She started on her way again, increasing her pace, not wanting to be late on her second week at work. A tingle etched down her back, and she glanced over her shoulder. That same man halted yet again and began fumbling through the pockets of his pants.

Lexie's heart tightened. Hiking her pack farther up her shoulder, she hurried forward. Finally at the museum, she circled to the employees' entrance in the back, retrieved the key from her pocket, and unlocked the door.

One last glance toward the street revealed the same man standing at the front of the museum, staring her way. Bolting inside, she slammed and locked the door, then leaned back against it.

She had no doubt now. She was being followed.

Barret didn't know what to expect when he knocked on Lexie's door the next morning. He checked his gold watch. 8:03 A.M. Would he find a kitten or a panther?

The door swung open.

Wearing her usual holey jeans and t-shirt, Lexie's stark green eyes met his and narrowed. Brushing away a strand of wayward hair, she cocked her head. "You," was all she said.

A panther.

A tired panther, by the looks of the shadows hugging her beautiful eyes.

Barret held up Bonnet's letter and smiled. "Peace offering?"

Snagging it, she examined every detail as if he might pull a fast one on her. "How could it be an offering, *Professor*, if it was mine to begin with?"

She had a point. For some reason, her snarkiness made him smile. "Please call me Barret, Ms. Cain."

"I won't be calling you at all." She gave a curt smile and started to close the door.

Of all the... Barret shoved his foot inside. "What have I done to upset you?" He put on his most contrite expression, hating he had to humble himself and beg to see Bonnet's letters from someone with apparently no education and no idea what she had in her possession.

She studied him for a moment. "Nothing to speak of. I just..." Sighing, she rubbed her eyes then pinned him with a sharp stare. "Since you asked, I find your arrogance and look-down-on-me attitude annoying. Now, if you don't mind. I'm tired."

Barret couldn't help but smile.

She put a hand on her hip. "What are you smiling at?"

"Your honesty, Ms. Cain. I find it refreshing. And for the record, I don't look down on you."

"Oh, really?" She huffed.

"Listen, how about I buy you breakfast? No strings attached."

She wrinkled her cute little nose. "I've been working all night."

Barret leaned against the door frame. "You still need to eat, right?"

One brow raised. "You don't fool me, Professor. You want my letters."

"I'll admit to being interested, yes, but I would also like us to be friends."

"People like you aren't friends with people like me."

"Is that so? Sounds like you're the one with the chip on your shoulder."

She bit her bottom lip, making him think she was considering his offer. But then her eyes narrowed, and she started to close the door yet again. "Thank you for bringing back the letter."

Barret had one card left to play, one he'd planned on playing at breakfast when she was sitting down. "Someone broke into my office last night."

Her angry expression transformed into one of curiosity. "What?"

"Let me take you to breakfast, and I'll tell you all about it."

Of course Barret took Lexie to one of the most expensive, posh restaurants in downtown Charleston, *The Palmetto Cafe.*

She halted outside. "I can't go in there in these ratty jeans."

"Don't worry," Barret said with a wink. "I know the owner."

Of course he did.

"And besides, they have the best Belgian waffles this side of the Mississippi." Holding the door open, he gestured for her to enter. Not only that, but once the hostess led them to a table, he pulled out her chair and waited for her to sit. It took her a minute before she realized what he was doing. A gentleman. How rare in this day and age.

She eased onto the seat, and he pushed her chair in before he sat across from her. His cologne showered her with the scents of musk, cedar, and rum. Spicy, refined, just like the Professor. Other scents wafted around her—bacon, sweet syrup, and coffee.

To say she'd rarely dined at such a fine establishment would be an understatement. She could count the momentous occasions on one hand. One, when George had married Mom and they'd hosted the reception at a chic restaurant, and the other time when she'd graduated from high school, and Mom insisted George take them both out to celebrate. Of course he'd ruined it by his complaining, along with his constant criticizing of her manners. She fingered her gold hoop earring.

The memory of her mother caused the ever-present pain in her heart to throb.

She shook it off as she took the menu from the hostess's hand, ignoring the snub the woman gave her before the attractive blond turned to smile at Barret. They exchanged pleasantries and idle chit-chat about this person and that, but Lexie wasn't paying attention. Her eyes were glued to the list of mouth-watering food *and* exorbitant prices.

Was this guy trying to impress her or make her feel all the more inferior? No matter. She might as well take advantage of the situation and order what she wanted, because she doubted she'd make it back here again.

Not unless she found Bonnet's treasure.

Another patron entered the restaurant, and the chatty hostess was forced to stop her flirting and get to work. Poor thing.

Lexie glanced at Barret over the top of her menu. "We could have just gone to McDonald's."

The lines between his eyes folded, and the strangest look overcame him as if the very idea were ludicrous, and she wondered if he'd ever been to a McDonald's.

Instead of answering, he merely said, "Order whatever you want."

She hadn't eaten anything since her burger at 8:00 last night. And the more she glanced over the items on the menu, the more her stomach seemed to leap and yap like a hungry dog. True, she wanted desperately to hear about the break-in at Barret's office, but she needed food first.

By the time the waiter approached, she was ready.

"I'll have the Eggs Benedict," she began, but the waiter had already jotted it down and turned to Barret to get his order.

"And French Vanilla coffee." She drew his attention back to her. "Sliced fresh pineapple, a side of bacon, grits with cheese and butter, and a fruit plate with vanilla bean yogurt."

The waiter lifted both brows at her as if she were some strange oddity, but Barret laughed, a deep comforting laugh that surprised her with its warmth.

He handed the waiter his menu. "And I'll have the Belgium Waffle and a cup of Mayan Roast."

The waiter scurried off, leaving Lexie sitting alone with Barret. Why did the man keep smiling at her? At least a day's stubble peppered his jaw and chin, so at odds with his sophisticated mannerisms. He wore a black business shirt tucked into expensive jeans. A silver chain peeked at her from within his collar. But it was his eyes that drew her in, a mixture of brown and gold like amber, hinting at a depth behind them. What concerned her, however, was what lingered in that depth—shark or minnow?

"Hungry?" he asked with an annoying grin on his face.

She fiddled with her pristine linen napkin before sliding it in her lap. "So, tell me about this break-in."

The waiter brought their coffee, and Barret waited until the man left. "My entire office was ransacked. They smashed the window on the door and reached in to unlock it, then searched through everything I own, books, drawers, shelves, papers…even moved my rug."

Lexie sipped her coffee, allowing the rich vanilla flavor to flood her mouth. Best coffee she'd had in a while. "What did they take?"

"Not a thing." He shrugged. "That's the weird part. I have some very valuable antiques—bullets and coins from the Civil War, arrowheads, extant copies of colonial documents, an old ship wheel from the 18th century." He took a sip of his coffee and shook his head. "Whatever they were looking for, they never found it."

She set her cup down on the china a little too loud as an alarming thought occurred to her.

Barret leaned closer. "With your apartment broken into just the day before and now my office, this can't be a coincidence."

"And the only thing tying us together are Bonnet's letters."

"Exactly."

"I don't understand. Why would anyone care?"

Barret took another sip of coffee. "The letters are definitely a valuable find, but only to historians. I suppose someone would pay a decent penny for them, but they'd be easily traced back to the seller. I just can't see it."

"Then it's the treasure they are after." Lexie eased a wayward strand of hair behind her ear.

Barret shrugged and shook his head. "Bonnet's treasure is only a myth."

"But what if these letters contain information that could lead to it? If whoever broke into my apartment and your office is after them, that's the only explanation that makes sense."

"Maybe. I do admit it's rather strange." Barret scratched the stubble on his chin.

Lexie bit her lip, her suspicions rising. "You must have told someone."

"No...of course not...wait." He glanced up, eyes widening. "The antiquities lab. They would have known."

Sighing, Lexie sat back. Should she show him the coin? Maybe that would convince him of the treasure. But could she trust him? He was well-educated and obviously wealthy. *Definitely* privileged and snobbish—just the type of person she should *never* trust. Not after she'd seen what George did to Mom, how he lorded his money and status over her like a master to a slave.

To keep her compliant.

Yet when Barret looked at her like he was looking at her now, his eyes searching hers as if he longed to know more about her, she could not deny the tingle that ran down to her toes. Not a beware-of-this-guy-he-has-bad-intentions kind of tingle either.

"I read one of Bonnet's letters last night," she blurted, if only to stop his penetrating stare.

Excitement flashed across his eyes. "Really?"

Stomach growling, Lexie glanced to where the waiter disappeared. Were they waiting for the chicken to lay the eggs? "Yeah, bunch of sailing stuff mostly. He captured a couple merchant ships, then cleaned the bottom of his ship... I forget what it's called."

"Careening," Barret said.

She pointed at him. "Yup. That's it. Then he sailed to Florida and ran into some war ship. I fell asleep before I found out what happened."

"Ah, the Spanish war ship. That was the beginning of the end for him." He spotted her empty cup, then gestured for the waiter and asked for more coffee. For her! His cup was still nearly full.

Dumbfounded, she watched as the waiter dashed away. "The language is so different from ours, and I'm not sure what it all means." It was the truth. She'd had difficulty deciphering the archaic words. What if Bonnet put a code in the letters about the treasure? She might miss it altogether.

Barret leaned forward. "I know everything about Bonnet. Perhaps I can help. We could read the letters together."

She could tell he was trying not to appear overly excited, but his eyes gave him away. "So you can steal the treasure?" Cocking her head, she gave him a playful grin, half kidding and half not. No doubt this man had enough treasure of his own. But didn't the rich love to get richer?

He laughed, a laugh that said he was enjoying her company, not the nervous laugh of a man caught lying. "Miss Cain, I promise you that you may keep whatever treasure we find."

She pursed her lips, studying him.

He arched one brow. "So, do we have a deal?"

CHAPTER EIGHT

"I've never seen anyone eat so much food in one sitting." Barret chuckled as he walked beside Lexie down Meeting Street on the way to his car. Even though she had asked the waiter to bag up the bacon and fruit, she'd easily consumed the rest.

Shielding her eyes from the sun, she smiled up at him and shrugged. "What can I say? I'm a healthy girl."

Healthy *and* beautiful. Despite her disheveled hair and holey jeans—or maybe because of them—she had an innocent beauty, untainted by all the makeup, jewelry, and designer clothing most young women wore.

And besides, he could honestly say he'd not had so much fun with a woman in ages.

Sunlight reflected off the three earrings in her left ear—an odd combination of a pearl, a silver clip, and a skull. He wanted to ask her about them and about the eagle tattoo on the back of her neck, but it wasn't the time.

Suddenly she stopped, yanked her pack off her shoulder, and pulled out her wallet. When she flipped it open, Barret could easily see she had only two fives inside. He was about to tell her there was no need to help pay for her breakfast when she took one of the bills, along with the Styrofoam container of her leftover food and stooped to hand them to a woman sitting on the sidewalk with a sign that read. *Homeless mother of two. Please help.*

The poor lady glanced up at her and squinted in the sunlight. Her hair hung in matted strands, and dirt smudged her face, but she smiled and took the offering. "God bless you, miss."

Rising, Lexie started on her way again.

Barret followed, trying to make sense of what he'd just witnessed. She must have seen the woman on their way into the restaurant.

"You ordered all that food so you could give her some."
He glanced back at the woman over his shoulder.

"Yeah, but I shouldn't have eaten so much of it." She
quirked her lips and rubbed her stomach. "I was just so
hungry."

"I didn't even see her sitting there," Barret admitted.

"Of course not. Most people get so used to the homeless,
they become part of the scenery."

Barret scratched the back of his neck, feeling a tad
insulted. "I wonder how one tells whether they are sincerely
homeless or whether they are scamming people for drug
money."

Halting, she stared up at him. Wind tossed her ivory bangs
across her forehead, and she brushed them away. "I don't care.
When I see a woman…a *mother*, it doesn't matter. My mom
and I were homeless for a while, and I'm going to do all I can
to help other women in that same situation. If she scammed
me, that's on her." Turning, she started on her way again.

Unusual shame tugged on Barret's cheerful mood. He had
no idea she'd been homeless. Of course he hadn't. He hardly
knew her. And suddenly, he longed to rectify that. "I didn't
mean to upset you." He fell in step beside her.

"You didn't. It's what most people think of the homeless."

Barret searched for the right words to say as he drove
Lexie back to her apartment, but for the first time in his life,
his jumbled thoughts formed no coherent sentence.

"So, what do you say, Miss Cain?" He pulled his BMW
into a parking spot. "How about we read the letters together,
and I help you find this treasure."

Skepticism raced across her eyes before she turned to gaze
out the window. Several minutes passed as heat rose in the car,
along with the sweet smell of her vanilla perfume.

Finally, she faced him again. "Tell you what, Professor.
I'll read one letter with you. If you can help me, I'll consider
letting you read the rest. Deal?"

He smiled, pleasantly surprised at her acquiescence.
"Deal."

He was also surprised when she invited him up to her apartment. Once inside, she shut the door, moved two chairs close together and then faced him with one hand on her hip. "Try anything and you'll regret the day you were born."

Barret didn't know whether to laugh or be once again insulted. For one thing, the lady couldn't weigh more than 120 pounds wet. For another, Barret would never take advantage of any woman. "You have my assurance, Miss Cain, I will behave the perfect gentleman."

She must have taken his grin for sarcasm. "I may not look strong, but—"

"You don't have to act tough for me," he interrupted. "I'm not the enemy."

"Hmm," was all she said as she opened the folder and pulled out one of Bonnet's letters. "This is the one I started last night but didn't finish." Then taking a seat, she gestured for him to sit, and held the paper between them.

⚓

My dearest one, I shall ne'er forget the sound of those mighty guns. The ferocious thunder pounds in my head even still. Sharp splinters of wood fired through the air. Thick smoke enveloped the deck. The Revenge shook like a wailing babe, every timber screaming in terror. I lost my balance and fell to the deck. I couldn't hear. I couldn't see. I couldn't breathe. I thought I'd died and gone to hell.

Numb and disoriented, Bonnet rolled on his side and dared to open his eyes. Smoke billowed from one of his cannons, hit by a shot. The gun crew, bodies twitching and blood spurting, slumped over the steaming six-pounder. Not two feet in front of him lay a man with both legs missing. Other bodies, severed by massive splinters, littered the deck. Blood formed pools that slid back and forth with the movement of the ship as the acrid smell of gun smoke, mixed with blood and bile, stung his nose. Rising on all fours, he tossed what little was in his stomach onto the wooden planks and tried to rise but toppled to the deck again.

Above the screams of agony, Carter barked the order to fire, and the *Revenge* belched a booming broadside that sent a shiver through the ship. Batting away the smoke, Bonnet tried to assess whether the shots hit their mark, but all he saw was the Spanish ship coming across the *Revenge*'s stern.

"They're gonna rake us!" one pirate shouted in terror.

Bonnet attempted to rise again. He was the captain. He needed to take command, do something, give an order. But his mind was so befuddled with shock and his heart so gorged with fear, he couldn't think what to do.

The last thing he saw was the red flash of the Spaniard's guns. Closing his eyes, he waited for the shots to hit, wondering if he should pray or not. No doubt God had already made up His mind to send Bonnet to hell. The ear-piercing sound of glass shattering was followed by the crunch and grind of wood smashing and the horrifying screams of the injured below deck. Blood streamed into his eyes, yet no pain came. Odd. Reaching up, he felt a large spear of wood stuck in his head. Blood covered his hand. Then all went black.

My most precious Melody, you cannot imagine my horror when I next awoke lying injured in my cabin to discover that half my crew was either dead or wounded. Carter and Mullet took over the ship and sailed us to Nassau, where I now find myself alone on the Revenge, anchored in the bay of that dreaded pirate haven. I fear my crew have abandoned me. Last I ventured into town, I heard snickers rising like the tide as mocking eyes followed my every move. I am a laughingstock, my dear, the wealthy gentleman who tried to play pirate! I am undone and long to see your lovely face and hear your sweet voice. You always believed in me, my sweet. Oh, how I wish I could sail this broken ship to Charles Town and run into your warm embrace. But alas, I have not proven myself a captain, nor acquired enough wealth to make you proud. How I shall accomplish that now, I have no idea...

Wind whipped through the broken window of Bonnet's cabin, fluttering both his candle and the feathers of his quill pen. Laying it down, he rose and plucked a book from the shelf. At least most of his books had not been destroyed by the cannon shot. In truth, the past week at Nassau, they had been his only companions.

A knock sounded on his door, and he spun, book in hand, to see an enormous, rather frightening man in both height and brawn, enter. "Captain Bonnet." Halting, the man removed his feathered tricorn, swung it out before him, and dipped his head.

At the respectful greeting, Bonnet stood a little taller, wishing he'd donned his waistcoat and cravat in order to receive his guest like a gentleman. A thick black beard covered the man's face and hung in braided strands down to his belly. Over his shoulders hung two silken bands, each housing two pistols.

Bonnet slowly closed his book and set it on his desk as the realization of who stood before him turned his blood to ice. The most feared pirate in all the Caribbean. Blackbeard.

"I barely recognized you, Edward." Bonnet dared take a step closer to the pirate captain who invoked fear by only the mention of his name.

"Aw, this?" Edward Beard waved a hand over his attire. "Terrifying, is it not? Though I do think it suits a person of our vocation."

Bonnet gestured for him to sit as he moved to the sideboard to pour his guest a drink. "You've changed much since I last saw you on Barbados." He poured his best rum into a glass and handed it to Edward. "I'd say pirating has served you well."

Blackbeard took the drink and slid into a chair, studying Bonnet.

Bonnet sipped his own drink, desperately needing the calming effect of the rum. Though he had been acquainted with Edward in his past life, the man who sat before him was as different from the boy he once knew as a vulture was from an innocent dove.

Edward smiled and tossed back his rum. "Indeed it has. Yet, I hear ye have not benefited from the same experience."

Heat swamped Bonnet's face, and he turned to gaze out his glassless window. No doubt the man had heard his crew mocking him in town. "I ran into a bit of bad luck with a Spanish war ship 'tis all. Before that, I had some success. Not as much as you, to be sure, but I am learning."

"I have no doubt, my friend. And that is why I have come."

Turning, Bonnet noticed the man's empty glass and poured him another. Edward's gaze lifted to his over the decanter—dark, piercing eyes that reached deep into Bonnet's soul as if he wanted to grip it and tear it from him.

Bonnet backed away, attempting to hide the shiver coursing through him. "What is it you propose, Edward?"

Blackbeard swirled the rum in his glass. "That ye allow me to send my carpenters over to start on repairs immediately. We'll get this old sinking bucket back into prime sailing shape for ye in no time. And I'll toss in the use of me surgeon to dress your wound"—he gestured to the bloody bandage wrapped around Bonnet's head—"and tend to yer wounded below." He swallowed the rum in one gulp. "Then I will provide a new crew for the *Revenge*. What say ye to that?"

Regardless of the flicker of hope in Bonnet's heart, suspicion rang deafening alarm bells. "Why would you offer me such kindness?"

"Because yer uncle was kind to mine, and because we are friends." Edward attempted to smile, but it disappeared as quickly as the rum.

"Though I am grateful, do tell me what is in it for you, Captain? I mean no disrespect, but you are a pirate, after all."

He chuckled and set down his glass. "I will assume command of the *Revenge* but only until ye fully recover from yer wounds. You may, of course, remain as captain and reside here in the captain's quarters during yer convalescence."

"And you'll relinquish command back to me when I am well again?"

"Of course. I have me own sloop to command. What need have I of two?" He tossed a braided strand of his beard into the air.

Bonnet wondered. Even so, what choice did he have? Without Edward's help, his pirating career was over. He had no crew, little money, and a broken-down ship. If he accepted Edward's offer, he would gain both, along with being trained by the best pirate captain alive.

Have naught to do with evil. Again, that nagging inner voice rose up within Bonnet.

Placing his hands on his thighs, Blackbeard pushed himself to stand, his over six-foot height looming over Bonnet. "Do we have a bargain, Captain Bonnet?"

Bonnet took the man's hand in a firm shake. "We do, Captain Blackbeard. We do."

My dearest, my luck has turned. You would not believe who entered my cabin this very day but Blackbeard himself. You may remember him from Barbados as Edward Beard. He has made me an offer I cannot refuse, and with his help, I shall soon be able to garner the wealth I need for us to finally be together. I will write later when my situation has improved and then send the letters to you when next we approach Charles Town. I pray you are well.

With my fondest and sincerest adoration,
Yours forever,
Stede

"How embarrassing to think I'm related to this man." Lexie rose and set Bonnet's letter gently on her bed. Sitting so close to Barret was muddling her thoughts. Not to mention that darn cologne of his. She typically didn't like men's colognes, but this one was intoxicating—all cedar and musk. Sighing, she turned to face him.

He leaned back in his chair, a stunned and pensive look on his face. "Yeah. Not the best pirate, was he?"

"He was completely inept. Out of his league. And the worst part was he didn't realize it and cut his losses when he should have."

"His is a tragic tale." Barret's voice was methodic, distant. "He ends up—"

She raised her palm. "Don't tell me. Despite his flaws, I'm starting to like him. Maybe we *are* related because I can understand his mindset, his decisions." She sat on the bed. "And all the bad luck that came his way."

Barret said nothing as he stared off into space, his mind obviously elsewhere. No doubt back in 1717. He rubbed the stubble on his chin as she'd seen him do when he was thinking. With that black hair, the tips of which curled at his collar, his strong physique and piercing eyes, he looked more pirate than professor.

Or maybe she simply had pirates on the brain.

Handsome or not, the question remained, could he help her find the treasure?

"So, tell me, Professor, what about this Spanish war ship? How was Bonnet defeated so badly, and why did his men desert him? Is Nassau the same place as today in the Bahamas?" She pummeled him with questions, to which he gladly and quite enthusiastically answered with more information than she needed *or* wanted.

When he finished, he leaned forward, elbows on his knees. The chain slipped out from beneath his shirt. A silver cross hung on the tip. Great. Was this guy some Jesus freak?

His gaze drifted to the letter. "This is such an incredible find, Lexie—may I call you Lexie?"

She nodded. Nobody called her Miss Cain anyway.

"There has been much research on who Blackbeard really was, but this letter..." His words trailed off as he slid deep in thought once again.

"I knew he was a bad dude," she said. "A vicious pirate, but that's all I ever learned about him."

Barret snapped his gaze to her. "Most historians believe his real name was Edward Thatch or Edward Teach and that he came from Bristol, England. Yet recently there has been some evidence that he was instead the son of Captain James Beard, who moved from Barbados to Charles Town. This letter"—He pointed to it as if it were made of gold— "proves that." He raked a hand through his hair. "No one could ever figure out why Blackbeard would have approached a failure like Bonnet in the first place. Now we know. They knew each other!"

Lexie smiled at the excitement on Barret's face. "You really get into this stuff."

"I'm an historian." He chuckled. "And I'm writing a book on Charleston pirates, so yes, this is a thrilling find."

And she must never forget that fact. The professor was only here for the letters, not to be her friend and not to feed her gourmet breakfasts. But he had proved useful. He knew a lot about Bonnet, pirates, and now this Blackbeard fellow. No doubt he would be able to interpret any clues about treasure in these letters.

Reaching in her back pocket, she pulled out the Spanish coin and handed it to him.

He nearly squealed with delight, if men did such things. "A doubloon! From 1718!" He flipped it over, studying it further. "Where did you get it?"

"My mother had it."

Rising, he moved to look at it beneath a lamp on the table. "What are these numbers and letters engraved in it?"

"I was going to ask you, *Professor*."

"Hmm."

Lexie inched to stand beside him. "So, do you think this belonged to Bonnet?"

"It could have. It's the right year."

"Do you think the engraving is a clue to treasure?"

"That would be a far reach." Barret sighed and faced her. "Listen I know you want the treasure, but these etchings could mean any number of things or nothing at all."

"Maybe the letters would help decipher them."

"Maybe." He rubbed the back of his neck, still staring at the coin. "There's never been any evidence linking Bonnet to any hidden treasure."

She cocked her head. "You just told me there was new evidence linking him to Blackbeard, didn't you? Why do you historians think you know everything?"

He grinned. "Good point."

She took the coin back from him. "How much is it worth, anyway?"

"You aren't thinking of..." He frowned. "You could probably get four or five grand for it."

"Whoa." Lexie swallowed and stepped away from him. That would certainly help her situation—pay rent for four or five months. But then what?

"I'm sorry. I get overzealous about such things," Barret said. "You're absolutely right. There could be treasure and this could be a clue. I want to help you, Lexie. I hope you'll let me."

She turned to face him and found the sincerity on his face matched his tone. "I might do that, Professor."

She could tell he wanted to say more, but instead, he nodded toward her bed. "I should let you get some sleep. I know you work nights."

"I have tomorrow off. But yes, I'm pretty tired."

The shadow of a man crossed behind the curtains of her front window, drawing her gaze. Nothing unusual about that, except he lingered, moving too slow for a passerby. Dashing to the door, she opened it and glanced down the walkway. A man, wearing a hoody, glanced over his shoulder at her before disappearing into the stairwell.

She knew that face. It was the man who followed her last night. She was sure of it! Her breath caught in her throat.

"What is it?" Barret pushed past her and stood just outside the door, looking both ways.

"There was a man...I thought...I think he's been following me."

"Which way did he go?" Barret hurried toward the stairs.

"Never mind. He's gone."

"Are you sure?" Halting, he gripped the railing and scanned the parking lot.

An odd sense of being protected warmed her, but she shook it off and stepped back into her apartment. Thank God the super had replaced the locks that day.

Barret appeared in the doorway, looking concerned. "With the break-in here and my office and now this, you shouldn't be walking from your car to work alone at night."

Raising her brows, she cocked her head. "Well, I really can't afford a bodyguard, now can I?"

He gave her a look of sorrow. Pity? Either way she hated it. "Why don't I walk you there each night?"

"What?" She waved him off, unsure she even heard correctly.

Leaning against the door frame, he crossed arms over his chest. "It's a quick trip from the university to downtown. I don't mind."

She huffed. Did he think she was born yesterday? "If you're worried about the letters, I don't keep them on me."

"It's not only the letters I'm worried about, Lexie."

The look in his eyes was so full of concern, so sincere and penetrating, she turned her face away. "Thank you for the offer, but I can take care of myself."

"Very well. Call me when you want to go over another letter." He handed her his card. "*Or* if you need anything."

Like a million dollars, an education, good job, and a family who loved her? "Sure." Maybe.

And with that he gestured for her to lock the door and walked away.

She *did* lock her door—double bolted. Then leaning back against it, she looked at his business card. *Charleston Southern University, Barret Robert Johnson, PhD, College of History.*

Her stomach tightened. Maybe she was as dumb as her ancestor Bonnet and she'd just made a deal with Professor Blackbeard—one that would lead to her destruction.

CHAPTER NINE

A week passed and Lexie had not gotten the courage up to call Barret, nor to even read another of Bonnet's letters. She'd skimmed the next one but found it so confusing, she knew she needed Barret's help. And that made her angry most of all. She hated needing help from anyone. Everyone she had ever known had let her down—her father, her friends, her co-workers, her stepfather, and if she admitted it, even her mother. Why had she gotten sick and left Lexie all alone in the world?

"Oh, Mom," Lexie breathed out as she swept the last of the dirt from the dungeon floor into the dustpan. "If you could see me now... cleaning up other people's trash." Her mother had wanted so much more for Lexie. A college degree, good job, decent husband, and maybe a chance at a normal, happy life. And she had suffered immensely in an unhappy marriage of her own to give those things to Lexie.

Lexie dumped the dust, gum wrappers, mud, and other tidbits she couldn't identify into the garbage bag, then walked to put the broom and the pan in a hidden closet off to the side where tourists never went. Back at the garbage bag, she closed the top and wrapped a zip tie around it, then set it down. Sweeping back a strand of her hair, she glanced over the museum dungeon to make sure she'd gotten everything before she left for the day—or night. A quick walk into the next alcove led her straight to where Stede Bonnet had been imprisoned. His likeness in the form of a wax figure sat on a stool, head in his hand, and chains around his wrists, and she wondered yet again if it bore any resemblance to the actual man.

At first Lexie had not wanted to believe they were related. Wasn't her family history tarnished enough without adding a pirate to the mix? Even when her mom had shown Lexie the research and documents she'd obtained through Ancestry.com and told her about the old chest she'd found in her grandmother's apartment after she died, Lexie had wanted no part of it. Yet now, she could not deny that only a relation of Bonnet's would have kept such valuable letters and passed them down through the years.

"Hey there, Mr. Bonnet Sir, you wouldn't want to tell me where you buried your treasure, would ya?" Lexie smiled.

No answer came except a harbor bell in the distance and the *pitter-pat* of what she could only guess was a mouse or rat. Shivering, she spun about, grabbed the garbage bag, turned out the lights, and headed toward the door. Quitting time, and, boy, was she tired.

Outside the museum, she glanced up at the sky where thick black clouds hid most of the light of the rising sun. The scent of the salty bay, fish, and the spice of rain swept past her nose in the incoming breeze as she began her five-block walk to where she'd parked her car. Hoisting her backpack farther up her shoulder, she glanced around, looking for anyone suspicious. She'd seen the same man at least twice in the last week, always wearing a hoody, always following, and always turning away when she spotted him over her shoulder.

She made it to Church Street before the rain started. *Great. Just great.* The drizzle rapidly turned into a torrent as thunder growled overhead. Dipping her head against the drops striking her face, she hurried her pace. Very few people were out and about, only delivery trucks and a few shop and restaurant owners. A shiver spun down her back. She snapped her gaze over her shoulder. Hoody-man was a block behind her. He stooped to tie his shoe. Lexie dashed forward. By the time she made it to the parking garage, water dripped from her hair, and her t-shirt and jeans were soaked through.

She cast a quick glance behind her. Lightning highlighted her stalker in icy silver. This time he didn't turn away, didn't pretend he wasn't following her. Instead he kept walking, methodically, intently. Thunder boomed overhead. Fear sent ice through her veins. She couldn't make out his face within his hood, but she no longer cared. She scanned the surroundings. No one was in sight. No one to come to her rescue. As usual.

Fishing for her car keys in her pocket, she darted up the garage stairs and then raced down the aisle where her car was parked. Thunder roared again, shaking the building and flickering the dim lights overhead. They sizzled and spat. Raindrops tapped on the roof, mocking her with their laughter.

There. Her car, just seven cars down on the left. She dropped her keys. The clanking sound echoed through the garage.

A hand grabbed her arm. Her heart crashed into her ribs. Pain etched into her shoulder. She screamed. The man spun her around.

"Where are they?" he demanded through clenched teeth. His hoody had slipped off his head, revealing a shock of red hair, a round, thick face, clean-shaven jaw, and small blue eyes that sat too close on his face. He towered at least a foot above her. The nostrils of his pointy nose flared as he added. "I won't ask again!"

"What?" she managed to squeak out.

"The letters. Where are they?" He shoved his face into hers so close she could smell his breath—coffee and something sweet.

Blood raced through her veins. Her breath seized in her throat. *Oh no. Don't let me pass out!* Instead, she used her last remaining strength to punch him in the gut. Her fist struck steel. Her fingers throbbed. She kicked him, but he leapt out of the way. She tried to punch him again, but he grabbed her wrist and shook her violently.

"This can be easy or hard, lady. You choose." Releasing one of her hands, he reached for her backpack.

"We choose hard." The male voice came out of nowhere. So did the fist that slugged hoody-man across the jaw. Releasing Lexie, he stumbled backward, but quickly righted himself. Eyes full of fury, he charged Barret. Yes, Barret. She could hardly believe her eyes as the professor appeared beside her.

Hoody-man swung at Barret, but the professor ducked in time and dove his fist into the man's stomach. Groaning, he gripped his middle and then quickly thrust his fist upward, clipping Barret's jaw. The man came at him again, but Barret blocked both punches with his arms with amazing speed before leveling another strike across the man's face and kicking him in the stomach. Hoody-man cussed, wiped the blood from his mouth, and then turned and disappeared into the shadows.

Lexie, unable to breathe, stared at Barret as he rubbed his jaw and faced her. His breath came fast. His fists were still clenched, and his eyes blazed from the heat of the fight. Yet ever so slowly, he reached out to her.

"It's okay, Lexie. He's gone."

She knew that, of course, but for some reason, her fear did not agree, and she remained poised for fight or flight. He attempted a smile, his eyes never leaving hers as he reached for her, nodding his assurance. Slowly, she allowed herself to breathe, but then started to collapse. Barret caught her before she hit the ground. Then lifting her into his arms, he pressed her against him. He was warm and firm, and the scent of his cologne flooded her nose. And for the first time in her life, she felt safe. If only for a moment.

Before she came to her senses. She pushed from him. "What are you doing here?"

"You're welcome," he returned with a quirk of his lips.

Lexie closed her eyes and listened to the *tap tap* of rain on the roof. Her head suddenly felt light, and she raised a hand to rub it.

"Here, you need to sit." She felt his gentle touch on her elbow and allowed him to take her keys. "Which one?"

"The old blue Honda over there."

Within seconds, he had the door opened and her sitting on the passenger side as he knelt before her. "Was that the man who's been following you?"

Nodding, she leaned sideways against the car seat, still facing Barret, wondering if she were dreaming. "Why are you here? How did you know…?"

He shrugged. "I didn't." A car started up a few aisles over, drawing his gaze. "If I tell you, promise not to be mad?"

"No." Her hands shook, and she shoved them between her knees.

He smiled. "I was worried about you. So, I've been keeping an eye on you after work, making sure you make it to your car."

"What?" She should feel indignant, furious, violated even, but for some reason she could not conjure up those feelings at the moment. Still, she did manage to force annoyance into her tone. "Don't I have enough people following me?" More importantly, why had she not seen him?

"Just in the morning before I go to work."

"Oh, is that all?" A traitorous smile tickled her lips, but she shoved it away. Why would anyone care about her? *The letters.* Of course it was the letters. Her hands were still shaking.

Barret grabbed them and cupped them within his. His strength surrounded her like a barricade, but she shook off the warm sensation it caused. He certainly didn't have the hands of a professor or the fighting ability of a man who worked with books for a living.

A car entered the garage and thrummed past them. Releasing her hands, and without asking, he swept her legs inside the car and shut the door. Before she knew what was happening, he hopped in the driver's side, inserted the key, and started the car. "I'm taking you home."

Barret was not taking no for an answer. He'd never met a woman so stubborn and independent that she willingly put herself in harm's way.

"No. Please." Lexie put her hand on his arm, but it was still shaking. She snagged it back. "You don't have to. I'm fine, really."

He slid the car in reverse and gave her a stern look. "No, you're not. Why won't you let me help you?"

Settling back into her seat, she sighed. "Okay. But just this once."

"He wanted the letters, didn't he?" Barret said as they exited the garage onto the street.

Lexie nodded, staring at the buildings passing by the window. "Don't worry, they are safe."

Barret suppressed a growl. "I'm more worried about you." Rain splotched the windshield and he turned on the wipers.

She didn't respond, didn't look his way, obviously didn't believe him. What had happened to this woman to make her so frightened of letting anyone in? Yes, the letters were important, but not as much as her life. As *her.*

He'd come to realize that when he saw the man attacking her. Rage had welled up inside of him that was only outdone by his fear. Not only a rage at the villain or a fear that a woman would be hurt, but a terror that *this* woman would be hurt. *Lexie Cain.* He'd only known her a few weeks, but she had left her mark on his heart. And he found himself wanting to know her, to protect her. Maybe it was just because she seemed so lost and alone. Like a stray kitten wandering the streets for scraps.

She remained silent on the short ride to her apartment, and though he sought for the right words to say, once again he found his thoughts jumbled in this woman's presence. Him? A professor accustomed to standing up before hundreds of students in a lecture hall. He'd laugh if it weren't so humiliating.

He pulled into her parking spot and shut off the engine. "I'll walk you to your door."

She gave him a strange look, then began fiddling with the strap of her backpack in her lap. "No need. I should thank you, I guess."

"If it hurts to do so, don't bother." He hoped his tone was as playful as he intended.

A slight smile curved her lips. "Where did you learn to fight anyway?"

"Here and there. High school wrestling team, took martial arts growing up."

She released a heavy sigh as if the news unsettled her. "The letters aren't in my backpack." She glanced at him. "Just so you know."

Thunder rumbled, shaking the car slightly as raindrops tapped on the windshield and slid down in rivulets.

"I'm sure you're keeping them safe." Actually, he wasn't sure at all, but what else could he say to this oversensitive woman? "How about we do this?" He turned sideways to face her, but something in the back seat caught his eye—two packs of Huggies?

He couldn't help but chuckle. "Something I should know?" He jerked his head toward the diapers.

She followed his gaze and smiled. "They are for my neighbor. She's a single mom and has trouble affording them on her own."

Barret allowed the revelation to wander through his mind, seeking a rational explanation. He found none. None except that this woman who barely had two pennies to rub together had a heart of gold.

"I should go." She reached for the door handle.

"Let me come by your work early in the morning. We can read the letters together, and then I can walk you to your car."

Her forehead scrunched as if he'd asked her to do a cartwheel. She shook her head.

"That way you'll be safe," he continued. "It's obvious this guy is not going to give up. I can call Adam to help. You remember him, the policeman?"

"I don't want his help." She bit her bottom lip, studying the water streaming down the window. "I don't need protection. Besides, I'm sure you have classes to teach during the day."

"The students just went home for summer break. All I do over the next few months is research, and reading Bonnet's letters is just that."

She eyed him suspiciously, and he wished more than anything she would trust him. But trust had to be earned from this lady.

"I have work to do," she snapped. "Unlike you, I can't sit and read letters all night."

"I'll help you finish your work."

"You? Dust, scrub, and sweep?" She laughed. "Now, *that* I would pay to see."

Though he felt a twinge of anger at her insult, he smiled. "You'll pay me too? It's a deal!"

She shook her head, but the twinkle in her eyes gave her away. "I don't know. I'd have to ask my manager."

"I'll show up an hour or two before you quit. Tell her about the attack and that I'm walking you back to your car. She can hardly argue with that."

Lexie eased a strand of hair behind her ear. "Maybe. Let me think about it." She held out her hand, palm up.

Confused, he stared at it, wondering if there was some new handshake he was unfamiliar with.

She arched a brow. "The keys?"

"Ah." He dropped them in her hand.

"How are you going to get back to your car?" She grabbed her backpack and opened the door. A wet mist, carrying the fresh scent of rain, swept into the car.

"I'll call a friend." Barret got out on his side and shut the door.

A beep sounded as she pressed a button on the fob, and before he could say another word, she made a dash for her apartment. "Goodbye, Professor."

He rushed after her, trying to avoid the puddles in his Italian leather shoes. "I'm walking you to your door."

She made no reply, just darted up the stairs, unlocked her door, and turned to face him. Strands of her hair escaped her bun in damp curls about her neck. A raindrop slid down her cheek. He fisted his hands to stop from wiping it away.

"Thank you," she said.

"For what?"

"I guess you saved my life."

For some reason, the half-hearted appreciation warmed him. "You're welcome."

"So I guess we can try this idea of yours. But only on a trial basis."

Excitement buzzed through him. "Sounds good."

"Meet me at the back door of the museum tomorrow morning at 4:00 am. Unless that's too early for a man like you."

He wasn't sure what she meant by *a man like him*, but he didn't think it was a compliment. Regardless, he was more than thrilled by her acquiescence.

"I'll see you then."

CHAPTER TEN

November 1717, Off the Island of Martinique, Caribbean

My most precious Melody,

How I long to see your sweet face again. Your radiant smile and the look of love in your eyes when last we saw each other is all that keeps me moving forward each day. You cannot know the pain I suffer every time we sail past Charles Town and I know you are so close. How oft I have nearly jumped overboard and swam to your side. But alas, our time has not yet come.

I dare to admit that I trusted my old friend Edward Beard, or Blackbeard as he is called. In truth the man has changed so much, I hardly recognize that a human heart still beats within his chest. I hesitate to regale you with details of his vicious and cruel exploits, but suffice it to say, we have had much success in the trade since he took command of the *Revenge*. We captured eighteen vessels off the coast of Virginia and Delaware, each providing the pirates valuable cargo and prizes.

Out of revenge for the hanging of Captain Bellamy's crew, a friend of Blackbeard's, he burned most of the captured vessels and behaved most maliciously to the passengers and crew. For these events, my love, I remained below deck, still recovering from my injuries and unable to *take a stand against a man who had won so many victories for the men.*

The wind has grown cold as winter approaches and we have sailed south for the islands. I have regained my good health, dearest, but I fear my pleas to also regain command of the Revenge fall on deaf ears. In truth, some days, I fear for my life...

Bonnet returned his pen to the holder, sprinkled sand on the paper to absorb the excess ink, then blew it off. The pad of footsteps approached the door of his cabin, and he quickly folded the letter and placed it inside a drawer of his captain's desk. 'Twould do no good if Blackbeard read that Bonnet feared him. He'd experienced enough of the man's cruelty to know his savagery fed off the terror of others.

Mullet, his quartermaster, burst through the door, long ago forsaking the respect due his captain by a knock. The stench of sweat, urine, and last night's fish dinner wafted in with him.

Did the man never bathe?

Rising, Bonnet drew a handkerchief to his nose. "Yes?"

"'E wants t' see ye." He glanced over the cabin that had been Bonnet's hideout for much of the past three months while he recovered. Books of every color and size lined his shelves, many of which had provided far better company than any human on board. A trunk stood open, overflowing with an assortment of fine cambric shirts, silk-woven waistcoats, neckcloths, and velvet breeches—most of which he rarely donned anymore. A sideboard housed two silver-lidded claret jugs filled with his favorite wine and several square-sided cut-glass decanters, along with weapons—cutlass, ax, two flintlock pistols, and a long knife—grown cold from disuse. And finally, in the corner, stood a bed that, though it lacked the comfort of home, Bonnet had grown accustomed to.

Mullet wrinkled his nose as if he'd entered a putrid dungeon before he snorted, spun on his heel, and left. The man wouldn't know fine belongings if a trunkful fell from heaven and landed on his head.

Regardless, Bonnet's fear began to rise. Blackbeard rarely summoned him, rarely gave him the time of day, save for partaking of an evening meal here in the captain's cabin with Bonnet and a few of his crew. Even then, the way Edward oft gazed at the opulent surroundings made Bonnet nervous that he would not stop at merely taking over command of the *Revenge*, but soon take over the captain's cabin as well, relegating Bonnet to one of the few lesser cabins. Or worse, to the crew's berth on deck.

Slipping on his embroidered brocade coat, Bonnet strapped on his sword, drew a deep breath, and headed aloft. Better to appear in his finest attire to remind Edward that Bonnet was above him in social rank. At the moment 'twas all he had in his favor.

"Ah, the gentleman arises from his bed!" Blackbeard spun from his position on the quarterdeck as Bonnet approached. "I do hope I didn't disturb yer rest."

If the sarcasm in his tone didn't frighten Bonnet, the pirate's appearance did that quite nicely. The man already stood a head above Bonnet with a chest as wide as a wooden trunk and just as thick. But 'twas the vile assortment of weapons strapped about his person and flung over his shoulder and the long braids of black hair hanging to his waist that made him appear more devil than man.

Swallowing down his fear, Bonnet offered a tight smile. "Not resting, Captain. As you can see, I am fully recovered and quite able to take command of *my* sloop yet again." There, he'd said it. And though he might suffer dearly for the challenge, he'd learned that if Blackbeard respected anything, 'twas when one was both direct and bold.

Blackbeard studied him with dark eyes long since deprived of inner light. In turn, Bonnet shifted his gaze to the white sands and lush greenery of Martinique, where they anchored in wait for passing prey.

"And why would ye wish to do that, my friend?" Blackbeard said, still studying Bonnet as one would a speck of dirt to be flicked from one's coat. "Ye are unaccustomed to the fatigues and cares of being a pirate captain. Surely ye can see that." He faced the bay as a blast of wind oscillated his braids back and forth like a pendulum, bringing with it the scent of salt, fish, and the rich loam of a verdant jungle.

Bonnet drew a breath to respond, but Blackbeard continued. "Would it not be better for a gentleman as yerself to live at ease in yer own sloop and not be obliged to perform, shall we say, any distasteful duties but rather follow yer own patrician inclinations?"

"Nay, it would not!" Bonnet barked, stomach queasy at the encounter. "We have had the same conversation many a time, my old friend, and each time I assure you I am quite hale and able to resume command."

"Yet 'tis I who possess the wherewithal to determine the condition one needs to captain a crew of cutthroats, and I fear ye will only do yerself and yer crew harm unless ye wait a while longer. "

Blackbeard's tone alerted some of the crew, who stopped to watch the altercation. "In truth, I begin to wonder yer usefulness at all."

Terror iced in Bonnet's veins. He'd seen the tortures Blackbeard had inflicted on his enemies. Gathering his voice, he raised his chin. "'Tis my ship and my crew. Both of which I paid handsomely to acquire." Even as he said it, the irony of using that as an excuse to a renowned thief didn't escape him.

More of the crew stopped their tasks and moved closer to the two captains.

Blackbeard uttered a guttural snort and fingered the handle of the long knife stuck in his belt.

And Bonnet knew his life hung on the precipice between their one-time friendship and the encroaching darkness of this man's heart.

"A sail, Cap'n, a sail!" The shout from above couldn't have come at a better time.

After offering Bonnet a threatening sneer, Blackbeard spun about, spyglass to his eye before he completed the turn.

"Weigh anchor. All hands aloft. Raise all sail!"

The pirates scrambled across the deck, some leaping into shrouds, many grabbing lines, while others dropped through hatches, disappearing below.

Happy to be ignored at the moment, Bonnet moved to the starboard railing and lifted his own scope to his eye. 'Twas a large vessel, around two-hundred tons, with at least sixteen guns, from what he could tell.

"Sheet home, lower topsails!" Blackbeard bellowed as he marched across the deck.

Carter repeated his orders, adding others with more promptness and respect than he ever had Bonnet's commands.

"Haul taut! Haul taut!" Carter shouted, and soon all sails were lowered, each one snapping to attention as they filled with wind.

The *Revenge* took off with a jolt and sped swiftly through the sea, white foam exploding over her bow and a salty mist spraying over the crew.

Bonnet clung to the railing, bracing his boots against the heaving deck, allowing the wind to blast over him, and wishing it would blast away all his problems as well. He felt impotent, naught but a useless gnat caught in the shadow of a pirate like Blackbeard, his crew, his very ship, under the man's enigmatic spell. Perhaps 'twould be best to cut his losses, disembark on the next civilized port they encountered, and formulate a new plan.

Before Blackbeard hanged him from the yardarm.

But what of Melody? How would he ever gain enough wealth to rescue her now?

Thus consumed with his thoughts, he didn't hear the order to fire. The cannon thundered, jarring his heart and causing him to leap slightly—an action he hoped the crew had not witnessed. But no one paid him any mind.

Their prey, however, paid great heed to the warning shot, quickly striking their colors in an act of surrender. A pox on Blackbeard's good luck!

Yet it soon became obvious the closer they came to the vessel and especially after they threw grapnels and boarded her that most of the crew of *La Concorde* were weak, sick, and unable to fight. Much to the pirates' chagrin, Bonnet noted, as they flew onto the deck of their prey, cutlasses raised and ready to shed innocent blood. Moans of disappointment saturated the air like a hospital full of agony-ridden patients as Blackbeard spoke in French to the captain. More moans ensued when they discovered the cargo consisted only of four-hundred slaves.

Bonnet witnessed all this from the deck of the *Revenge*, smiling at Blackbeard's misfortune and wishing all the while he had the courage to unhook the grapnels and sail away from the devilish pirate. But he had neither the courage, time, nor the loyalty of the crew who remained on board. Still, 'twas nice to dream.

Bonnet must still be dreaming, for when Blackbeard returned to the *Revenge* and approached him, he wore an unusual smile on his face, one that seemed to crack the stiff lines around his mouth.

He slapped Bonnet on the back. "Today is yer lucky day, my friend!"

My most precious Melody, mayhap God has not turned his face from me yet, for my fortune has taken a grand turn for the better! I daresay, I misjudged my old friend Edward. He has granted me back my sloop, along with my crew, and I find myself a captain once again. Edward has refitted and converted a French slaver we captured into his new flagship, renaming her Queen Anne's Revenge and adding cannons up to forty guns. After putting the crew and slaves on the island of Bequia, per my insistence, we have now set sail to prey upon ships passing the Windward islands. Thus far we have captured the *Great Allen* out of Boston and the *Margaret* from New England. If you hear of atrocities committed on these raids, dearest, you must know that I do not approve of Edward's barbarous methods and soon hope to part ways with him as I believe I have become quite a skilled captain on my own.

You own my heart, dearest. I hope to come to you soon,
Ever yours,
Stede

CHAPTER ELEVEN

*L*exie leaned on the top of the broom handle and sighed. Though Barret had finished reading the letter, he stared at it as if it were more precious than gold. She smiled. He looked more like the pirate he read about than a professor as he sat on an old barrel in the Exchange dungeon. Why, with a few adjustments to his clothes, he would fit nicely next to Bonnet among the wax figures.

"So, he finally got his ship back?" she asked, pulling him from his trance.

He looked up and nodded. "The details he gives, especially about his state of mind, are invaluable."

"I'm glad you think so." She began sweeping again. "Any hints of treasure?"

"Not yet. At this point, it sounds like he didn't have any wealth to speak of." Barret carefully put the letter back into the folder, then yawned. Stretching his hands above his head, he stood. "Let me help."

"Not used to getting up this early, eh?" She teased.

He grabbed a dustpan and stopped to set it on the floor. "I don't know how you do it, working graveyard."

She shrugged and swept the pile of dirt she'd accumulated into the pan. "You get used to it."

Barret dumped the trash into the open plastic bag.

"Thanks for your help. I'm nearly done and have an hour left to kill."

"My pleasure."

"Was it?" She had to admit it had been entertaining watching Barret attempt to sweep and then mop the floors of the main museum above them. And dust? He acted like he'd never seen a dust cloth in his life. But she had to give him credit. He had tried and not complained. Well, he might have complained a little.

Leaning her broom against a wall, Lexie headed for the displays.

"I didn't realize you'd been homeless. How long?"

Barret's question jarred her, and she wondered what had led him to ask such a thing.

"Just six months." Longest six months of her life. She slid under the chain keeping the public out of the display. Plucking the feather duster from her back pocket, she lightly swept it over the wax figures, not sure she wanted to talk about it.

"What happened?"

"Mom and I ran into some bad luck. She lost her job and her current boyfriend left her." She dared to look at him and found pity on his face. She hated the pity most of all.

"I'm sorry."

"Don't be. We survived."

"What happened to your dad?"

She flattened her lips. "Why do you care?"

"I want to get to know you better, that's all."

But why? That was the real question. "My dad left us when I was a baby." She moved to dust Bonnet, wondering whether he'd had a father who cared. She'd always heard from the many shrinks George had sent her to—trying to fix her—that the absence of a loving father was the root of her rebellious lifestyle. If that were true, then Bonnet, no doubt hadn't had a good father either.

"I'm sorry."

"Stop saying that!" Her shout came out louder than she meant.

"Okay." Barret held up his palms.

She sighed. "My dad is in prison, if you must know. Armed robbery." She'd said it to shock him, to get him to stop asking questions.

But all he did was stare at her. His mouth opened as if he wanted to say something—probably *I'm sorry* again—but then he pressed his lips together and swallowed.

She returned to her dusting.

"I bet it was difficult for your mom raising you alone," he said.

"What would you know about it?" She moved to dust another pirate, instantly regretting her harsh tone yet again. Barret may be nosy, but he didn't deserve her anger. Still... "I bet your parents are together, right? And they sent you to the best Ivy League schools. Let me guess." She spun to face him, a sarcastic grin on her face. "Captain of the football team? Prom king?"

When he didn't answer, she knew she'd guessed right.

He crossed arms over his chest. "Yeah, I had a good life. I have no complaints, but I make no apologies either."

Touché. The man could hold his own. She'd give him that.

"What does your mom think of you moving to Charleston to chase pirate treasure?" he asked.

Lexie's stomach sank. "She's dead. Died of cancer last month." Pain scorched through her heart at the words spoken aloud, and she wondered when it would stop, if ever. But at least she'd finally silenced the professor.

After several more minutes of dusting, all the while sensing Barret still standing there, she turned to face him. "It's obvious we have led very different lives. Let's just drop the getting-to-know-each-other-business and stick to deciphering Bonnet's letters."

He smiled. "Whatever you want." Yet she had a feeling he wasn't giving up so easily.

After she finished, she was surprised when Barret helped her put the broom, mop, and dust cloths away, then tied and set the garbage sack by the door. She'd been rude to him. Unnecessarily. In fact, she wouldn't have blamed him if he'd walked out. Sure, it was the letters that kept him there, but they didn't force him to help her. *Or* be polite. He even followed her upstairs to do a final inspection of the upper museum before they both bought a soda from the machine and sat down for the rest of her shift.

"Friends again?" He held up his soda can to toast hers, and she tapped it in return, an unavoidable smile on her lips.

"I ask too many questions. Occupational hazard, I'm afraid." He sipped his coke.

She drank her cream soda, savoring the sweet bubbly taste. "It's okay. I just don't like talking about myself."

"Noted."

"What do you suppose it was like for Bonnet?" Lexie asked. "To his crew he probably seemed like an inept coward, but he must have had some courage to attempt to captain a pirate ship." She huffed. "And to argue with Blackbeard."

"I agree. I don't think I'd attempt either."

She doubted that. Barret leaned forward on his knees and stared at the floorboards, his cologne finally making its way to her nose...tantalizing, sensual. The man had fought off her attacker without a second's hesitation. Not many men would have done that for a near stranger.

"What would it be like to sail one of those old ships?" Lexie wondered out loud, not expecting an answer.

"Have you ever been sailing?" Barret looked up.

"Never been on a boat at all."

Shock sprang from his eyes, and he smiled as if he held a grand secret. She shifted her gaze from his penetrating stare, wondering why warmth suddenly flooded her.

He reached his hand out for hers...to hold? To squeeze? She didn't know. Leaping to her feet she glanced at her watch. "I'm off the clock. Let's go."

⚓

Barret had always been able to woo any woman he wanted with his charm, wit, kindness, and good looks. But not Lexie Cain. Most women enjoyed it when he took an interest in their lives and their pasts. But not Lexie Cain. She was an enigma, a puzzle he longed to solve. Not merely for the challenge but because he truly wished to understand her.

He had put up with her sarcasm and rebukes. He had helped her with her menial work, something he had never done for anyone. At home, they'd always had maids to do such things. Good grief, he'd even gotten up at 3:00 a.m. just to help her read Bonnet's letters. And though he admitted he had a personal interest in that, they could read the letters anywhere. In truth, he'd come here to protect her. Yet she rebuffed his every attempt to grow closer.

Fascinating.

Now, as they walked side by side down Broad Street on the way to her car, he longed to say something to regain her trust, to begin again on the path to friendship. But what? He sensed her exhaustion as she slogged along the near-empty sidewalk. The rising sun cast glittering gold over her skin and hair, making her look almost angelic. At least when she was quiet.

She'd been right about him. His parents *were* still together, and he'd been sent to the best schools. "I wasn't captain of the football team," he blurted out to hopefully make her smile.

She did as she glanced up at him. "But captain of...?"

He frowned. "The baseball team."

She laughed.

Darn it! He wasn't about to tell her she was right about the prom king too.

"I don't suppose you'd like breakfast?" he asked as they turned toward the garage. Thus far, he'd not spotted anyone following them.

"No, thank you. I'm too tired. Besides, don't you have to get to the university?"

"I keep my own hours over the summer."

"How nice for you." A hint of sarcasm rang in her tone, but he also sensed a longing within her. He'd watched her slip a timecard into a machine to mark her time served at the museum before they left. In all his life, he'd never had to do such a thing.

"Rain check then. I know you like to eat."

She chuckled.

They mounted the steps in silence and approached her car, their footsteps echoing through the garage. Barret scanned the area, searching for anyone lurking about, but found no one. Good. Maybe the creep had given up.

Lexie's startled gasp snapped his attention first to her and then to where she was looking. She dashed for her car before he could stop her.

The driver's side window was smashed in and the door ajar. Pebbles of glass littered the oily garage floor beside her car.

"Wait. Don't touch anything!" he shouted as he yanked his phone from his pocket and began dialing his friend Adam. But the woman was already sitting in the driver's seat, despite the glass.

She leaned over, opened the glove box, and rummaged through the belongings inside.

"Adam." Barret stooped beside Lexie. "Yes, I know you're on duty. That's why I'm calling. It's Lexie Cain, the woman's whose apartment was broken into? Now, it's her car. Yeah…I figured it was easier to call you directly than 9-1-1. Yup. Okay. We are in the garage on King Street, second floor. Thanks."

He pressed the red button and slipped the phone into his back pocket. Lexie remained in the driver's seat staring straight ahead as if she were watching a movie that made no sense.

"They took it," she said, her voice scratchy.

"What?" Barret grabbed her hand and squeezed.

Her gaze shifted to him, tears moistening her eyes. "The coin."

"The antique doubloon?"

She nodded.

Barret didn't know whether to feel angry or sad. "You kept it in your car?"

She ripped her hand from his. "In the glove box. I didn't think…"

Drawing a deep breath, he retrieved her hand. "It's okay. It's just a coin." He cringed at his own words. "At least you have the letters." He glanced at the backpack she'd dropped by the car.

He tugged on her arm. "Let's get you off the glass. The police are on the way."

Much to his delight, she not only allowed him to help her from the seat but didn't resist when he embraced her. In fact, she fell against him and began to sob. "Why is this happening to me?"

Barret wrapped his arms around her and held her tight. She smelled of vanilla and woman, and he drew in a deep breath.

"I don't understand," she continued, whimpering. "What do they want? Why do bad things always happen to me?"

"Bad things happen to everyone." Barret rubbed her back, confused at where the tough, independent woman had suddenly gone. Not that he was complaining.

She nudged away from him, swiping at the tears on her face. "Bad things don't happen to you." Backing away, she leaned against the car, crossed arms over her chest, and stared into the garage.

All Barret wanted to do was hold her again. Instead, he pondered her statement. True, rarely had anything gone wrong in his life or in his family's lives. In fact, his life had been pretty good thus far, and he could only attribute that to one thing—his faith in God. "God blesses those who believe in Him," he finally said.

A slight pursing of her lips was the only initial reaction he received. Several seconds passed before she shot him a pointed stare, her green eyes firing ice. "You aren't one of those crazy religious types, are you?"

Barret groaned inwardly. "If you mean do I believe in God, then yes, I guess so."

She shook her head, grabbed a strand of hair and began twirling it.

"You believe in God, don't you?" he asked, knowing he was pressing the issue.

She wouldn't look at him, but her words came out strong and full of pain. "If I admit there's a God, then I must also assume he hates me and my family. Therefore, no, I do not believe in God."

For some reason, her statement sent a palpable ache through his heart. He'd never been good at sharing his faith, but he'd never encountered such anger at God either. Best to change the subject.

A car roared into the garage on the ground floor below him. Probably Adam.

"Well, there's one thing you've convinced me of," he said.

She eyed him suspiciously. "What's that?"

"That Stede Bonnet's buried treasure is most certainly not a myth."

CHAPTER TWELVE

*L*exie kissed Ellie and drew in a deep breath of her sweet scent—lollipops, bubble bath, and innocence. How she longed to have a child of her own someday, but she had promised herself long ago that she would not subject anyone else to the curse that hung over her family.

Ellie giggled as she scooted off the couch and flew the unicorn figurine Lexie had brought for her through the air. "Miss Lexie, see? She can fly!"

"Yes, I see. All unicorns can fly. Didn't you know?" Early morning sunlight filtered through the window and shone on the toy's glittery wings.

Tracy giggled as she entered the room, two mugs in her hand. "She so rarely gets something new to play with. How can I thank you? *And* for the groceries." Handing a mug to Lexie, she wiped moisture from her eyes. "I don't know what we'd do without your help. Victor hasn't sent the child support check this month and the welfare money ran out."

"What's his story? What happened with you two?"

Tracy sat across from Lexie and sighed. Brown, silky hair hung to the shoulders of her stained t-shirt. Even with her ragged, exhausted appearance, she was quite pretty. She lifted fawn-colored eyes to Lexie. "You know the usual sad love story. High school sweethearts. Got married too young. I was three months pregnant on our wedding day." She glanced at Ellie. "I think he resented being tied down." She stared off into space, and Lexie could see the pain in her eyes.

"He had a wandering eye." Tracy released a heavy sigh. "And then a wandering body." She shrugged. "One day, he just didn't come home."

"I'm so sorry. I can tell you loved him."

"I did. Once. But he gave me the greatest gift of all." She glanced at Ellie. "So how can I complain? If only the man could be found so he could help us financially."

Setting her mug down, Lexie grabbed Tracy's hand. "I won't let you go homeless. I won't. Don't worry."

"But you hardly make enough to support yourself. It's too much."

"I do okay." Lexie retrieved her hot cocoa and took a sip. When she found Bonnet's treasure, she would buy Tracy a house with a big backyard for Ellie to play in.

"If only childcare wasn't so expensive, I could get a job," Tracy said. "You are a true friend, Lexie Cain. Not many people would help nobodies like us."

That much Lexie knew was true. Memories flooded her of begging on the streets of Richmond, huddling against her mother from the cold and rain. She had been only six then, but the memories were as vivid as if it had been yesterday. So few had even glanced their way, the rest turned up their noses and crossed to the other side of the street.

Ellie plopped to the floor and began to build a home for the unicorn with her blocks. Tracy smiled at her daughter, so much love pouring from her eyes that Lexie's own eyes teared up. Her mother had loved her like that—had always loved her. At least Lexie had that to cling to.

"But"—Tracy sipped her coffee and smiled at Lexie—"I hear you caught the eye of one of the most handsome and wealthy bachelors in the city."

Had she? Stunned, Lexie stared into the cocoa swirling in her cup. "I wouldn't go that far. He's just helping me with some old letters my mom had."

"Ah, so him picking you up later today for some special event is only about some silly letters?" Humor twinkled in Tracy's tired brown eyes.

"I have no idea what he wants." It was true. She also had no idea why she'd agreed to go.

"Honey, if you can't figure that out, you don't know men." Tracy chuckled.

Lexie smiled, unwilling to admit to the spark of joy Tracy's statement caused. "It's probably some historical thing about this pirate he's researching." Whatever it was, Barret wouldn't tell her when he called yesterday to invite her. "Just dress for warm weather and bring sunscreen," he had said.

After the car incident, Barret had driven her home and called a glass company to come replace the window. By the time she'd woken for her night shift, the window was fixed. Barret had overslept and had not made it to the museum in time to read a letter but had walked her to her car. Still, he refused to allow her to pay for the window, which only infuriated her. The last thing she wanted was his charity. Charity from people like him meant she owed him, and she didn't want to owe anyone.

"Well, I think it's exciting." Tracy set down her coffee and sat back in her chair. "You should go for it!"

"I'm not going for anything, Tracy. I don't want a relationship, especially not with someone like Barret Johnson. We are too different. He's a snob, educated, religious, and has lived a life of privilege."

"But he's *so* handsome."

Lexie laughed. "I admit to being attracted to him. What girl wouldn't be?" Yet it seemed more than that. When he'd held her so tightly in the garage, comforting her during her weak moment, she'd felt cared for, cherished, even safe. And yes, her body had reacted to being so close to him.

"I think you should give him a chance."

"He won't want a chance when he finds out about my past." She suddenly regretted agreeing to join him today. What if he really *did* have romantic intentions?

"Regardless, enjoy your day."

"We'll see." Lexie set down her mug and stood. "I better get some sleep. He's picking me up at 4:00." An hour earlier than she normally got up for work, but she had the night off tonight.

After hugging both Ellie and Tracy, Lexie headed to her apartment, suddenly doubting she'd get much sleep in anticipation of what she was now beginning to believe was a date.

"Okay, open your eyes!" Barret refused to release his grip on Lexie's hand, anxious to see her expression when she saw his surprise.

It wasn't what he expected.

Instead of the delight, joy, and excitement, her delicate brow furrowed as she glanced over the marina looking confused. "Are we going fishing?"

Barret chuckled. "No. Sailing!"

Wind whipped hair into her face, and she snapped it aside and gave him a confused look. "On what?"

"Right in front of you. The ketch."

Her gaze wandered down the long dock before landing on the boat right in front of them. "*This* is yours?"

"Yes. Well, my family's. You said you'd never been sailing, so I thought it would be fun to take her out."

Finally the smile came, the slight twinkle of excitement in her eyes. "Out to sea?" She shielded her eyes from the afternoon sun.

"Why not?" He tugged her toward the boat. "This way you can better relate to Bonnet."

Though she wore a stunned, slightly uneasy expression, she allowed him to take her hand and help her leap onto the main deck. The boat rolled, and she wobbled.

Barret gripped her elbow to steady her and gestured toward the folder in her hand. "You brought the letters."

She gave a sheepish grin. "I thought maybe that's why we were meeting."

"Here, let me put them in the seat locker so they don't get wet." Before she could protest, he took them, opened up the padded top of the locker, and slipped them inside.

Derek hopped up from below, his glance taking in Lexie with an approving grin.

"Derek, this is my friend Lexie. Lexie, Derek, my deckhand."

Lexie nodded toward him.

"All set to go then?" Derek said.

"We're waiting on two more." Barret scanned the marina toward the dock house. "They should be here soon."

"They?" Lexie asked.

"Yeah. I hope you don't mind. I invited Adam and his wife."

"The cop?"

Barret nodded, hoping he hadn't blown things. If there was one thing he knew about Lexie, it was that she was distrustful of everyone and everything. They'd spent hours together already, and yet he felt he hadn't even broken the surface of this fascinating woman. If she thought this was a date or even suspected that he had a romantic interest in her—which he did—she would bolt as fast as a rabbit from a hound. And he couldn't have that.

At the moment, as she glanced around nervously, he suspected she might just do that anyway. She wore a green tank top stuffed into jean shorts that revealed way too much of her shapely legs. Wind tossed loose strands of her light hair, which was pinned up in her usual crazy style—a style he was beginning to like very much. But it was the tattoo on her upper arm that caught his gaze—one he hadn't seen before. A daffodil. Odd. She didn't seem the type to have a flower tattoo.

Finally, she drew a deep breath and smiled. "Sounds like fun."

Whew! So far so good.

"Ahoy there!" Adam's shout echoed over the blue water, and soon he and Christy arrived, all smiles and excitement, thanking him for the invite and conversing with Lexie as if they'd known her all their lives. Which is what Barret had hoped. Christy was the sweetest woman he'd ever known—a good Christian lady who truly loved others and could make a mouse in a cathouse feel safe and comfortable.

"Let's get on our way, then!" Barret turned to find Derek to assist him with the mainsail. He could easily sail the boat by himself, but he wanted to free up his time to spend with Lexie and his friends. As he headed to check the halyard, he lifted up a prayer that Lexie would have a wonderful time, for he doubted that she'd experienced many of those in her life.

Lexie didn't know whether to be thrilled, scared to death, or awestruck. Not only had she never set foot on a boat before but had never seen one as magnificent as the *Dignity*, the name painted on the bow. Wind whipped past her as they made their way through Charleston Bay toward Fort Sumter and the sea beyond, and she felt as though she were a sea gull flying low over the azure water, free and wild. She wanted to close her eyes to revel in the sensation, but for some reason, she couldn't keep them off Barret.

Dressed in jeans and a black t-shirt—so unusual for him— he and his deck hand had unhooked the boat from the dock, started the motor, and then navigated them slowly out of the marina into the bay. Now, they pulled ropes and adjusted sails, calling orders to one another as if they'd sailed the seas together forever.

Derek, a young man with sun-bleached hair, khaki shorts, and no shirt or shoes, looked the part perfectly.

But Barret? The pretentious professor? He looked as comfortable sailing this boat as he did in his office at university. More pirate than professor, she had always thought.

Soon the engine was cut and the sails ballooned with wind, taking over propelling the boat. Without the noise of the motor, other sounds—the waves lapping, the wind whisking, and an occasional gull squawking filled Lexie's ears. And a peace settled on her that she'd rarely experienced. Odd.

Christy leaned toward her. "Isn't it magnificent? Being out here?"

Smiling, Lexie nodded, her gaze unavoidably dropping to Christy's baby bump. "How far along?"

"Five months." Christy caressed her belly, glancing at her husband sitting across from them. Their eyes met and Lexie was shocked at the amount of love she saw in that one look. George had never looked at her mother that way. Not once that

Lexie had seen. Had he ever loved her? Or had it just been lust? Her mother had been a beautiful woman. A sudden sorrow swept over her, but she shook off all thoughts of the past. Today, she wanted to savor every minute in the present.

Soon, they sailed past Fort Sumter and blasted out into the open sea, the bow rising over an incoming wave and plunging down the other side. A spray of salty mist showered over Lexie, and she smiled as she gripped the side railing to keep from being thrust overboard. Derek and Barret scrambled across the deck, tugging on various ropes and adjusting the sails to catch the wind as they flapped above her, thundering like massive sheets of leather. Finally, they filled up like balloons and jerked the boat to the right.

Rays from the sun low in the sky over Charleston heated Lexie's skin and shimmered over foamy waves. Adjusting her sunglasses, she shifted in her seat to face the east, amazed at the endless expanse of water stretching to the horizon.

Once the craft settled again and began a smooth sail toward the south, Barret joined them, breath coming fast and exhilaration lighting up his eyes. He sat beside her and ran a hand through his wind-blown black hair. A hint of his cologne broke through the smell of salt and the sea that swirled around him. "What d'ya think?" he asked.

She wanted to laugh. What would any sane person think of such a wonderful gift? "It's… it's incredible."

"You should have seen her face the entire time," Adam interjected. "Sheer enjoyment."

Heat swamped Lexie. Were her emotions that obvious?

Barret gripped her hand in his. "I'm glad."

"I'm just glad I don't feel seasick," she said. "Like Bonnet did when he first went to sea."

He laughed. "Good thing, because I brought dinner." Rising and keeping Lexie's hand in his, Barret gestured for his friends to follow him as he led her down a set of narrow stairs to the deck below. She was stunned to find a kitchenette and dining area—much nicer than the one in her own apartment— along with two bedrooms and a bathroom. All paneled in rich wood and decorated in brass. Savory smells emanated from the oven as Barret led her to sit at the dining table.

Adam did the same with his wife and joined Barret in the kitchenette.

Christy smiled at Lexie. "Nice to have men wait on us now and then."

Lexie had never had anyone wait on her, man or woman, but she returned the woman's smile.

Within minutes, the two men had placed platters of savory food on the table, handed out plates and silverware, and filled cups with sweet tea.

"Let's give thanks," Barret said as he slid beside her on the seat. Then bowing his head, and with Adam and Christy joining him, he thanked God for the food and the boat and the relatively calm seas and asked that God keep His watch over them. Everyone said Amen except Lexie. She had no patience for useless prayers, especially ones of thanksgiving. She'd had so little to thank God for in her life.

The boat rolled over a wave and everyone settled their plates and glasses before conversation and feasting began. Lexie helped herself to everything, her mouth watering at the assortment of delights.

She faced Barret. "So, you sail *and* cook? A man of many talents."

Adam laughed and Christy smiled, both gazing at Barret.

"I take credit only for the sailing. I couldn't boil an egg if you paid me," Barret responded joyfully. "I ordered this from Purlieu, my favorite French restaurant."

Of course he had. And it was delicious. Parisian herb gnocchi for appetizer, *Prawns Meuniere and tortellini la foret* for the main courses and chocolate mousse for dessert. That made two fancy meals Barret had served Lexie, and both times she ate so much, she felt like a stuffed goose.

Not only was the food good, but, surprisingly, the company was too. Lexie was not a huge fan of cops. She'd had her fair share of run-ins with the law in the past. Yet she found Adam intelligent, kind, and down to earth. She liked Christy even more. The woman came from humble beginnings, the daughter of a mailman and an elementary school teacher, and Lexie felt an immediate bond with her. Not to mention she was funny and kind and had a sarcastic wit that made Lexie smile.

The deck tilted. "So, how did you two first meet?" Lexie asked as she settled her shifting plate.

"Ah, a funny story." Adam glanced at his wife. "I was a rookie on the force, my first week, in fact, and me and my partner got this strange call from an hysterical woman who said it was a matter of life and death."

Christy gave an indignant huff. "Well, it was. Just not for me."

Adam chuckled. "Turns out her pet was stuck in a tree."

Lexie took a bite of tortellini. "Don't you call the firemen for that?"

"One would think." Adam gave his wife a sly glance.

Christy sipped her tea. "I called them first, but they wouldn't come."

"I wouldn't have either if I'd known what kind of pet you had," Adam said.

"Which is why I didn't mention it to 9-1-1."

Grabbing his tea, Barret sat back and laughed.

Lexie couldn't imagine what type of pet would scare a policeman. "How bad could it be? Feral Cat? Ferocious dog?"

Adam's gaze landed on Lexie, his brows raised. "Try skunk."

"Skunk?" Now it was Lexie's turn to laugh.

"You'd be surprised what great pets they make." Christy turned up her nose. "They are very sensitive and intelligent creatures."

"Until they spray you," Adam said.

"I can't help it you picked Pepe up wrong."

"Pepe?" Lexie laughed so hard, she nearly sprayed everyone with tea. "Like Pepe le Pew?" She glanced at Barret and found his eyes upon her, joyful and approving.

"Anyway." Adam lifted his wife's hand to his lips for a kiss. "It was love at first sight."

"Or spray," Barret added, and they all laughed.

Lexie enjoyed the looks the couple exchanged, looks of such intimacy that could only come from knowing someone deeply and loving them anyway. Oddly, a gnawing emptiness grew within her at the realization she would most likely never know that kind of love. At least no one in her family ever had. Divorce seemed to be a family pastime, a weekend event, as natural as taking a family trip to the beach.

The boat bounced, and Lexie settled her plate, finally putting down her fork. "I'm stuffed."

Adam reached into his duffle bag and handed her a black box. "I have a gift for you."

"For me?" Lexie could not imagine...

But Adam only smiled and held it out to her.

Taking it, she quickly read the words on the outside *Taser Police Stun Gun*. "What?" She glanced up at him.

"Listen, Lexie." He swallowed his last bite of mousse. "Your apartment and your car have been broken into. I know Barret is walking you home from work, but he can't always be there. I want you to have this. It's the same stun gun they give us at work. I was going to get you an actual gun, but"—he shrugged—"I wasn't sure you knew how to use one."

"Oh, no, no. I'm glad you didn't," she said. "I really don't like guns." Even though she already owned one. Why she kept it, she couldn't say except it had been a gift from her mom. Lexie had never taken it out of the lock box it had come in. She'd seen too many people die from guns, including her best friend. She looked down at the Taser. "I can't take this." She shook her head. "I'm sure it's super expensive and besides, I don't know how to use it."

"I'll teach you. It's easy. I'd feel"—he glanced at Barret and Christy—"we *all* would feel better if you had some form of defense. At least until we catch whoever is after you."

After her? The words sounded so ominous, so frightening. Perhaps because she could no longer deny them. She glanced at Barret, and he gave her a nod of approval.

"Okay, thanks. I'll pay you back."

"No, you won't. It's a gift."

She hated gifts. They always came with strings. But she spotted no such strings in the concerned look in Adam's eyes. Or in Christy's, who smiled her way. Lexie had never trusted cops, thought they all had it in for her and her family. But Adam seemed different.

Barret scooted off the seat and stood. "Now that that's settled, let's go above. It's beautiful this time of evening when the sun is setting."

Lexie was more than thrilled to comply. When they'd first come below for dinner, she'd wanted to suggest they eat up on deck. She'd wanted to spend as much time as she could gazing at the sea and feeling the wind in her hair before the day ended and they had to return to land. But it wasn't her place to say. She was merely grateful to be on this expensive boat eating such a lavish meal with such nice people. It was a dream for someone like her who grew up eating fast food and hanging out with less than savory sorts.

Above deck, Adam led his wife to the side where they sat together arm in arm. Barret conferred with Derek at the wheel before offering his hand to Lexie, a gleam in his eye. Against her better judgment, she took it and followed him to the bow of the boat, only stumbling twice on the jostling deck. He placed her hands on the railing, then took a stance beside her, the wind blowing his hair back as he stared over the sea.

Rays of the setting sun fluttered gold and maroon ribbons over the waves and glittered in their foamy caps.

"So beautiful." She closed her eyes, enjoying the wind caressing her face, the sound of the sails, the splash and gurgle of the water, the smell of brine and fish and freedom. She released a deep breath, suddenly longing never to return to her old life, to leave all her problems and struggles behind on land.

"So, are you kidnapping me to the Caribbean?" She dared a glance at Barret.

His lips curved in a sensuous smile. "Would you like me to?" He winked.

Yes, yes! No, no! What was she thinking? "I do wonder at your intentions, Professor," she teased. "Or should I say Professor Pirate?"

"Pure as the wind-driven snow, I assure you, Miss Cain," he replied with another wink.

Which made her suspicious. She turned toward the sea again. "I can see why Bonnet loved the this... why he left his sad life in Barbados."

"Really?"

"Yes. There's freedom out here, a wildness that seems to sweep away all responsibilities and problems."

He nodded. "Maybe you *are* related to him."

She must be, for they both seemed to make mistake after mistake.

"Why don't we read one of the letters before the sun sets?" Barret said.

"Good idea."

"I'll get it." Barret walked away as if he'd walked on a pitching deck his entire life. Maybe he had.

Lexie lowered to sit on the deck, shoved her feet between the thin steel rails and waited to be whisked back in time onto a pirate ship. What better way to end a perfect day.

CHAPTER THIRTEEN

Nassau, March 1718

My dearest and most precious Melody,

Much has occurred since I last wrote. I fear you will find a plethora of varied emotions within this letter, for such is the life of pirates...good times and bad, successes and failures, life and death. Hope and disappointment. Once again I find myself in that wicked pirate haven, Nassau. I laugh, for I suppose I am one of those wicked pirates now. Yet, news abounds of a pardon offered by King George to all pirates willing to give up the trade, lay down their arms, and surrender to any Royal Governor in the Caribbean. To do so by September of this year will absolve said pirate and his crew of any prosecution for crimes committed upon the seas.

I longed to take this pardon, my love, for I have found myself but a prisoner on board Edward's flagship, the Queen Anne's Revenge. He has removed me from command of Revenge and put his second in command Richards in charge. For what? My failure to take as prize a twenty-six gun, four-hundred-ton merchantman, Protestant Caesar! When at the very least I should have been praised for such a brave attempt. I do believe these foul-mouthed, ignorant ruffians hold animosity toward me for my status and education, which may have played a part in their decision. Yet 'tis my ship and my crew! But how can I resist a devil like Blackbeard?

Hence, I was on my way to receive the aforementioned pardon when I discovered 'twas only valid for acts of piracy committed before January 5th. Saint's blood! I had attacked the *Protestant Caesar* after that date. Therefore, my love, I am back on board the *Queen Anne's Revenge*, for where else could I go where I would not be arrested and hanged? At least among Blackbeard's armada of four vessels and four-hundred pirates, I am protected. In addition, I can still receive my share of any treasure we acquire, to be added to the wealth I accumulate for our life together.

Nevertheless, I have good news with which to end this letter! On my advice, Edward has decided to prowl the waters outside Charles Town. While he is thus engaged, my love, I will do all in my power to come ashore and find you.

At last, I shall see your lovely face and feel you in my arms,
    With every hope and prayer toward that end,
    I am eternally yours,
    Stede

Bonnet stood at the larboard railing on the quarterdeck of the *Queen Anne's Revenge* and gazed toward Charles Town, a lump of longing in his throat. Thus far, they had been lingering just outside the entrance to the harbor for five days. And in that time, Blackbeard had captured nine vessels. *Nine!* Bonnet had witnessed the skill and bravado of his old friend, taking note of each command, each action, committing them to memory in the hopes he would learn from them and add to his skill, should he ever be given back command of the *Revenge*. What he didn't wish to learn from Blackbeard was his heartless cruelty—a lack of natural empathy for his fellow man. Bonnet oft pondered what caused a man to lose that part of him which was distinctly human.

Meditating on these thoughts, while also planning a way to sneak ashore, Bonnet watched as Blackbeard's crew pillaged their recent prize, *Crowley*, a passenger ship heading to London.

"I do hope he does these innocents no harm," David Herriot said from beside Bonnet, as numerous passengers were shoved up the ladder and onto the main deck from the cockboat below.

"I would prepare yourself for the worst, my friend." Bonnet adjusted his tricorn against the blazing sun. *Friend.* Aye, he considered Herriot a friend, for they'd been prisoners together aboard this devil's ship for a month now, though odd friends that—Bonnet, being a pirate, and Captain Herriot the respectable captain of the *Adventure*, a log-cutting vessel that had the misfortune of sailing into the same lagoon off Turneffe where Blackbeard had been anchored.

Together they watched as dozens of terrified passengers flooded the main deck of *Queen Anne's Revenge*, most of the women crying, the children clinging to their parents, and the men's faces stark with fear. A few of the men hid that fear behind defiant expressions that faded when Blackbeard rose onto the deck from below like a black Leviathan from the deep. Dressed in all black, he eyed the passengers as he moved toward them, the thump of his knee-high jackboots drumming ominously over the deck. Long braids of black hair swung about him in the breeze, brushing over the three brace of pistols draped over his shoulders. He stood at least a head above the tallest man there, his wide shoulders casting an ominous shadow on the deck. Sunlight gleamed off the hilt of his cutlass as his piercing gaze took in each terrified face. He stopped before a man who stood in front of the mob, apparently their leader, and uttered a snort that sent a shiver through the crowd.

One woman screamed, another fainted, and two children began to wail.

Against his will—and against knowing pirates shouldn't feel such things—Bonnet's heart ached with sorrow for these poor innocents.

Blackbeard ignored them. "And, pray tell, who are ye?" he asked the man, who, much to his credit, met Edward's gaze straight on.

The ship careened over a wave, and the man plucked a kerchief from his pocket and dabbed at his forehead and neck. "Samuel Wragg at your service, sir."

"Sir, be it?" Blackbeard chuckled and gazed over his crew, who joined in his mirth. Finally sobering, he faced the man again. "And just who is Samuel Wragg?" He lowered his gaze to a small boy, no older than four standing staunchly beside his father. Brave boy. He neither cried nor clung to his father's breeches.

"I am a merchant from Charles Town and a member of the Carolina Provincial Council bound for London to meet with the Lords Proprietors to request more funding."

At this, Blackbeard's brows lifted, and a slow smile spread across his leathery skin. "We have an important catch here, men!" he shouted over the deck. Removing his tricorn, he swept it before him in a mock bow.

Still the man did not cower. Bonnet's respect rose for him, along with his fear. Brave or not, he obviously had no idea who he was dealing with.

"With respect, Captain Blackbeard," Mr. Wragg began as a blast of briny wind whipped his hair in a frenzy.

"Respect be it? I see I need not introduce myself."

"What is it you want?" Wragg continued. "The *Crowley* is a passenger ship with very little merchandise on board, as I'm sure your pirates have discovered."

Blackbeard glanced to the ship drifting off their starboard quarter and scowled.

"Why not return us to our ship and allow us to proceed to London?"

Queen Anne's Revenge rolled over a wave, and Bonnet both braced his boots on the deck and himself for Blackbeard's fury. One thing the devil didn't like was being told what to do.

Yet, much to Bonnet's surprise, Blackbeard merely sighed. "Nay. I have at least one important citizen with which to bargain. I shall see if we have more." His imperious glance over the mob sent them shrinking backward. "And then I will use you, Mr. Wragg, as leverage to get what I want from your fair city."

Unable to watch Blackbeard interrogate the poor passengers further, Bonnet excused himself and returned to the cabin he shared with Herriot. He'd brought several of his books and other personal items over from the *Revenge*, and thus occupied much of his time reading or, when Herriot was present, in discussing politics, philosophy, and world events. After months of having only ignorant cullions to converse with, 'twas quite refreshing to finally have someone who could carry a conversation on more subjects than rum, booty, sailing, and wenches.

He had just settled down to continue reading *Paradise Lost* by Milton when Blackbeard's bosun, Ignatius Pell, a dreary looking fellow with an earring in his nose, burst through the door and informed Bonnet he was wanted in the captain's cabin for a vote.

A vote, indeed. Merely an illusion of democracy on an autocratic ship. Nevertheless, the fact that Blackbeard included him in anything of import gave Bonnet hope.

By the time he arrived and slipped in the back, they were already discussing the fate of the ill-begotten passengers and their plan to plunder Charles Town. Blackbeard might be the most evil man Bonnet had met, but he was not stupid. His plan was simple. Two pirates would row into the city with a list of demands. If not met, all the passengers of the *Crowley* would die a horrific death and their heads sent to the governor. If they *were* met, the passengers would be released unharmed.

Bonnet hoped with all his heart the governor understood that Blackbeard was a man of his word. He also hoped to be one of the pirates sent ashore. This was his chance! Hence, when a call for volunteers was made, Bonnet, a lump in his throat, stepped forward, along with several other pirates.

Blackbeard's pointed stare, however, focused on Bonnet. "And why would I send the likes of ye?" The other pirates laughed.

Bonnet adjusted his woven-silk waistcoat. "Because, Captain, of all your men here, I am the most educated, the most accustomed to the language and dealings of gentlemen, particularly those who hold office. Who better than I to negotiate with Governor Johnson?"

Laughter subsided, replaced by muttering and grumbling as Blackbeard held his penetrating stare at Bonnet. The deck rose and fell. Timbers creaked, and Bonnet did his best to stand tall and not stumble. The stench of sweat and rum saturated his lungs.

Finally Blackbeard snorted. "By God ye finally make some sense, Bonnet. So be it." He scanned the other men in the room. "Stiles and Bane. Go with him."

Making every attempt to hide the glee on his face, Bonnet nodded. *Gadzooks!* He'd done it. He was going ashore! He would soon see Melody!

Upon returning to his cabin, he gathered his weapons, quickly washed his face, and changed his shirt before hurrying on deck where a boat was being lowered. Blackbeard had once again brought over the passengers from the hold of the *Crowley* to inform them that their lives lay in the willingness of Governor Johnson to meet his demands.

'Twas then that Samuel Wragg once again boldly addressed Edward. "I beg your indulgence, Captain, but might I suggest that I accompany your two pirates if only to express more adequately and truthfully the danger in which we find ourselves and thus to induce the governor to more readily submit to your demands in order to save lives."

Blackbeard shoved his face into the poor man's. "D'ye find me a fool, sir? Ye are the most valuable possession I have. I'll not be givin' ye up for anything short of a chest full of gold and silver."

The surrounding pirates cheered.

Mr. Wragg squinted in the afternoon sun. "I will gladly leave my son here as proof of my return."

Blackbeard dropped his gaze to the boy and snarled. "Nay. Ye." He pointed to a well-dressed man standing behind Wragg. "What be yer name?"

The man swallowed hard, his chest billowing, but to his credit, he stepped forward. "Mr. Marks, sir…I mean, Captain."

"Go." Blackbeard waved him away before ordering his men to take the rest of the passengers back to the hold of the *Crowley*.

Bonnet couldn't crawl down the ladder into the cockboat fast enough. Stiles, Bane, and Mr. Marks soon joined him, and he shoved off from the *Queen Anne's Revenge* before Blackbeard changed his mind.

The afternoon sun that only a moment before had been hot and bright was soon swallowed up in a bank of dark clouds as he, Bane, and Stiles picked up oars and began rowing. Good. At least it wouldn't be so hot on the trip to shore, for they had a long way to go. Hot, nay. Windy? Aye. Unfortunately, the gust was against them, making their progress slow.

Bonnet's muscles ached. Removing his waistcoat, he tossed it aside. Waves rose, causing the little boat to leap like a deer on the run. Water foamed over the sides and soaked his shoes. Beside him, the pirates grunted and groaned from exertion. Mr. Marks clung to the railing, a look of terror on his face. 'Twas then that a torrent of rain unleashed upon them as if God Himself were trying to prevent them from reaching shore. In the distance, Bonnet could see the buildings of Charles Town stretching upward toward a cauldron of low black clouds.

So close! He was so close! He would not let a little rain stop him now.

Behind them, he could barely make out the blurry hulk of the *Queen Anne's Revenge* rocking in the water.

Lightning flashed a white trident across the sky.

Thunder roared. The little craft quivered.

"Should we return to the ship?" Mr. Marks shouted over the din, terror sparking in his eyes.

"Nay!" Bonnet brayed. "Nay!" He would never go back.

The pirates merely shook their heads and kept rowing. A wall of water crashed over them. Bonnet's eyes stung from the salt. Mr. Marks let out a yelp. The boat tipped to larboard. Bonnet settled it with his weight.

Lightning coated the water in silver. Another wave struck. The boat rose and plunged, careened left and right, jumping and yawing like a toy in a child's hands.

Water dripped from Bonnet's hair, chin, and clothing. The thick rain obscured all but a few feet in front of them.

"Keep going!" he shouted to Stiles.

A wave rolled toward them from the distance, rising... taller and thicker as it came, like a bear lifted on its haunches, foaming at the mouth in anticipation of its next meal.

Bonnet whispered a prayer.

Mr. Marks screamed.

Stiles stared wide-eyed. Bane crossed himself.

The wave struck. Bonnet was shoved under water. Sounds became muted and gurgled. He thrust his arms forward and kicked his legs, gasping for air.

He broke the surface. The roar of the storm filled his ears as water filled his mouth. He spit it out and searched for Marks. Flailing arms and legs appeared beside him, and he grabbed Mr. Marks by the coat sleeve and dragged him to what appeared to be a spit of land to his left. At least Bonnet hoped it was land.

Stiles, who thank God could swim and had Bane in his grip, shouted, "This way. Land!"

Bonnet dragged Marks up onto the sandy beach and collapsed beside him. The last thing he remembered was the raindrops stinging his cheek and the distant wail of an unhappy sea gull.

"Get up, Bonnet! Wake up!"

The nagging voice rode through Bonnet's mind, jabbing his consciousness.

He didn't want to wake up. Surely, he'd drowned in Charles Town Bay and would awake to find himself in the fires of hell. Yet.... he felt no heat at the moment, only a shivering, damp cold.

"Wake up!"

Bonnet pried his eyes open to see a monstrous face of dripping aged parchment and two vacant blue eyes.

Screeching, he jerked to sit, pushing the demonic entity away. *Nay.* He rubbed his eyes. Not a demon. 'Twas Stiles staring at him with annoyance as if he'd missed an important appointment.

"Nice to 'ave ye join us," he said, gesturing over his shoulder to Mr. Marks pacing across the beach and Bane sitting with his head in his hands.

Bonnet coughed, spewing out a spray of water. "I nearly drowned, man. Have a care." He glanced over the bay. Though the storm had passed, the clouds remained gray and the waters rough. "Where are we?"

"Dunno." Stiles coughed out water. "One o' the islands guardin' the entrance to the bay be my guess."

Bonnet ran a hand through his wet hair and attempted to rise, gazing into the distance at Charles Town. A bay of water stood between him and Melody, but it might as well have been an ocean.

"We are closer to the *Queen Anne's Revenge.*" Stiles must have seen the longing in Bonnet's eyes, for he nodded toward Blackbeard's ship in the distance. "Best t' make a swim fer it."

"Nay. We had a job to do. We must try and make it to Charles Town. That is"—Bonnet smirked—"unless you would prefer to face Blackbeard and tell him you failed?"

Panic crossed Stiles's blue eyes as Mr. Marks pointed to what appeared to be a wooden hatch cover laying on the beach. "We could use that to hang onto while we paddle to Charles Town." Apparently, the man was as anxious to escape Blackbeard as Bonnet was to see his lady.

Bonnet and Stiles went over to examine it. 'Twas definitely large and sturdy enough for all of them to hang onto, and it would float well enough. "An excellent idea." Bonnet smiled.

An hour later, it seemed the worst idea Bonnet had ever agreed to, for the four men found themselves drenched, out of breath, and exhausted to the point of barely being able to hang onto the wood. Between the wind, waves, and currents, they made little progress toward town, and it soon became apparent, they would all drown in the harbor with no one the wiser.

Bonnet leaned his head onto the sodden wood, his breath heaving, his lungs aching, and his arms and legs cramping. *Oh, God. If you're there. Show mercy. Let me see Melody one more time. If you grant me this request, I vow to quit pirating.* He lifted the silent plea to heaven, not expecting an answer.

Stiles, Bane, and Marks clung to the hatch, unable to move, unable to even speak. Bonnet closed his eyes, waiting to die.

"Ahoy there!" The voice was distant and muffled. "Ahoy!"

With his last shred of strength, Bonnet lifted his head, blinked, and glanced over the endless gray water. A boat appeared out of the mist.

He raised one arm to wave and started to slide off the hatch. Mr. Marks grabbed him but had not the strength to maintain a hold. Water surrounded Bonnet as he slipped beneath the waves into silent bliss once again.

A firm hand grabbed him and hoisted him over a railing. His head hit wooden planks, and he opened his eyes to see Mr. Marks and the pirates beside him.

An aged man with long gray hair and a wide toothless smile stood over them. "Looks like we caught some odd-looking fish today, gents!" He laughed.

By the time they reached Charles Town, Bonnet had regained some of his strength. He and Stiles and Mr. Marks thanked the fishermen profusely for saving their lives and then proceeded down the wharf into the center of town, nearly empty now due to the hour, which Bonnet guessed to be around 9:00 p.m.

Mr. Marks announced he was going to request an audience with the governor in the morning.

Stiles and Bane went off to find some rum and warm wenches.

And Bonnet, renewed energy in his step, went in search of Melody.

CHAPTER FOURTEEN

"That's it?" Lexie flipped over the parchment, anxious to read more, desperate to know if Bonnet ever found Melody. But there was no writing on the back. Of course. There never was.

"Careful now." Barret settled her hand and gently removed the letter from her grip. "This paper is over three hundred years old."

"Sorry." Lexie shrugged and faced the sea, "I wish I'd brought the next letter."

Barret slipped the aged parchment—still in its plastic sleeve—gently inside the folder. "Well, I will tell you one thing since Bonnet probably won't write it in his next letter. He *did* make it to Charleston, though only after a storm and a shipwreck. He and those with him nearly drowned swimming across the bay until a fishing boat rescued them."

"I'm just glad he made it." A gust swept over her as she attempted to stand. The boat leapt over a wave, and she nearly fell. Would have fallen if Barret had not leapt to his feet, grabbed her arm, and settled her.

"Guess I haven't gotten my sea legs yet." She gripped the railing.

"Not surprising. It takes a while." Placing the folder inside a seat locker, Barret joined her and gazed over the sea, a mixture of lustrous dark blues now that the sun had descended beyond the trees. A half-moon she hadn't even noticed had risen just above the horizon, announcing the coming night and giving a host of stars permission to begin their nightly show.

Since Lexie worked most nights, she'd forgotten how beautiful the sky could be, especially away from city lights.

Per Barret's orders a half-hour ago, Derek had turned the boat around, heading back to Charleston, and Lexie found herself disappointed that Professor Pirate wasn't whisking her off to a Caribbean adventure. But she was being silly. So not like her.

"To think Bonnet was right here on this very sea. And Blackbeard too," she exclaimed.

Barret smiled and placed his hand over hers on the railing. "Look who's getting into history."

His hand swallowed hers up in a covering of rough warmth. She shouldn't allow it. She shouldn't. But for some reason, this night, under the stars, with the smell of the sea surrounding her and romantic pirate adventures on her mind, it felt right.

They both remained quiet for several minutes, and she was glad for it. She wanted to soak in all the sights and sounds around her—the splash and gurgle of the sea, the thunderous flap of sails, the mad rush of wind past her ears, and the way the moonlight sprinkled silver gems atop waves.

The twinkling lights of Charleston came into view as they rounded the corner of Morris' island and entered the bay.

Behind them, she could hear Christy and Adam laughing and enjoying one another's company. Lexie dared a glance at Barret, wondering if she'd ever have such intimacy with a man, a bond that reached beyond the physical into one's soul.

He glanced at her, and she quickly shifted her gaze away, her face flooding with heat.

"It's beautiful out here at night," he finally said, but when she faced him again, he wasn't looking at the scenery.

Flustered, she released the railing and hugged herself. Bad idea. The bow rolled over a wave, and she careened backward.

Right into Barret's arms. Warm and strong, they encircled her like a shield—a dangerous shield.

She pushed from him and lowered to sit on the padded seat, hoping to squelch whatever strange emotions had overtaken her. "To think this is where poor Bonnet and those other men nearly drowned." She glanced across the dark waters toward Charleston. "Such a huge distance to swim."

"And in the dark." Barret added, crossing arms over his chest.

How the man was able to keep his balance on the teetering deck, she had no idea. Perhaps *he* was the one with pirate blood in his veins. She smiled. He stood so strong and confident, his black hair blowing in the wind, that she suddenly found her tongue as tied up in knots as her emotions.

Thank God Barret soon excused himself to help Derek with the sails, leaving her to thoughts she'd rather not entertain. So she didn't. Instead, she kept her gaze on the bay and her mind on appreciating her last moments aboard this boat. This may very well be her last time at sea. Unless she found Bonnet's treasure and she bought a fleet of sailboats. She smiled at the thought.

Soon sails were lowered and tied to masts, and Derek fired up the engine in order to navigate the craft safely back into the marina. Once the boat was tied in place, Barret jumped onto the dock and extended his hand to help her. Her first steps were as unsteady as they had been when she'd boarded the boat. But finally, she got her land legs again and said her goodbyes to Adam and Christy. Facing Barret, she thanked him for the wonderful evening and started for her car, hoping to get away from him as fast as she could.

Of course he followed anyway. Apparently, he'd assumed the role of her bodyguard. Something that was starting to annoy her. She needed to rely only on herself. That way she wouldn't be hurt when the inevitable disappointment came.

At her car, she turned to face him. Light from a nearby streetlamp gave her a glimpse of his handsome features, though most of him remained in the shadows. She saw enough, however, to know he was smiling at her. "Thank you, again. I really enjoyed myself."

"I'm glad. I thought you might." He took a step closer. "It was fun reading Bonnet's letter right at the very spot where he and Blackbeard had been. Kinda made it come to life."

His close presence sent her blood racing, and she suddenly longed to be in his arms again. Especially because of the way he was looking at her… as if she were a precious treasure to cherish and protect.

"It did." Lexie fumbled with her keys and pressed the button to unlock her car. The beep echoed across the near-empty parking lot. She needed to get out of here. And quick. Something strange was happening between her and Barret. And she didn't like it one bit.

Reaching around her, he opened her car door. Always the gentleman.

"Maybe we can read the next letter tomorrow?" he asked as she inched around the open door toward her seat.

"Maybe." She refused to look at him. "Thanks again." She was almost free. Almost out of his reach. But then he took her hand. A pleasurable shiver coursed through her as he lifted it to his lips for a kiss, as gallant and chivalrous as they did in the old days. Who *was* this guy?

At the moment, she didn't care. She just wanted him to kiss her.

He brushed hair from her face and stroked her cheek with his thumb. She couldn't move. Couldn't breathe.

And then he lowered his lips to hers.

Barret had wanted to kiss Lexie all night. He'd resisted the urge more than once, wanting to take things slow, be cautious with this magnificent, yet somehow deeply-wounded woman. Lexie Cain reminded him of a cat stuck in a tree, unwilling to allow anyone to come to her rescue, and the last thing he wanted to do was scare her and make her climb higher, out of his reach. But as she stood there in the moonlight, her green eyes shifting between his with a longing in them he could not deny, his willpower blew away with the wind.

Ah, her lips were so soft! Her taste so sweet! He wrapped his arms around her and drew her close. Her curves fit perfectly against him. The sweet scent of her vanilla perfume drove him mad as she responded to his kiss with a hunger that surprised him. He ran fingers through her hair, pulling strands from that crazy bun she always wore, and pressed her closer, deepening the kiss.

She moaned, kissing him back, allowing him liberties he never expected. Heat flooded him. His emotions soared. And a longing rose within him to know this woman in every possible way.

Then she was gone—her lips removed, the warmth of her body replaced by cold wind—and Barret's face exploded with a stinging pain.

Shock deflated his passion. He raised a hand to his cheek and stared at the enigma of a woman who one minute kissed him like a lover and the next assaulted him like an enemy.

Anger—no, more like horror—filled her eyes as she turned, leapt into her seat, and slammed the car door in his face. The engine started, and she squealed away, leaving him standing there in a cloud of dust and exhaust, baffled at what had just happened.

But he knew one thing. He was falling in love with Lexie Cain.

What is wrong with you, Lexie Cain? Lexie mumbled to herself as she pulled into her parking spot, locked her car, and made her way to her apartment. Once inside, she bolted the door, slid to the floor, dropped her head to her knees and sobbed. Though she couldn't say why. She'd had the time of her life! And she'd *wanted* Barret to kiss her. She blew out a sigh and batted the tears from her face. And wow, what a kiss it was! Like none she had ever received. The boys she'd kissed in high school and college were just that, mere boys, interested in the pleasure she could provide them. Barret's kiss was different. It didn't seem to come merely from passion or pleasure, but from an affection that yearned for more intimacy, yearned to *give* rather than take.

What kind of crap was that? She'd obviously lost her mind.

Rising, she flipped the light switch and headed to the bathroom where she plucked a tissue from the box. Dabbing it on her red eyes, she gazed into the mirror, searching her face for any remaining sanity. The last thing she needed right now was a relationship. Her heart was too tender, too vulnerable after the loss of her mother, not to mention several broken hearts in her past. If she'd learned one lesson in life, it was that men were the cruelest species in the animal kingdom. When they saw a female they wanted, they put on their best behavior for the chase. They charmed, they spent money, they flattered, and they made promises they never intended to keep. But once they hooked their prey, they grew bored and tossed their prize to the alley while they went in search for the next conquest. She'd experienced it herself, had seen it happen with her mother and George, who Lexie was sure had been unfaithful.

One more broken heart, one more broken promise, would send Lexie over the edge. The edge of what, she didn't know, but she knew it would be a dark place of no return.

And Barret Johnson was just the type of man with the power to pull it off—handsome, successful, and charming. He knew how to speak to a woman, knew how to make her feel safe and cherished. And he had money and boats to shower upon her, making her pliable for the attack.

Well, not her! She turned on the water and splashed it over her face. Then grabbing a towel, she patted her skin, and threw back her shoulders. "You're better than this, Lex, stronger than this," she said to her reflection.

You've always been stronger than me, honey. Her mother's voice was so clear in Lexie's head, she nearly turned around, expecting to see her. *You'll do far better than me. You'll achieve great things in this life for God.* Lexie didn't know about the God part, but she had soaked in her mother's praises, rarely given until she had taken sick and turned to God for comfort—and a healing that never came. True. Lexie had been the strong one during her mother's last months, but that was only because she had to be. There was no one else. No one to lean on.

And the same was true now.

She must remember that.

Still, she could not deny her attraction to Barret, her longing to be truly loved, to not feel so desperately alone anymore. But that kind of love was a fairytale that filled women's dreams in movies and romance novels. Real life was quite different. She needed the professor's expertise to decipher Bonnet's letters. That was all. The worlds they came from couldn't be farther apart. He was born to privilege, wealth, and an honorable family name. She was born in poverty to a family of criminals that extended all the way back to Bonnet. Barret had the best education while she'd barely finished two years of junior college. He had a prestigious job and held the respect of the community. She was a night janitor, cleaning up tourist's old coffee cups and gum wads. He believed in God and had hope for the future. She possessed neither of those things.

He could have any young woman he wanted. Then why had he set his sights on her?

No. She needed him, but she would keep their relationship strictly on a friendship basis. Nothing more. Nothing less.

CHAPTER FIFTEEN

*L*exie's phone began playing the theme song from *Pirates of the Caribbean*. Barret. She'd programmed the tune to his number so she wouldn't be tempted to glance and see who was calling. If she saw his name, she feared she'd pick up.

And she wasn't ready.

Leaning over, she swept the last of the dirt into the dustpan, set aside the broom, grabbed a cloth, and headed back upstairs to look over everything in the museum in case she missed something. Ms. Anderson was a stickler for absolute cleanliness and had already chastised Lexie for a few smudges on the glass covering the displays.

It had been three days since they'd been sailing, three days since she'd seen or spoken to the infamous professor. During that time, he'd left several voice messages apologizing for his behavior and asking to meet and talk in person. The man was persistent, she'd give him that. But why? They hadn't known each other long. What did he want from her? Could this all be about Bonnet's letters and his silly research book?

You are using him, too.

The voice came from within her, loud and clear, though she hadn't been thinking along those lines. It was true, though. If not for his help with the letters, she wouldn't risk seeing him again.

After ensuring everything in the upper museum was in perfect shape, Lexie descended into the dungeon once again. She liked to end her shift where Bonnet's wax figure sat, a penitent look of despair on his face. Oddly, it made her feel close to him, and she often carried on a conversation with him as if he were really here in prison, as if it were 1718 and she was bringing him his daily meal.

The pirate theme song blared from her phone again. Lexie had needed this time away from Barret. To clear her head, get her priorities straight, to remember the task she'd come to Charleston to complete. The treasure. It was all about the treasure and starting over, removing the curse that had followed her family for centuries. She leaned against the brick wall beside Bonnet's cell and realized that curse had begun right here in this dungeon with his imprisonment.

"You were not a bad man, were you?" She sighed. "You didn't wish anyone harm. You only wanted your freedom and to get enough wealth so you could be with the woman you loved. What was wrong with that?"

She half expected him to answer her, to nod and affirm her opinion of him. But he remained staring at the stone floor.

Fate had frowned on a good man, had cursed him to a life of crime, punishment, and unfulfilled dreams. Like so many of her ancestors. Too many.

It stops here.

It stops now.

"I will find your treasure, Bonnet. And I will put it to good use. Not just for myself, but for others. As I believe you would have done if given a chance." Her voice echoed across the brick ceiling with authority, bolstering her courage, her determination to stay the course. She couldn't change Bonnet's history. But she could change hers. With his help.

And Barret's, unfortunately.

Her phone sang the pirate song once again, and this time, fishing in her pocket, she pulled it out and pressed the green button. "Yes, Professor Pirate."

"Thank God," replied the deep and far-too-sexy voice. "You're okay?"

"Of course. Why wouldn't I be?" She put the phone on speaker and set it on a barrel, her annoyance rising.

"Maybe because some thug is following you and your apartment and car have been broken into?" Now it was Barret who sounded annoyed.

He had a point.

"And you wouldn't let me walk you home the past three mornings."

Lexie picked up the broom and put it in the closet. "I needed a break."

"From me? Why? 'Cause I kissed you?"

Yes. She headed back toward the phone. It was exactly the kiss and the strange emotions it stirred within her. "Not everything is about you, Professor," she spat back.

Silence.

"Okay. Okay. I was just worried when you didn't answer my calls. Do you still want to read the letters together, or do you need a break from that as well?" He sounded mad, but she couldn't blame him.

She hadn't read any more letters since that night. She couldn't say why exactly. She was dying of curiosity to find out if Bonnet found Melody, but somehow it wouldn't be the same without Barret.

"I'll meet you at City Lights Coffee at 2:00 p.m. I'll bring the next couple of letters."

"Sounds good. Can't wait."

She clicked the red button before he could say anything else. It was rude and she knew better, but she needed to squash any hopes he had for anything but friendship.

With Taser in hand, she locked the museum door and started down Broad Street toward the parking garage. Thankfully, no one seemed to be following her anymore. Maybe they'd given up, moved on to more lucrative crimes. Besides, all she had were a bunch of ancient letters that may or may not lead to treasure that may or may not exist. When she put it that way, her efforts seemed a bit foolish. But it was all she had.

Back in her apartment, she double locked the door, took a shower, put on her comfy pj's and crawled into bed. Everything ached, from her feet to her brain and then down to her heart. Too much to think about, too much pain, too much hard work.

"God, help me." With those odd words on her lips, she drifted off to sleep.

And was awoken by a thunderous crash!

She sprang up in bed, rubbed her eyes, and peered into the darkness.

Sunlight drifting in through her open door revealed a large dark figure moving toward her.

Before she could scream, a hand slammed over her mouth.

Her heart crashed into her ribs. She gasped for air. She punched the man's arm.

He forced her down onto the bed.

"Where are the letters?"

She tried to kick him, but her legs got tangled in her blankets.

The Taser!

Reaching onto the bedstand, she felt for the small object.

"I said, where are the letters!? Give them to me or die right here!" He shoved her deeper into the mattress, so hard, she thought she'd break through the box spring to the floor beneath.

His breath blasted over her, foul and hot. She felt his spit on her forehead.

There. She grabbed the Taser, clinging to it like a lifeline. Now, to turn it on.

"If you scream, I'll kill you," he growled.

Kill? Did he say kill? She was far too young to die. She had her life to live, treasure to find, a curse to lift. She couldn't think. Shock and terror buzzed through her, fogging her brain and blurring her vision.

He slowly released his hand.

She switched the Taser on, shoved it into his gut.

And pressed the button.

Barret, pulse racing, and more terrified than he'd been in a long while, burst through the open door of Lexie's apartment. Two officers stood in the center, one dusting the dresser for prints and the other kneeling to examine something on the carpet.

Blood?

Dear God, no!

Another policeman emerged from the bathroom and placed his hand on the gun at his hip. "Who are you? This is a crime scene. Get out."

"Where's Lexie?" Barret scanned the room for any sign of what had occurred. Blankets and sheets bundled haphazardly on the bed. A lamp lay shattered in pieces on the ground, and wood-spiked holes lined the door where locks had been. "Where's the woman who lives here?"

"You a friend of hers?" The kneeling officer stood and faced Barret as he put something he'd found into a small bag.

No blood. Barret allowed himself a small measure of relief. When Adam had called him to tell him that he'd heard over the radio that a woman had been attacked in her apartment, the same apartment as Lexie, Barret had raced across town, even running a few red lights in the process. He feared the worst. He still did.

"Yes, I'm a friend."

"Barret Johnson?" the officer with the gun asked.

Barret nodded. "Yes. Where is she?"

"Adam said you'd probably show up. He took her downtown for a statement. Said to tell you she's okay. Just shook up."

Barret didn't thank them, didn't say goodbye. He dashed to his car, leapt in, and raced to the police station. After asking the officer at the desk where she was and getting nowhere, he was about to throw a fit when Adam appeared and gestured for him to follow.

"She's all right, Barret," he said as they moved past large rooms filled with officers at their desks, several of whom were on the phone.

Barret spotted her before she saw him. She sat in a small room with a table and two chairs, speaking to a woman officer. Wrapped in a blanket, with her hair askew, and her face flushed, she looked like a little frightened girl, not the usual in-charge, independent Lexie Cain. And he wished more than anything he could hold her and make all her fears go away.

Pushing past Adam, he opened the door, dropped before her, and took her hands in his. "Are you all right?"

Though tear tracks lined her cheeks, she smiled and nodded.

"She's a tough one, this one," Adam said, following him inside. "Fought off her attacker with the Taser I gave her." He turned to the woman officer. "Did you get everything?"

"Yes. For now." Rising, she closed her notebook and left.

But Barret's mind continued to spin around the word *attacker*.

"What happened?" he asked her.

She sniffed, pulled back her hands, and shook her head. "I was sound asleep, and this guy broke in, held me down on the bed." She drew a shaky breath and swallowed. "Told me he'd kill me if I didn't give him the letters."

Growling, Barret stood, his anger rising to near boiling. He ran a hand through his hair and met Adam's gaze.

"She Tased him, Barret." Adam's brows rose above a proud smile. "She Tased him good. So good, he took off."

Sounded like her. Barret huffed and glanced her way. A hint of pink satin peeked from beneath the blanket. Pajamas? And was that a print of Hello Kitty? He would expect her to sleep in a black t-shirt, certainly not anything feminine and pink. Another dichotomy from a woman who was full of them.

Pulling up a chair in front of her, he sat down. "Did he hurt you?"

She shook her head, her eyes still glazed with shock.

Adam sat on the table. "You didn't recognize him?"

"He had a mask on."

Barret rubbed the back of his neck. "I told you it wasn't safe to stay there."

She shot him an angry gaze. "Where else am I going to stay? It's not like I can afford to live in a gated community."

No, but *he* could. He could set her up like a queen if she'd allow him. He leaned back in his chair, vacillating between hugging her or yelling at her. "Well, you can't stay there anymore. I know someplace where you'll be safe, okay?"

One brow arched sarcastically. "Let me guess. Your place?"

Adam laughed.

Barret would join him if the situation weren't so dire. "Do you think so little of me?"

She flattened her lips. "No."

"It's my parents' condo. It's close to your work."

"But isn't—"

Barret silenced her with a finger pressed to her lips. A bold move and one he didn't think would work, but in her traumatized state, she allowed it.

He looked her straight in the eyes. "You need a safe place. And I'm not taking no for an answer."

"What about my things?"

Her easy acquiescence shocked him, though he did his best to hide it. She must really be frightened.

"I'll have Christy run by your apartment and get some essentials," Adam offered.

Thankfully, this seemed to appease her.

Barret was beginning to think that protecting Lexie Cain would be a full-time job. However, it was a job he was more than happy to sign up for.

CHAPTER SIXTEEN

When Barret had offered his parents' townhome for Lexie to stay in, she'd expected a semi-nice small place in the middle of historic Charleston or perhaps across the Ashley river on the mainland. What she didn't expect was a luxury 3500-square foot, four-bedroom home on Bay Street facing the harbor.

"This is your parents'?" She hated the awe in her voice, the obvious amazement from someone who had never seen such luxury.

"Yes." Barret placed the small suitcase of her things on the foyer floor—the *exquisite marble* foyer floor. A winding staircase rose on her right while a door opened on the left to a room filled with sunlight. A hall led toward the back, where more sunlight streamed in from other rooms.

Barret closed and locked the door. "Let me give you a tour."

Lexie had no words as Barret led her around the home. It was huge, filled with gorgeous furniture—down-stuffed couches and chairs, mahogany tables, porcelain floral lamps, and crystalline chandeliers. Each room had high ceilings with fancy-carved crown molding and wainscoting decorating the walls. Huge double-paned windows looked out upon gardens on one side and the bay on the other.

Yet Barret just swept her through each room as if there was nothing special to be seen. Finally, he led her back down the stairs to get her things. "You can choose whatever bedroom you want."

"But what about your parents? Won't they want to come stay here?"

"No. They haven't been here in months. It's just a vacation home."

Vacation home? Lexie suddenly felt like grabbing her suitcase and bolting out the front door. She didn't belong here.

"How much does a place like this go for?" She stopped at the bottom of the stairs and looked up at him.

Barret shrugged and glanced around. "About three mil, maybe more."

Against her will, Lexie's brows shot up. The room suddenly spun, and she wobbled slightly.

Barret caught her and drew her close. His warmth seeped through the shirt he'd lent her—an old t-shirt that hung down to her knees. His scent permeating the fabric had been driving her mad the past hour, but now with his closeness, it overwhelmed her. She wanted to push from him but found she couldn't. Not good. Being attacked obviously was affecting her reason.

Finally, Barret moved away and led her through a door into a sunlit room filled with comfy couches and elegant furniture. A tall grandfather clock stood by the bay windows overlooking Charleston Harbor. Bookcases stuffed with books and trinkets reached the ceiling, and she moved past them, admiring the various vases, candlesticks, pictures, and other objects that made the room look more like a museum. Stopping before a singular set of glass shelves set in one corner of the room, she picked up what looked like a silver bowl. On the lid was a silver-covered sculpture of a lion, while floral designs were etched along the sides.

"You have good taste." Barret approached. "That's a French tureen, crafted during the reign of King Louis XV."

"What?" Lexie's hands shook as she replaced it on the shelf. "Good grief, wasn't that like three hundred years ago?"

"Ah, you *do* know some history."

She stared at it, wondering if the king of France had actually touched it. "Is it real silver?"

Barret nodded, obviously happy with her interest.

"Whoa. It must be worth a fortune."

"Yeah, a couple hundred thousand, I guess."

What? Lexie had never held such a valuable object. "Why isn't this in a museum somewhere?"

Taking her hand, Barret led her to one of the couches. "My father likes to keep his treasures close." He helped her lower onto a couch. "You must be exhausted." He eased beside her, thankfully keeping some distance between them. In all honesty, in her present state, she doubted she could resist him if he took her in his arms—those muscular arms she'd seen fight off bad guys before. Despite all the warning bells within her, she wanted to be held by this man, to feel his strength around her. She wanted to feel safe in a world that was growing increasingly unsafe. Good grief, she needed to snap out of it.

"I can't stay here, Barret." She leaned back onto the cushions and drew her knees up to her chin—if only to keep him from holding her. Sunlight streaming through bay windows shone over her pink pajama pants, making her feel all the more ridiculous.

How could she be tough and strong wearing shiny pink Hello Kitty pajamas? How embarrassing!

Barret rubbed his chin where morning stubble sounded like sandpaper. His brown eyes that matched the rich mahogany of the tables around him assessed her with concern and a hint of amusement. "Of course you can. It's empty. No one has been here for months."

Lexie glanced out the window at the bay where sunlight spread a sheen of diamonds over the blue waves. Her thoughts drifted to the homeless, the hungry, the widows and orphans who lived on the streets, who cuddled up in corners of rat-infested, urine-stenched alleyways. While this house stood empty. Anger surged at the injustice. Yet when she glanced back at Barret, she found she could not maintain her fury. Not when he was offering this place to her, a woman he barely knew, a woman to whom he'd shown nothing but kindness.

"I will pay rent for the time I'm here. Which won't be long, by the way. I intend to find another apartment."

"I don't want your money, Lexie. And this is the safest place for you. It has a great security system that calls the police the minute anyone tries to enter without a key."

Of course it did.

"Where are you going to find that?" he added.

"I will not accept your charity, Barret."

"Yet you give your charity to others and expect them to take it."

She bit her lip. The man had a point. Still, she did not want to owe him anything. But neither did she want to put herself in a situation where she could be attacked again. "Tell you what. Help me find Bonnet's treasure, and I'll use it to pay you what I owe for rent."

Barret smiled. She wished he hadn't. His smile did odd things to her insides, especially when it reached his eyes with an intensity that spoke of a deep yearning within him.

A yearning for what?

"You have a deal, Ms. Cain. But only if you allow me to walk you to and from work again."

⚓

Barret expected her quick denial. Instead she sighed and shifted those gorgeous green eyes between his as if searching for his sincerity. She bit her lip again, tugging on it with her teeth the way she did when she was confused, unsure. And he wanted more than anything to kiss those lips again and hold her in his arms. He hated she'd been attacked, scared out of her wits. If he ever found the man who'd done it, the villain would regret being born. But for now, Barret's job was to make sure this precious woman was not only safe but that she *felt* safe.

Right now, she looked incredibly small, vulnerable…and beautiful. Her silky alabaster hair was even more askew than normal, her cheeks flushed, her eyes fearful. She wore an old t-shirt he'd had in his car. Though it hung baggy on her small frame, just seeing her in it did strange things to him, as if her wearing it made her his… belonging to him, under his covering of protection. And his need to protect her grew even more. He was seeing another side to the strong independent Lexie Cain, and he found he liked it just as much, if not more. "I wouldn't have pegged you for the Hello Kitty type." He grinned, nodding at her pajamas.

She huffed. "Can't a girl have a childhood fetish?"

"Of course, but I would have figured you were more into—"

"G.I. Joe? Trucks? Superheroes?" she snapped. "Am I so unfeminine?"

"I was going to say Legos." He rubbed the back of his neck. "And you are anything but unfeminine."

Looking away, she grew somber. "I had a Hello Kitty doll when I was a kid. It was the only toy I had. I loved that doll."

Barret was suddenly sorry he'd teased her. Yet, it pleased him that she opened up to him about her childhood. "So, what about me walking you to and from work?" he asked again, hoping to change the subject.

"I guess it's okay," she finally said, tilting her head, "but only if you have time, and only if the letters continue to help you with your research."

Nodding his agreement, his eyes drifted down to her lips. He supposed he should apologize for their kiss, but he wasn't sorry at all. Instead, before he did something that would earn him another slap, he quickly rose. "I'll show you how to set the alarm, and then I should leave you to get some sleep."

For some reason, terror streaked across her eyes.

"Or…" he lowered to sit on the coffee table perched in front of the couch. "I could stay while you sleep. If that would make you feel better."

She frowned and fiddled with her small gold earring. "I don't think I can sleep. How about we read Bonnet's next letter?"

May 1718, Charles Town, Colony of Carolina

My most precious Melody,

I cannot find the words to express my joy of the past few days. Seeing you, even for a short while, has given me strength to carry on with what I know I must now do. I must find a way to accept the pardon offered by King George, take the money I have thus acquired, and spend the rest of my life with you, my love.

Bonnet halted and set down his pen, his thoughts drifting to the two most wonderful days of his life. He was once again on board the *Queen Anne's Revenge*, stuffed within the tiny cabin he shared with Captain Herriot. But it mattered not. He would soon be free of this place.

Bonnet had encountered no obstacles in finding the residence of the infamous Reverend Thomas Rogers, Melody's father. The man always made a host of friends and foes where'er he went with his boisterous proclamations of eternal judgment and doom. When Bonnet had asked various citizens of the man's whereabouts, drunken sailors cursed at the mention of his name, whilst the few upstanding citizens wandering about that night had proclaimed the reverend's godly attributes and how pleased they were when he joined St. Phillip's church. Either way, Bonnet quickly found the Rogers' home, his heart all but leaping through his chest at being so close to Melody. 'Twas a humble house just inside the walled city, closed up and dark for the night, but Bonnet could not find it in himself to leave. Hence, he curled up beneath a tree across the street and waited for morning.

He could still so vividly remember his first glance of her when she exited the house, straw hat upon her ivory curls, basket on her arm, and servant following close behind. 'Twas like when one first approached heaven and saw an angel leaving by the gate, a glorious creature all light and wonder, not meant for the darkness of this world, yet scattering it with every step she took.

He followed her, watched her adoringly as she wandered through the open market, lingering here and there at items of interest. But always accompanied by the woman servant.

Didn't her father realize there were ruffians running about town? Surely 'twas not safe for two women to walk alone without protection? Anger burned within Bonnet as he slunk through the crowd, ignoring the cautious looks he received as if he were one of said ruffians! Egad!

He glanced down at his attire. He wore a gentleman's attire—a fine cambric shirt, embroidered waistcoat, black breeches and jackboots—all a bit stained, not to mention wrinkled from dried salt water. Mayhap 'twas not his clothing, but the various pistols and knives stuffed in his belt and baldric and the cutlass at his side. He surprised even himself that he'd not lost them, nor his boots, in the bay. In truth, he'd grown so used to them, he'd forgotten they made him look more pirate than gentleman. He hadn't considered they might frighten Melody. He should remove them. He should bathe and find new attire.

Too late. When he glanced up, she stood across the sandy street, staring at him with eyes wide and mouth open as if she were seeing a ghost. By the powers, he hadn't meant to surprise her thus.

He smiled.

Stunned, she started across the street, unaware of a carriage heading toward her. Her maid screamed. Bonnet charged forward, gripped her by the waist and hoisted her out of the way just in time.

The driver uttered a foul curse. "Look where yer goin', ye daft-witted woman!"

Gasps from the crowd filled the air. A few clapped their approval.

But all Bonnet saw was the look of love in her blue eyes.

"Stede!" She grabbed his arms and squeezed them. "You're real. I thought I was dreaming."

"I told you I would find a way to see you." More than anything, he longed to kiss her, but people were beginning to stare. 'Twas a small town and one in which he was sure gossip spread like the pox. He took a step back.

Sunlight glittered in her light hair fastened atop her head, allowing ringlets to dangle at her neck like jewels. She wore a lavender overgown open in the front and laced across, revealing white ruffles beneath. Her brilliant sapphire eyes continued to stare at him in wonder.

"You are far more beautiful than I remember." He bowed gallantly before her.

Pink blossomed on her cheeks as she looked around, embarrassed. Her servant sidled up behind her, gazing at Bonnet with suspicion.

"And you, sir, look like a handsome pirate." One of Melody's delicate brows arched.

He retrieved her straw hat from the dirt and shook it off, handing it to her. "There *are* rumors." He winked.

She glanced around at the people still looking their way. "How are you here? How did you... How long..." she seemed to be tongue-tied.

Taking her elbow, he led her down the street and turned a corner to a quieter part of town. The servant followed, a look of disapproval on her face.

"Miss, we shouldn't," she protested. "Your father expects us home soon."

"It will be all right, Omelia. He is an old friend. A dear, beloved friend," she added in a hushed tone that only Bonnet would hear. "Remain here. I shall only be a few feet away," she instructed the maid.

They stood in a narrow alleyway between two brick buildings amongst puddles of slop and refuse, but they might as well have been standing in the Great Hall at Windsor Castle for all Bonnet cared. Regardless, he withdrew a handkerchief and handed it to Melody who covered her nose.

"How long are you here, my love?" she asked.

"Not long, I fear."

Voices and the rattle of a carriage drew his gaze to the street. He must be on guard should someone recognize him. "A day at most. I am escorting one of the hostages from the *Crowley* to give Blackbeard's demands to your governor."

She lifted a gloved hand to caress his face. "When I heard Blackbeard had blockaded the city, I knew you were with him. I knew it! I could sense your nearness."

He closed his eyes beneath her heavenly touch.

"Oh, my sweet, my precious angel, how I have missed you." He rubbed a thumb gently over her lips, longing for a kiss. But Omelia glared at them from a few yards away. "When can I see you...*alone?*"

"Tonight. After my father falls asleep. I will slip out my window."

"I will be there." He gestured toward the nervous maid. "Will she say anything about me to your father."

"Nay, not if I ask her not to. I trust her. She's a bit overprotective, but we are friends."

"Until tonight then. I cannot wait!" Resisting the urge to pull her into his arms, he lifted her hand to his lips for a kiss. He felt her tremble, elating his heart and granting him encouragement that the lady's affections were as strong as ever.

Bonnet picked up his pen again and dipped it in the ink.

That night we spent together, my love, was the most glorious night of my life. I shall never forget it, nor your declarations of love that warmed my heart and filled me with hope for a future I dared not think possible.

Bonnet halted, remembering Melody's sweet face in the moonlight, gazing up at him from the blanket he'd spread beneath a Southern Magnolia tree in the woods near her house. He'd chosen a private place where no one would be passing by in the middle of the night.

"Please don't leave me again, Stede," she had said. "I hate it here in this barbaric town. My father restricts my every move, fills my days with obligations and duties, and limits my friendships." She shook her head, moisture glistening in her eyes. "He wants me to marry a rich merchantman, some old man who attends St. Philips." Tears streamed down her cheeks.

Bonnet's insides crumbled. "I will not allow it!" He wiped her tears and drew her close. "I will not allow it."

She pushed from him and sat up, wiping at her face. "He said within the year."

Bonnet moved behind her, and drew her back against his chest, encasing her with his arms. He buried his nose into her hair. Her scent of jasmine and rose sent his senses whirling. "I need more money. Just a few more conquests and I'll have enough for us to live comfortably."

"There may not be time." She turned to face him. "What if Blackbeard doesn't capture any more ships? What if you are caught?" Sobbing, she fell against him. "I'm so frightened, Stede. I'm so frightened."

He held her while she spent her tears, longing to comfort her, to tell her everything would be all right. In the distance, a night heron sang a mournful song. Wind stirred the leaves above them as the scents of pine and maple and earth wove around him—so different from the smells he'd grown accustomed to at sea.

"There, there, my love." He patted her back. A cloud moved away from the moon, dappling her with silver light. "When you left Barbados you seemed content to spend your life without me. And yet here you are so full of love. What has changed?"

Moisture once again filled her eyes. "I've had to endure a life, a place, a city in which you are nowhere to be found. That alone made me realize how much I love you."

"Enough to run away with me? To shame your father and mother, to live with a man who cannot marry you?" He hated to dissuade her, to offer her any reason to turn him down, but he had to know her true feelings.

A moment passed, a tender moment when she searched his eyes, her breath coming quickly. She bit her lip and then smiled. "I would do anything to be with you, Stede. Anything.

I don't care how much wealth you have accumulated. I shall be happier than a princess in a palace merely to live in a hut on a beach with you."

'Twas at that exact moment that Bonnet felt he truly began to live. Every second before, he had only been moving through life, dazed and empty, numbly attending duties and responsibilities dictated by social mores and societal restrictions.

But now, he came alive, every nerve, fiber, and cell exploding with vibrant hope and joy!

He had kissed her then, full and deep, exploring, yielding, loving, a kiss brimming with magnificent possibilities. And then he'd held her until the first light of dawn sprinkled over the morning mist.

"You have my word, Melody, I shall quit the trade, take the pardon, gather my wealth and return to you before the year is out."

They stood close to her home, near the open window of her bed chamber. "Will I see you before you must leave?" she asked.

Bonnet took both of her hands in his and lifted them to his lips. "I will try. Edward expects our soon return, and he is not a man to cross. But I will try."

And with that, he gave her one last kiss and watched as she gathered her skirts, darted across the field and disappeared inside her window.

CHAPTER SEVENTEEN

onnet did not see Melody again. By the time he
returned to town and found Mr. Marks, the governor
had already given him the chest full of booty Blackbeard
demanded. Trouble was, the two pirates, Bane and Stiles were
missing. In truth, missing was not the best description, for
Bonnet soon discovered from several citizens that the two
pirates had been strutting about town like besotted peacocks,
brandishing weapons, insulting and terrorizing everyone they
saw, women, children, and even pigs and chickens. They had
stolen with impunity, and even threatened to ravish any young
woman they saw to their liking, whilst the citizens felt unable
to string them up like they deserved for fear of Blackbeard's
repercussions.

To make matters worse, the *Queen Anne's Revenge* had
weighed anchor and sailed into the harbor, opening their gun
ports in a threat to pummel the city to dust. Some citizens had
left the city. Others stayed in their homes. All were in a panic.

Hence, Bonnet, along with Mr. Marks, were forced to
search the city for the two pirates and bring them back to
Blackbeard, along with the treasure, before Edward unleashed
hell. A threat Bonnet knew Edward was not only capable of
following through with, but one which would provide him
great enjoyment.

They found Stiles and Bane drunk and unconscious in a
tavern, and after dragging them to a boat, they quickly rowed
out to the *Queen Anne's Revenge*.

Hence, Bonnet had been unable to wish his sweet Melody
adieu.

Regardless, he would see her soon enough. Soon enough.

The deck tilted as the mad rush of water purled against the
hull, reminding him that Blackbeard, along with the other three
ships in his fleet, had set sail for North Carolina.

Bonnet dipped his pen once again in ink, intending to tell Melody how the passengers of the *Crowley* had been relieved of their valuables and most of their clothing, but were returned to Charles Town unscathed. He also wanted to tell her that the chest Blackbeard had demanded did not contain silver and gold as one would expect, but medicines, in particular mercury, which was used to treat syphilis. But then, he thought better of it. 'Twas not a thing to which a lady should be exposed. Truth be told, neither story would do him much credit in her eyes. Hence, he would simply tell her he loved her and would see her soon.

He started to write those very sentiments when a pirate knocked on his door. "'E wants to see ye."

The 'E would be Blackbeard, and that was never a good thing. Bonnet quickly dusted the words he'd already written, then blew over them, put the parchment away, and set the pen down.

An hour later he returned, his heart even fuller than when he left.

My dearest, my most precious, you shan't believe what good fate has befallen me! Or mayhap God Almighty has shone His favor on me at last. Edward has given me back command of the Revenge! Not only that, but he desires to leave the pirating trade as much as I! Together we have set sail for Topsail Inlet, where, whilst the Queen Anne's Revenge is being careened, he and I will venture inland to Bath and receive the governor's pardon. My love, this is what I had hoped for! Freedom, not only from this heinous trade but from any punishments due me from my actions whilst I was thus engaged.

Edward has further plans to then sail to St. Thomas and receive privateering papers from

Denmark to attack Spanish ships. Egad! He longs to be a legal pirate now and has asked me to join him. I agreed, but only to appease his ill temper, for I have other plans, plans to come rescue my lady love and sail away to a glorious horizon of love and happiness.

Until that day arrives, you have my heart, precious. Hold onto it with tender care.

I am and always will be affectionately yours,
Stede

Barret had not been able to keep his eyes off Lexie the entire time she read. He loved the sound of her voice, so soft and smooth, yet always with a hint of sorrow lingering at the edge. She read every line with excitement, yearning, joy, and sorrow as if she had traveled back in time three hundred years and was witnessing the events herself. Yet, toward the end of the letter, her eyes kept blinking and she yawned, and he remembered she hadn't slept in quite a while.

She set the letter down and stared at it. "I'm so happy for him. He got to spend time with Melody, and she professed her love. *And* then he got his ship back. It seems things are looking up for him." Leaning back onto the couch, she looked at Barret. "But I know his good luck doesn't last long."

He shook his head. "Yeah, I wouldn't get too attached to him."

"Too late." She smiled. "I feel like I know him. Like I understand him, you know? He's my distant relative, after all." She hugged herself and closed her eyes.

"I should let you get some sleep," he said. "Do you have to work tonight?"

"No…" Her voice dragged out like she spoke through molasses. "I have the night off."

For very different reasons, Barret was equally ecstatic over the contents of this particular letter. No historian had ever found evidence that Bonnet had a lover in Barbados, and certainly not that she had moved to Charleston. By all accounts Bonnet had *not* been part of the crew sent by Blackbeard into town to collect the ransom. To discover otherwise was an astounding find! Barret couldn't wait to write his book. With these authentic letters to back up his claims, his book would become a best-seller among the colonial historical societies and could potentially win him an award from the American Historical Association, something that would fast-track his career.

Snoring snagged his thoughts back to the present... *and* to Lexie who, with mouth open, had fallen sound asleep on the couch. Snoring! He smiled. What a delightful woman. Rising, he nudged her to lay down and then found a blanket in a hallway closet and returned to cover her. After placing the letter back in its sleeve, he sat across from her.

What a rare moment to look at her without appearing to be a letch, to admire her features without being too forward. She looked so small and vulnerable when she was sleeping, innocent even. Wisps of ivory hair lay across her forehead while her long lashes fluttered over her golden cheeks. Her lips, slightly open now, were full and pink and so...so *kissable*, especially when they weren't spouting defiance and sarcasm.

One thing he knew. He had to tell his parents she was staying here on the off chance they decided to take a mini-vacation and pop in on a strange woman living in their house. That wouldn't go well with his father, Judge Gregory Barret Johnson, at all. He would have her arrested immediately and locked away before she had a chance to explain.

But how to tell him? His father had never been one to offer lodging to poor strangers. Barret had hoped, if things progressed with Lexie, to introduce her slowly to the family. But now, he'd have to rush things.

Her snores grew deeper, and she let out a whimper that sounded more like a little girl than a grown woman. He smiled.

The barbecue. The family summer barbecue. He'd invite her to come. It would be the perfect fun, relaxing event for them to get to know her. He hoped they would love her as much as he did.

But how could they not?

Rising, he placed a gentle kiss on her forehead, careful not to wake her.

"Lord, please watch over this precious angel," he whispered before he left her to rest.

The next day, after giving Lexie sufficient time to catch up on her sleep, Barret caught himself whistling as he walked up to the front door of his parents' townhome. He wasn't sure if Lexie had to work tonight, and he wanted to honor his promise to walk her to the museum. Of course, he was also interested in reading another of Bonnet's letters. But, oddly, as he approached the door and knocked lightly, he found all his thoughts, *all* of his anticipation, was just on seeing her again, on being with her.

Either he was the biggest fool ever, or God had finally brought Barret the woman of his dreams. He scratched his stubble, waiting for someone to answer the door. Dreams might be a bit of a stretch, for Lexie was a handful. A fun, exciting, wonderful handful. He'd never felt this way about any woman, and he'd dated quite a few in his twenty-six years.

A breeze, ripe with the scent of fish and salt waved over him as he knocked again, a bit louder this time. Could she still be asleep at 4:00 in the afternoon? Alarm cut like a razor. Maybe she was hurt, injured! Maybe the people after the letters had found her! Groping for the keys in his pocket, he found the right one and unlocked and opened the door. A quick punch of the code on the alarm box by the door disarmed it.

He charged into the parlor where he'd left Lexie sleeping.

And came face to face with the barrel of a double-action revolver.

It shook in the hands of the woman who held it. Not Lexie, but a brown-haired woman, young and with a small child clinging to her leg.

"One move and I'll shoot," she said, breath coming hard and eyes narrowed.

Barret wasn't sure quite what to make of her, though he assumed from the look in her eyes that she was serious about shooting him. Even so, he felt no fear. What woman would shoot an innocent man in front of her small child—a rather adorable child peeking at him with a smile from behind her mother's blue jeans.

He raised both hands in the air. "Who are you and why are you in my house?"

Her brow wrinkled. The gun shook even more. "*Your* house?"

Barret extended his hand for the gun. "Give it to me, or I'll have you arrested for trespassing."

"Professor Johnson?" She took a step back. The little girl began to whimper.

And then it dawned on him. "You're Lexie's friend. The one she helps out now and then."

"Yes." She lowered the gun. "And you're Barret. I should have known. She said you were handsome."

Delight soared through him. "She did?"

The gun still shook in her hand. He reached for it, and thankfully, she gave it to him. He switched on the safety and headed into the foyer. "Is she upstairs?"

"No, she's not here," she shouted after him. "Listen, Mr. Johnson, I'm sorry to have pointed a gun at you. It's just that Lexie said some people are after her, and she didn't tell me you were coming by, so I just assumed... I'm really sorry."

Fear streaked across her eyes as she sank onto the couch and drew the little girl in her arms.

He didn't know whether to be angry at having a gun pointed at him, furious that Lexie invited a friend over to *his* house, or sorry he'd scared this poor woman and her child.

He decided on all three. "It's all right. It's a natural reaction. I didn't mean to frighten you or your little girl." He glanced at the gun, a Ruger SP101 .357 Magnum. Yes, he knew his guns, the benefit of having a policeman for a best friend. "Where'd you get this?"

"Lexie. She said she's had it for a while."

Of course. But hadn't she said she was afraid of guns? And why take the Taser from Adam? Scanning the room, he walked over and placed the weapon atop a stack of books on a shelf, high out of the little girl's reach. "I'll leave it there in case you need it. Which I doubt you will. This place is very secure." He faced the woman. "What are you doing here, anyway?"

"I'm Tracy, and this is Ellie. We are friends of Lexie's." Brown un-styled hair hung to the woman's shoulders, which were so slight, he wondered how they held up her head. In fact, the rest of her was thin and frail as well. Was it genetic or due to lack of nutrition?

The little girl peeked up at Barret from her mother's chest, glanced over him as if assessing the danger, and then obviously deciding he posed none, slid from her mother's lap and approached him. "Are you a pirate?" she asked.

Laughing, Barret stooped to her level. "I am. But a *good* pirate." He tapped her on the nose, and she giggled and ran back to her mother. Barret hadn't had much experience with kids, but this girl warmed his heart.

"Lexie was babysitting for me," Tracy said, drawing Ellie back into her lap. "I need to find work, and I had a couple of interviews." She sighed and blinked as afternoon sun streaming through the window shone on her face. Moving aside, she continued. "She's been helping me with food and money. She's such a great friend. When I got back, she asked me to stay for dinner."

Though he guessed Tracy to be in her early twenties, the exhaustion lining her face made her look much older. Based on what Lexie had told him, there was no Mr. Tracy involved, and therefore, the poor woman was trying to support herself and raise a little girl on her own.

"I see," he said. "And she's out getting food?"

"No. She volunteers at the women's shelter on her days off, so she went over there for a few hours. She told me I could stay here and when she got back, we'd order pizza. But I can leave. This is your place, after all." She started to get up, but Barret lifted a palm.

Women's shelter? "No. Stay. Any friend of Lexie's is welcome here." Unless they were criminals or drug addicts. But Lexie didn't know any of those types, did she? Memories rose of her handing money to a homeless woman. Good grief, what if she invited vagabonds to stay here? Or women from the shelter?

"The shelter downtown?"

"Yes. I think so."

"Thank you," And with that, he pivoted, rearmed the alarm, and left his own townhouse with a stranger inside. Something he would have never done a week ago. But then again, he'd been doing a lot of strange things since he'd met Lexie Cain.

CHAPTER EIGHTEEN

*B*arret had to admit that he'd never ventured into this part of town, nor had he ever considered visiting a shelter. His father had always warned him to steer clear of such seedy places and the vagrants and gangs who inhabited them.

"Not that we shouldn't pray for them and help them out now and then," he had said. "But remember, son, bad company corrupts."

Yet when Barret entered the front door of the women's shelter, and the older lady at the desk greeted him with a huge smile, he felt nothing but peace and hope in this place. A huge wooden cross hung on the wall behind the woman with a Scripture painted beneath it.

Pure and undefiled religion before God is this: to visit orphans and widows in their trouble, and keep oneself unspotted from the world. James 1:27

Odd, but Barret didn't remember hearing that Scripture before, and he'd been in church his entire life. It was even more odd that a woman who could hardly afford to take care of herself would spend her free time helping others. *And* give money and help to a single mom like Tracy. Truly Lexie was a complex puzzle—one he would love to solve.

"Can I help you, sir?" the lady asked.

Only one other person was in the waiting area, a young woman sitting in a chair, staring straight ahead with a look of shock on her face. One of her eyes was puffy and red.

"Is there a Lexie Cain here? She volunteers."

The woman beamed. "Lexie? Of course. You a friend of hers?"

"Yes. I've come to pick her up," he lied, well sort of. That was his intent, though they'd had no such arrangement.

"Such a lovely girl," the woman said. "She's one of the few volunteers we can count on. She's always on time, and she brings food and clothing to help. The women here just love her. I'll go see where she is." Rising, the woman went through one of two open doors behind her.

Barret stood there stunned, unable to think clearly. He knew Lexie had a heart for the downtrodden, but this? Devoting time and money to those in need when *she* was the one in need. He didn't know whether to chastise her or hug her.

A song drifted to his ears through one of the doors, a sweet, mournful melody that oddly touched his heart. From the other door came the sounds of women talking, babies crying, and children laughing.

Finally, Lexie appeared, and against his will, his heart leapt in his chest. She wore her usual blue jeans and t-shirt, her hair pinned up in its crazy way. One strand fell across her flushed cheeks, and she batted it away as shock filled her expression.

"Barret, what are you doing here?"

"Tracy said you'd be here."

The lady returned to sit behind the desk again.

"Are you finished?" he asked. "Can we talk?"

"Yeah, my shift is over." After saying her goodbyes to the woman, Lexie headed out the door with him.

A blast of summer heat swamped him, along with the stink of garbage and urine that seemed to permeate this part of town.

"What's this about, Barret?" Halting, she shielded her eyes from the setting sun, and stared up at him. "I don't appreciate being stalked."

⚓

The word *stalked* was perhaps a bit harsh, but it got Lexie the reaction she hoped.

Shock and dismay.

She wanted him to know she didn't appreciate him following her around town, and that just because he helped her out with a place to stay didn't give him *certain* privileges. She intended to tell him just that, but he took her hand and pulled her out of the earshot of passersby.

"Stalking? Are you kidding me?" Instead of getting angry, he laughed and shook his head. "There are people after you to hurt you, Lexie, to steal your letters, remember? Then you don't answer your phone, and it won't let me leave a message. I was worried about you. That's all."

She suddenly felt like a heel. "Okay, I'm sorry about the stalking comment. That was unfair."

"You think?" He raked back his black hair and let out an exasperated sigh, giving her a look that was both chastising and... something else she didn't want to admit—concern, care, something deeper? He stood there, towering over her, a Greek god with dark chiseled features and deep mahogany eyes, and it almost seemed a dream that a man like him would worry about someone like her.

It *was* a dream, a foolish dream. She pushed past him and headed toward the parking lot where she'd left her car.

He fell in step beside her.

"I guess you met Tracy," she said.

"Yes, at the other end of a gun."

Halting, she faced him, flinging a hand to her mouth. "Oh no! I'm so sorry. I wanted her to have some protection."

He raised a brow. "Turns out you own a gun *and* a Taser now." He gave a slanted smile.

She bit her lip and continued walking. "I hate the gun. I hardly ever remove it from its case. It was my mother's." A present from George, who had a collection of guns. Lexie had only kept for protection when all else failed.

"And your phone? Are you avoiding me?"

"It's off." She didn't want to tell him she'd been unable to pay the bill. He'd no doubt offer to pay it for her, and she didn't want to argue with him.

They reached the lot, and she found her car. Fishing for her keys in her pack, she faced him. "So, you see I'm fine. No need to worry."

"Please turn your phone on, Lexie. You might need it if something happens. Also, I'd like to know you're okay. I thought we were friends."

The way he said friends, with a twinge of sorrow, caused her to blink. She glanced down at his white tennis shoes standing in a puddle of grease. All because of her. "We are. I'm sorry."

He shifted his stance and glanced around as if making sure no one was after them. Protecting her? "So, you going to work? Need me to walk you?"

"No, I have the night off. I'm ordering a pizza and hanging out with Tracy." She bit her lip. "Hey, how about you join us?" It's the least she could do to make up for being such a snark.

He smiled, that slightly slanted, sensuous, grin of his that reached his eyes with such promise. "Love to. Meet you there."

Lexie regretted inviting the handsome professor before she even drove from the parking lot. He had remained long enough to ensure she was safely in her car and on her way before he turned to walk to wherever he'd parked his BMW. He waved at her as she passed, but she didn't wave back. Her plan to remain friends would be difficult the more time she spent with him, and here she'd gone and invited the man to dinner. "Good grief, girl. You're dumber than a box of rocks."

Yet she had to admit that three hours later as the four of them sat around the dining room table in Barret's townhome, their tummies full of pizza and their hearts full of cheer, she was having a good time. Barret and Tracy hit it off right away, which was itself a surprise since they had nothing in common. But Barret was a charmer, full of jokes and stories that kept them entertained. Then, of course there was Ellie, giggling and dancing around the dining room like an innocent little fairy from another world where there were no problems or heartaches.

Even more surprising was Barret's interactions with Ellie. Lexie would have supposed someone in his position would ignore the child or be annoyed at her silly comments and interruptions. Yet he played with Ellie, tickled her, spun her around, listened enraptured to every word she said and even at one point, held her in his lap. If somebody had poured a bucket of ice water on Lexie's head, she wouldn't have been more surprised.

Ellie, sitting in his lap, gazed up at him adoringly. "Can you teach me how to be a good pirate like you?" she asked.

They all laughed, and Lexie added, "Professor Pirate."

Grinning, Barret kissed Ellie's forehead. "Okay, but you must learn to say this in a pirate voice. *Avast, ye may be gettin' wet!*" He said the phrase as good as any pirate, then glanced up at Lexie and shrugged. "From Disney World's pirate ride."

She smiled, picturing him in pirate garb, standing feet spread apart, fists at his waist, on the heaving deck of a tall ship. And, against her will, a flood of pleasurable heat swirled in her belly.

Thank goodness he returned his attention to Ellie or he might have seen her reaction.

The little girl repeated the phrase over and over until she got it perfectly. Barret praised her and gave her a big hug as she leaned against his chest and yawned. Within minutes, she fell asleep in his arms, curled up against his chest as he shared a pirate story with them from the history of Charleston. Lexie couldn't take her eyes off the vision—his muscular arms surrounding the girl, protecting her, encasing her in warmth. Just like a father should do, like a father both Lexie and this little girl had never known.

She looked away as he finished his story, and Tracy rose from her seat. "That was so fascinating. I never knew such things about our history." She pointed toward her daughter. "I guess I should be going. Poor Ellie needs her sleep."

"I'll carry her to your car," Barret offered as he cuddled her close and stood. Always the gentleman.

At Tracy's car, while Barret strapped Ellie into her car seat, Tracy turned to Lexie. "I like him. A lot. He's a keeper." She winked, then slid into the driver's seat and closed the door.

Of course he was a keeper. A woman would be a fool to think otherwise. Lexie walked beside him back to the townhome, a sudden uneasiness stirring within her. It was precisely that he *was* such a good catch that made him dangerous, a man that could rip out her heart and stomp it into dust.

"I see why you want to help her out," he said as he unlocked the door and allowed her to enter first. "She's really nice. And Ellie is precious."

"Isn't she?" Lexie smiled and entered the front living area, her favorite room in the house. Though it was dark out, the huge bay window had a great view of the harbor, where moonlight streaked wavelets in glistening silver. She sank onto the couch, wondering if Barret would stay. She could hardly throw him from his own house.

He seemed to be having similar thoughts as he leaned against the door frame and glanced around awkwardly. "Thanks for letting me join you tonight."

She shrugged. "It's your house."

"No." His tone was serious as he walked toward her. "While you are here, it's your home. I don't want you to feel like you can't get rid of me if you want to."

Her heart rarely wanted to get rid of this man. It was her mind and her reason that wanted to cast him as far from her as she could.

"In fact, I should let you get some sleep." He walked to the bookshelf and pulled her gun down from atop a stack of books. "Before I forget." He laid it on the table. She shivered at the sight. Her best friend had been killed by such a weapon, a drive-by shooting for some gang retaliation. Thing was, she and her friend weren't even in a gang, though they dressed the part to look cool.

"Hey, how about you join me at church tomorrow?" Barret asked.

Another shiver overtook her as she stared at him, unsure she'd heard him correctly.

At her questioning look, he added, "You know, a building people go to each Sunday to hear about God and be inspired."

Lexie drew her knees up to her chest. "No, thanks. I don't need any inspiration." Besides, the last place she ever wanted to go was church.

He sat in a chair across from her and leaned forward, elbows on his knees and a grin on his face. "How about if I make it worth your while and take you to visit Melody's gravesite afterward?"

"Bonnet's Melody?" She unwrapped her legs, nearly springing from the couch. "You found her?"

"Yup. Right here in the historic district too, walking distance from the church." Oddly, the small cross he wore around his neck slipped out from beneath his shirt as if urging her to agree.

She bit her lip. Of course she'd love to see Melody's grave. She was her great, great, great... not sure how many greats, grandmother. She glanced at Barret with a sly smile. "Now that you told me, you know I could find it on my own."

He chuckled. "Yeah, but where's the fun in that? Let's go see it together."

"And church is the price." She arched a brow.

"A small price to pay."

"For you, maybe."

"You might even enjoy it."

She doubted that very much. Yet the mention of Melody's name got her excited about reading the next letter. "Hey, since you're here, wanna continue Bonnet's journey?"

Once again he flashed her that smile that would stop a war. "Let's do it."

CHAPTER NINETEEN

June 18th, 1718, Bath, Carolina

My Most Dearest and Precious Melody,

I post this letter to you from the capital city of Bath to your north, though, alack, one would be hard-pressed to call it a city and more inclined to call it a disgrace to be named a capital, for there could be no more than twenty homes shabbily erected on a dirt street, and poor homes at that.

You shan't believe this, but Edward, the great Blackbeard, ran his ship aground as we sailed into the inlet, and unable to free her as she had a considerable list to starboard, he abandoned the vessel, transferred all his goods, treasure, and men to my sloop, Revenge, and also to the captured Adventure. Hence, he was unable to accompany me on my journey and sent me on my way inland from Topsail Inlet with five of my men and several lucrative gifts to obtain a pardon from Governor Eden.

I am most pleased to announce to you, my darling, that the Governor was more than happy to not only grant me said pardon but to issue me a commission to sail to St. Thomas to seek a Letter of Marque from its governor! Not that I plan on becoming a privateer, but 'tis good to have options.

I am, therefore, returning to the Revenge, where 'tis my utmost joy to inform you that I intend to sail straight for Charles Town and steal you away aboard my ship to some exotic location where we will live out our days in loving bliss. Though I'd hoped to procure more treasure to provide you with a living to which you are accustomed, you have convinced me such things matter not to you, only that we are together.

You are a rare and precious find, my love. I cannot wait to see you again. Soon, my darling, soon.

Ever your devoted servant,
Stede

Bonnet brushed aside a thicket of leaves and emerged onto the sandy shore of Topsail Inlet, his men behind him, and the Governor's pardon in his pocket. Oddly, instead of three ships at anchor, only two remained, his sloop *Revenge* and the *Queen Anne's Revenge,* which lay battered and broken in the incoming surf. No doubt Edward had spotted worthy prey passing at sea and went in pursuit upon the *Adventure.*

Plucking a handkerchief from his pocket, Bonnet dabbed his forehead, then ran it across the back of his neck. Two days of tromping through grueling heat, thick forests, and swamp land would have drained him of all patience and energy, if not for the hope of a glorious future tucked safely within his waistcoat.

Tucker came up beside him. "Where'd they sail off to?"

"No idea," Bonnet replied. "Let's find out. Get the boat ready."

Within minutes, the men retrieved the small craft they'd hidden in the brush and soon, after a fierce paddle across the inlet, they thumped against the thick hull of the *Revenge*.

No face appeared from above, nor had any sentries been spotted on duty as they rowed toward the sloop. Not a sound, a stomp of foot, song, or voice could be heard. Bonnet's nerves tightened. Something was wrong, *terribly* wrong.

"Ahoy there!" he shouted upward while one of the men, Richards, tied the boat to an iron hook on the hull and flung himself onto the steps leading upward. Halfway to the top, he drew his cutlass and peered over the side.

Bonnet did the same as he mounted the steps behind him.

The thump of Richard's boots on the deck without any accompanying shouts or pistol shots encouraged Bonnet to join him. 'Twas a ghost deck—lines left scattered about, an empty barrel on its side, a scattered deck of cards, and not even a ship mouse to be seen. Sunlight shifted ghoulish shapes over the wooden planks as the sloop rocked in the inlet.

The other pirates joined him, scratching their flea-infested hair and peering about, pistols drawn.

"Search the ship!" Bonnet ordered, though he already knew what he would find. An alarming suspicion, a *traitorous* suspicion, had begun to take root deep in his soul, growing like a malignant cancer intent on strangling all his hopes and dreams. Soon, the men returned with the report that not a soul was on board...

And neither was a gleam or glimmer of any treasure.

Bonnet's treasure!

Blackbeard had betrayed him.

Slumping to sit on a barrel, his cutlass limp in his hand and clanking hollowly against the deck, Bonnet felt as though his heart had been keelhauled and tossed to the depths.

The pirates began cursing and spitting and searching for any rum they could find. But of course, there was none. A pirate like Blackbeard would not leave even a drop to ease their pain.

It had all been a ruse. Blackbeard had not sailed the *Queen Anne's Revenge* into a sand bar by accident! Bonnet ground a fist into his forehead. How stupid could he have been? Blackbeard was an expert sailor. He had only done so to trick Bonnet into leaving him alone with all the treasure.

So he could steal it!

Sheathing his cutlass, he rose, marched to the railing, and gripped the sea-worn wood until his fingers hurt. He glanced out to sea and blinked at the afternoon sun reflecting off waves. "Where are you, you bloody devil?" Bonnet would find him and make him pay! He needed his portion of the treasure. Saint's blood! He needed it for Melody. For their life together. Bonnet's grief boiled into fury, a fury that would not be quenched until he had his revenge!

At least he had his sloop, aptly named at the moment. But why had Blackbeard left it? Why not steal it as well? Perhaps God had granted Bonnet a speck of mercy, after all, for, unbeknownst to dear Edward, Bonnet had been pilfering treasure from the hold and storing it in a secret place in his cabin.

Shouts drifting on the wind from the west drew his gaze. A group of pirates waved at him from a wooded shore several yards from where Bonnet had emerged. The group grew larger as more men joined them from the trees. He couldn't recognize them from here, but he assumed 'twas his crew, at least most of them. Blackbeard would not have wanted to risk a mutiny should any of them remain loyal to Bonnet. That he hadn't killed them was to the villain's credit.

It took the entire afternoon to rescue them in the one cockboat left to Bonnet by his nemesis. It took only a few minutes for them to tell him the crew of the *Adventure*, along with Bonnet's friend Herriot, had been marooned and left to die on an uninhabited spit of land nearby. Or so they'd heard Blackbeard say.

Hence, once Bonnet got the *Revenge* underway, he scoured the barren strips of land lining the coast and quickly found his friend. Leaping from the boat, Bonnet tromped through the surf onto the sand, and Herriot nearly fell into his arms.

"We'd lost all hope, my friend," he breathed out, then stepped back and gripped Bonnet's arms. "He left us no food or water and with no trees to build a raft, we expected naught but a lingering death." His face was red and cracked from the sun and his lips chapped, but his eyes filled with hope once again.

"I am most pleased to have found you." Bonnet scanned the shore where at least twenty men gulped water from jugs his men had brought with them. Herriot took another swig from his, allowing the water to dribble over his bearded chin and then lifted his face to heaven and thanked God Almighty.

Saint's blood! 'Twas Bonnet, not God who had rescued the man. No matter, he was overjoyed to be in his company again.

Once everyone was brought on board the *Revenge*, Bonnet ordered his men to ready the sloop to sail to St. Thomas. His temper having cooled, allowing reason to return, he knew 'twas best to receive his commission to privateer and use it to, once again, acquire enough wealth for his life with Melody. What he had stored in his cabin would not be enough to last them all their days, and besides, he wanted to lavish her with luxury, not whisk her away to a life of poverty. It grieved him greatly that their happiness would be delayed yet again. But Blackbeard had left him no choice.

Standing at the larboard railing, he gazed over the rolling waves of the sea, kissed tenderly by the orange and red rays of the setting sun. Behind him, the pirates hustled to and fro, hauling lines, adjusting sheets, some cursing, others whistling. Below deck, Herriot and the other passengers were being fed and cared for. Bonnet closed his eyes and listened to the sounds of the ship and the sea, sounds that had become soothing to him—the slap of waves against the hull, the creak and groan of wood, the snap of lines and flap of canvas, and the mumblings of men who had spent their lives at sea. His emotions? A vile brew of potions that could be his undoing if he allowed them to poison him—fury, anger, sorrow, and a desperate need to be with Melody.

"Halt, there! Who are ye and want d'ye want?" A pirate's shout behind him, along with the cock of a pistol, spun Bonnet around and sent him charging across the deck to the starboard railing. A small boat approached the *Revenge,* filled with four sorry-looking souls and two large barrels.

"We's sellin' fresh apple cider!" the oldest man shouted back. "Thought ye looked a bit thirsty is all."

Groans rumbled from the pirates. "Got any rum?" one of them shouted down at the craft.

"Nay, but I swears this cider will quench yer thirst as well as any!" the old man smiled, revealing but two lonely teeth remaining on his top row.

Bonnet had no time for this tomfoolery. He had an hour or two of daylight left in which to begin his trip south. "Begone, man. We need none of your cider."

Growling, the man snapped orders to the others, and they began to row away.

"Wait!" Bonnet shouted. "Have you seen any other ships around here?"

Removing his floppy hat, the man scratched his head. "Aye, but it'll cost ye."

Bonnet reached inside his pocket and tossed the man a silver coin.

He caught it and smiled. "We did see a ship, didn't we, gents?" He glanced over his friends. "About a day's sail north o' 'ere, anchored in Ocracoke Inlet. The *Adventure,* weren't it?"

His friends nodded. "Aye, 'twere the *Adventure,* fer sure. They bought some cider from us. I ne'er forget a customer."

Bonnet sent them on their way. *Blackbeard.* Just a day's sail from here. Punching the railing with his fists, Bonnet took up a pace, pirates scattering before him. If he took the blackguard by surprise, with his ten guns to Blackbeard's eight, he just might be victorious. Anchored in a safe inlet, Edward would be deep into his cups. He would not expect

Bonnet to attack. If Bonnet was successful, he could get back his treasure and start a life with Melody right away.

Halting, he stared out to sea yet again and stroked the royal pardon tucked safely in his waistcoat pocket. Yet the safer route would be to forsake his revenge, sail to St. Thomas, and become a privateer. The safer and much *longer* route. Would Melody even wait for him another year, or two? Or would her father marry her off to that wealthy merchant?

Ignatius Pell approached, his greasy hair tossed by the incoming wind. "Where to, Cap'n?"

Where to, indeed? Bonnet sighed. Closing his eyes, he lifted up a prayer, his first in decades. *God, if you're there, I need some wisdom. Tell me what to do.*

He waited, listening, quieting his spirit.

St. Thomas.

The words echoed within him, soft and yet somehow authoritative. Had God just spoken to him? Couldn't be. Surely 'twas just the wind or his own foolish imagination.

Pell cleared his throat. "Cap'n?"

June 21st, 1718, At Sea

Precious Melody,

I pray this letter finds you in good health and happiness and that your heart still belongs to me as mine always will to you, my love. I hesitate to inform you of my recent misfortune, but as it seems, my old friend Edward has betrayed me and run off with all the treasure I had garnered for our life together.

Bonnet dipped his quill in ink as the *Revenge* rolled over a massive swell. The deck tilted to port as bare feet thundered above him, adjusting sail. 'Twas good to be back in the captain's cabin where he belonged, but these rough seas were doing no credit to his exemplary penmanship. Resuming his letter,

Hence, with royal pardon in my pocket, I am pursuing Edward in order to retrieve what is mine. Never fear, my dear, I have learned much under his tutelage and I know I can best him. Once I have treasure in hand, I shall set sail for Charles Town and we shall be together forever. Nevermore shall we be parted, my dearest.

Pray for me, if you will. Blackbeard is a formidable foe, but we have goodness and justice on our side.

He'd wanted to say God, but he knew deep down the Almighty had told him not to pursue Blackbeard. Even so, should God be looking down on him, surely His favor would land on Bonnet and not on murderous Edward.

I am ever your humble and adoring servant, Stede

CHAPTER TWENTY

L exie should have told Barret she wasn't going to church the second she opened the door and saw him cringe. A barely noticeable cringe, but she'd known him long enough to spot it. Still, when he followed it up with that sensuous smile of his, the cringe faded from her memory.

Until now.

Until she walked into the beautiful sanctuary of Mercy Community Church and realized her mistake. She was way underdressed. For some reason, she'd thought churches had modernized and people could wear jeans and a nice shirt—her nicest shirt, in fact—a button-down collared lavender shirt with a white lacy camisole underneath. But apparently, she'd been wrong. Dresses and suits stretched as far as the eye could see, while above them eyes scoured her with looks of disapproval. Well, not everyone, but enough of them to make her squirm.

Barret must have sensed she was about to turn and bolt, because he grabbed her hand and placed it in the crook of his elbow, holding it there as they proceeded down the aisle. A few people smiled his way, but the music started, and Barret quickly found them a seat. *In the back*, thank God.

Although now that she thought about it, it seemed a bit sacrilegious to thank God for that.

Good heavens! What was she doing here? Her heart thumped so wildly against her ribs, she thought Barret would hear it. Instead, he grabbed a hymnal from the pew in front of them and gestured for her to stand. Her hands were so clammy, she feared she'd leave a mark on the book as she held one side and sang a hymn called *Be Thou My Vision*. She couldn't tell you what the words said, nor those of the next hymn… or the next. Her thoughts were occupied with finding a good reason to excuse herself and leave. But Barret's strong baritone voice beside her, belting out the songs as if he meant every word, kept her in place. If she left, she'd embarrass him in front of his friends, and he didn't deserve that.

Finally, they sat back down. Announcements were made, jokes were told, a Scripture was read, and prayers were said. All the while, Lexie did her best not to shift and wiggle on the red cushions of the pew and reveal her discomfort. A collection plate made of beautiful wood and inlaid with velvet passed before her. For some reason, she felt guilty for not tossing anything in it. Especially when Barret placed an envelope inside.

Crossing arms over her chest, she lifted one hand to finger her gold earring. Her mom would be glad to see her here, but Lexie still hated church. It was a place where God made people feel guilty—guilty for not giving enough, doing enough, following all the rules. And people put up with it because they were afraid to die and even more afraid to end up in hell. If there even *was* such a place.

Barret gazed at her sideways, offering a comforting smile, but she only frowned in return. No sense in pretending she was enjoying herself. If they were to remain friends, he would have to respect her lack of faith.

The pastor or preacher or whoever he was moved to stand behind the podium and began his sermon. Too bad Lexie couldn't just close her eyes and zone out. Instead, she tried to fill her thoughts with other things—seeing Melody's grave, continuing Bonnet's adventure, and finding his long, lost treasure. Only money would change Lexie's life and remove her family curse, not some distant God who didn't care about her.

Yet, no matter how hard she tried, the preacher's words kept barging into her brain. *Choices.* He kept talking about choices in life and how God created us with free will so we would choose Him out of love and not by compulsion. He spoke of an enemy who did his best to get us to make wrong choices at every turn and a loving God who continually enticed us to choose the right path. He quoted a verse from Isaiah,

Your ears shall hear a word behind you, saying, "This is the way, walk in it," "Whenever you turn to the right hand or whenever you turn to the left."

She bit her lip. Growing up without a father and with a mother who was often too busy working, Lexie had no one to give her guidance, no one to tell her which way to go, what decision to make. And she suddenly wished she'd had that. Would she have listened? Would her life had turned out differently?

The preacher went on to quote verse after verse about how the Lord blesses those who "walk in His ways." He explained how the Israelites continually refused to listen to God's instructions, how God wanted them to live in the promised land in peace and prosperity, yet they rebelled over and over. After years of God's patience, He finally gave them over to their enemies. Not because He wanted to. Not because He was mean or a bully. But simply because they had chosen that path and because of their free will, He could no longer protect them. Like Adam and Eve, they'd been given a choice. Choose life, choose to follow God, or choose to rebel and follow God's enemy.

Lexie shifted in her seat. Like she said, this religion stuff was all about following rules and guilt. But then the preacher spoke about the love of God, that even in our bad choices, He never gives up on us. He pursues us and keeps giving us chances. The preacher explained that it's not all about this world and our happiness here, but that God wants to bring us to heaven when our time is finished. And all the choices we make either lead us to heaven or lead us to hell.

Now Lexie really squirmed. So much so that Barret tried to take her hand in his, but she withdrew.

Ah, and here it came, the spiel about how God sent Jesus, His only Son, to die on the cross for our bad choices... blah blah blah. She'd heard all of that before from her mother on her death bed, begging Lexie to say a prayer of repentance and receive Jesus before it was too late. But, even if this Jesus was truly God, Lexie wanted nothing to do with Him. He hadn't lifted a finger to help her and her mother all the years when they'd lived in roach-infested apartments eating SPAM out of cans or when they'd been on the street, cold and hungry, begging for food. Not even when her mother had cried out to Him in the agony of cancer. Nope. Lexie didn't need a God like that.

She closed her ears to the rest of the service—an altar call, more prayers, and an ending song. Afterward, people crowded the aisles, making a fast exit impossible. Instead, Lexie had to endure being introduced to several of Barret's acquaintances and friends. The man was certainly popular, but what did she expect from the charismatic, good-looking professor? She, however, did not seem to have a speck of his charisma. Most of his friends were polite enough, shaking her hand and smiling, but behind the smiles, disapproval prowled. Some even asked her a few questions—"What do you do, Miss Cain? Where are you from?"—to which Barret answered in her stead that she was new in town, worked at the Exchange museum, and was helping him with research. He didn't tell them *what* she did at the museum. No doubt that would be too embarrassing.

Finally, after most of the crowd dispersed, Barret stood in the aisle by their pew, scanning the sanctuary as if he were looking for someone. He waved at an older man standing next to the preacher, who turned to acknowledge Barret but whose gaze quickly shifted to Lexie.

"Come. I want you to meet my father."

"Your father?" Holy cow, his father wasn't the preacher, was he? "Who is he?"

"There, standing by Pastor Greg. He's one of the elders of the church."

She didn't know what an elder was, but from the way the man was staring her down with censure, she didn't want to know.

"I can't." She tugged out of his grasp. "Maybe another time." She'd had enough condemning looks to last a lifetime.

Barret stared at her a moment, then glanced back at his father, but by then, the man had disappeared with the preacher through a side door.

Breathing a sigh of relief, Lexie spun and sprinted out the door into the bright sunshine, ignoring loitering church-goers...ignoring the aching emptiness in her soul.

Barret frowned at his father's disappearance. He'd informed the man last night that Barret was bringing a special guest he wanted him to meet. Why would he completely ignore him? Shaking his head, Barret turned to escort Lexie out of the church, but she, too, had disappeared, leaving her vanilla fragrance and a string of onlookers behind. Smiling at them, he hastened after the fascinating woman. He found her hurrying down the sidewalk in front of the church as if she couldn't get away fast enough. Of course, he noticed her squirming and sighing throughout the service, but he hoped it was because she was being convicted by the presence of God and the great sermon. At least that had been his prayer.

"Lexie!" He caught up to her. "Where are you going?"

She kept walking. "Far away."

"That bad, huh?" Rubbing the back of his neck, he fell in step beside her.

Halting, she faced him, glanced back at the church, and huffed. "It was okay, I guess. They just aren't my kind of people is all. I'm not into this religious cr—stuff."

Religious *crap* was what she was going to say. Barret frowned, feeling the sudden urge to defend his church. "These people are decent and upstanding, some of the nicest people you'll ever meet."

She placed a hand on her hip. "Then why were some of them staring at me as if I were a cockroach to be stepped on?"

Confused, Barret searched his memory for any slights his friends might have given her.

"At my hair, my clothing?" She gestured to the wild and adorable way she pinned up her hair and then down to her jeans. "And my tattoo?"

True, some of the more prudish parishioners might have found her attire a bit unorthodox, but had they been rude? He'd been so nervous about her hearing a good word from the pastor, he truly hadn't noticed anyone giving her disapproving looks.

"I don't fit in, Barret. If you can't accept me the way I am, then maybe we should stop hanging out."

"I accept you as you are, Lexie. You know that."

"Then, please, no more church for me, okay?" She started on her way.

Barret's heart suddenly felt like a stone. How could he pursue anything deeper with this woman if she didn't believe in God, if she wasn't saved? Yet, maybe... maybe God wanted him to convert her. Maybe that was why their lives had been thrown together.

He walked beside her with renewed joy. "Still want to see Melody, or are you too upset?"

"I'm not upset. I appreciate you inviting me, Barret. Let's just drop the subject. And yes, I'm dying to see Melody's grave!"

"Very well, as the lady wishes." He gave her that smile he knew she enjoyed, and sure enough, she smiled back at him sweetly.

The sun was shining, and a cool breeze blew in from the bay, making it an easy choice to walk the eight blocks to the cemetery at St. Philip's instead of drive. Lexie remained quiet and pensive as they strolled along, and Barret thought it best to leave her to her thoughts. Maybe she was thinking about the sermon, after all. One could only hope.

She stopped before the iron gates of the western cemetery and glanced back at the large church across the street with its massive steeple poking into the blue sky and yard filled with gravestones. "Two cemeteries? How do we know which one?"

"The churchyard was originally only for church members, and this western cemetery was for—how did they put it?—'strangers and transient white people.'" Barret laughed. "But eventually they ran out of room at the yard, so members are now buried here in the western side."

She nodded with a huff. "Transient white people, eh? I suppose this is where Melody was buried, though, if I remember correctly, her father was the preacher at this church."

"Rector, yes, but I suppose she must have done something that disqualified her."

"No doubt it had to do with Bonnet." Wind swept over them, fluttering through her hair and tossing pearly bangs across her forehead. She brushed them away and stared forlornly at the graves. "And I have an idea what it was."

To his delight, she took his hand in hers and dragged him through the open gate where gray stones—some standing, others lying on the ground—dotted the lush green grass. Huge maple and oak trees spread leafy branches over the scene, offering shade to the departed, while the scent of earthy loam, salty sea, and unrealized dreams swirled about the place.

"This way." He led the way, still holding her hand, but she tugged him to stop, her gaze riveted to a head stone.

William Johnson
Son of M. Aaron and Mrs. Isabel Johnson
Died September 2nd in the Year of Our Lord 1759
Aged 2 years and 5 months
Mournful Parents here I ly
As you are now, so once was I
As I am now so you must be
I pray each other again will see

"So sad." Lexie withdrew her hand and sighed. "He was only two."

"Lots of children died young in those days," Barret offered, though it didn't seem to lessen her sorrow, as frowning, she moved down the row and stopped before another stone. Did this woman never cease to surprise him? He'd thought her only interest had been in Bonnet's treasure, not in any real history.

Underneath
Lieth the Body of Robert
Comonly called Burdkins
Who died July 27, 1793
Aged 63
Here lie I at the eternal door
Here lie I because I'm poor
The farther in, the more you'll pay
Here lie I as warm as they

Lexie chuckled, then quickly covered her mouth and gave him a sly look. "I suppose I shouldn't laugh at the dead."

"I don't think they mind." Barret glanced at the few people milling about and spotted a crowd around Colonel Rhett's tomb. He should show Lexie the tomb of the man who caught Bonnet, but then changed his mind. Maybe later, after they finished the letters. No sense in upsetting her further. Church had been enough.

"Let's go pay our respects to Melody." He led the way to the far end of the cemetery by the stone wall and stopped before her grave.

Birds chirped a happy tune above them in the trees as Lexie reverently slid beside him, her eyes locked upon the gravestone.

Her lies the body of
Melody Rogers
Daughter of The Reverend Thomas Rogers and
Rachel Rogers
Died March 6, in the year of our Lord
1743, in the 45th year of her Age.
A troubled life finally come to rest

Lexie released a burdened sigh, then knelt to the damp grass. "A troubled life," she breathed out, pain in her voice.

Stooping beside her, he flung an arm around her shoulder, but said nothing. There was nothing to say. Through the letters, they had both come to know Melody, to feel her pain and join in her dreams. Even though the end of the story was already written, it was hard to face that her life had not turned out as she hoped.

Lexie ran her hand over the leaves covering the grave. "Just like my mother. A troubled life. Perhaps it is the way things are meant to be for our family."

Barret shook his head. "I don't believe that."

"You don't know my family," she snapped, but her anger quickly faded as she gazed back at the grave. "I wonder how she came to be buried here. My mother told me that Melody had lived most of her life in Virginia."

Barret had no idea. What he did know was that this woman's sorrow affected him in a way no one else's ever had. He wanted more than anything to hold her, wipe away her tears, take away her pain. *And* the pain of her family that haunted her. It was true. He didn't know much about her family, but he wanted to. He wanted to know everything about this woman. But now was not the time to ask. Instead, he watched the way the breeze danced through her hair and twirled the ivory wisps dangling about her neck, the way rays of sun streaming through the branches lit her golden skin, the way her lips puckered when she was thinking, and those green eyes of hers, so filled with pain.

Finally, after several minutes, she rose. "Thank you for bringing me here. I feel closer to her now for some reason." She wiped the moisture from beneath her eyes. "You must think I'm silly for getting all emo over someone I never knew."

"I have never thought you silly. Foolish sometimes, a bit crazy, but never silly."

She laughed. "Fair enough." But her smile soon faded as her eyes focused on something behind Barret.

Spinning around, he saw two men duck behind a monument. One of them looked like the man who had attacked Lexie in the parking garage. "Wait here." He marched in their direction, angry when he heard her footsteps following him. Would the woman ever listen?

Nearly at the stone monument, Barret glanced over his shoulder at Lexie to once again order her to remain where she was. When he turned back around, a powerful fist struck him across the jaw.

His world spun. Pain seared across his face. He blinked, trying to focus. Lexie screamed.

The fist struck him again, this time in the gut. Holding his stomach, he barreled over, but managed to get a good look at his attacker—a huge beast of a man with red hair hanging to his shoulders and tattoos covering both arms. The man from the parking garage. The man behind him was just as tall, but smaller in size. Barret charged the beast, using his head as a weapon. They both crashed to the ground.

A woman screamed in the distance. Gasps and shouts rose all around.

"Call the police!" one man said.

But all Barret could think of was whether Lexie was okay?

No time to check. The large man pinned Barret's arms to the ground and struck him on the forehead with his own head. Barret's world went blank. He gasped for air, willing himself to focus. The beast released him and rose. Barret swept his feet across the man's legs, and he toppled like a hewn tree. Leaping to his feet, Barret grabbed the man by his shirt, lifted him from the ground, and gave him a left punch to the gut and a right across his jaw. The man stumbled backward, fell, and his head struck a gravestone. He rolled to the ground.

Barret glanced around and found Lexie picking up a large rock and heading toward them. Crazy woman!

The skinny man grabbed her by the waist.

"Let go of me!" She struck his head with the rock.

Not hard enough, however. The brute only shook his head and continued to drag her away.

Sirens screamed in the distance.

Fear and anger consumed Barret. A bestial roar emerged from within him as he charged the smaller man and knocked him away from Lexie. Stumbling backward, the fiend remained on his feet. Hatred burned in his dark eyes. Plucking something from his belt, he charged Barret.

Where was Lexie? There, picking up the rock! Barret headed toward her while trying to shove the man aside.

Pain, raw and penetrating, burned in Barret's side. He collapsed to the ground. The larger man finally stood and was heading toward them when the other man shouted, "Police are coming. Let's get outta here."

They both raced away as a crowd formed around Barret and Lexie.

She dropped to her knees before him, her expression filled with fear. "Oh, my gosh, you've been stabbed!"

CHAPTER TWENTY-ONE

*L*exie had seen blood before. Lots of it, in fact—a good friend's blood during a gang shooting, blood from fights during her time in Juvie, and more than she ever wished to see of her own mother's blood. But the sight of Barret's blood sent a chill through her like none other. Ripping off her outer shirt, she bundled it and pressed it hard against the wound in his side. A crowd formed around them.

"Call 9-1-1!" She shouted just as two police officers broke through the mob and approached.

One of them leaned to speak to a radio on his shoulder. "We need a bus at 146 Church Street Western Cemetery ASAP."

Lexie continued to press the wound. Her lavender shirt turned brown. Panic set every nerve on fire. "Don't you die on me, Professor!" Yet one glance in his eyes revealed nothing but peace. He smiled. "I'm okay, Lexie. Don't worry."

How could he be so calm?

"Step aside, ma'am." The policewoman nudged Lexie away and took over holding the wound.

The rest of the afternoon became a blur of panic, fear, a ride in the ambulance, and a dash into the emergency room. Lexie was shoved outside two swinging doors and told to wait.

Waiting was not her strong suit. She paced. She bit her fingernails. She tried to pray, but the words would not come. She should call someone—his parents? But her phone was still dead, and she didn't know their numbers anyway.

The police officers who had helped Barret entered the waiting room and asked her a bunch of questions about what happened. She gave them a description of the men and told them they had attacked Barret for no reason. Which was true. What she neglected to tell them was that one of them had attacked her before and that they were probably after the same pirate treasure she was seeking. Even hearing those words in her head sounded crazy. No way she was going to tell them.

"Very well, Miss Cain." The woman closed her notebook and stood. "We'd like you to come down to the station and work with a sketch artist as soon as possible, and"—she glanced over her shoulder at the doors leading to surgery—"we would like to speak with your friend when he's...when he's able." She gave Lexie a smile that said the poor woman had seen too many victims die before she'd been able to talk to them.

Which did nothing to lessen Lexie's fears.

A call came in on the man's radio and they both nodded at her and left, leaving her alone with *those* fears that seemed to rise with each passing minute.

Finally, a doctor in blue scrubs pushed through the doors and headed her way. "Are you Lexie?" he asked, but all she could see was the blood on his gown.

The doctor raised his brows. "Barret's girlfriend?"

Girlfriend? Ah, yes, that's what she'd told the paramedics so they would allow her in the ambulance. "Yes, that's me."

The doctor smiled. "He's going to be fine."

A tidal wave of relief passed over her so strong, the rest of the doctor's words flowed along afterward in wavelets of wonderful phrases—"No vital organs, minimal damage, slight blood loss"

"We'll keep him a few hours for observation, but he can go home soon."

"Can I see him?"

"Of course."

The first thing Lexie saw when she was led to the small enclosure in the emergency room was Barret lying on a bed with his eyes closed. The next thing she saw was the large white bandage on his right side. But it was the various monitors beeping and buzzing by his bedside that finally drew her attention and sent her pulse racing.

The scent of rubbing alcohol, disinfectant, blood, and death filled her lungs, and she nearly turned and bolted out of there. She would have done just that if Barret hadn't opened his eyes at that very moment, saw her, and smiled. *Smiled?*

She hated hospitals, their smell, the fluorescent lighting that made everything look creepy, the sterilized walls with strange artwork, the howls of pain, the people dressed in blue paper that crinkled when they walked. And all the beeps and buzzes of the machines! She hated that most of all.

"Are you all right?" Barret attempted to sit, wincing in pain.

Lexie dashed for him and forced him back down. "Yes. What are you doing?"

"I'm okay." He moaned.

"Sure you are." It was then Lexie noticed the man wore no shirt. Funny it wasn't the first thing she saw when she'd entered the room, but whoa, the man's muscle tone was stupendous. The small silver cross he wore laid perfectly in between his firm pecs.

"You checking me out?" He grinned.

Heat swamped her face, and she shifted her glance away. "Don't be stupid. I was just looking for wounds."

His grin didn't fade.

"How can you joke around? You were stabbed."

"I'm well aware." Pushing against the mattress, he attempted to sit up and winced.

Lexie touched his arm, hating to see him in pain. "Do you want me to call your parents?"

He shrugged. "No need to worry them. I'll be out of here in a couple hours."

"But still, I'm sure they'd want to know."

He reached for her, and she slid her hand in his. He felt warm and solid and strong. "Are you okay, Lexie?" he asked.

She stared at him, stunned. He was the one who'd been stabbed and yet he was asking how she was? Honestly, it was getting really hard not to fall head over heels for this guy. And that scared her most of all. "I'm so sorry, Barret. All this is my fault. They were after me, not you." She pulled her hand away and uttered something she'd been pondering for a while but something that nearly tore her guts out to say. "For your own safety, you really shouldn't see me anymore."

Not see her anymore? Just the notion made Barret's heart ache more than his side was doing at the moment. He felt the loss of her soft hand immediately.

She took a step back, hugged herself, and glanced around. Blood stained the white camisole she was wearing, and he remembered she'd used her nice blouse to stop his bleeding. He also remembered her sitting in the ambulance, insisting she was his girlfriend when they'd tried to kick her out, and the way she'd held his hand and looked at him with such concern. She'd been so brave at the cemetery, but now only fear and unease tainted her expression, as if she would dash from the room at any moment. Ah. He was a fool! Of course. Hadn't her mother died of cancer? Hospitals surely brought back horrid memories for this poor lady.

"That's not going to work for me," he said matter-of-factly. "Not seeing you. Besides, I don't blame you, Lexie. None of this is your fault."

"No, but I don't have to include you in my mess."

"Too late." He wanted her to glance his way, to see his smile and the care in his eyes, but her gaze kept shifting nervously around the room. "Besides, I have *you* to protect me," he added to lighten the mood. "I seem to remember you bashing a rock over one of those men's heads." He still couldn't believe she'd done that. What a brave lady!

"Lot of good it did." She huffed and gave a half-smile. "Thick-skulled jerk."

"You should have stayed away like I said."

She shot him a pointed gaze. "No way. I'm not going to stand there and watch you get beat up."

He smiled. "What do you mean beat up? I had them both in the palm of my hand."

Lexie laughed and shook her head. "Okay, Mr. Tough Guy. If you say so."

He tried to keep his eyes off the lacy silk camisole she was wearing that left little to the imagination. "Anyway, I am worried about you. These guys are getting more violent, taking more risks. I'm going to hire a fulltime bodyguard for the townhome."

Her cute little nose scrunched. "Don't be ridiculous. That's way overboard."

Exactly what he'd thought she'd say. "Okay, then. I guess I'll have to move in."

A loud beep echoed down the hall, drawing her gaze as several nurses sped by with a cart.

Several seconds passed—seconds in which Lexie appeared to be having trouble breathing. Finally, she faced him, hugged herself, and seemed to relax a little. One brow playfully arched. "I beg your pardon, Professor Piety. Doesn't that go against your religion?"

"Hmm." He rubbed his chin. "I don't recall anything in the Bible about not protecting the woman I lo—an innocent woman." He hoped she didn't notice his mistake. A thrill passed through him at what he'd been about to say. He was definitely falling in love with her. But he doubted she was ready to hear that. "Besides," he continued, hoping to cover it up. "I would just be there for protection. Nothing improper."

She bit her lower lip, tugging on it. She was about to say something when the curtain swept open and a nurse rushed inside. "Good day, Mr. Johnson." After smiling at them both, she glanced at the monitors, wrote something down on her chart, then moved to peek beneath Barret's bandage. "Looks good." Reaching behind him, she helped him move to the edge of the bed and swing his legs over. Pain radiated across his stomach, but he tried not to show it, nor utter a single grunt. He didn't wish to stay overnight in a place that made Lexie so uncomfortable.

"Now, stand up for me, please." The nurse took a step back and watched as Barret stood. The room spun, his side exploded in agony, and he blinked to clear his vision.

"Dizzy?

"No, ma'am."

At this, the nurse smiled. "Very well. Then you may get dressed, Mr. Johnson." And out she went as fast as she had entered.

Grabbing his shirt from the chair, Lexie tried to help him put it on, but he waved her away. "I'm good, thanks." As much as he enjoyed her being close, he was not an invalid.

A voice blared over the intercom, calling a Dr. Tatum to Surgery One. The patient in the next enclosure moaned for a nurse. A scream blared down the hall.

Lexie looked more nervous than ever.

Barret hurried buttoning his shirt.

Finally, a doctor entered, chart in hand. "I'm releasing you, Mr. Johnson. Here's a couple of prescriptions." He began scribbling on a pad. "One is an antibiotic and the other for pain." He tore off the paper and handed it to Lexie. "Take good care of him, miss. Clean and rebandage his wound every day, and if he gets a fever, bring him back." He looked at Barret. "You should see your doctor in a week and have him check your wound. You're a very lucky man, Mr. Johnson."

And before they could thank him, he disappeared behind the curtains.

"Well, looks like you've been assigned my nurse for the next few days," Barret said.

She chuckled. "It's the least I can do when I'm the one who got you stabbed."

He grabbed his things from the stand—phone, wallet, and keys—and stuffed them in his pocket. "Your place or mine?"

She gave him a sassy look. "They are *both* yours."

"Then yours. Mine looks like a bachelor pad."

"Well played, professor." Taking his arm, she shook her head and led the way from the room. "Looks like you're moving in with me after all."

As it turned out, Lexie was a much better nurse than Barret would have guessed. By the time the cab pulled up in front of the townhome, it was dark outside. She helped him out of the car and onto the couch in the living room, made sure he was comfortable and had water, then ran out to get his prescriptions filled. Despite the piercing pain in his side and a massive headache, he was enjoying her tender care and concern.

Now, she sat in the chair beside the couch, her feet drawn up on the cushion as she read out loud from a book she'd pulled from the shelf, *The Confederate South Carolina*. He knew she wasn't interested in the topic and only read it to entertain him, which endeared her to him even more.

Light from a nearby lamp showered her with golden rays, glittering over her skin and glistening in her ivory hair. And sitting there in the dark room, the sound of her voice so soothing and sweet, she was like a burst of sunshine in a dark world—all warm and bright and beautiful. His gaze landed on the small daffodil tattoo on her upper arm.

"Why a daffodil?" he asked, interrupting her.

She looked up at him, then glanced down at her ink. A sadness overcame her, and she fingered the gold hoop earring in her right ear. Several seconds passed, and Barret regretted the question.

"My mother used to call me her little daffodil," she finally said.

Barret didn't know how to respond to such a sweet sentiment. "You loved her."

"Very much." She gave a sad smile and fingered her earring again.

"She give you that?" He gestured toward her ear.

Lexie nodded.

He wanted to ask her about the eagle on the back of her neck but thought it best to wait for another time. "I want you to meet my family."

She gave him a curious look. "Why?"

"They'd love you."

"I don't need anyone to love me."

Hmm. Maybe try a different tactic. "We're having a family barbecue in two weeks. Come with me and meet everyone. I want you to see we are not the rich, religious prudes you think we are."

She raised one delicate brow. "I never said that."

"You didn't have to."

She dropped the book to her lap. "Is this part of my penance for getting you stabbed?"

"If that's what will make you go."

Her lips curved as a twinkle appeared in her eyes. "Ah, Professor, there's only so far I'm going to allow you to milk this."

He smiled. "So it's a date."

"We'll see." She set the book down on the table. "You must be tired. Why don't you get some sleep? I'm going to head upstairs."

He didn't want her to leave. Not yet. He was enjoying her company far too much. "How about we read another Bonnet letter instead?"

CHAPTER TWENTY-TWO

July 1718, Ocracoke Inlet, Carolina Province

My Most Precious Melody,

I pray you are well, my dearest, in good health and happy. Do not forsake your faith in me, sweetheart, for we shall soon be together again. 'Tis my misfortune, however, to have somehow missed Edward and his ship, *Adventure*, once again, for we now find ourselves in the empty inlet in which those miscreant purveyors of cider and lies informed us he had anchored.

Hence, I called a meeting of council to decide our next course of action. Our first order of business resulted in a unanimous vote for Robert Tucker to become quartermaster. I must admit to being opposed to the crew's choice, for there lurks something in Tucker's eyes which sets me ill at ease. However, he is highly skilled and the men respect him. Therefore, I gave him my vote as well.

I fear, my love, you will not be overjoyed at my next bit of news. Allow me to explain before you cast your affections aside. You see, we are quite short of provisions, with only a bit of rice which would not be enough to fill our bellies should we attempt to sail to St. Thomas. 'Twas my desire to send a scouting party ashore in search of food, but to my utmost dismay, the council voted to head north to pirate the busy seas off the Virginia coast. 'Twas Tucker, you see, who led the charge and convinced them.

What was I to do, my love? These men would as easily tossed me into the sea should I have forbidden them their desire. 'Tis the way of these depraved ruffians. Egad! I have a pardon in my pocket, which I do not wish annulled. Therefore, I finally convinced them to rename the *Revenge*, the *Royal James*, and to call me Captain Thomas henceforth. In this way, any acts of piracy will not be to my charge. I also convinced them to compensate the ships we seize for any goods stolen.

I must end this letter, my precious, for we are readying the sloop to set sail. You have my promise that as soon as we have restocked our provisions, I will come for you.

Until then, you are always in my heart. Now and forever,

Affectionately yours,
Stede.

"Blast them all to hell!" Bonnet poured himself a drink and moved to look out the stern windows of his captain's cabin. Through the salt-encrusted haze, foam-capped waves of an azure sea spread toward a gray horizon. Rays from a sun high in the sky lit the waters in patches of diamonds— diamonds Bonnet wished were real and lining his pockets.

His friend Captain Herriot stretched out his legs before him as he sat in one of the leather cushioned chairs. "Truly, Stede, what sort of characters did you imagine pirates to be when you set out upon this silly adventure?" He laughed. "Kind, benevolent, generous, honest? They are but ignorant thieves. 'But these, as natural brute beasts, made to be taken and destroyed, speak evil of the things that they understand not; and shall utterly perish in their own corruption.'" He quoted from the Bible, as he so often did.

Bonnet spun to face his friend. "Then why did *you* join us?"

Herriot shrugged. "I had no choice. You see, I prefer to live."

"Humph." Bonnet sipped his rum. "I beg you, sir, please cease quoting Scripture. I fear God abandoned me long ago."

"Perhaps 'tis you who abandoned Him?" Herriot smiled, stood, and poured himself another drink.

Bonnet longed to chastise his friend, but he felt no anger at his affront. No doubt he was right. But what did it matter now?

The sloop rolled over a wave, creaking and groaning as the flap of sails above reminded Bonnet he should be on deck, directing the crew, and not here in his cabin drinking. In truth, he was still overly distraught from what he'd witnessed two days earlier. Not to mention that his crew seemed to have no further need of him.

"Cheer up, my friend." Herriot lifted his glass. "Thus far, you and your crew have amassed quite a fortune. Odd's life, no sooner did you set sail, than we took two prizes straight away."

"Indeed. Quite fortunate." Bonnet and his crew had taken the two merchant ships with ease, commandeering their provisions of pork, bread, and molasses. Much to his surprise, the pirates honored his command to pay for the goods by offering rice in exchange. However, their benevolence did not extend to the next thirteen vessels they captured, which they pillaged with impunity.

"I would say this man Tucker is a natural born pirate," Herriot offered.

Bonnet repressed a growl and sat on the window ledge. "Indeed, and with all the cruelty of Blackbeard himself." He shook his head. "The way he stormed on board the *Fortune* and fell to beating and cutting its crew with his cutlass. Even severed one poor man's arm." A shiver ran through Bonnet as the scene replayed in his mind.

Herriot sipped his drink. "Barbaric. And 'twould seem that quality is the only one these blackguards respect."

"If you are saying the man appears to have taken over the ship, I quite agree."

"The crew do call him 'Father'." Herriot laughed. "Though he wouldn't be any father I'd wish to have."

"An odd title, indeed, for such an evil man." Bonnet slammed the remainder of his rum to the back of his throat and tossed the glass into the corner. It shattered, startling Herriot from his thoughts.

Setting down his drink, he leaned back in his chair and leveled a serious gaze at Bonnet. "You need to resume command, Stede. Take control of your ship. Then the men will respect and follow you. Fear and brutality is the only language they know."

He was right, of course. But hadn't Bonnet tried that once before? It had ended with many of his crew dead, his sloop severely damaged, and him injured. Perhaps he'd be more skilled at it now. Yet...he couldn't help but wonder if he would ever possess enough sadistic brutality to be a pirate captain.

The deck canted as the ship veered to larboard, and the mighty sea dashed against the hull in its endless soothing dissonance. Bonnet gripped the edge of the window ledge. What choice did he have? He needed more wealth, and in order to get it, he must captain this ship.

A knock preceded Mullet, his former quartermaster and now bosun's mate, bursting into the cabin without permission. Halting, he sneered at Bonnet. "Tucker says t' come on deck, Cap'n. We spotted a ship at anchor."

Bonnet stood and blinked to clear the rum from his mind. "You'll wait until I say enter before opening the door, Mullet, or there'll be hell to pay." He said the words in his most threatening tone, but Mullet simply shrugged and left, muttering to himself.

"A plague on that man!" Bonnet growled, ignoring the smug look on his friend's face. Nor did he like being summoned like one of the crew. Still, he grabbed his cutlass, slid it in its sheath and marched out the door.

He emerged from the companionway to a blast of hot wind, spiced with brine and sweat, the crew lowering sails, and Tucker with spyglass to his eye at the larboard railing. Hand on the hilt of his cutlass, Bonnet approached him. "What goes on here? Why are we stopping?"

For a moment, the man refused to answer. Finally, he lowered the scope. "'Tis a ship, *Cap'n*"—he slurred the title— "Looks t' be a sixty-ton merchantman anchored in that inlet up ahead. Ye said ye wanted t' know when a ship were spotted."

Though slightly shorter than Bonnet, Tucker was an imposing man, nonetheless, with long brown hair that blew in the breeze and an untrimmed beard dangling from his chin. He wore the usual pirate attire, open shirt, short breeches, a brace of pistols and a cutlass at his side. But 'twas his eyes which disarmed men. Narrow slits of darkness that seemed capable of sucking the soul out of anyone they gazed upon. Thankfully, he didn't look at Bonnet.

Bonnet grabbed the scope from Tucker and focused on the ship. Indeed, she appeared to be a worthy prize. Not well-gunned, with only what appeared to be eight cannons on board, she sat low in the water, which meant her hold was stuffed with goods. "Let's take her," he commanded, but before he even replaced the spyglass in his belt, Tucker was ordering a boat to be lowered.

"Aye, aye, Father." William, one of Bonnet's crew, saluted Tucker as he sped off.

Bonnet gripped the railing and squeezed. He'd deal with him later.

"We'll row right up t' 'er an' pretend t' be that bone-headed cap'n, Thomas Read, from the sloop *Fortune* we jist captured." Tucker announced the plan before Bonnet could even offer an opinion. "If that be okay wit' ye, *Cap'n*." Finally, he glanced at Bonnet and smiled.

Bonnet wanted to say no, that he had a better plan, but in truth, he did not. "Very well, but I order you to be about the business of pilfering her goods and leave her crew alive and unharmed. This senseless killing has got to stop, Tucker. I won't stand for it."

The man only snorted in return before he joined his fellow pirates in the small boat and shoved off from the *Royal James*.

Raising the spyglass to his eye, Bonnet watched as the small craft approached the merchantman, and after some discussion, a rope ladder was tossed overboard to welcome the newcomers.

No sooner, however, did all the pirates climb aboard than they drew their cutlasses and the merchantman's crew raised their hands in surrender. Would Tucker obey Bonnet's charge? 'Twas hard to tell from so far away. Hence, Bonnet paced the deck, thinking to lift up a prayer for the poor crew's safety but then laughed at the idea. A pirate praying for God's mercy! He must surely be losing his mind.

Finally, the boat returned, rowed by two pirates and carrying a tall, weather-worn man with light hair upon which perched a captain's hat.

"I welcome you aboard the *Royal James*, sir." Bonnet approached him after he climbed on deck. "And you are?"

"Peter Manwareing, captain of the *Francis*." He handed Bonnet a stack of documents.

Grabbing them, Bonnet perused the contents—the ship's merchant papers and cargo manifest.

"Ah, I see you travel from Antigua to Boston." Bonnet glanced over the list of goods on board. "Rum, molasses, sugar, cotton, and gold coins. Excellent."

"Vile miscreant," the man spat.

A pistol shot echoed across the water from the *Francis*, along with shouts, a fiddle, and the sound of revelry. Bonnet faced the man. "I would watch your tongue, sir, for 'tis only I who stands between you and a rather barbaric death."

"And with whom do I have the misfortune of speaking?" Captain Manwareing asked.

Bonnet dipped his head. "Captain Thomas of the pirate ship *Royal James*, at your service."

After Bonnet secured Captain Manwareing below deck, he sent the pirates back with instructions for Tucker to return at once with a report on the contents of the hold and the state of the prisoners.

An hour passed, then another... and another, all the while sounds of revelry—ribald songs, pistol shots, screams, and laughter—echoed over the dark water.

Enough of this! Marching across the deck, he found Daniel, his bosun, sleeping under the quarterdeck. "Get up, man! Gather the crew and hoist topsails! Robinson, Levit!" he shouted, storming down the ladder to the berth. "Get up, men. Man the tiller!"

Once the sleepy crew lumbered onto the deck, grumbling and rubbing their eyes, Bonnet ordered them to bring the *Royal James* alongside the *Francis* at once. Within minutes, they approached the ill-fated vessel. Grappling hooks were tossed, and the ships hauled together with a mighty crunch.

Armed and angry, Bonnet leapt on board the captured vessel with twenty of his men, found the top deck empty, and stormed down the hatch below. There he found Tucker passed out in the corner of the captain's cabin and the rest of the men he had sent over in similar condition. The few who were still conscious were engaged in a game of dice over what appeared to be a bucket of gold coins. A young man sat huddled in the corner.

Furious, Bonnet ordered his men to bring Tucker and the rest back to the *Royal James*, then turned to the young man. "And who might you be?"

The man slowly rose. "Name's James Killing, first mate of the *Francis*." Though he was clearly frightened, his tone and demeanor showed courage.

"Where are the rest of your crew?"

Killing was more than happy to lead Bonnet to the hold where the pirates had tied and imprisoned his friends. Several of them had bloody wounds and one was near death. Bonnet ordered them released and their wounds tended. Then ascending to the top deck, James Killing following behind, Bonnet ordered all the goods brought from the hold onto the *Royal James.*

To his surprise, with Tucker indisposed, Bonnet's crew obeyed his commands. And just as the sun peered over the horizon and spread golden rays over the sea, the last of the cargo was brought on board.

After positioning ten pirates to guard the *Francis,* Bonnet ordered Killing to follow him to his cabin. He wanted an account of what Tucker and his men had done, and Killing would be the one to ask.

James Killing, a sturdy man with brown hair and piercing blue eyes, stood nervously before Bonnet's desk, shifting his gaze over the cabin.

"Well, sir," he began. "The first thing they begun with was the pineapples, which they cut down with their cutlasses. They asked me if I would not come along and eat with them. I told them I had but little stomach to eat. They asked me why I looked so melancholy. I told them I looked as well as I could. Then they raided our rum and sugar and made bowls of punch and started their drinking and singing songs, and pointing their blades at our crew, terrifying them. We feared for our lives, Captain. We did."

"Sit down." Bonnet gestured to a chair. "You have naught to fear from me."

James slid into a chair, but sat at the edge.

Bonnet smiled. He considered himself a good judge of character, and he liked this man. Smart, brave, and honest. Hard qualities to come by for a pirate. "Why not join us, Killing? I can see you are a brave man with skills at sea. Pirates can earn more than twenty years' of a merchantman's wages in a single raid."

Killing swallowed nervously. "I am not fit, Captain, for your trade. I have no inclination for it."

"Humph." Bonnet leaned back in his chair as his anger rose. Whether 'twas from lack of sleep or the insubordination of Tucker and his crew, he didn't know, but he found he had lost his patience. "Here's your choice, Mr. Killing. Either you join me and my crew, or I will leave you on a deserted island to face a slow, agonizing death."

To his credit, Killing didn't blink. Instead, he released a heavy sigh. "Then I suppose I shall join you."

"Excellent." Bonnet dismissed the man with orders to return to the *Francis*, take command, and follow Bonnet's ship when they set sail.

After he left, Bonnet poured himself a drink. He'd seen the cargo as it was hoisted aboard. 'Twas a good haul, indeed. His share, added to what he'd already stashed away, would make a grand start to his life with Melody. Rubbing his eyes, he gazed out the window as footsteps and shouts thundered above. But first he needed to restore order on board his ship. He must make the men respect him again. And the only way to do that was to inflict punishment and fear.

August 8th, 1718, Cape Fear River, Carolina Province

Dearest Melody,

I am happy to inform you that we have had much success in the trade of late and hence, find our hold full of valuable goods. In addition, I have procured a bundle of gold and silver coins that will greatly aid us in our life together! Soon, my love. Soon, I shall come for you and we will never be parted again.

These gains, I fear, have not been without their challenges. This band of ignorant cutthroats I call a crew have neither respect for their superiors nor compassion for their inferiors. On the one account, they either ignore or blatantly disobey my every command, while on the other they enact such cruelties on those we capture that I dare not describe them to you, for your sensitive female nature could not handle the report.

Hence, dearest, to my utter distaste, I have forced myself to inflict punishments upon this crew, for 'twould seem to be the only way to maintain control. These whippings have found success thus far, for the crew appear to be following my orders once again.

Hence, the *Royal James* and our two prizes set sail from Cape Henlopen and have arrived here at Cape Fear River, where I plan on careening my sloop. Never fear, precious, we are safe enough in this protected inlet and well stocked with provisions. So much so, I may remain a few months to wait out the storm season in the Caribbean. I still intend to sail to St. Thomas to receive my privateering papers with which I can legally acquire all the wealth we need. You deserve to live like a queen, my love, and I intend to surround you with every luxury the world offers. Do not despair. I believe but a few more prizes as a legal privateer should provide me with the wealth I require... then...

A knock on the door startled Bonnet from his pleasant thoughts.

"Enter!" He set down his quill pen and rose as Hewet, his helmsman, entered. At least the man had not burst in without permission. Perhaps Bonnet's punishments were indeed working.

The man drew off his hat. "Tucker wishes t' inform ye that the goods 'ave been moved to the *Fortune* an' the men be ready to tip o'er the *Royal James* for careenin'."

"Very well. Order half the crew onto the *Fortune* and half onto the *Francis* and tell Tucker to commence."

The man sped off and Bonnet lowered to his chair and glanced at his letter. He was tired of writing to Melody, tired of not seeing her, of not being with her. Tired of living amongst such uncultivated, uneducated, brutal ruffians. Tired of sleeping with one eye open and always looking behind him lest one of his men stab him in the back and toss him to the sharks.

Footsteps pounded above as shouts echoed through the wooden planks. His gaze landed on the window seat beneath the stern windows, and a glorious idea sprouted in his mind. Picking up his pen, he dipped it in ink,

I must close this letter, dearest, but I believe I have reached an epiphany, a plan, if you will, to end this hideous charade and begin our lives sooner than expected. For I have all the fortune we need right here in my very hands. Hence, all I require is the privateering commission so I can no longer be arrested, and we will be free to live our lives as we wish!

I will be in touch soon, my precious.

Eternally yours.
Stede

After sprinkling powder over the ink and blowing it off, Bonnet closed and sealed the letter. Then stuffing it inside his waistcoat pocket, he grabbed his knife and turned to the stern windows. Kneeling, he jabbed his blade into a barely noticeable seam in the wood and pushed. The plank popped open on one side. He smiled and opened it, peering into the dark hole. A cloud of dank, moldy air enveloped him. Unbeknownst to anyone but Bonnet, he had instructed the ship builders to install a secret compartment in his cabin—a place no one would find or suspect. He couldn't say why he'd done it, save for the fact that, even before he embarked on this adventure, he'd known pirates could not be trusted. Reaching in, he retrieved the large sack, having some difficulty squeezing it through the opening. Then, replacing the plank, he slid the knife into his belt and opened the bag.

Still there—the jewel-encrusted Spanish dagger, bar of gold, and string of rare conch pearls, doubloons, a chalice, silverware, jeweled necklaces, and rubies that Bonnet had painstakingly stolen one by one from Blackbeard's treasure. A fortune, to be sure, but not quite enough to secure his life with Melody. Yet, did he not have sacks of gold and silver coins in the holds of his ships from his last few raids? True, the pirate code demanded he share all plunder with the crew, but what did he owe a mob of bedeviled rogues anyway? Would they not as quickly steal everything Bonnet had if given the chance?

He smiled. The difficult part would be sneaking the treasure off the ships and finding a place to bury it ashore. He would have no trouble doing so alone as long as none of these miscreants saw him. But he had two things on his side, three, if he counted their dull wits—the cover of night and their overindulgence in rum.

After returning and securing the treasure back behind the bulkhead, he left his cabin, hope making an appearance in his soul for the first time in a long while.

CHAPTER TWENTY-THREE

*L*exie halted before the display of Bonnet and leaned her broom against the brick wall. Despite the early morning hour, sweat moistened her neck and arms. She'd been working extra hard this past week, barely finishing all the cleaning before quitting time. Mrs. Anderson said it was due to the summer tourist season and that things would quiet down when school started. The weather would cool too. Both things would make life better for Lexie.

"Or maybe I'll find your treasure, Bonnet." She smiled. "And I won't have to clean up other people's messes anymore."

The poor man always looked so dejected, sitting there on the stool with his head in one hand. But how could she blame him? He'd had such high hopes for a wonderful life with Melody only to find himself here in this very spot.

On such nights as these when she was alone and could hear the surf just outside the dungeon walls, she felt as though she, too, was imprisoned here along with him, suffering his fate, enduring his dashed hopes and fears. The last letter she and Barret had read had left Bonnet filled with renewed joy at a plan to get the treasure he needed. *Right in his very hands* he had said.

"What did you mean?" she asked him.

But only the *drip-drip* of a faulty toilet upstairs and the howl of wind outside answered.

Barret said that maybe Bonnet intended to steal from his fellow pirates. He'd been thrilled at the idea, but mainly for Lexie, because it meant there was actual treasure that Bonnet could have buried somewhere. But would Bonnet do such a thing? Take a risk with such cutthroats? Surely they would discover his betrayal.

After glancing over both shoulders to make sure she was alone, she stepped over the chain and entered the display—

something Mrs. Anderson forbade her to do. But she needed to be near him, wanted to kneel beside him and look at his face. Careful not to disturb anything, she did just that. So lifelike! So real, down to the slight wrinkles on his forehead and the brown hair hanging in his face.

"Did you even look like this?" she asked, wanting so badly for him to look at her and answer.

She rubbed her eyes. She was being foolish.

Someone knocked on the back door. Startled, Lexie quickly exited the display, her heart pounding. It had been a week since Barret had been stabbed, and every morning like clockwork, Adam had come to walk her home. Per Barret's request, of course.

Actually, she was happy for the escort. Especially after what happened to Barret. Thank God the professor was healing nicely. Trouble was, they hadn't been able to spend much time together, nor read another letter. Whoa, but the man could sleep! When she was awake, he was asleep and vice versa. At least she'd been able to feed him, dress his wounds, and give him his medicine each day.

Grabbing her broom and dustpan, she put them away and stopped at the door. "Who is it?"

She expected to hear Adam's voice, but instead, Barret's deep baritone sifted through the wood.

She flung open the door, unable to keep the smile from her face. He must have noticed it because his eyes lit up, and he returned her smile.

"Surprised to see me, Sunshine?" he asked.

Sunshine? "Are you okay?" She ushered him inside and shut the door. He certainly looked okay, especially from behind in his tight jeans and t-shirt. By the ease with which he walked, no one would know he'd been stabbed a week earlier.

"Should you be up?" She gestured toward a barrel for him to sit.

"Yeah, I'm good. I feel much better." He squeezed her arm. "I'm okay, Lexie." He smiled again, *that* smile of his, and she shifted her gaze away.

He was definitely feeling himself again.

"All because of you and your excellent nursing."

"Give me a break." She chuckled. "I just tossed some food and medicine at you once a day, that's all."

"You did more than that, and you know it." He took her hand and raised it to his lips for a kiss.

The gesture still surprised *and* delighted her. "I think you were born in the wrong era, Professor Pirate."

Still holding her hand, he winked. "You may be right about that." He continued to stare at her with those deep mahogany eyes as if he were imagining them in a different life, a different time. His ebony hair curled slightly at the tips around his neck, and though he had shaved recently, the shadow of stubble lined his jaw. His cologne of musk, jasmine, and rum saturated the air between them, sending her senses in a whirl.

Good grief, she wanted him to kiss her! To hold her. To make her feel safe again in his strong arms. He must have wanted the same, for his gaze dropped to her lips, and he began to lower his own to meet them.

But then she saw the imprint of the cross he always wore beneath his shirt, and she plucked her hand from his and backed away. They were from two different worlds. She must remember that.

Pain crossed his eyes. "I wasn't going to bite, Lexie."

"I would have preferred that to a kiss." She tried to make light of the situation.

"Am I that bad a kisser?"

Hardly. Their last kiss had been so incredible, Lexie had lost all sense and reason. "You'll do, I guess." She teased, but his frown remained. "Okay, listen. I just think we should remain friends. Okay?"

Uttering a sigh, he rubbed the back of his neck. "I don't think that's what you really want."

Anger stormed through her. "How do *you* know what I want? Could you be more full of yourself? Do you expect every woman to throw herself at you? I'm sure all your cute little coeds do, but I'm not that naive and dumb. It takes more than a studly guy to turn my head."

Instead of getting mad, he grinned. "Studly?"

"Oh, you're impossible!" She placed hands on her hips, trying her best not to laugh. How did this man make her so mad one minute and so happy the next?

"Okay, okay." He raised both hands. "I surrender. Friends it is."

"Good." Then why didn't she feel good about his easy acquiescence? "How about we read another letter? I'm keeping them here at the museum in my locker now."

"Ah, good idea. Probably the safest place for them. But I can't stay. I need to go to work today." He opened the door and held it for her.

Disappointed, Lexie gathered her purse, keys, and shut off the lights. "But you're still wounded."

"I'm better, and I only sit at a desk. I need to make an appearance. The fall semester will start before I know it."

A blast of salty air struck Lexie as she turned and locked the door. "But I'll see you when you come home, right?" What was she saying? She sounded like some needy female who couldn't live without a man around.

He started walking, an odd sense of sorrow surrounding him. "I moved back into my place. It didn't seem right to take advantage of your kindness when I'm able to get around."

Lexie's heart sank. "Of course. I understand."

"But don't worry. I've enlisted Adam to walk you to work each evening, and I hired a bodyguard to sit in front of the townhome when you're there. *And* I still plan on walking you home each morning."

Oddly, she hadn't even thought about her safety. "You don't have to do that."

"Yes, I do. Those scumbags are still out there."

They both walked in silence the rest of the two blocks to Barret's townhome. Lexie always enjoyed this time early in the morning when the city was quiet and the air fresh. Only a few delivery trucks rumbled about, along with shop owners opening up their shops and fishermen heading out for an early morning catch.

Finally, they mounted the steps to the front door, and she turned to face him, unsure what to say. He stopped on the step beneath hers. Even so, he was still taller than she was. She glanced down to where she knew he'd been stabbed.

"You should have your doctor look at your wound."

He smiled, that smile that said he knew what she was thinking. "Yes, Mom."

"I'm serious, Barret."

Wind blew a strand of her hair into her eyes, and he reached up and brushed it aside, then ran his fingers over her cheek.

A thrill tingled through her. "I wish you wouldn't do that."

His eyes shifted between hers, but he said nothing.

Reaching in her pack, she fumbled for her keys. "So, you *will* go to the doc, right?" She could think of nothing else to say.

"I will. Promise. As long as you keep your promise."

Confused, she stared at him.

"That you'll come to my family's barbecue on Saturday."

Shoot. Had she agreed to that? She frowned. He was standing so close again, she couldn't think.

"You promised." He tapped her on the nose and stood back. "They are expecting you." And with that, he turned and descended the stairs, whistling a tune.

Barret could tell the minute he picked up Lexie that she was nervous about meeting his family. For the life of him, he couldn't figure out why. They were just ordinary people. Very wealthy, important people, but still just regular folk. She kept saying that she and Barret were worlds apart, but in truth the only difference he could see was money and religion. The money made no difference to him. Her faith he would have to work on.

Excitement soared through him that she would meet his family. They were good, kind, Christian people, and he was sure they would love her as much as Barret did. To him, it was the first step in what he hoped was a long and eventually serious relationship.

He smiled and glanced her way as he veered his BMW onto the freeway. Despite her misgivings, he could tell she liked and admired him. Of course, he hoped her feelings ran deeper, and based on her reactions when he'd been stabbed, he was sure they did. He could also tell she was attracted to him, which didn't hurt.

Yet there she sat in the passenger seat, squirming about and biting her nails. At least she'd not worn her Metallica t-shirt, but rather a very nice, modest green blouse, which matched her eyes perfectly. In addition, she'd worn her jeans without the holes in them. She looked beautiful and perfect. Well, except for the tattoos and earrings, but surely that wouldn't upset his parents.

Maybe if he brought up her favorite topic, it would help relax her. "Have you thought any more about Bonnet's strange plan to get more treasure?"

She glanced his way. "A little. I'm anxious to keep reading."

"Me too. Maybe later, since you have the night off." Barret hoped that after the barbecue, if all went well, he could spend some time with Lexie at the townhome.

"Sure. We'll see." She gazed back out the window at the passing scenery. "I'm sure that if he did get more treasure and hide it, he would have given Melody clues to the location."

Barret agreed. "Guess we'll find out." More importantly, Barret was getting some great information for his book—a book that would no doubt skyrocket his career. He couldn't wait to tell his father about it.

An hour later, he pulled into the circular driveway and shut off the engine. "Here we are."

Lexie said nothing. Instead she stared out the window at the front of his parents' house. "This is your family's house?"

"Yup. Grew up here."

Unease lined her forehead. "I don't know, Barret...I...I...."

"You're going to love them, and they will love you. Come on." Hopping out, he circled the car and helped her from the passenger seat.

"Hello!" he shouted as they entered the front foyer.

Kim descended the spiral staircase, a sarcastic smile on her face and her eyes all over Lexie.

"Brother dear," she said. "Long time no see." She halted before Lexie. "So this is the ex-con you've been hanging out with."

CHAPTER TWENTY-FOUR

E x-con? Is that what the young, attractive woman had called Lexie? She swallowed as the woman, who looked a lot like Barret, stared at her with a sarcastic smile on her face and pity in her eyes. Lexie should say something, deny it, ask how she knew? But she couldn't find her voice.

"What are you talking about, Kim?" Barret laughed. "Where's Mom and Dad?"

"Out back with the others." She flung a handful of beautifully cultured French nails in that direction.

"Lexie, this is my sister, Kim. Kim, Lexie."

"A pleasure." Kim gave that fake smile again, as if she knew something Lexie didn't, before she turned and headed down a hallway. "Come on. Dad is anxious to see you. Seems you've been rather busy lately, brother."

Impeccably dressed in textured satin slacks, a silk *V*-neck blouse, and jewel-studded red pumps, Kim walked with a grace only money could instill. Her dark hair was cut short in a cute style, and Lexie guessed her to be close to her own age.

She wanted to bolt. Her feet wouldn't move. Had the ex-con comment been a joke? Did Barret's family know about Lexie's past? How could she ever face them now?

Barret extended his elbow for her to grab. "Don't mind her. She's always been a little hoity-toity."

"I heard that!" Kim shouted over her shoulder.

Barret leaned to whisper in Lexie's ear. "You'll like her when you get to know her."

Somehow Lexie doubted that. Everything within her said to run, run as fast as she could and get as far away as she could from this place. But now that she was here, she'd embarrass Barret in front of his family, and she didn't want to do that. Besides, she'd been running her entire life, running away from her family, from the curse upon them, from boys who used her,

her stepfather who abused her, and from people like Kim who always thought they were better than her.

Time to stop running.

Holding her head high, she placed her hand on Barret's elbow and allowed him to lead her through a long hall decorated with oil paintings on the walls and marble busts and painted pottery on tables. The luxury passed by in a blur as Kim's pumps *tap-tapped* on the wooden floor, sounding out the drum roll of Lexie's execution. She led them through a set of glass French doors onto a wide porch, then down a set of stairs into the largest and most beautiful backyard Lexie had ever seen. Roughly a dozen people milled about on a perfectly manicured lawn over which tables and plush chairs were set. Lush, flowering bushes lined the porch and a low brick wall separating the main house from another building. A waterfall poured from a steaming hot tub into a large pool whose waters were the same color as the Caribbean. Orange lights were strung over the entire scene, making it seem magical. Beyond the pools, the lawn extended several yards toward a long wooden dock that sat upon a glistening lake.

Lexie didn't have time to take it all in before an elderly man sauntered up to them, a drink in his hand.

"Dad." Barret released her hand and gripped his father's in a firm shake.

"Son." The elder man quickly examined Barret before shifting his gaze to Lexie. Tall, like his son, with thick, graying hair, a strong jaw, and penetrating eyes, the man had a presence—a commanding presence—that caused Lexie's nerves to tighten.

"So this is Miss Cain." His gaze immediately shifted from her eyes to her hair, her earrings, and then down to her clothes. "A pleasure to meet you."

She couldn't tell if he meant it or not, and she was usually good at such things, but the man wore a shield over his eyes.

"Thank you for inviting me, Mr. Johnson."

He glanced over his shoulder and upon spotting a woman, waved her over. "Amelia and I always love to meet Barret's friends."

The woman, who must be Barret's mother, floated over to them on a cloud of white satin and lace. Her brown hair draped in perfect curls to her shoulders, her makeup was expertly applied, and a string of pink pearls lined her graceful neck. She halted beside her husband, showering Lexie in a mist of what must be very expensive perfume, for it smelled heavenly.

"Lexie, dear. Such a joy to meet you." She extended both hands to grip Lexie's. "Oh, Barret, she's simply adorable."

Adorable? Lexie had never been called that before.

"Gregory, why are you letting our son and his date stand here? Come, dear, let me introduce you around."

Date? Before Lexie could protest, the woman entwined her arm within Lexie's and pulled her away. She cast a look of terror over her shoulder at Barret, who, thank God, got the hint and followed. Not that she minded this woman's kindness, but Lexie felt like an ant intruding upon the king's picnic.

Weaving in and amongst tables laden with all manner of appetizers, fruit, biscuits, and punch, Mrs. Johnson introduced her to several cousins, an uncle in a wheelchair, two nieces, and a nephew in his twenties who blatantly stared at Lexie as if she were a stripper.

"And you've met Kim." Mrs. Johnson halted before the woman, who turned from chatting with a friend to smile once again at Lexie. "She's my eldest daughter and has a masters degree in childhood development and psychology," she said with pride.

"Oh, Mom." Kim lifted one shoulder. "Always bragging about me."

"Well, why shouldn't I?" Mrs. Johnson suddenly took on a southern accent. "I have wonderful children." She glanced at Barret, who had been pulled away by one of his cousins. "My son has a PhD in history, and…" she scanned the crowd. "There. Let's go meet Evelyn." She pulled Lexie's arm. "She is in med school at Clemson, second year."

Of course she was. Lexie's insides spun into a cyclone. Was there no one in this family who wasn't a genius?

Yet, as they walked up to Evelyn, Lexie would not have guessed she was in med school. She sat alone on the edge of the pool, her pant legs rolled up and her feet dangling in the water. She wore regular jeans and a plain black t-shirt, and her light hair hung down her back in no particular style.

Lexie liked her even more when she stood to meet her. An odd piece of costume jewelry hung around her neck, two earrings pierced one ear, and not a lick of makeup tainted her face. Yet it was more than her appearance. There was something in her eyes that was genuine.

"Oh, dear," Mrs. Johnson drew her daughter aside and whispered, though Lexie could hear every word.

"Can you find nothing else to wear? And what did I say about those earrings?"

Lexie couldn't help but smile. Ah, she must be the black sheep of the family.

Evelyn only shrugged. "It's just a barbecue, Mom." Moving back to Lexie, she cocked her head and studied her. "Pleasure to meet you. You don't look like the sort Barret usually dates."

"We aren't dating." Lexie offered, just as Barret strolled up.

"Lexie and I are just friends," he said. "I told you that, Mom."

The woman fingered her pearls. "Very well." She turned to Lexie again. "Would you like to meet our youngest?"

Did Lexie have a choice? Apparently not, as the woman tugged her back across the lawn to a young lady leaning against a tree trunk, phone to her ear. Thankfully, Barret followed.

They halted before her as Mrs. Johnson cleared her throat.

Clearly annoyed, the teenager said, "Hold on," and lowered the phone to her shoulder with a huff. Black hair hung to her waist in curls while designer jeans that surely costs hundreds clung to her teenage figure. A cute floral blouse completed a pleasant look if not for the scowl on her face.

"This is Marsha. She's first in her junior class at Porter-Gaud. She's our little horse lover."

"You ride horses?" Lexie asked just to make conversation.

"She does," Mrs. Johnson answered for her. "Dressage. She's won an entire mantel-full of trophies, haven't you, my dear?"

Marsha only smiled. "I guess so."

"It's horribly cruel to horses." Barret sipped his soda.

"It is not!" Marsha protested. "Mom, make him stop saying that."

"You know that's not true and it upsets your sister."

"Mom, can I go out with Victor and a few friends?" Suddenly Marsha's frown transformed into a look of innocent pleading.

"Darling." Mrs. Johnson cast Lexie a smile before taking Marsha by the arm a few feet away. "We have guests. Can't you stay home one night?"

Marsha growled. "Whatever." And walked away.

Lexie withheld a smile. A rebellious teenager, the most normal thing she'd seen yet.

Spinning to face them, Mrs. Johnson smiled again, though this time, it seemed tight enough to break her face.

"Well, I'll leave you two to mingle. I must check on the cooks in the kitchen." She fluttered away, patting her perfect hair.

Barret stared after her before turning to Lexie. "Want something to drink?"

"Sure."

Together, they went and grabbed two glasses of punch and then sat on one of the lounge chairs by the pool.

"So you've met the family." Barret's expression was priceless, one that was an odd mixture of embarrassment and pride.

Lexie sipped her drink. "They seem very nice." Pretentious, cold, and very rich, but mostly nice. She glanced at Barret's father speaking with a group of men his age. "How often do you see them?"

"Not often." Barret followed her gaze. "Maybe every couple of months. We are all pretty busy."

Though it had only been Lexie and her mom in their family, they had always been affectionate. Hugs and kisses abounded, especially if they hadn't seen each other for a few days. Barret's father had given him a handshake as if Barret were a colleague, and his mother had not touched him at all. In fact, neither of them had asked their son a single question. *How was he doing? How was his book coming along? What had he been up to?* Did they even know he'd been stabbed? It all seemed so odd to Lexie. Even his sisters had barely given him the time of day.

"My dad is a judge, a magistrate," Barret said with pride as his gaze remained on the man.

Lexie swallowed. "No kidding." She had never liked judges. At least the ones she'd been put in front of. That explained why she'd felt uncomfortable in his presence.

"And your mom?"

Barret smiled. "My mom? She runs everything." He chuckled. "She volunteers at church, runs local charities, and she's on so many committees, I've lost track. She also manages our tea plantation."

Lexie's brows shot up. "Tea plantation?"

His lips quirked. "I didn't mention that?"

Lexie only sighed.

"Yeah, we own a tea plantation not far from here. We grow seven flavors of tea in our gardens and brew the finest Sweet Southern you'll ever taste. We also give tours."

Of course they did. Lexie squirmed on her seat.

"I'll take you there sometime."

Lexie sipped her punch, a sweet fruity drink that had no alcohol in it. Something she desperately needed at the moment. She didn't want to see the tea plantation. She didn't want to even be here.

"Everyone in your family is so smart and accomplished."

"Yeah." He raked a hand through his hair. "We've been blessed. When you live right, go to church, and follow God's commandments, good things happen."

Against every urge within her, she stopped from tossing her drink in his face. "So, you're saying because I haven't done that, that's why my life has been hard?"

He grew serious, his eyes searching hers. "I meant no offense, Lexie. I don't know what your life has been like. I'm just saying I believe God has blessed our family."

The look in his eyes was so loving and sincere, it cooled her anger instantly. Blessed, eh? She glanced at all the luxury and wealth, the good food, the jewelry and fine clothes, and yet... something seemed missing. Something that was the most important thing of all.

Dinner was served buffet style, and Mrs. Johnson fluttered about, making sure everyone was happy and had what they needed. Barret and Lexie sat at one of the tables with his father, sisters, and a few cousins, all chatting between bites about various topics—investments, politics, the Johnsons' new thoroughbred, travels abroad, and the recent economic collapse—none of which Lexie knew much about, so she remained quiet. Neither did anyone address her, or Barret, for that matter.

Excusing themselves, Barret suggested they take a walk down the dock to look at the lake.

Alone at last. Lexie was beginning to feel her nerves unwind slightly when Evelyn approached from behind.

"Father wishes to see you in the study, Barret. Alone."

"What for?"

A sassy look overcame her. "Guess you're in trouble."

Growling, Barret turned to Lexie. "I'll be right back. Okay?"

She didn't want him to leave. She didn't want to be alone with his family, but she supposed if she had her pick, it would be Evelyn.

Barret stormed down the dock, shaking the wood beneath her as he went.

Evelyn faced her, a grin on her face. "So, how's it going in the lions' den?"

Lexie chuckled. "As well as can be expected I guess."

"Well, if I were you, I'd leave, because it's going to get a lot worse."

⚓

Barret marched into his father's study and found both his parents waiting for him. Odd. On the way, he'd forced down his anger at being pulled away from Lexie. They were still his parents and deserved his respect.

"What is it, Father? I have a guest to entertain."

"Indeed. That is why your mother and I have summoned you." His father circled his large oak desk and pointed to one of three plush leather chairs. "Sit."

His mother wrung her hands and remained standing by the wall of bookshelves on the left side of the room.

The sweet smell of his father's pipe, combined with the scent of leather and old books, swirled beneath Barret's nose, springing memories to mind. Not all of them good. How many times had he stood right here and been chastised severely as a child? And though he was now twenty-six and a man of his own, he couldn't help but suddenly feel like a child at his father's mercy.

He slid onto the seat and waited.

"I see you are quite taken with Miss Cain," his father began.

"I like her a lot." Suspicion rising, Barret forced down further anger until he knew what this was about.

"What are your hopes for this relationship?"

Confusion scraped across Barret. Was this the 1800's? Did he need his father's permission? "Why? Is there a problem?"

His father frowned and blew out a sarcastic huff. "The problem is, son, she's an ex-con."

Barret leapt to his feet. "What are you talking about?"

"Sit down." His father ordered, but Barret refused.

"Please, dear," His mother emerged from the shadows, a worried look on her face. "Listen to your father." Her tone was more pleading than commanding.

"When you first mentioned her name, I did some digging." His father sat back on his desk and crossed arms over his chest.

"Why would you do that? You've never checked on any of the other women I've brought home."

"None of the other women you've brought home have tattoos and skull earrings and look like they've never brushed their hair in decades."

Now, Barret *was* angry, and he didn't care if it showed. "Your friends at church told you what she looked like."

"I have my sources."

Lexie had been right. People *had* been giving her condemning looks. "So what? She has a couple of tattoos and wears weird earrings. You don't even know her!"

"You know what the Bible says about tattoos, dear," his mother said.

Barret's father expelled a deep breath. "I don't have to know her. I checked up on her and she's been in prison—juvenile prison, but still prison."

Something inside Barret twinged at the news. "For what?"

"Two times for shoplifting and one for a gang involved shooting."

Shooting? "I refuse to believe that." Lexie was terrified of guns. Shaking his head, Barret moved to the window overlooking the backyard. He spotted Lexie and Evie on the dock, talking. Wouldn't she have told him something that important?

"It's true. I can show you the records. And," his father continued in his superior tone, "her father is in prison for armed robbery, and her mother has a record for prostitution."

Barret already knew about Lexie's father.... but her mother? Prostitution? The words marched through Barret's mind like stormtroopers on an evil rampage.

"Did you know most of her relatives either are or were in prison? Her grandfather, his father, two uncles and a niece. In fact, as far back as I looked, she comes from an entire family of criminals."

A cloud of numbness fell on Barret as he took in each word, each pronouncement of guilt on Lexie and her family. He knew she'd come from poverty, but this!

He spun to face his father, knowing he would find an arrogant smirk on his face. "So, she did her time, and now she's out trying to live a decent life. Isn't that what you, as a judge, hope for when you put someone away?" Why he felt the need to defend Lexie, he couldn't say. Well, actually he could say. He loved her, and he hated hearing her name slandered. Maybe she hadn't divulged all of her past to him, but did that make her a liar? Did that make her a bad person? No, he knew her. She had a good heart.

His father's jaw stiffened, and his mother stepped forward again. "These aren't our kind of people, Barret. You can't get involved with her. Surely you know that."

His father raised one eyebrow. "Any association with her would put an irreparable stain on our family name—a name that has been held in the highest esteem in this county throughout the generations, something we and our ancestors have worked hard to achieve."

Barret was well aware. It had been drilled into him over and over as a child. "Let me get this straight. Even if she has been rehabilitated, wants to live an honest, good life, and has nothing to do with her family, you still hold all this against her. And for what? *Our* reputation? She's a human being."

His father gave him that look Barret had known all his life—a look of disapproval, of pride, and a will that would not be broken. He turned to his wife. "Talk some sense into him, dear."

She looked at Barret with all the pleading of a mother to her child. "Son, there are so many lovely young Christian ladies out there from good families. Why choose someone like this? With those tattoos and the way she dresses, not to mention her family history, we can hardly present her to society."

Barret could *hardly* believe his ears. Were his parents that pretentious, that concerned with appearances? Why had he not seen it before?

He crossed arms over his chest. "I thought Jesus said to love everyone, especially the poor and downcast."

"And we do, son," his mother said. "But he didn't say to marry them!"

"Okay. I've heard enough." Barret's gaze drifted between his parents, and for the first time in his life, he felt he hardly knew them. Or maybe he really didn't know himself. "You've told me your wishes. Now, leave me be." Then turning, he walked out of the room.

His father's voice followed him like a booming decree. "We order you to stop seeing her at once. I will not have our family name destroyed over some sultry itch you wish to have scratched!"

Sultry itch? Of all the...! Barret made his way back to the dock with every intent of grabbing Lexie and taking her as far away from his family as possible.

But only Evie remained, sitting on the edge staring out across the water.

"Where is she? What have you done with her?"

She gazed up at him, her face scrunching. "What have *I* done? She left. I think she called a cab."

"Why would she do that? What did you say?"

"I told her that Dad was going to tell you about her past. Warned her she'd be better off leaving than staying."

So, everyone knew. Everyone but Barret. Grinding his teeth, he raced down the dock, through the house, and onto the front driveway. His car was still there, but no Lexie. Plucking his phone from his pocket, he punched her name.

No answer.

He texted her. "Where are you Lexie? Please answer me."

Nothing.

Terror ripped through him. Had he lost her forever?

CHAPTER TWENTY-FIVE

N o sooner had Evie—as Evelyn had told Lexie she preferred to be called—explained that her parents knew all about Lexie's past, than she thanked the kind woman for the warning and did what she'd been wanting to do ever since she'd arrived. She bolted! The hour ride in the Uber back to the townhome gave her plenty of time to think. No wonder everyone at the barbecue had been so aloof. No wonder no one had asked her any questions about herself. And no wonder they had looked at her with both pity and censure. It hadn't just been her clothing, hair, and tattoos. Well, all except Barret's mother. She had truly seemed kind to Lexie, introducing her around to everyone as if she wanted to make her feel comfortable. Then again, maybe she was merely keeping up the appearance of a gracious hostess. Lexie could never figure out rich people.

Her phone buzzed during her entire ride home. And it kept buzzing even now as she unlocked the townhome and punched in the alarm code. Setting down her things, she locked the door, then finally checked her messages. It was Barret, of course, flooding her with texts asking where she was and how she was doing.

Setting the phone down, she made her way to the kitchen to make some hot cocoa. Even though it was eighty degrees outside, there was something about hot cocoa that always soothed her nerves—nerves that couldn't take reading Barret's texts at the moment.

He knew. He now knew everything about her. About her family, her sordid past, her time in prison...all things she intended to tell him eventually but had never found the time.

Or maybe she was just a coward. Worse, a pretender. Maybe she wished she could truly erase her past and remake herself into someone else, someone respectable, honorable, and good.

Someone Barret would be proud to love.

Good grief, what was she thinking? She didn't want him to love her. She didn't want to love him. Then why did she care so much what he thought of her?

"I'm going crazy." She poured boiling water into the mug of cocoa mix and stirred. The sweet chocolate scent filled her nose, loosening her tight muscles.

Maybe it was for the best. Once he accepted the truth, he would no doubt keep their relationship strictly about reading the letters together. Then she wouldn't have to work so hard at resisting him. Like she said, they were from two different worlds.

That truth couldn't have been more obvious than it had been tonight.

The doorbell rang.

Heart leaping, Lexie rushed down the hall, groped through her pack for her Taser, flipped the on switch, and crept up to the door. "Who is it?" she yelled as she stood on tiptoes to look through the peephole.

Tracy. Lexie blew out a sigh.

Setting the Taser on a side table, she unlocked the door and swung it open.

"Oh, Lexie..." Tracy sobbed. "Thank God you aren't working tonight."

"What's wrong? Come in." Lexie stepped aside to allow her friend and little Ellie inside. Only then did she notice the two suitcases the woman carried.

No sooner had Lexie shut the door than Tracy dropped the suitcases and fell against her, crying. "I had nowhere else to go."

"What happened?" Lexie nudged her back and then escorted her and Ellie into the living room. "Here sit." She leaned over to the little girl. "How are you, Ellie?"

She smiled. "Good, but Mommy's sad."

"Well, don't you worry about that. We will make her happy again, okay?"

The girl nodded.

"Would you like some chocolate milk?"

Ellie bobbed her head up and down, her eyes sparkling.

Darting to the kitchen, Lexie mixed up some chocolate milk and another hot cocoa and returned to find Tracy sitting on the couch, head in her hands, and Ellie playing with the pirate ship Lexie had given her.

She handed the little girl her milk and Tracy her mug of cocoa.

Tracy cupped her hands around it as if it were made of gold. "Thank you." Her eyes were red and puffy and her face flushed.

"What happened?" Lexie sat beside her.

"They raised the rent on my apartment, and I couldn't afford it anymore." She sipped her cocoa. "That's why I was looking for work."

Lexie placed a hand on her arm and squeezed, ignoring her buzzing phone.

"They evicted us, Lex." Tears streamed down Tracy's cheeks. "I thought I had more time, but they tossed our stuff out and changed the locks."

Anger soured the cocoa in Lexie's stomach. "Don't you have a couple of months before they can legally do that?"

"My lease was up, so no. I couldn't pay the rent hike, so he gave me two weeks to move."

"Why didn't you tell me?"

"I wanted to, but you have so much going on." Setting down her cup, she glanced at her daughter, who had lain down on the rug, her eyes drifting closed. "I'm so sorry. I didn't know where to go." She rose, picked up Ellie and placed her on the sofa.

Once again ignoring her buzzing phone, Lexie grabbed a quilt she'd used to cover Barret and placed it over the little girl. "You and Ellie are staying here for as long as you want. I mean it."

Tears flooded Tracy's eyes. "What about Barret?"

"I'm sure it will be fine." Actually, she wasn't sure after what he knew about her. But she'd figure that out later.

"I don't know what I'd do without you, Lexie. You're a godsend." She hugged her and Lexie returned her tight embrace.

"I'm here for you, but I doubt God sent me."

Tracy laughed and sobbed at the same time. "Either way, I'm so grateful."

Lexie's phone buzzed again.

"Someone is trying to get ahold of you."

"Yeah, it's Barret."

"Trouble in paradise?"

Lexie snorted. "It's hardly paradise. But if it was, it's now Paradise Lost."

"I'm so sorry." Tracy frowned.

"It's okay. I'll tell you another time. Let me go up and get a bed ready for you and Ellie, okay? It's getting late."

"Thank you. I'll carry her up."

After getting Ellie settled in for the night, showing Tracy the bathroom and the toiletries she could use, Lexie shut off the lights, made sure the door was locked, then stood looking out the front bay window.

The bodyguard, whom Barret had hired to watch over the place, sat in his car across the way. She smiled, feeling warmth flood her at the thought that Barret had not called him off his post.

Upstairs, she put on her pj's and crawled into bed. Only then did she look at some of his texts.

I'm sorry about my family, Lexie.
Are you okay? Please call me. I need to know
I'm worried about you.

Then a little while later

Don't be mad but I had Adam trace your phone. I'm glad you're safe at the townhome.

A little while later

I'll leave you alone now.
I hope to hear from you soon.

He traced her phone? Was that even legal without a warrant? Yet, instead of being mad, she felt cared for, loved even. And right now, that was the last thing she wanted to feel.

The night passed in a fitful cyclone of short naps, TV show repeats, books, and hot cocoa. She hadn't really wanted to sleep anyway because that would throw off her graveyard clock. Now, as she took a sip of coffee, she found herself back at the bay window, squinting at the glistening rays of morning sunlight spearing through the glass into the living room. She would have to catch a few hours of sleep before she went to work that night, but for now, she wanted to make sure Tracy and Ellie had everything they needed.

What Tracy *really* needed was a good job and reasonably priced childcare or else she might end up on the street like Lexie and her mom. Not if Lexie could help it. She would do everything in her power to stop that from happening. She huffed. Who was she kidding? She could hardly take care of herself. Yet...*if* she found the treasure. She blew out a sigh. So many things would change, so many problems solved. But first, she and Barret must figure out Bonnet's clues.

An hour later as Tracy was making them pancakes and Lexie was playing fairies with Ellie, the doorbell rang.

After checking the peephole and seeing a delivery man holding flowers, Lexie shouted through the door for him to set them down and leave. Flowers or not, she didn't trust anyone. After he left and keeping her Taser before her, she opened the door, knelt to get the bouquet and then shut and locked it again.

"Holy cow, look at those flowers!" Tracy turned from flipping over a pancake. She set down the spatula and whistled. "I think those are Juliet roses, though I've never seen any. And look at these daffodils. So beautiful."

Lexie set the vase onto the counter as a whiff of sweet rose filled her nose. The pink and peach roses were truly exquisite with petals the likes of which she'd never seen before. But the daffodils warmed Lexie down to her toes. These had to be from Barret.

"Lordy, girl, you have a wealthy admirer," Tracy said. "Read the card."

Grabbing the folded note, Lexie opened it.

Good morning, Sunshine. I'm sorry for everything, Barret.

Short and to the point.

"Barret." Lexie said.

"Girl, whatever problems you have with this guy, I'd work through them. Nobody has ever sent me flowers like that." Smoke rose from the pan. "Oh no!" Tracy turned to take the pancakes off before they burned.

If Barret's intention was to soften Lexie's heart toward him after what his family had done, it was working, because at the moment her heart felt as syrupy as the bottle of Aunt Jemima sitting on the counter.

Thankfully, even with Tracy and Ellie in the house, Lexie was able to get a few hours of sleep before work. She was also thankful that in the summer months it was still light out when she walked the few blocks to the museum. Adam never showed, so with Taser in her hand, she tried not to think about the men who were following her—the men who were desperate enough to stab Barret. Why would they bother unless there was some truth to the tales of hidden treasure? Regardless, she had not seen them in awhile or sensed anyone following her. Maybe they had given up.

With earbuds in place, blaring Evanescence, the first six hours of cleaning the museum went by faster than usual. Now she only had to sweep and dust the dungeon and empty the garbage and she was done. Good. She'd spend the rest of the time talking to Bonnet, or maybe she'd read a letter, though she still needed Barret to explain some of it.

With a can of Pepsi in hand, she descended the steps and flipped on the lights. The dungeon came to life as the ever-so-light *pitter-patter* of little feet echoed through the chambers. The sound always made her squirm, though she'd never actually seen a rat. Setting down her can, she began sweeping, making her way over to Bonnet to say hi.

Yes, she'd obviously lost her marbles. Laughing she continued her cleaning as she offered the pirate her usual greeting. "Ahoy there, Bonnet!"

Tap, tap, tap.

Lexie snapped her gaze to the door. It was far too early for Barret, even if he *was* coming. Setting down her broom, she inched toward the door, if only to make sure she'd locked it on her way in.

Pound, pound, pound.

Heart racing, she stopped before it. No peep hole to look through. It was probably best to not say anything either. No sense in alerting whoever it was that someone was inside.

"Lexie?" Barret's deep voice penetrated the wood and wrapped a blanket of warmth around her heart.

Against all logic and reason, she snapped open the bolts and flung open the door.

"Hey, Sunshine." His grin disarmed her.

"Hey," was all she could say as an unexpected swamp of shame nearly drowned her. He knew. He knew everything. Yet... she saw no disgust in his gaze. Quite the opposite.

He rubbed his chin. "Can I come in?"

"Oh, sorry. Yes." She stepped aside. "I didn't think you would come."

"Why wouldn't I?" He turned to face her as she locked the door.

No matter what Barret's father had told him, she might as well just spit it out, put it all on the table, get it over with.

"Because I'm a criminal with a record from a family of criminals."

"That's why you left, isn't it? Evie told you my father knew."

She brushed past him and picked up her broom. "I'm surprised they even allowed me in their home."

He gently grabbed her elbow and spun her around. "I don't care if your entire family is imprisoned at Gitmo for terrorism. Nor do I care that you once committed a crime. Do you know why?"

She tried to tug from him, but he wouldn't let go. No, she didn't want to know why. She didn't want to talk about this at all. A mixed bag of emotions raged within her—fear, shame, sorrow, and worst of all, hope.

"Because I know who you are *now*, Lexie. And you're kind, smart, clever, generous, funny, and...and...well, just plain incredible." Nothing but sincerity beamed from his eyes. And something else that made her pulse race.

She finally managed to retrieve her arm. No one had ever called her such wonderful things. He must be lying. But why would he? What did he want from her? "You don't know me," she snapped.

"I think I do, but if you'd like to share your past, I'm happy to listen."

She began sweeping. "Don't you already know it?"

Barret sighed and sat down on a barrel. "Just facts. Not what really happened."

Lexie had no desire to resurrect painful memories. None of them would cast her in a good light. And for some reason, she longed for this man to believe the things he'd said about her.

"Like, why were you in juvenile prison? What did you do?"

"I stole food from a grocery store. My mother and I had nothing to eat for two days. I was sixteen."

Silence, except for the swish-swish of her broom echoed through the room. When she glanced his way, he stared down at the floor, sorrow tugging on his features.

"I'm sorry, Lexie. That wasn't fair."

She shrugged. "It is what it is. I suppose your father told you about the gang affiliation too?"

He nodded.

"I wasn't in a gang." She leaned on the top of the broom. "My best friend and I thought it would be cool to pretend we were, so we painted on gang tattoos and walked down the street, acting all tough. I was only fourteen." Emotion clogged her throat, and she couldn't go on.

"My father said there was a shooting."

Lexie's vision clouded with tears. "A rival gang drove by and shot at us. My friend was killed. She died in my arms before the ambulance arrived." Turning, she batted her tears away and began sweeping again.

Strong arms grabbed her from behind, spun her around, and drew her close. She pushed against him, but he held her tight. He felt so good, so warm and strong, and she wanted to cry, to pour out all the years of pain into his arms. But she couldn't. She couldn't show her weakness.

"I'm so sorry, Lexie."

"They arrested me for being in the gang, but finally released me when the tattoo washed off."

They stood there for several minutes, Lexie trying to get ahold of her emotions, and Barret encasing her in strength—a strength she had longed for all her life, from a father, a stepfather, and boyfriends who wanted nothing from her but sex.

Finally, he released her, and she stepped back, lowering her gaze. "No big deal." Turning she began sweeping again, but he touched her hand, stopping her.

"I'm sorry my father investigated you. I'm sorry my family was so rude and unkind. And most of all, I'm sorry for taking you there."

Cocking her head, she raised one brow. "I told you I didn't want to go."

"Next time I'll listen. Deal?"

Next time? Why was he being so nice? Why wasn't he at least showing a tiny bit of repulsion at her past? A smidgen of disgust and disapproval? "I told you we were from two different worlds."

Barret rubbed the back of his neck. "I'm not sure I'm that crazy about mine at the moment."

Lexie studied him. The man was handsome as always, especially when he wore his jeans and black t-shirt. His silver cross hung over his shirt today, winking at her as if the God he served wasn't judging her either. Stubble shadowed his strong jaw, and his black hair was askew, not normal for him. He looked at her as if he were examining a precious vase, something to be cherished and protected.

Impossible. She looked down. "Thank you for the flowers. They are lovely."

He took her hand and raised it to his lips for a kiss.

Warmth spiraled up her arm, across her shoulders and down to her toes, as an overwhelming sense of relief and... *love*... swept through her.

She was suddenly jealous of her hand. No! She mustn't kiss him. Regardless of how accepting he was being, how could he ever relate to the life she'd had? Somewhere down the road, it would cause more problems than not. Right? Good grief, why was she so confused?

His gaze dropped to her lips.

She stepped back, turned, grabbed the broom, and began sweeping again. "I guess your parents don't want you hanging around me."

"I don't care what they want. I'm a grown man."

That's for sure. All grown up and *all* man. She shifted her gaze away before he caught the look of admiration in her eyes. "Let me finish up here and then maybe we could read Bonnet's next letter?" Maybe that would keep her from doing what every part of her wanted to do… run into his arms and kiss him deeply.

He looked disappointed…for a brief moment…before he smiled. "I'd like that very much."

CHAPTER TWENTY-SIX

September 26th, 1718, Cape Fear River

Dearest Melody,

I have excellent news. The success of my plans to ensure our future fortune has far exceeded my own expectations. As I suspected, though these ruffians can smell gold from a mile away, they are but ignorant clodpoles when faced with the cunning mind of an educated, well-bred nobleman. Thus, beneath their insidious noses I have hidden our future in a safe place where man nor beast shall ever find it...

"Saint's blood! What is it?" Bonnet set down his pen and glanced up to find Tucker and two pirates marching into his cabin.

"Cap'n." Tucker spat the title as if it hurt his lips. "We've spotted two masts in the river o'er the trees. It be my guess they be merchantmen what's got stuck in the mud at low tide. What say ye if we sent boats under the cover o' night to check it out?"

Bonnet rose, growling. That would have been *his* plan if he'd been given the information and been allowed to form one. Blast this man for his constant attempts to take charge! Pushing past Tucker and his men, Bonnet ascended to the quarterdeck, plucked his scope from his belt, and focused it above the tree line toward the sea. Footsteps pounded behind him.

Indeed, there appeared to be two ships grounded in the mud. "Very well, Mr. Tucker. I agree. Send two boats with twenty men each and as many muskets and pistols as each man can carry." He smiled as a blast of wind swept over him, carrying the scent of the sea and hint of autumn. Two more prizes would bring more wealth, and more wealth would ensure he and Melody would live long and happy lives in comfort. "If they are worthy prizes, board them and signal me to join you."

Tucker grunted and leapt down the quarterdeck ladder, his lackeys following like apes behind him. At least Bonnet's recent punishments had instilled a small measure of fear among the men, though Tucker still looked at him as though he'd sooner sup with cockroaches than obey his orders.

Several hours later, and well after midnight, Bonnet paced the deck, waiting for Tucker's signal—a shout, a pistol shot, anything to indicate the success or failure of his mission. Though the night was cool, sweat beaded on his neck and arms. Snoring rumbled, and he glanced at the two watchmen on duty, one on the foredeck and one on the quarterdeck. Both awake. Good. He didn't feel like inflicting punishments at the moment. Wind whistled through the trees lining the river as the sound of a night heron and the splash of a jumping fish met his ears. Wait, not a fish.

Leaning over the railing, he peered at the rolling dark waters and saw the bows of two boats heading toward him in the glint of the moonlight.

Grabbing a lantern, Bonnet held it over the railing. "Who goes there?"

"It be us." Tucker's raspy voice replied, bearing none of the glee or vainglory one would expect from pirates who'd captured a prize.

No sooner did they clamber over the railing and thud their bare feet upon the deck, than Tucker began to growl and cuss. "Beat to quarters!" he shouted. "Prepare for battle!"

Bonnet grabbed his arm and spun him around. "What's this about, Tucker? You will not give commands without my permission!"

The belligerent man tore his arm from Bonnet's grip and spat on the deck. "They's not merchantmen but two heavily armed sloops bearing the king's colors."

One of the other pirates stepped forward, eyes as wide and white as the moon. "Come here to capture us, no doubt, Cap'n."

Shock buzzed through Bonnet, igniting every dormant fear he'd ever had.

"They'll come fer us," Tucker said. "Brimstone and gall, they'll come for us at high tide."

Bonnet could only stare at him, his mind refusing to accept the news.

"Orders, Cap'n?" Tucker scratched his lice-infested hair and gave Bonnet a sarcastic grin.

Bonnet took a deep breath and glanced over the dark sloop, lit only by a few lanterns hanging on the masts. The men who slept on deck had been jarred awake by Tucker's shouts and now stood rubbing their eyes, waiting for Bonnet's orders. Other pirates who slept below would need to be awakened immediately. There wasn't a moment to lose. They had but hours to ready the sloop for battle against two of His Majesty's warships. *Two.* And with Bonnet trapped like a fish in a net.

All these things passed through his mind as his predicament became all too real. Finally, gathering his strength and the courage he'd obtained over the past year, Bonnet shouted across the deck, "Prepare for battle, men! Clean and ready the guns, bring up shot and powder from the magazine, remove all bulkheads, net and sand the decks, extinguish the galley fire, and gather all the weapons we have!" Bonnet listed everything he had learned, and thankfully the crew sped off to do his bidding.

Then turning, he marched up the quarterdeck, down the companionway and back to his cabin. He slammed the door behind him and leaned against it. "Saint's blood! How did they find me?" They had to be from Charles Town. Word had reached Bonnet of a beloved Charles Town hero, a Colonel William Rhett, who was appointed to hunt down pirates. Exactly why Bonnet had determined to not sail anywhere near Charles Town until he had his pardon and privateering papers in hand.

Now what was he to do? Moving to the sideboard, he poured himself a glass of port as the thumping of feet rumbled like thunder above him, along with the grinding of gun wheels, slam of bulkheads, and shouts etched in terror. He couldn't blame them.

As he slammed the port to the back of his throat, his gaze landed on his unfinished letter to Melody. He must finish it and send it ashore with his most reliable man before dawn. But first, he would speak to Manwareing, the captain of the *Francis* imprisoned in the hold. Fury coursed through Bonnet. He was so close to fulfilling all of his dreams! And he was not going to allow some bilge-sucking, daft, son of a princock stop him now. "Saint's blood!" He tossed his glass against the bulkhead, where it shattered into a hundred pieces that glittered in the lantern light.

Most precious one, it seems I have encountered a bit of bad luck, for we find ourselves trapped in the river by two British war ships. 'Tis my belief they hail from your city of Charles Town and are captained by one William Rhett. I only inform you of this should you hear news of the ensuing battle. A battle which I am confident to win, my dear. Hence, never fear. However should a portion of our prisoners escape during said encounter, I have read the contents of a letter to Captain Manwareing of the Francis to be delivered to Governor Johnson after I am victorious over these insidious forces he has sent to capture me. Your governor should know the sort of man he entangles himself with, a man who will burn and destroy all vessels going in or coming out of South Carolina in retribution.

Forgive me, my love, for I fear you have not seen this side of me, but we are so close to seeing our dreams fulfilled. I will not be put off!

Alas, before you turn your heart from me, I have spared Manwareing's life along with all of our prisoners and have ordered them moved to the Francis *and the* Fortune, *the two prizes which sail with us, for we have neither the skill or manpower to use all three in battle.*

My darling one, do not be alarmed. When dawn breaks, my plan is to maneuver around the warships, well out of their gun range, before the tide frees their keels from the bottom of the river. Once upon the sea, I intend to sail straight away to St. Thomas with my pardon.

My love, all these plans depend on many things, not the least of which is that I must abandon my ship and crew before they inspect the hold and discover my treachery. Do not fear for me, only pray that if God has any mercy at all, he will surely see the good in both our hearts and grant us the future we desire.

You are forever in my deepest affections,
Stede

Barret sat back against the brick wall and watched as Lexie finished reading the letter. Her hand trembled, and she seemed to be having trouble putting the precious document back into the folder. Finally, she managed it and then glanced at the wax figure of Bonnet.

"He didn't make it, did he?"

Barret sighed. "No. He put up a good fight, though. In his attempt to veer around Rhett's ships, he ran aground and got stuck."

She faced him, her eyes moist. Was she that attached to Bonnet?

"That's terrible."

"Well..." Barret leaned forward, elbows on his knees. "Rhett's ship got stuck too." He smiled. "So they both just kept shooting at each other."

"With cannons?"

"Pistols and muskets. Both their decks were too tilted to be able to aim their cannons."

Rising, Lexie walked over to Bonnet's cell. "So he was trapped."

Barret joined her. "Yeah, both of Rhett's ships rose off the river bottom first and headed toward Bonnet. Word was he wanted to fight, but his crew opted for surrender." He studied the wax figure of the man they'd both come to know. "Rhett sailed his two warships, Bonnet's *Royal James*, and the *Francis* and *Fortune,* into Charleston harbor on October 3rd, 1718."

Several seconds passed as she stared at Bonnet's figure. "Poor guy. He was so close."

Barret shrugged. "But now he was near Melody."

"In prison?"

"I bet he found a way to see her." Barret winked. Though history provided no clues.

"You *know* something. Wait." She held up a hand. "Don't tell me. I want to read about it." A long, slow smile spread across her lips. "But did you hear what he said about the treasure?"

"Yeah. Incredible." All these years Barret had believed Bonnet's buried treasure had just been a myth. "Seems like he must have hidden it somewhere around Cape Fear."

"I was thinking the same thing. I just wonder how he managed to sneak it off the ship beneath the pirates' noses."

Barret shook his head. "Or how he made the sacks in the hold look full. Clever man if he pulled it off."

She looked back at Bonnet. "But where did you put it?"

Barret glanced at his watch. "Shoot. I have an appointment at the college." Though at the moment, he wished more than anything to stay with this woman here in the dungeon, looking at Bonnet and reading his letters.

"Sure. I need to get some sleep anyway."

On the short walk home, Lexie was unusually quiet. He was beginning to know her well enough to realize something was on her mind. However, *his* mind was on keeping an eye out for the creeps who had attacked them. He would not be caught off guard again.

He glanced her way, thinking of her past—of her family's past. After he'd recovered from the shock, he had to admit he had struggled with the revelation. In fact, he'd been up all night, unable to sleep, unable to stop thinking that he'd fallen in love with a criminal from a family of criminals. His father had been right about one thing. Any serious association with her would forever tarnish his family's reputation. His father might even be excused as an elder of their church, his mother cast from women's society groups, Barret's own reputation at the university questioned. He had prayed. He had sought God's will. And in the end, he found he hadn't the strength or the will to break things off with her. Besides, he could influence her for the better, help her find God and change her life.

At the townhome door, she turned to face him. Though shadows hugged her eyes, the morning sun glistened over her slightly tanned skin, transforming it into gold. Green eyes the color of the tropical sea gazed at him, shifting between his as if searching for the answer to some question. A burst of wind, carrying the scent of salt, fish, and flowers, twirled through her hair.

"Spit it out, Lexie. I know you want to say something."

She smiled. "Tracy and her daughter Ellie are staying here with me for a while."

"Okay." Barret let the information sink in.

"She got evicted, Barret. She had nowhere to go. I'm helping her find a job. Is it okay? I mean, it's not my home." She spat out the words in quick succession as pleading filled her tone.

"Of course." Barret took her hand in his. "Let me do some digging. I might be able to find her something." Why hadn't he thought of that before? He knew just the thing.

She breathed out a sigh of relief. "I don't know how to thank you."

"On your next night off, let me take you to a nice dinner."

She tugged on her bottom lip and gave him a look of censure. "We can't, Barret. You know that. We have to keep things strictly friend—"

Barret didn't want to hear it. Instead, he wanted more than anything to kiss her. So he did. He took a chance and placed his lips on hers, silencing her protests. Then wrapping his arms around her, he drew her close, deepening the kiss.

Instead of pushing him away and slapping his face, she fell against him and received his kiss with more passion than he expected.

She moaned, inciting him to continue, to explore and caress and taste. Moments passed in which Barret lost all sense and reason, all desire to ever let this woman go. He wanted more of her...and more and more... *No.* He withdrew, his breath coming fast. Her breath was heavy too as she stared at him in wonder.

"I'll take that as a yes for dinner," he said. And before she could respond, he descended the steps and walked away.

CHAPTER TWENTY-SEVEN

L exie couldn't sleep. Maybe it was the gardener next door running his weedwhacker. Maybe it was Ellie's giggles as she ran through the house playing.

Or maybe it was Barret's delicious kiss still tingling on her lips.

Good grief, why had she allowed him to do that? It was best to keep things simple, friendly, platonic. And, as usual, she'd gone and done the opposite. No, Lexie Cain could never do the right thing, the rational, logical thing. Just like the rest of her family, she had to live by her emotions, by her desires, and let caution fly by the wind.

And boy did she *desire* Barret Johnson. Not just in the physical sense. Those came and went with every passing good-looking guy. No, with Barret, she wanted much more—to know him in every way possible, to spend every waking hour with him, to hear the tenor of his voice, his laughter, and watch the way he rubbed his chin when he was deep in thought. She couldn't get enough of him. And that made him all the more dangerous.

Still.... That kiss! As Bonnet so often said, Saint's blood, what a kiss!

Sitting up, she swung her legs over the edge of the mattress and yawned. Maybe she should just give in to her feelings for him. He sure didn't seem to mind that his parents hated her. Yet would it work in the long run? The last thing she wanted was to come between him and his family.

Too confusing to think about without coffee. She would grab a cup, spend some time with Tracy and Ellie, and then maybe try a nap later on.

Downstairs she found Ellie opening a cupboard beneath a bookshelf and placing one of her toys—a fairy—inside, while Tracy stared at her laptop.

"You're up early." Tracy looked up. "Sorry. Were we making too much noise?" She glanced at Ellie. "No, Ell. Don't put your toys in there. I'm so sorry." Setting her computer aside, she moved to her daughter, retrieved the fairy, and shut the cupboard. "She likes to hide things. Always has."

Lexie laughed. "I think it's cute. I found a dragon in my bathroom cupboard yesterday."

Tracy shook her head. "Well, it won't be so cute when your boyfriend finds pirates, dragons, and fairies all over his house."

"He's not my boyfriend." Lexie sipped her coffee and slid onto a chair, smiling at Ellie, who had returned to play with a set of blocks.

Tracy sat back and grinned. "Not what I saw early this morning."

A hot flush swamped Lexie. "Oh my, did you see?"

"Not much. Enough." Tracy teased. "I'm happy for you. He's a good catch."

Lexie cupped her mug, relishing in the warmth. "I haven't caught him. I'm afraid he's the one who's caught me." She looked around. "I am living in his house, after all."

"Well, there are worse things to be caught by."

Maybe. Maybe not. "What were you doing up so early anyway?"

"I'm having trouble sleeping, too. Though not for the same reasons." She blew out a sigh and glanced down at her laptop. "Seems I'm not qualified for much. And the things I *am* qualified for don't pay enough for me to afford childcare."

The treasure. Lexie must find the treasure. She could help so many people. Not to mention herself. "I'm sorry. Keep looking. Something is bound to—"

CRASH!

The bay window shattered as something large and solid flew past Lexie's vision.

Ellie screamed, and before Lexie could get up, Tracy was on top of her daughter, shielding her with her body.

Barret's phone *dinged* with a text message. He would check it later. At the moment he was interviewing grad students for his vacant teacher's assistant position. He glanced at the young man sitting across his desk from him, looking more nervous than a turkey at Thanksgiving. Short hair, wire-rimmed glasses, and a bow tie on his hand-me-down suit made him look the perfect part of a history professor.

"So, as I was saying," Barret continued. His phone *dinged* again. "Excuse me for a moment." Reaching in his pocket he pulled it out. The message was from Adam.

Lexie in trouble. Townhome broken into. Better come right away.

Leaping to his feet, Barret tore from the room, shouting, "Sorry, have to reschedule." He didn't even care that he hadn't locked the door. He didn't care about anything but Lexie and her safety at the moment.

The drive downtown was a blur of annoying traffic, stop lights, and a heart that felt as though it would crash right through his chest. He barely remembered parking, barely remembered anything except Lexie's face as he shoved past the police standing around the open doorway.

"Wait. Who are you?" one of them asked.

"The owner," he responded without stopping.

Lexie fell against him and allowed him to swallow her up in his arms. On the couch, behind her, Tracy, with Ellie in her lap, was talking to Adam.

"We were just having coffee…" Lexie said, pushing from him. "Just talking, and it came through the window." Her green eyes sparked with fear.

Only then did Barret notice that a strong salty breeze swept through the room. His gaze landed on the shattered bay window and the thousand glass shards spread across the carpet.

"Are you hurt?" His glance took in her cute Hello Kitty pj's but found no blood.

"We are all fine." She hugged herself. "It just scared us. And there was a note attached."

"Note?"

"Adam has it."

Barret stormed toward his friend, who was just finishing up with Tracy, and took the note from Adam's grip.

Give us the letters or we will kill all your friends, including the professor and the little girl. Place them in PO box 1779 by midnight tonight.

The little girl? What kind of freaks were these people? Growling, Barret ran a hand through his hair. "I can't believe it." He glanced at the broken window, then at Lexie comforting Tracy and Ellie, and then back at Adam.

"Seems whoever they are, they are serious, Barret. Are these letters they want more important than your life, than Lexie's life?"

No, nothing was that important. But still, his anger burned. "Are you suggesting we give in to their demands? Let them know they can terrorize law abiding citizens whenever they want?"

Adam frowned. "Of course not. I just don't think I can get the manpower to watch over Lexie and her friends—or *you* for that matter—24-7."

"I can take care of myself."

Adam glanced in the direction of the knife wound. "Yeah, right."

Ignoring him, Barret ground his teeth together. "Did you talk to the neighbors? Did anyone see anything?"

"Yup. And no. And I've taken both the ladies' statements. Nobody saw a thing."

"What about the bodyguard I hired?" Barret glanced outside.

"There wasn't one here when we arrived." Wearing a glove, Adam held up a key. "To the PO box. I'm taking it and the brick to the lab to look for prints or DNA. Other than that, I have no leads."

Barret groaned. Where the heck did his bodyguard go? "Thanks. I appreciate everything you're doing."

"I'll bring it back before midnight, just in case you want to comply with their demands. Either way, we will send a couple of guys to watch the post office."

Barret wanted to say that he never would give them what they wanted, but as he glanced at Lexie and her friends, he wasn't sure what to do.

Adam gripped his shoulder. "Take care of her. Call me if they remember anything."

And just like that, Adam and his police officers left. Barret locked the door and set the alarm before he realized how foolish that was with a wide open front window.

Lexie started his way, but he held up a finger as he did a quick search on his phone for the number of the glass company his father used. He stepped out into the hall, and within minutes, he arranged for them to come and fix the window immediately.

When he returned to the living room, Ellie seemed none the worse for the incident as she sat on the couch playing with her doll. Lexie and Tracy sat beside her.

"The glass company will be here within the hour. They'll clean up the mess and install a new shatter-proof window." He sat on the chair facing them and stared at what must have been Lexie's half-finished cup of coffee.

"That must be costing you a fortune." Lexie shook her head, clearly distraught. "And it's all my fault. I shouldn't be staying here." She squeezed Tracy's hand. "I'm so sorry you got involved in this. Now they are threatening..." Her gaze landed on the little girl and tears spilled down her cheeks.

Barret had never seen her cry this hard, and in all honesty, it moved him so deeply, stirred such raging emotions, he had no idea what to do. So he sat there like a fool.

Tracy, on the other hand, plucked a tissue from a nearby box and handed it to Lexie. "Don't be silly. We'd be on the street without your kindness"— she snapped her gaze to Barret, as if she suddenly remembered it was *his* house— "Without both your kindnesses. None of this is your fault."

Lexie dabbed at her tears, then blew her nose. "I'd die if something happened to any of you."

"Well, nothing will." Barret stood. "Because I'm moving in permanently."

Lexie had always prided herself on being independent, on needing no one, but when Barret charged in that morning with his arms held wide, she felt like a little girl longing for a safety she'd so rarely experienced. Not only did that moment in his arms wipe away her fears, but she felt as though she'd come home. *Finally* home.

Now, as he took charge like a pirate captain on his ship, she couldn't help but admire him even more.

He handled the workmen who came to replace the glass, directing them to task. He made a fresh pot of coffee and helped settle Lexie, Tracy, and Ellie in the family room, which was connected to the kitchen in the back of the home. Then as if that wasn't enough, he ordered a delicious breakfast for all of them from one of his favorite restaurants.

None of them were terribly hungry, well, all except Ellie, who inhaled her French toast with extra syrup as if she hadn't eaten in a week. Barret even played with the little girl, helping her reconstruct the castle she'd been building when the brick hit.

For some reason, watching him interact so sweetly with the little girl mesmerized Lexie. Even Tracy couldn't take her eyes off them. "As I said before, you've got a keeper there," she whispered, tossing a piece of bacon in her mouth.

An absolute keeper, but for someone far more worthy.

Lexie knew he had more important things to do, like his job, like the appointment he had that morning. But still he stayed—until the window was installed and the workman were paid, until all of their nerves had finally unwound and laughter returned to the house.

A call from Adam sparked those same nerves again. Taking his cell, Barret moved to another room, out of earshot. No doubt he was protecting her from bad news, though she heard bits and pieces of the conversation. Enough to know that there were no prints or DNA on the brick, key, or note.

Barret returned wearing a tight smile she knew was for all their benefits, but she had to know the truth.

"What about the post office box?"

Barret frowned. "Eavesdropping?"

Lexie eased a wayward strand of hair behind her ear. "Can't help it."

After glancing at Ellie playing with her blocks, Barret sat on a stool at the counter. "The listed owner of the box doesn't exist, apparently, but the police are going to stake out the post office from now until after midnight to see who shows up."

Lexie's gaze swept over Ellie, so young and innocent, and then to her friend whose eyes still sparked with fear. And the toast in Lexie's stomach suddenly soured. She cupped her mug of hot cocoa and stared at the swirling chocolate. "Maybe I should just give them the letters."

"No!" Tracy shouted, startling them all. "I won't let you do that. Not if you're doing it for us. I know how much these letters and the treasure means to you. Don't let these bullies scare you." She placed a hand on Lexie's arm. "Please."

Barret smiled at Tracy as Lexie felt her eyes moisten once again. "The treasure means nothing to me if it comes at the cost of hurting my friends."

"Let's just wait and see what happens tonight," Barret said. "In the meantime, I hired a fulltime bodyguard to stay here when I'm at work."

"*In* the house?" Lexie wasn't sure she liked that idea.

"A friend of mine. He's trustworthy, I promise. And he won't bother you." He glanced at his phone. "He'll be here any minute. Then I gotta get back to work for a bit."

Tracy nodded. "Thank you for all you're doing, Barret. And for being so kind to Ellie and me."

His gaze landed once again on the little girl. "She's precious."

Lexie wondered what sort of father he would make. Scattering such dangerous thoughts, she stood. "I need to get some sleep before work."

Barret's dark brows collided. "You're not going to work. Not after this?"

"I have no choice. I need the money, and I've already taken off too many days."

His deep mahogany eyes assessed her for a moment before he nodded. "Okay, I'll tuck you in."

Tuck her in? Was he kidding? Was she a child in need of a bedtime story? Yet as he gazed at her with such tenderness, she found she couldn't say no. In fact, a soothing bedtime story from such a man sounded like a great idea.

Up in her bedroom, Lexie suddenly felt like a teenager on her first date, nervous and awkward. The second Barret entered the room, his masculine presence swallowed up every inch of air, including what was in her lungs. Grabbing a pillow for security, she sat on the bed and gazed up at him. He seemed equally uncomfortable as his eyes lowered to her lips.

"Going to kiss me again?" She teased, if only to break the awkward tension.

The right side of his lips quirked in a grin. "If you want me to."

Of course she wanted him to. What kind of question was that? "Is that why you came up here?"

He stooped beside the bed and took her hands in his. "I didn't come up here to seduce you, Lexie, if that's what you're implying. I just wanted a moment alone to make sure you're okay. To ask if I can do anything else to make you feel safe."

Lie in bed next to her and hold her while she slept. Sweet heavens, what was she thinking? "You've done more than enough. Thank you, Barret. You're a good friend."

"After that kiss, wouldn't you say we are more than that?"

She wanted to say yes, that she'd be honored to be his girlfriend, that she couldn't get him out of her mind—*or* her heart. But instead she just smiled.

"I'll take that as a yes." He tapped her on the nose and rose. "Now, off to sleep with you."

Reluctantly, Lexie laid down and allowed him to pull the covers up to her chin.

He kissed her forehead. "Sleep well, Sunshine." Then he left, closing the door.

And despite all the frightening events of the day, Lexie slept better than she had in a long while.

CHAPTER TWENTY-EIGHT

October 10, 1718, Charles Town, Provost Marshal's Home

My Most Precious Melody,

As I'm sure you have heard, I and my crew have been captured and brought to your fair city. Alas, though 'tis unfortunate news, I am sure you are unaware that I am not being held in the dungeon of the Court of Guard along with my fellow pirates but have been treated with the respect due a man of my station. As it turns out, Provost Nathaniel Partridge knew my father and uncle in Barbados and was a member of the same Parish of Christ Church in which my family presided. What fortune, my love! Indeed, I am kept prisoner but surrounded by every comfort I could hope for. In addition to the Provost Partridge's excellent company, my good friend Captain Herriot, along with my boatswain, Ignatius Pell, have joined me here, having agreed to testify against their fellow pirates for immunity.

Never fear, my adoring one, but I expect such a deal to be forthwith offered to me as well. Hence, once I gain my freedom, we shall ever be together. I must say that I had not expected things to turn out quite as fortuitous as this, for it is now assured that my crew will never learn of my treachery.

I beg you to come to me, my love, as soon as you are able to get away, for I am allowed visitors and have thus received several gentlemen who respect my position, merchants who benefited from selling pirate goods, and ladies who view me as a sort of hero who preys on the rich to give to the poor.

However, my love, none of them could ever compare to you.

Please come soon. I fear I shall die if I don't see your angelic face.

Ever yours,
Stede

October 18th, 1718

Bonnet sat sipping his tea when a knock came on the door of the provost's home. Herriot, who sat across from him, glanced up from the book he was reading, whilst Pell remained at the window, staring out at a freedom that was denied them by the two armed guards standing in the room.

The setting sun drew the last rays of light through the window, making Bonnet wonder who could be calling at this hour. Surely 'twas too early for the crowds of protest to form around the house as they had been for the past several nights, nor would any of them dare intrude upon the provost's privacy. Bonnet and his friends had just partaken of a delicious meal— joined by the provost and his wife—the likes of which Bonnet had not tasted since he'd first set sail.

Sounds reached his ears, wonderful sounds that gave him hope. The door opened, and the provosts' voice mixed with a feminine one—a sweet voice that stirred every drop of Bonnet's blood. Rising from his seat, he faced the door of the parlor, praying he was not dreaming.

A vision appeared around the corner, an angelic vision that made Bonnet wonder if he were in heaven. But nay, surely he would never be allowed entrance to that glorious city, and hence, would have to enjoy bliss in the brief moments allowed him here on earth. She floated toward him in a gown of blue taffeta with a bodice of braided ribbon down the front and a low neckline edged in a white lacy ruffle. Radiant curls that outshone the sun dangled from her pinned up hair and danced over a neck that would make a swan envious. But 'twas the look in her blue eyes that made his heart melt.

"Miss Rogers." He spoke her formal name so as to not embarrass her in front of the others.

The provost entered after her and gave a sly grin. "She claims she knows you, Bonnet."

"Indeed, we are well acquainted." Bonnet took her hands in his and lifted them to his lips for a kiss.

"I thought she was one of your admirers, but then I recognized her name from Barbados." Provost Partridge moved to a sideboard and poured himself a glass of port. Tall and lithe, he sported a wig of long brown curls and a mustache that appeared to sink beside the corner of his lips.

Herriot cleared his throat and stood, whilst Pell spun to face them.

Bonnet made introductions, all the while wishing more than anything to be alone with her. They had much to discuss and, beside all of that, he longed to kiss her.

"Nathaniel, my good man." Bonnet turned to his friend. "I beg your indulgence, sir. Is there some place private where the lady and I may talk?"

Nathaniel sipped his port and examined Bonnet with a spark of suspicion, but then he shifted his gaze to Melody and her sweet smile was the end of him.

"It can do no harm, I suppose." He called for a servant, a plump elderly lady with gray hair pulled in a tight bun and a lacy mobcap atop her head. "Miss Charlotte, will you escort Captain Bonnet and Miss Rogers to the library and remain as chaperon."

Bonnet growled inwardly, but he knew 'twas the best he could expect under the circumstances.

Once settled on a velvet settee with the maid sitting upon a stool near the open door, Bonnet faced Melody. "What has delayed your coming, my love?"

"You must forgive me, Stede. I heard you were here the moment you arrived, but my father is suspicious and has kept a firm eye on me since."

"Where is your lady's companion?"

"Outside waiting." Melody glanced toward the single window in the room overlooking the back garden, her light curls brushing over her creamy neck. "And watching, on the chance we were followed." She faced him, her eyes racing between his. "Stede, I fear for you. Will you hang? I could not bear it."

"Nay. Do not worry yourself so." He kissed her hands. "Do you not see all the support we have garnered? Why, each night crowds assemble outside and also at the Court Guard to protest our imprisonment."

"So, 'tis true? I have heard the rumors but dared not hope."

Her sweet scent of jasmine and rose drove him to distraction. "Nay, there are many merchants who have benefited from selling our goods and also citizens who believe us to be noble in our efforts to steal from the rich and help the poor, though I admit that the only poor I hope to aid are you and myself." He chuckled.

Melody arched a single brow. "And women admirers I hear?"

He shrugged. "The gentler sex do seem to adore a handsome swashbuckler."

"Well, they shan't have you, for you are mine." She smiled.

"I want none but you." And at the moment Bonnet wanted nothing but to kiss her. He glanced at the maid, who had leaned her head back onto the wall and closed her eyes. What luck!

He started lowering his lips to Melody's when she rose from her seat.

"I have disturbing news." She moved to the window, glanced at the lady servant, and continued in a hushed tone. "A meeting of the General Assembly was held at my house, an emergency meeting." She sighed and peered into the shadowy evening. "One of the guards stands out here."

"Aye, Nathaniel, no doubt, moved him there should I attempt an escape through the window." Bonnet would have expected no less from his cunning friend. "But what of this meeting?"

"They passed an act for the more speedy and regular trials of pirates. Stede," Rushing back to him, she sat and gripped his hands. "They will bring you to court soon."

"Nay, not me, my love. 'Tis for my crew no doubt, wasting away in the Court of Guard dungeon." Bonnet attempted a smile to reassure her, but it faltered on his lips, for he could not swear to that. Regardless of the support of Charles Town citizens or the provost's friendship, Bonnet might have to face the consequences of his actions. His only hope was the pardon from Governor Eden and the corresponding commission to seek a Letter of Marque from the governor of St. Thomas. If he could escape and make his way to that island, his life would be spared. He was sure of it. If he could not escape, he could at least use the pardon to his advantage at court.

"Nonetheless, surely they will put you to trial after them." Melody lowered her gaze, her chest rising and falling beneath her lacy ruffle.

A rap on the door brought both their gazes up to see another servant enter. A young, blushing maid whom Bonnet had befriended and to whom he had conveyed his romantic tale of love for Melody. "The mistress has need of you, Charlotte, in the kitchen."

Charlotte shook the sleep from her body, looked up at the young maid, then gestured toward Bonnet and Melody. "Very well. What of them?"

"'Tis of no concern of ours," the maid answered before following Charlotte out. "He'll not escape." Then winking at Bonnet, she left, closing the door.

Wonderful woman!

Bonnet smiled at Melody. "You think me a prisoner, but alas, I have arranged for us to have some time alone."

Melody glanced after the maid and then back at him. "I do say, Stede, you could charm a starving man from his last meal."

"Then allow me, my precious, to charm you with every bit of my love. Will you grant me this gift?"

"I shall."

October 22, 1718, Charles Town, Provost Marshal's Home

Dearest,

I have thought of nothing else but our indescribable moments alone together four nights past. You have entrusted me with your most precious gift, and I shall cherish it forever. I had hoped you would visit me sooner, yet I know how difficult it is for you to escape your father's keen eye. I long to see your face, to hold you in my arms. My heart aches for another moment with you.

Alas, word has reached me that the pirate Christopher Moody has set his sights on Charles Town and even now anchors outside the entrance to the harbor to prey on every passing ship. Some say he intends to enter the city and rescue his fellow brethren of the coast, including myself, but I have my doubts. Regardless, my darling, this may be my chance to escape. If I could but get myself to Sullivan's Island and hail down Moody, I am sure he would bring me aboard and take me to St. Thomas posthaste. I find myself deprived of my weapons, to be sure, but I still have my pardon tucked safely within my pocket.

I hesitate, my love, to ask you this, but will you find a way to come for another visit and bring lady's attire, large lady's attire?

I know 'tis much to ask of you, but I fear 'tis my only chance for freedom, and thus, our only chance to be together.

I await your response and yet another chance to see you.

Forever yours,
Stede

Barret admitted to being a little nervous going on his first official date with Lexie. It wasn't like he hadn't spent a great deal of time with her in the past month. Heck, he'd even moved in with her yesterday. Strictly platonic, of course. And against every natural urge within him, he would keep it that way. He would honor God's commandments.

He glanced at her sitting in the passenger seat as he turned into the parking lot of Halls Chop House, one of the best and most expensive restaurants in downtown Charleston. Maybe he could change the trajectory of her life. Maybe he could open up her mind and heart so she would believe in Jesus and start living right. Then maybe his parents would accept her. Surely they would. They were good, God-fearing people who loved everyone as the Lord commanded.

Regardless, he hoped tonight would be the beginning of a wonderful romance. He hoped Lexie loved the ruby and diamond tennis bracelet he got her. And he hoped his good news about Tracy would endear him to her even more.

He also hoped there would be no discussion of villains and threatening letters. No one had shown up at the P.O. box last night. Though Lexie had seemed disappointed, maybe it meant they'd given up. That was Barret's fervent prayer.

After parking, he quickly exited the car and rushed around to open her door. He knew it was old-fashioned, but he hoped she wouldn't mind his chivalry. She smiled as he assisted her from the car. Good sign.

"Whoa," she whispered as they entered the front door of the restaurant. A dozen savory scents spun around them, eliciting a growl from Barret's stomach. Thankfully, the light music and conversation of patrons drowned it out.

"You're going to love this place," Barret said as the hostess took them to their table, the small two-seater in the corner he had requested. Candlelight flickered from within a glass globe set upon a white linen tablecloth. Sparkling wine glasses, a single pink rose in a vase, and real silverware completed the romantic setting. Light classical music filled the room, accompanied by the hum of conversation and clink of glasses.

"I have no doubt I will love everything, but what does it all cost?" Lexie raised a brow at him after he scooted in her chair.

"Don't worry about it." Barret took his seat across from her. Oh, how he longed to ensure this woman never had to worry about money again, a blessing he'd enjoyed his entire life.

"What'd you think of Bonnet's last letter?" Barret asked as a waiter brought their menus. He had wanted to hear her thoughts ever since they'd read it together at the museum early that morning, but she'd been so tired and he'd thought it best to get her home and in bed as soon as possible. After she'd gone to sleep, he had gone to his apartment, gathered a few things, and then moved into the living room downstairs. Then, leaving the bodyguard there to watch over them, Barret had gone to the university. Not only did he have to finish interviewing for the teacher's assistant position and finish his syllabus for next semester, but he had a far more important mission.

Lexie set her napkin in her lap and gazed at him over the candle flickering between them. My, but she was lovely. She wore a long floral sun dress—casual, but classy—that clung to all her curves. In fact, this was the first time he'd seen her in a dress, and he found her more alluring than ever. She'd even put her ivory hair up in a less-than-crazy style that still left several silky strands dangling around her neck. Though she rarely wore makeup, she'd applied some mascara, a bit of rouge, and some lip gloss which only enhanced her beauty. Excitement sparkled in her green eyes as she looked at him. "I'm so happy he's finally with Melody, well, sort of with her, but I'm sad that he's caught, even if this provost guy is being nice to him. But"—she gave him a sassy grin—"sounds like he might escape?"

The waiter came by and Barret ordered a bottle of Chateau Montrose Grand Bordeaux, then faced her with a smile. "You told me not to tell you." Besides, he didn't want to ruin her good mood.

Her smiled faded anyway. No doubt she remembered that Bonnet's story had already come to its conclusion—a sad conclusion.

"I like him too." Barret reached across the table for her hand.

She took it and gave him a squeeze. "I think it's hysterical that some of the people in town, particularly the ladies, were protesting his arrest."

Barret shrugged. "Everyone loves a pirate, right? Look at how popular Johnny Depp is." He chuckled. "Handsome, adventurous, courageous, daring. I guess there's something incredibly romantic about them. Plus, Bonnet had education and status in his favor."

She leaned toward him, a coy smile on her lips and sparkle in her eyes. "Do you think they did it?"

Warmth flooded Barret. He knew exactly what she meant by "it", and he found her straightforward manner captivating. "Well, I guess they would have to have done"—he cleared his throat— "at some point, or *you* wouldn't be here."

She smiled as the waiter returned with the wine, uncorked it, and allowed Barret a sip for his approval. Smooth as ever. He gave the expected affirming nod, and the waiter poured them both a glass. Soon another waiter came to take their orders.

Lexie ordered crab soup for an appetizer and fillet mignon with wild mushroom risotto and Pancetta-roasted Brussels sprouts for her main meal—more food than most men Barret knew could eat. But he loved that about her. All the other women he'd dated ordered salads and seafood and then picked at their food as if they were terrified of it. But not Lexie. He loved watching her eat and enjoy every bite. She even had room at the end for Key Lime Meringue pie.

"You're smiling at me." She set down her fork and sat back with a satisfied look on her face.

"Am I?"

"Did I eat too much? Oh, no." A look of shame crinkled her expression. "I'm so sorry. This must have cost you a fortune. George always told me I embarrassed him with my appetite."

"George?"

She flattened her lips. "My stepfather."

"Lexie, I love watching you enjoy your food. Seriously. And I don't care about the money. In fact, I have good news that I hope will be even better than that key lime pie." He glanced down at her dessert plate, empty except for a few crumbs.

"I don't know, Professor Pirate." She smiled and pressed a hand over her stomach. "It will have to be pretty good news."

Barret sipped his wine, thankful that his full stomach softened the effects. "What if I told you that I think I got Tracy a job."

It took a moment for her face to blossom in an expression of complete joy. "What? Serious? I would say you were incredible, wonderful... the best friend ever!"

Barret would settle for that at the moment. "I contacted the Early Childhood Education department head and as part of the program, they run a preschool there on the campus. It just so happens she is looking for a fulltime worker to help with the kids."

Lexie gripped her hands together.

"I told her about Tracy, and she's anxious to meet with her, but honestly, unless Tracy shows up stoned, she's got the job." He hated to brag, but he had a great deal of influence at the university.

Squealing, Lexie nearly leapt from her seat.

"The best part,' Barret added, "it comes with free childcare for Ellie. In fact, Tracy would be right there with her the entire time she's working."

This time Lexie did jump up and embraced Barret in a hug so tight, he nearly fell backward. Her sweet vanilla perfume tantalized every inch of him, and he never wanted her to let go.

People began to stare. Lexie returned to her seat, her eyes moist with tears. "I can't believe it. She's going to be so thrilled. I can't wait to tell her! How can I ever thank you?"

"No need, Lexie. I'm happy to help." He played with his fork, suddenly embarrassed by her praise. "I should have thought of it sooner."

Sitting back, she sipped her wine and smiled.

He couldn't take his eyes off her, the way she seemed to glow from within. His gaze landed on the three earrings in her left ear. "Do those have meaning?" He gestured toward them. "You always wear the same ones."

She reached up to touch them. "Sort of, I guess. The skull is my family's curse, the pearl represents hope. I got it from a story my Mom told me from the Bible about a pearl of great price."

Barret nodded, pleased to hear her mention the Bible. "The one the merchant sold everything to acquire."

"Yes." She fingered the clip in the middle. "And this one is a bridge between the two. Hopefully, a bridge I can cross."

A lump of emotion balled in Barret's throat. "Of course you can. And you will."

Her eyes moistened, and she glanced out the window onto the dark street.

"And the eagle tattoo?" Barret knew he was pressing his luck by asking so many questions. Maybe it was the wine, but she seemed willing to answer, and he didn't want to pass up an opportunity to know her better.

She rubbed the back of her neck. "Freedom. It represents freedom."

He wanted to ask her freedom from what but thought better of it. Maybe freedom from her past, freedom from poverty. Perhaps this was the perfect time for his gift. Reaching into his pants' pocket, he pulled out a small box and handed it to her.

She looked at him quizzically.

"Just a gift, Lexie. Something nice I wanted to give you."

Shaking her head, she lifted the top and her eyes widened. "What?" She stared at it a few minutes, then snapped it shut and handed it back to him. "No way I can take this."

CHAPTER TWENTY-NINE

Why did Barret have to ruin a perfectly lovely evening by giving her such an extravagant gift? Lexie huffed and drank the remainder of her wine. Already her head felt as though it were floating on a cloud—a lovely sensation, but one that reminded her that it was always best to keep her senses *and* reason sharp. Too many times in her past, when she'd been high or drunk, she'd made the worst decisions, done the most damaging things she later regretted. But the evening had been so special, the food so good, the company alluring, that she thought a little wine couldn't hurt.

The bracelet was gorgeous. What surely had to be rubies and diamonds sparkled in the candlelight—elegant but not gaudy. She'd never seen anything so beautiful. *And* so costly.

"I can't take this, Barret." She ignored the look of pain in his eyes as he fingered the jewelry box.

"Why? It's just a gift. Something beautiful for a beautiful lady."

"It costs too much."

He blew out an exasperated sigh. "Why are you always worried about money?"

"Because I don't have any, Professor." She instantly regretted her harsh tone. "I know that's a hard concept for you to wrap your rich mind around, but it's the truth."

Barret reached for her hand. "Please, Lexie."

She hesitated but finally grabbed it.

"I'm sorry. I meant it only as a token of my affection and admiration for you, and maybe as a good way to start our relationship."

"You can't buy me, Barret."

"Not trying to." He set down the box and sat back, running a hand through his hair. "I wouldn't want you if I could."

The statement, along with the look of love in his eyes, poured cold water on her anger. He meant no harm. She knew that. Releasing a heavy sigh, she smiled. "Our relationship?"

"We're dating, right?" There was that grin of his again, the one that disarmed her every defense. "I want to get us off to a good start. It's just a bracelet, Lexie, not an engagement ring. Please take it. It would mean a lot to me." He handed her the box again.

Opening it, she stared at the glittering jewels. "You aren't going to turn into a monster, are you?" She blurted out, no doubt due to the wine.

His forehead wrinkled. "What?"

"Sorry." She picked up the bracelet and sat back in her chair. "My stepfather used his wealth to seduce my mom. But once she married him and became dependent on him for everything, including me, he turned into a monster. He treated her terribly."

"And you think I would do such a thing?" He looked hurt.

"No." The denial came from her heart, but in her head, she wasn't convinced. She'd trusted far too many people in her life, only to be burned later on. She glanced down at the bracelet. This thing would feed a family for months. How could she ever wear it on her wrist?

"Say you'll keep it."

"If I do, it's mine, right? No strings attached."

Confusion, followed by delight, crossed his deep eyes. "You never fail to surprise me, Sunshine. But the answer is yes, of course."

Lexie slipped the bracelet on her arm. "Then, yes. Thank you, Barret."

"How about we ditch this place and go for a moonlight walk?" Rising, he held out a hand for her.

On the ride to the waterfront park, Lexie couldn't keep her eyes off of the bracelet. It sparkled and shimmered beneath every streetlight they passed and even more so out in the moonlight as they walked down the pathway bordering Charleston Harbor. Joe Riley Park was small with a single gravel path bordering the harbor, along which benches were placed. A light breeze blew over Lexie as she walked beside Barret, filling her nose with the scents of the sea and the loamy rich smell of marshland. And, of course, Barret's cologne of musk, cedar, and rum. Moonlight cast silver gems over the bay, making it look like a magical place from another world.

Barret stopped and leaned on the railing, gazing over the water, deep in thought. Another thing she liked about him. He wasn't the type who always had to fill the air with chatter. He was a deep thinker, and often she had no idea what was on that mind of his.

She inched beside him. "No wonder Bonnet loved the sea. It's not only beautiful but full of mystery and adventure."

A moment passed before he answered. "Like you."

She smiled. The man knew how to flatter a woman. She'd give him that.

Another couple passed behind them, and Lexie felt Barret tense beside her. There were still people after them. She had not forgotten. She had simply *wanted* to forget tonight.

"Should we be out here?" She glanced around. "Vulnerable?"

Easing an arm around her shoulders, he drew her close. "Don't worry. I will never let anything happen to you."

He said the words with such conviction and confidence that she found herself believing him. Odd that she trusted a man, but this particular man had more than proven his ability to fight, to protect, along with his willingness to put himself in harm's way for her. It was the thing of romance novels, chivalry of days long ago, knights and ladies, and all the things women's liberation taught this generation of females to avoid, to disavow, to spit on. She'd always embraced the notion that women could do anything a man could do, that they didn't need a man to protect them. But for some reason, here in his strong arms, she felt safe, loved, cherished even, and she wouldn't want it any other way.

He rubbed her arm, then turned her to face him. His black hair blew in the breeze as his dark eyes locked upon her. "It's all going to work out. You'll see. God protects us."

She huffed. "He might protect you, but I doubt he does me."

"But, you forget, you're with me." He chuckled, brushed a strand of hair from her face, then lowered his lips to hers.

His breath warmed her cheek, smelling of wine and spice, and she wanted nothing more than for him to kiss her, fully and deeply.

But a gunshot cracked the night air!

Before the echo of the shot even faded, Barret forced Lexie to the ground, covering her with his body. "Are you hit?"

"I'm fine." Her voice squeaked.

He scanned the area around them, looking for any movement in the shadows. Nothing.

"Let's go. Run!" Grabbing Lexie's hand, he dragged her down the path and across the yard, diving into a line of trees. He stopped to listen for anyone following. Nothing but the lap of waves on shore and a distant siren met his ears. His breath heaved between them. Lexie's too. He felt her tremble. He had to get her out of here. Fast! Sprinting for the car, he groped for his keys in his pocket, unlocked it, and had Lexie in the passenger seat before he allowed himself a breath.

He ran for the driver's side, steeling his gaze all around for anyone moving. Then leaping inside, he started the engine and took off with a squeal.

"They shot at us!" Lexie's voice spiked with terror, but to her credit, she did not cry, did not start sobbing or shaking.

"Yeah, but they missed."

Nothing else was said as he parked the car and got Lexie safely inside the townhome. Tracy and Ellie had long since gone to bed, and the bodyguard reported nothing unusual had occurred. After dismissing him, Barret made Lexie a mug of hot cocoa, then sat beside her on the couch.

With her legs propped up against her chest, she hugged herself and stared into space. Shock. She was going into shock. He needed to comfort, soothe her anyway he could. He handed her the mug. Took her a minute to see it, but finally she accepted it and smiled.

"Sorry the evening ended this way." Barret had so wanted to give her the perfect, romantic night out. And these goons had ruined it! Fury raged in his veins. He shook his head. Maybe he shouldn't have risked taking her to the park, but it seemed the perfect ending to a great date.

"Not your fault." Her phone beeped, and setting the mug down, she reached for it in her purse and answered. For a moment nothing was said, but then the voice—a deep, angry voice—spoke loud and clear, so loud, Barret heard every word.

"Next time we won't miss."

Grabbing the phone from Lexie, Barret shouted. "Who is this?"

"Give us what we want, or someone will die." *Click.*

Growling, Barret wanted to toss the phone against the wall. Instead, he set it on the table. He wanted to cuss, to call them a not-so-nice name, but he'd been raised to never say such things. "Jerks, blackguards!"

Lexie laughed. "Who says blackguards anymore?"

Barret smiled, happy to have lifted her mood. "I guess history professors do."

She sighed, her laughter fading back into fear. "They are not going to give up, are they?"

"Honestly, Lexie, I don't know. But I don't think these guys are killers. They had a clear shot of both of us. It's like they missed on purpose... a warning, you know?"

"That doesn't make me feel any better." Her lips slanted. "I should just give them what they want. It's not worth it." She looked at him, her green eyes clouding with moisture.

"No." He walked to the window and raked back his hair, more frustrated than he'd been in a while. "We are too close.

All I gotta say is it must be a vast fortune for them to go to all this trouble."

"Told ya." Her tone was playful.

He turned to see her grinning. "Another thing I love about you. You're brave. How many women... how many *men* would be making a joke after getting shot at?"

"Maybe it's my way of coping. I'm not brave, Barret. I'm scared to death. Not for me, but for you, Tracy, and Ellie, everyone I care about." Her bottom lip quivered.

"And yet another thing I love."

"Love?" She grinned. "Strong word, Professor."

He returned to sit beside her, taking her hand in his. "Strong feelings."

She lowered her chin, a slight blush rising on her cheeks as she glanced at the bracelet he'd given her. It looked so beautiful on her wrist, and he longed to erase the past hour of their date.

"Well, let's not allow a little thing like being shot at ruin our evening. Want to read another letter?"

She pulled on her earring. "I want to so badly, but I think I've had too much wine. Can I just lie here on the couch with you for a while? I don't want to think about anything right now."

Could she lie on the couch *with* him? Was she kidding? "Of course."

His phone played *The Imperial March* from Star Wars. His father. Something must be wrong, He never called Barret this late. "Dad?"

"You at the townhome?"

"Yes." How did his father know that?

"Come by my office tomorrow. 8:00 a.m. sharp. I need to speak to you." *Click.*

"Dad?" Nothing. Barret stared at the phone. He knew that tone. Whatever his father wanted to speak to him about, it was not going to be pleasant.

Barret spent a restless, yet oddly wonderful night. He supposed being shot at was the cause of his restlessness, but in fact, it seemed his father's call had done the most damage. Barret could not figure out what he had done to earn the disdain he'd heard in his father's tone. Could it still be about Lexie? Yet how could his father know whether Barret was still seeing her or not? *The townhome.* He'd known Barret was in the townhome, and that fact disturbed him greatly.

Regardless, the wonderful part of the night had been that Lexie had fallen asleep in his arms as they curled up together on the couch. The rise and fall of her chest, her deep breathing and light snoring warmed every inch of him. He was delighted she felt safe and secure with him, that she trusted him to protect her and to not try anything improper. His head leaned on top of hers and all through the night her sweet scent filled his lungs, both exciting and soothing.

Never had he felt this way about a woman. Never had he wanted more than anything to protect, to hold, and to cherish this lady forever. And though his physical attraction to her was strong, thoughts of being with her in that way did not consume his mind. Not even as he held her all night. He simply longed for her to sleep in peace and feel safe.

So he stayed awake for many hours, enjoying the moment, pondering what had gotten his father's hackles up, until finally he drifted off as well. Sunlight shining in his eye jarred him awake, and one look at the clock told him if he didn't get going, he'd be late to see his father—tardiness, an unforgivable sin.

Now, as he mounted the steps to the courthouse, he finished the last sips of his macchiato, tossed the cup in the garbage, and entered through the glass doors to meet his fate. Through the security scan, into the elevator to the 4th floor, then down the hall he marched, greeting people he knew along the way.

"Barret." His father said as if Barret was unaware of his own name. He rose from his desk and thanked his assistant as she ushered Barret inside and shut the door, sealing his fate.

"What's this about, Father? I have work to do at the university." Barret glanced around the judge's chambers, all of which reflected his father's harsh, strict, and perfect demeanor in every way. Sharp angular oak furniture, elegantly carved and stuffed, sat upon expensive and elaborate Persian carpets. Bookshelves reached for the ceiling, lined with every law book written throughout the centuries. A large window brought in the only light from the back of the building that faced a garden across the street.

His father, dressed in an elegant three-piece suit, studied Barret with that same penetrating stare Barret was sure he used on many of the defendants in his court. "Barret, I'm disappointed in you."

Barret had already figured that one out. "What did I do this time?"

"You were stabbed, and I had no idea until my friend Doctor Trankin mentioned it to me the other night." For a moment, a look of concern crossed his father's eyes.

Barret breathed out a sigh. Maybe the man was truly just concerned. "Yeah, sorry, Dad. It was nothing really, just a flesh wound. They released me the same day."

His father gestured toward Barret's side. "Are you okay?"

"Yes, it healed nicely." Surely that wasn't all he wanted to talk to Barret about.

"So, you were protecting that *woman*." The judge studied Barret as one would a convicted criminal.

And here it came. "If you mean Lexie, yes. We were minding our own business, and two men attacked us."

"Just like that," his father said with skepticism. "For what reason?"

Barret didn't want to disclose the fact that someone was after Lexie and her letters, though he had an idea his father already knew. His father knew everything that went on in Charleston, which was why Barret suddenly realized how foolish he'd been. "We were merely wandering around the cemetery at St. Philip's."

"Humph." Judge Johnson's frown could frighten a staunch warrior. "We'll leave that question aside for a moment. More importantly." His eyes narrowed. "Why are you allowing vagrants to live in my townhome without my permission?"

Barret's heart seized. Here was the real reason he'd had been summoned. Not concern over his wound. "I thought it was the *family* townhome and therefore my decision as well."

His father's face reddened, his cheeks swelled. "You thought wrong!"

"I—" Barret began to talk but his father held up a hand.

"Not just this Lexie person but a homeless woman and her brat! This is unacceptable, son. Unacceptable! Next, you'll invite half the bums in town to live in my house. *My* house! Do you realize how many valuables I have in that house?"

Barret crossed arms over his chest, refusing to cower before this man. "They won't take anything."

"You're too trusting. These people will do anything, beg, steal, lie, *anything* to survive."

"I invited Lexie to stay there for her own safety. And Tracy and Ellie were evicted from their apartment. They are friends of Lexie's. Was I supposed to let them sleep on the street?"

"Evicted no doubt due to drugs or negligence," he spat out. "And there are shelters for these kinds of people, Barret. Lots of places for them to stay."

"I made a judgment call. They are good, decent people."

"*You* made a judgment call. I fear your judgment has gone askew ever since you started dating that... that... criminal. I ordered you to stop seeing her."

Fury inflamed Barret's tongue, enticing him to spit out his true feelings to this man, but he knew if he did, he'd say something he would regret. Instead he stood there, staring at his father, the man who had raised him, the man who had taught him about honor and decency, charity and goodness, the man who was a pillar of the community and an elder at their church.

And he suddenly realized he didn't know him at all.

The judge sat back on his thick, oak desk and continued his tirade. "I heard about the brick and the glass. Were you ever going to tell me about that?"

"Eventually. I had it fixed. Replaced with even better glass. No harm done."

"No harm done?" He growled. "I checked with the chief of police who looked up the report for me. Seems someone is after Lexie Cain, threatening to kill not only her, but you as well by association. Is that what you want? To die for this slut?"

That was it. "How dare you?" Barret took a step toward the man, his hand fisting. "She's no slut, Father! You don't even know her. What happened to your Christian charity?"

His father shrank back, surprising Barret. "Your mother and I give plenty to charity. What happened to your common sense, boy?" Releasing a deep sigh, he shook his head, his tone softening. "Your mother and I are merely worried for your safety."

Barret huffed. "I think you're more worried about your reputation and your townhome."

For a moment, the anger returned to the judge's eyes. "I'm sorry to do this, son, but I will not allow these people to remain in my home. Send them packing and do it soon, or I'll be forced to take action."

CHAPTER THIRTY

*L*exie woke with both a start and a smile. Odd combination. Instantly she turned to look behind her, but she knew before she did that Barret was gone. She rubbed her arms. The feel of his strong ones wrapped around her all through the night remained, even as his masculine scent filled the air as if he'd only just left. In the corner, two suitcases sat open, evidence of him living there—protecting them.

As she swung her legs to the floor, memories flooded her of their glorious evening together, the wonderful candlelit meal, the walk in the moonlight, the *shot*! Cringing at that last event, she glanced down at the bracelet still on her wrist. Rays of morning sun set it aglow in sparkling brilliance. She fingered the string of rubies, set apart by three glimmering diamonds. She'd never been given such a gift.

She'd never had a man protect her with his life either. Before she'd even realized they'd been shot at, he'd covered her with his body like a shield. Who did that? Who reacts so quickly, so courageously, at the risk of his own life?

A hero, that's who. A modern-day hero. Lexie had not believed they existed. But after he had held her all night and not once tried to hook up with her, she now knew without a doubt they did.

And for some reason, this knight in shining armor had chosen her to be his lady.

She was not good enough for him. She'd tried to tell him that on multiple occasions, but the fool would not listen. Sooner or later, he'd probably find out—something from her past would rise to haunt her or she'd do something stupid that would turn him off.

And Lexie would get her heart broken. Yet, she found she could no longer resist him. Much like Melody, who would have been better off sending Bonnet packing, Lexie would treasure every moment she had with Barret—for as long as they lasted.

Giggles preceded Ellie dashing into the room, wearing her mermaid pj's. "Lexie, Lexie!"

Lexie swallowed the little girl up in her arms. "How's my little mermaid, this morning?"

"I'm a pirate today," the girl announced as she perched on Lexie's lap and repeated the phrase Barret had taught her. "Avast, ye may be gettin' wet!"

Lexie laughed as Tracy appeared around the corner, cup of coffee in her hand. "Sorry. When I saw you sleeping here, I tried to keep her from bugging you."

Lexie took the mug and sipped it. "You're an angel."

Tracy chuckled, but then her lips curved in a coy grin. "So…you and Barret?" She glanced at the couch where Lexie sat, her eyes sparkling with mischief.

Lexie laughed. "It's not what you think. We, ah…we, um."

"Oh, I see." Tracy said with a smile.

"Stop it. We just fell asleep together. That's all. He was the perfect gentleman."

"Like a prince," Ellie said.

Lexie kissed her forehead. "Just like a prince, my darling."

"Princes love fairies," she added.

"Do they?" Lexie hugged her. "Well, everyone loves you."

Ellie laughed, scooted off Lexie's lap and dashed from the room, no doubt to get some toy.

Alarm shot through Lexie. "Where's the bodyguard? What's his name, Matt?"

"Oh, my gosh! What the heck?" Tracy rushed toward Lexie and dropped to the couch beside her, her eyes on the bracelet. "Is it real?"

"Knowing Barret, I guess so."

"He gave this to you?" Tracy fingered it with care. "He must really be serious." She stared at Lexie, her eyes wide. "You're so lucky to have such a guy."

"I don't have him, Trace. And I don't know if I'm gonna keep it."

"I'll take it!" Tracy laughed. "You're nuts if you don't. But whatever." She sat back with a sigh.

"Matt?" Lexie raised her brows.

"No worries. He's right outside the front door. He didn't want to stand here while you were sleeping."

"Geez, I'm so sorry." Lexie rose and rubbed the sleep from her eyes, glancing down at her now-wrinkled dress. "We should ask him in. I need to shower, anyway." Should she tell Tracy they'd been shot at? No. Why stress the poor woman out? "Do you still need me to babysit today?"

Tracy gave her a pleading look. "Yes, but only for an hour. I have an interview, but it's close by. At 10:00. She glanced at the grandfather clock as Ellie bounced into the room carrying two fairies and a dragon.

"Of course." Lexie wished more than anything she could tell Tracy about the job Barret had gotten her, but she wasn't sure it was a done deal.

"Come, sweetheart, let's go play with those in the family room." Tracy ushered Ellie out, then stopped at the front door. "I'll let Matt in, and you go shower."

The warm shower felt wonderful. The hour playing with Ellie precious. But soon, Lexie drove around town running a few errands, all the while terrified of being shot at again. Barret had told her to stay home, to allow Matt to walk her to work, but she refused to be held captive in her home. She refused to cower to these thugs. After making a quick stop, Lexie walked into the women's shelter, not only to offer her help for a few hours, but to offer something that would help these poor women greatly. Even so, with every hour that passed, her thoughts were filled with Barret. She wondered how his meeting with his father had gone. She wondered if she'd see him soon, or perhaps he'd come to the museum later. She wondered why he hadn't called.

She was behaving like a foolish high school girl with her first crush.

So, by the time Matt walked her to work, she determined to put Barret out of her mind. Not an easy task. Shoving earbuds in her ears, she listened to her favorite bands while she worked, keeping her mind on her job and doing her best so Mrs. Anderson would be pleased. Even though it was demeaning work, Lexie owed the woman her best for hiring her, an ex-con, whether she'd known that fact or not.

By 4:00 a.m., Lexie's shoulders and arms ached, but she was happy to descend into the dungeon to finish her shift. Walking to Bonnet's cell, she greeted him kindly, as had become her custom. And as usual, he didn't respond. She smiled. If he actually did, she'd probably die of a heart attack.

A knock rapped on the back door. Barret? Her hopes rising, she moved closer. "Who is it?"

"Me, Sunshine."

She couldn't open the door fast enough. Nor could she control the huge smile on her face.

He sauntered in, closed and locked the door, then took her in his arms. "Miss me?"

He felt so good. Warm, strong, like a barricade of protection and care.

She hated to admit it, but there was no sense denying it anymore. "Yes."

He nudged her back. "Yes? That's a first."

Shrugging, she walked away. "Don't get a big head about it, Professor Pirate."

"Oh, I don't think you'll let me do that."

Lexie picked up her broom and began sweeping. "What did your father want?"

"Nothing important."

He said the words with such sorrow, she faced him. Barret was rarely sad, but now that she looked at him, she sensed something was upsetting him.

"Want to talk about it?"

"No. I want to read another letter. You?"

She smiled. "I thought you'd never ask."

October 24, 1718, Charles Town, Provost Marshall's Home

Dearest, beloved Melody,

By the time you receive this, I shall be free. And if all goes well, I shall be in route to St. Thomas to procure my ultimate freedom from any further condemnation. Be patient, my dearest, I vow to return to you immediately and hence, to sweep you away to a life of loving bliss and elegant luxuries, which you heretofore have not enjoyed, but which you greatly deserve.

Until then, my love, you are always in my thoughts,
Stede

Dressed in a too-tight gown with a shawl over his shoulders and a lacy bonnet covering his head, Bonnet slunk down the quiet streets of Charles Town, keeping to the shadows. Thankfully, only a sliver of a moon afforded any light, along with the few flickering streetlamps perched along the way. He glanced at Herriot beside him and nearly gave their position away by a chuckle. The man looked ridiculous in a petticoat, yellow silk overgown, and mobcap, stumbling along with difficulty in all the fripperies women were expected to wear. Still, Bonnet was thankful for the company, though it had taken some convincing—convincing to the tune of a quarter of the treasure Bonnet had buried. Nevertheless, he needed the help if their escape would be successful.

It had been easy to escape the provost's home. Bonnet had no trouble in charming the younger housemaids to keep the guards—should he say—*distracted*, whilst Bonnet and Herriot crawled through one of the windows. At well-past midnight, Nathaniel and his wife were fast asleep. As was most of the small town. Only the distant sound of a pianoforte and the lap of waves met Bonnet's ears.

Halting, he looked both ways before crossing the empty street, then proceeded to slip beneath the palisades at Vanderhorst Creek. The stink of fish and brine swamped him as he crept in the darkness toward the gurgle of water slapping the shore. Finally, a canoe, along with three men who stood in the sand, came into view.

God bless Tookerman! Bonnet halted as—without saying a word—two of the slaves leapt into the boat whilst the other gestured for them to follow.

"I told you we could trust Tookerman," Bonnet whispered to Herriot as they settled on the rocking thwarts of the craft.

Herriot only grunted as the last slave shoved the boat from the shore and leapt in.

Bonnet smiled. Richard Tookerman was one of the city's richest merchants who had grown wealthy off smuggled pirate goods. 'Twas he who, with a wink and a nod, had offered his services to Bonnet during a visit at the provost's house. How could Bonnet resist?

In truth, at the moment, he couldn't stop smiling, not even when they rowed halfway into the harbor and a chilled northeasterly wind blasted over them. Shivering, he drew up the shawl, but he didn't mind the cold. That, along with the teeter of the boat, the splash of waves, and the smell of the sea—all combined into the sounds and senses of freedom. Free at last!

He peered into the darkness and spotted his ship, *Royal James,* at anchor at Rhett's wharf. Like a long-lost lover, he mourned the loss of her. They had enjoyed many adventures together, along with many defeats. Would he ever captain her again? Perhaps not.

His gaze shifted to the fading buildings of Charles Town as his thoughts shifted to Melody. "I shall return for you, my love," he whispered, but the wind soon swept his words away.

Melody pressed the letter to her bosom and thanked Mrs. Partridge for being discreet. 'Twas obvious Bonnet had charmed the lady, but who could blame her? Stede had a captivating way about him that was undeniably alluring.

The elder lady patted her coiffure and smiled. "I didn't wish it to fall in the wrong hands, Miss Rogers, if you know what I mean."

Melody's father, for one.

Nodding, Melody turned to leave the provost's home when Nathaniel Partridge stormed through the front door and tossed down his hat. Barely acknowledging Melody's presence, or perhaps unaware of it, he shouted, "I've been relieved of my position! Can you believe it?"

Mrs. Partridge gripped her hands together. "You are no longer provost?"

"Replaced by that imbecile, Conyers." He marched to the sideboard and poured himself a drink.

Quite unlike the provost to imbibe in spirits, especially at this early hour. Melody should leave this personal exchange between husband and wife, but she couldn't move, so desperate was she for any news of Stede.

"Ridiculous!" Mrs. Partridge took a step toward her husband but hesitated at the fury on his face. "Why would the governor do such a thing? Bonnet's escape had naught to do with you!"

Nathaniel tossed the drink to the back of his throat and set down the glass so loud, Melody jumped. "The governor thinks otherwise, my dear. At best, he finds me negligent, at worst complicit."

"Unheard of! This is madness."

Nathaniel strode to the window, where midmorning sun enhanced the lines of age and exhaustion on his face.

"Governor Johnson has ordered a search with hue and cries, expressed by land and water through the entire province. And a seven-hundred-pound sterling reward for Bonnet's capture."

Melody flung a hand to her throat.

"Seven-hundred pounds," Mrs. Partridge exclaimed. "My, my." She approached her husband and leaned her head on his shoulder. Flinging an arm around her, he drew her close.

Melody had heard enough. Neither of the Partridges seemed aware of her presence. Hence, she slipped out the door and onto the street, where she was joined by her companion.

With such an enormous reward, everyone in town would be looking for Stede.

November 5, 1718, Charles Town

My beloved Stede,

I shan't know whether I will ever send this letter nor to what address I would post it if I could, but I feel compelled to write you, nonetheless, of the proceedings which have occurred in Charles Town these past days. Yet, I have another, more selfish reason for writing to you that I dare not admit, for it does no credit to my rational mind. Speaking to you, if only with pen and parchment, makes me feel as though you are near, and I find myself longing to see your face and feel your arms around me during this precarious time.

Allow me to explain. Four days after you escaped, the Vice-Admiralty court convened here in town to try your fellow pirates. Though I was hesitant to witness the proceedings for fear of finding them overly alarming, I attended for your benefit, Stede, for I knew you would be anxious to be informed of the fate of your men.

The court itself is a spurious imitation of justice. One judge, ten assistant judges, the attorney general, and assistant attorney general all sat upon a bench staring down at your men as if they were but rodents to be squashed beneath one's boots. The pirates were denied legal counsel and were given a jury of twenty-three, all who had prejudices against them. Four eyewitnesses testified, including Ignatius Pell, that traitorous dog whom I met at the provost's home, Captain Peter Manwareing of the *Francis,* his first mate James Killing, and Captain Thomas Read of the *Fortune.*

That infamous Judge Nicholas Trott presided, a most heinous and despicable man, if I am permitted my opinion, which rarely occurs. I have no doubt you have heard of him, a self-righteous princock, who lords it over those beneath him and abuses the privileges God has granted him. I am ashamed to say that he is also a friend of my father's.

You may be proud to hear that all thirty-three of your pirates pleaded not guilty, though each had little defense. One man, a Robert Tucker, stepped forward and explained in great detail how you, my dearest, wished to sail to St. Thomas for the Emperor's commission, but due to lack of provisions, was forced back into piracy. Though I recall you did not like the man, 'twould seem he attempted to defend you in the end. However, 'twas when Captain Manwareing and Captain Read gave their testimonies that the most damage was done.

I shall spare you any further details, but suffice it to say that twenty-nine of your men were found guilty. The other four were able to convince the court that you had forced them into piracy on pain of death. Alas, the last words Judge Trott spoke still ring in my ears, giving me nightmares. "You shall go from hence to the place from whence you came, and from thence the place of execution, where you shall be severally hanged by the neck, till you are severally dead."

My dearest, I suffer through these long nights in agonizing prayer for you, that you are safe and well and receiving your pardon at this very moment. I long to see you again.

Soon,
Yours always,

Melody

CHAPTER THIRTY-ONE

On the walk home from work, Lexie's mind and heart spun from Bonnet's and Melody's letters. Melody, no doubt, had never posted her letter, or it wouldn't have been included in the batch handed down through the years. Regardless, Lexie was glad for the chance to peek into the lady's heart.

Taking a deep breath, she smiled. She loved this time of day when the sun sheepishly peeked over the horizon, dew littered the ground, and the air smelled fresh and pure as if the world had a janitor like her who stayed up all night to sweep and clean. So few people were out, that the city seemed to breathe a sigh of relief at the silence. Even Barret remained quiet all the way home. Another thing she admired about him. He seemed to sense when to speak and when to enjoy the peace.

"How about we stop by and pick up some donuts for Tracy and Ellie?" Barret broke the silence, tossing her compliment to the wind. But she wasn't annoyed. Donuts sounded like the perfect idea.

The bodyguard Barret had hired to watch the house thought so too as Barret handed him a maple bar through his car window. The man thanked him, announced he'd return same time tomorrow, and then sped off as Barret and Lexie mounted the steps to the townhome. Matt would no doubt be arriving soon to keep watch over them during the day. Guilt assailed her at the money Barret was spending on security, but she knew it was pointless to try and change his mind.

No sooner had he unlocked and opened the front door, than Ellie came bouncing down the hallway and leapt into his arms. Taking the wobbling box of donuts from his hand, Lexie quickly shut the door, punched in the alarm code, then stood smiling at the way Barret embraced the young girl and how her little hands wrapped around his neck. What a great father he would be. She swallowed down a burst of emotion at the longing in her heart to have had such a father herself.

"And just what are you doing up so early, my little princess?" He kissed her cheek.

She giggled. "I'm not a princess. I'm a fairy."

"Oh no. I don't think fairies eat donuts, do they?" He glanced at Lexie, pretending alarm. "Only princesses can eat donuts."

Ellie's eyes widened in horror before she flattened her lips. "But fairy princesses can eat donuts. And that's what I am!"

Barret chuckled and set her down. "Of course."

Ellie ran down the hall to the kitchen. "Mommy, Mommy, Lexie and Barret brought donuts!"

Barret winked at Lexie and gave her that smile that would melt a thousand hearts.

Once in the kitchen, he opened a cupboard, no doubt seeking paper plates or napkins. Instead, he pulled out a pirate ship. "What be this?" He glanced at Ellie. "Hidin' yer pirate ship, little one?"

Giggling, she grabbed it from him and said, "Avast, ye may be gettin' wet!"

"Good job, my little pirate." He swept her up in his arms again as Tracy offered an apology.

"No need," he said, setting the little girl down. "This is your home."

The four of them enjoyed their donuts over coffee, hot cocoa, and laughter. The sorrow Lexie had sensed earlier in Barret seemed to fade as he grew increasingly excited every time he looked at Tracy. Finally, shoving away his half-eaten second donut, he faced her.

"I have some good news, Tracy."

She looked up from wiping crumbs off Ellie's face. "Yes?"

Lexie could hardly keep from leaping off her seat at what she knew Barret would say.

"There is a fulltime position for you at Charleston Southern University as a childcare preschool assistant. That is, if you want it."

Silence, except for the drip of the facet infiltrated the dining room. Tracy blinked. Several times, in fact... as if she were trying to wake up. "What?" she finally said.

"A job." Barret smiled. "You know, you work and they pay you?"

"For me?"

He nodded. "The department head owed me a favor. It's all yours if you want it. And it includes free childcare for Ellie."

Trace jumped up, circled the table, and all but leapt into Barret's lap, squealing like a girl who had just been proposed to. "Thank you! Thank you! Thank you!"

"Whoa." Barret hugged her, a look of shock on his face. "You're very welcome."

Lexie's heart nearly burst for joy at the scene as Tracy stepped back and shook her head. "Why would you be so kind to me?"

Barret gave a confused look. "Why wouldn't I?"

Tracy lowered her chin as tears spilled down her cheeks. "I don't know what to say."

Rising, Lexie gave her a hug. "Told you it would be all right." They both laughed and cried together.

Barret reached into his pocket and pulled out a card. He handed it to Tracy. "Just contact this lady, and she'll arrange a time for you to come in, meet her, and fill out the paperwork."

Taking the card, Tracy kissed it. Then turning, she kissed Barret on the cheek. "You are a prince among men."

Lexie quite agreed. Gathering the empty cups and plates from the table, she started for the kitchen.

"Let me do that," Tracy said. "You've been working all night. Go on to bed. I'll get this."

"Thanks, Trace." Lexie set the dishes on the counter. Exhaustion weighed heavy on her eyelids, on her entire body for that matter. She hated working graveyard. Everyone she loved was awake during the day. If only she could find that treasure.

"Yeah, let's get you to bed." Barret rose from his chair.

Tracy raised a brow and grinned.

"I mean, let me tuck you in...." His face grew red. "Oh, never mind. You know what I mean." He tousled Ellie's hair as she played with one of her fairies, and then escorted Lexie upstairs.

As Lexie emerged from the bathroom in her pj's and crawled into bed, she realized it might not be the best idea to have Barret in her bedroom, not the way she was currently feeling about him. Part of her wished he'd make his move, like so many other men in her life had done, but part of her knew she'd be disappointed if he did.

Barret sat on the bed and raised his brows. "Some letters we read tonight, eh?"

"I loved hearing from Melody. I didn't realize she'd written some of them. Did you learn anything cool for your book?" She was babbling like a nervous teenager with him so close. Thankfully, he didn't seem to notice.

He nodded, his eyes lighting up as they usually did when he spoke of history. "Amazing details that have never been known."

"I'm glad they are helping you."

"I wish they'd give you what you want as well."

"I *do* need the money, Barret. Yet I find myself more caught up in Bonnet's story than worrying about the treasure. Weird, isn't it?"

"No, I guess he has a way of affecting people even three hundred years later, especially the ladies," he teased.

Commotion sounded from downstairs. It sounded like the front door opened and several people entered.

Footsteps pounded up the stairs, and Barret's father appeared in the open doorway.

"I should have figured you'd be here, polluting my bed with this whore!"

Barret stood, fury raging through his veins. "How dare you say such a thing? How dare you come barging in here like this?"

Judge Gregory Johnson stepped forward, his eyes aflame. "How dare *I*? This is my house! I asked you to get rid of these vagrants and what do I find instead? You here sleeping with one of them. Committing a sin right in my bed!" His angry gaze swept over Lexie as if she were nothing but a pesky gnat.

Barret fisted his hands, trying to stop from slugging his own father. He wanted to explain that Lexie had worked all night, that Barret was only tucking her in, but he knew what it looked like, and to say otherwise would be fruitless. One glance at Lexie revealed a myriad of emotions on her face—fear, shock, and anger among them. Barret stepped in front of her, blocking her from his father's view. "You are wrong, Father. About many things. But what good has it ever done to tell you?" Fury burned in his father's eyes—a fury that Barret had shrunk from all his life. But no more. "Can we take this downstairs?"

"By all means," his father hissed. "Pack your things, Miss Cain. You're leaving today," he added before he stormed out.

Turning toward Lexie, Barret knelt and took her trembling hands in his. "Don't worry. Let me deal with this."

"I'm so sorry, Barret. I should never have moved in here." Her green eyes shifted between his, fear and sorrow streaking across them.

Which only angered him more. "It's not your fault." He kissed her hands, then went downstairs where his father awaited him in the front living room. Tracy and Ellie sat on the couch while a policeman stood by the bay window.

"The police, Father, really?"

"I didn't know what I would find or whether I needed help to get rid of them. Honestly, Barret, what has gotten into you lately? Ever since you met that…that *woman* upstairs."

Ellie dislodged from her mother and ran to Barret

He drew her up into his arms and pressed her head against his shoulders, wishing he could close the girl's ears as well. "Are you going to arrest this poor woman and her child?"

His father stared at him with disgust. "Are you involved with this one too? Is this a homeless shelter or a harem?"

"That's enough, Father! Tracy is a friend who needed a place to stay. I already told you that. There is nothing sinful going on here."

Movement behind him caused Barret to glance over his shoulder. Lexie, fully dressed, with suitcase in hand, entered the room. Running to Tracy, she sat beside her and took her hand in hers. A look of sorrow and shame passed between them.

"Nothing sinful, you say? Not buying it, Barret. I raised you better. You *know* better. Fornication is a sin, along with disobeying your parents. I explicitly ordered you to get rid of these people."

Ellie trembled in his arms and gazed up at him. "Why is that man so mad, Barret?"

Barret hugged her tight. "Can we not speak this way in front of the child, please?"

Standing, Tracy moved to take Ellie from Barret's arms and faced his father with all the dignity and kindness of a saint. "I'm sorry for any trouble we have caused you, sir. I will go pack and leave immediately."

"I'll help." Lexie started after her, but Barret's father raised a hand. "No. You are the cause of this, and I want you to hear what I have to say."

She hesitated, staring at the judge as if pondering whether to obey. Good for her. Finally, she remained but did not sit back down.

Barret faced his father. "You only told me yesterday to toss them out. How are they supposed to find a place so soon?'

"I don't care. Lazy drug addicts do not deserve to live in such luxury, son. You are only enabling them to continue. The Apostle Paul said in 2nd Thessalonians that if a man doesn't work, he shouldn't eat."

"What the heck?" Lexie shook her head in disgust. "I have a fulltime job."

"Then why are you and your friend mooching off my son?" He snickered. "Ah, unless you are giving him special favors in return."

"That's it!" Barret charged his father with the full intent of striking him, but the policeman, no doubt a new recruit, stepped in his way.

"You're going to hit me now?" For the first time in Barret's life, the man looked truly alarmed. "When I'm only here to protect you? This woman is not only enticing you to an eternity in hell, but she is putting you in danger. Your very life! I will not have it. At least not in my own home!" He stormed through the room like a raging bull, examining every vase, book, and knick-knack.

"Mr. Johnson. I will leave today. There's no need for this anger toward your son. And for the record, we are not sleeping together."

"And I'm to believe *you*?" he spat without turning around.

Barret went to stand beside Lexie, taking her hand in his and offering her a look of comfort. "Don't worry," he whispered. She smiled in return, a tender smile, a sad smile. He would sweep her far away from here this minute if he could, but he knew from experience that it was best to allow his father this moment of anger. They were, after all, in his home, against his wishes. Once the man had exhausted his fury, Barret would take the ladies and find another safe place for them. No harm done, except to his relationship with his father, and after his embarrassing and cruel display, Barret doubted it would ever heal.

"Aha! It's missing!" Judge Johnson spun on his heels, a look of gloating victory on his face.

Barret released a heavy sigh. "What are you talking about?"

"The French tureen. It's gone!" His father gestured toward the shelf where the antique had been. Empty.

Barret gulped.

"Do you know how much that was worth?" his father continued? "Silver crafted for King Louis XV?"

A slow wave of terror spread from Barret's heart, across his chest, down his arms and legs until numbed shock took over. Visions of how much Lexie had admired that particular antique when they'd first arrived played over and over in his mind. He remembered how her eyes had lit up as she examined it. What was the one thing she wanted most in the world? Treasure, money, wealth!

He glanced down at her.

"What?" Her forehead wrinkled. "*I* didn't take it. Why are you looking at me like that?" Pulling her hand from his, she stepped away.

"Go search the other woman's things," Barret's father ordered the policeman, who immediately rushed out. "Let's see what's in your suitcase, Miss Cain."

Confusion stomped through Barret's mind.

"I didn't take it." Lexie repeated in a stronger tone, her glance shifting between Barret and his father. "I'm not a thief."

The judge moved toward her, his penetrating eyes full of censure. "Not according to your police record, miss. Now, shall we?" He gestured toward her suitcase. "Or did you already hock it like the bracelet my son gave you?"

A sharp pain jabbed Barret's heart, a palpable pain. He glanced at Lexie. Hocked it? "You…what?" He longed for her to deny it, tell him it was a mistake, reach into her backpack and pull it out as proof.

But she didn't. Instead, she looked down and bit her lip. "I'm sorry, Barret. It was…it was worth so much… it could feed so many." She glanced at him, moisture in her eyes.

The judge snorted. "I told you she was a thieving liar, only after your money."

But his father's words spun more confusion in his already bewildered thoughts, and he found he couldn't form a coherent sentence.

"I gave it to the women's shelter," she offered, pleading in her gaze, pleading to be believed. But could he?

"Sure you did, missy," the judge said. "Now, where's the tureen?"

Ignoring him, she frowned at Barret. "You don't believe me, do you? I didn't take the tureen. Neither did Tracy."

Barret stepped back and shifted his gaze out the window, too stunned, too confused to speak.

His father got up in Lexie's face. "Nevertheless, we will search all your things. Then afterward, you and your girlfriend will leave and never come back."

CHAPTER THIRTY-TWO

*I*n those magical, waking seconds when one's mind slinks down the long tunnel of slumber toward the bright light of consciousness, Lexie caught a glimpse of pain awaiting her. Desperately, she retreated, clinging to the sweet bliss of sleep.

Yet the more she clung, the more her grip loosened until, finally awake, all the pain of Barret's betrayal crashed over her. It was bad enough he had not defended her to his father, but he truly believed she was capable of stealing. From him! He had not denied the accusation or blown it off as ridiculous. In fact, he had looked at her with all the doubt and condemnation of a prosecutor. Being tossed from her home, being called a criminal and a slut, both were nothing compared to the pain of Barret's treason. Yes, treason. Because one didn't treat someone they loved that way. They gave them the benefit of the doubt. They trusted before they accused.

She was a fool. A sucker for a handsome face and a charming pirate. Just like her ancestor, Melody. And look where that had gotten her. Alone, pregnant, and impoverished.

Sitting up, Lexie rubbed her eyes and headed for the tiny kitchenette. She tripped on something and stumbled, glancing back to see Thomas the Train, one of Ellie's toys, lying in the middle of the small living area. She smiled, stretched, and took the last two steps. Though Lexie was thrilled for Tracy, she missed Ellie now that Tracy was taking her to work every day. At least Barret had kept his word about the job at the university.

After they'd all been tossed out of the townhome, it hadn't taken long to find this rental in an extended stay hotel, complete with a single bedroom, living area, one bathroom, and small kitchen. It was all they could afford until Tracy got her first couple of pay checks. After that, they would look for a two-bedroom apartment.

Lexie poured boiling water into the mug and stirred, glancing over the living area that was smaller than her bedroom at the townhome. In the corner stood a day bed, covered with rumpled sheets and blankets where Tracy and Ellie slept, while strewn across the carpet were toys and clothes and dirty plates from last night's dinner. Quite the culture shock from where they'd come from, but Lexie had lived in worse.

Taking a sip of her cocoa, she savored the sweet chocolate taste and glanced at the clock on the stove. 4:30 p.m. She had only an hour to shower and eat something before Matt showed up. Another thing Barret had kept his word about. For the past three nights, Matt had both walked her to work and back home, while another bodyguard sat outside their hotel during the day. How Barret had found them, Lexie could only guess. Perhaps Adam had traced her phone again. Either way, she didn't want to accept his protection anymore. Not if he thought her a thief. But she had Tracy and Ellie to think about. Besides, she'd spotted men following her again, lurking around corners, staring at her from a distance. They wouldn't try and shoot her. At least she had that assurance. They were after the letters, and they needed her alive and well until they had them.

Which they never would. If only Lexie could find the treasure! Then the letters would be meaningless to these scumbags, and she could put the treasure in a bank or vault somewhere. This nightmare would be over, the fear, the looking over her shoulders, her uncertain future.

And spending time with Barret.

One thing she knew for sure. She would never trust another man. Ever. She would never allow her heart to be broken again.

Finishing her cocoa, she headed toward the shower. Tonight she would read another letter or maybe two or three. She hoped she wouldn't need Barret's expertise to decipher any further clues. No. She didn't need him. She would find the treasure without him.

She had no choice.

November 9, 1718, Charles Town, Guard House Dungeon

Dearest, most precious Melody,

I write to you with great dismay and despair. You have no doubt heard that I have been captured yet again, but instead of being imprisoned in the comforts of a respectable home, I find myself in the dungeon. I can hardly blame those in charge, my dear, but 'tis most disagreeable here. Rats and refuse abound, along with ill-tempered, illiterate men who reek worse than bilge water. 'Tis hell on earth, my love, but allow me to regale you with the tale of how I came to be here....

Bonnet lowered his pen, thankful the guards had granted him his request of quill and parchment with which to write his lady love. His thoughts drifted to the western end of Sullivan's Island, where he and Herriot and Tookerman's slaves had been forced to take refuge from the cold nor'easter which had blown in upon them rather suddenly. Strong, icy winds that cut like a razor had prevented them from rowing any farther in search of Moody's ship.

On the final day upon that ill-fated island, Bonnet tossed another log onto their fire and then squatted, reaching out his hands to the heat.

Across the flames, Herriot peered from the blanket he huddled beneath. "'Tis been ten days, Bonnet and still no sign of Moody. How long are we to rot away on this bug-infested island with naught to eat, shivering to our bones?"

Bonnet frowned. Wind whipped over him as if to prove Herriot's words, and he lifted up the edges of an overcoat that did little against the cold. At least he'd thought to bring a change of attire, or he would have been forced to wear a woman's gown the entire time. Ignoring Herriot's constant complaining, Bonnet stood and lifted his scope toward Charles Town. Dozens of merchant ships hugged the walls of the city—ships that would be able to travel in these stormy conditions but would hesitate if a pirate loomed offshore— which gave him hope that Captain Moody still lurked nearby. He would not give up. He could give up. Moody was his only chance of survival.

Moving away from the fire toward the ocean side of the island, Bonnet scanned the horizon as he did several times a day, searching for any sign of Captain Moody and his ships. Naught but a sheet of blue sprinkled with white-capped waves met his view. He sighed and lowered his glass, started to pray, but thought better of it.

"Surrender at once!" The command came from behind him, jerking every nerve to alert. Reaching for the long knife stuffed in his belt, he spun about to see at least a dozen armed men approaching from the back of the island, Colonel William Rhett in the lead. Mewling popinjay! How had Bonnet not heard him? And where was the man he'd put on guard?

Before Bonnet could determine what to do, a shot rang through the air. From whom, he had no idea, but the result was a barrage of musket fire assailing them from all around. Bonnet dove behind a rock, wishing he'd brought his pistol. Gunsmoke filled the air and his lungs as shots whizzed past him. A moan. A scream. And then all went silent.

"Come out to meet your fate, Bonnet. 'Tis over," Rhett shouted.

Bonnet peered over the rock, his worst fears realized. Two of the slaves were on the ground, moaning in pain from bloody wounds while Herriot lay by the fire, still as the doldrums. Rhett and his men had reloaded their muskets and stood at the ready.

Bonnet was surrounded.

Rising with all the dignity he could gather, he held his hands aloft and walked to where Herriot lay. Shot through the head, his friend stared vacantly into space.

And that is how I lost my good friend, my dear. That is to say, as good a friend as I have had this past year. I mourn him deeply as I sit here in the filth and squalor. My only encouragement is that he has been spared the horrors of this place, along with the humiliation and agony of a public hanging. Which I suppose to be my fate now, my precious one, for only yesterday twenty-nine of my crew were forcibly hauled from this dungeon to be paraded about town and hanged at White Point. I have no doubt you heard of these horrid events, and I pray you were not present to view such barbarity. 'Twas my utmost horror to witness many of them weeping like babes, begging for their lives, while others trembled incessantly, or vomited the meager food they'd been served. Wide, terror-streaked eyes stared at me as they were dragged out of my cell. Brave men, ruthless pirates all, reduced to squealing poltroons in the face of an enemy that comes for us all one day—death.

At that moment, my dear, I would have done anything to spare them such an ending. At that moment, I wished more than anything I had not encouraged their crimes, had not influenced their debauchery, for will not the Almighty hold me even more guilty than they?

These thoughts consume and torment me in the darkest hours of the night. Was there a better course for my life? A better option for happiness?

One in which God would, indeed, smile down upon me?

I am at a loss whether to ask you my next question. I feel as though I will die if I do not see you soon. Yet, I do not wish you to witness this place, nor see me in this condition. There is yet one small hope, my love. I hear Captain Moody still lurks outside Charles Town Harbor and that your governor has sent four vessels to capture him. Should Moody, by God's merciful grace, win against their forces and enter town a victor, he will surely release me from my shackles.

Let us both cling to that hope. Pray for me, my love.

I am forever yours,

Stede

Bonnet dusted the ink, blew it off, and sealed his letter. He had no idea if Melody would receive it, or if her father had grown suspicious and intercepted her correspondences. But he had to try. He must hear from her or he feared he'd go mad.

The thunder of distant cannons shook the cell walls, raining dust onto his head. The battle had begun over an hour ago, and ever since, Bonnet had prayed, pleading with God for Moody to be victorious. Though praying for a pirate's success would surely damn Bonnet to hell, what was he to lose if that was to be his end anyway? Perhaps God would find a shred of mercy for him, after all.

Rising from his seat, he moved to the iron bars, the shackles on his feet clanging over the cold stone. He called the guard and handed him the letter to Melody as another cannon blast roared in the distance. He was about to return to his seat when shouts and jubilant cheers rose from what sounded to be quite a crowd above him on the ramparts of Half-Moon Battery.

"A plague on it!" he cursed. That could only mean one thing. Moody had been defeated.

Only it wasn't Captain Moody, but a Captain Worley and his crew who soon joined Bonnet in the dungeon. Thirty of them in fact, many horribly wounded. Their cries and moans throughout the long night only reminded Bonnet that all hope was lost.

⚓

Barret couldn't remember a time when he'd been more miserable. Ever since his father had accused Lexie of thievery and tossed her from the townhome, he'd been unable to sleep, unable to eat, barely able to think. Now, at two in the morning, he found himself wandering around the townhome in the dark like he had the past two nights. Why? He couldn't say except Lexie's presence lingered here, her laughter bubbled through the halls, her smile appeared before him in visions—brief and fading. He even smelled her sweet vanilla scent. But that couldn't be. His father had hired a crew of maids to sanitize the place from floor to ceiling.

Still… just being here brought him a speck of comfort, helped to clear his mind so he could figure out what had happened. He dropped onto the living room couch and ran his hand over the soft cushion, remembering how they'd slept all night in this very spot, arm in arm. Had he been so smitten by her, so overcome by her beauty and fascinating personality that he'd not seen she was just a common thief?

He shook his head and rubbed the back of his neck. It just didn't make sense. If she took the tureen, why was she still in town? Surely with such a treasure in hand, she'd leave, seek out whatever criminal contacts she had, and find a buyer for it. She wouldn't continue working as a janitor, cleaning up other people's slop. Would she? Most likely Bonnet's treasure would be nothing compared to the value of that tureen. Yet she remained. A ploy to deceive? If so, she was a smart one. He'd give her that.

Moonlight spun silver eddies through the bay window, giving the room a milky, ethereal appearance. A vision of little Ellie twirling and dancing, armful of fairies, made Barret smile. He missed her. He missed them all. He missed opening a cabinet or drawer and finding a toy hidden inside.

Wait.

Ellie liked to hide things.

Punching to his feet, Barret glanced at the empty spot in the case where the tureen had been, then around the room. Hope daring to rise, he began opening every drawer and cabinet. He shoved his hands behind stacks of books. He opened the coat closet in the hall. Nothing. He was being foolish, of course.

Breathing hard, he entered the living room again. A strange light, more golden than the moonlight, filtered in through the window, catching his eye. Perhaps from a streetlight? Still, it seemed to land on the bay window seat, hover there for a minute, and then disappear.

Barret didn't hesitate. Charging forward, he shoved the pillows aside and lifted the seat. Only darkness met his gaze from inside the storage compartment. He plucked his phone from his pocket and turned on the flashlight.

There, at the bottom of the chamber, the silver tureen winked at him in the light.

CHAPTER THIRTY-THREE

*S*itting cross-legged on the floor of the dungeon, Lexie set the letter she'd just read gently in her lap. Fighting back tears, she gazed at Bonnet, wondering if the pose they'd put him in was the very one he took when news of Moody's defeat reached his ears. Shackles gripped his ankles and arms as he leaned his head on one hand, a look of despair on his face.

She had the sudden urge to find the key, free him from his chains, and help him escape on a ship. Silly girl! She was getting too involved, cared for him too much, felt his pirate blood racing through her veins. She could understand his need for true love, his need to be free, his need for wealth. She felt all those same desires. Was she then doomed to the same fate as he? Was there no other course for all those born from his blood? It would seem so if her family history was any indication. What she didn't know was whether the path of her life was set in stone. Or were there multiple paths from which to choose? Did God exist? And if so, wouldn't He lead His children down the right path?

Bonnet believed in God. Nearly everyone in that era had. Why, then, hadn't the Almighty directed Bonnet's steps?

A knock rapped on the back door. Lexie looked at the clock. 4:00 A.M. It couldn't be Matt. He never came before her quitting time at six. Besides, she still had cleaning to do.

Ignoring it, she slipped the letter back into the folder and rose to her feet.

The knock came again. This time followed by a deep voice she never thought to hear again.

"Lexie, you there? Open up. It's me."

She froze, angry that Barret's voice made her heart leap and sent a thrill down to her toes. Pushing those sensations aside, she marched to the door. "Aren't you afraid I might steal something from you?"

Silence answered her, followed by a sigh. "Will you let me come in and apologize?"

Lexie bit her lip. No way. She shouldn't. If she did, she'd be allowing him to break her heart all over again. Silently cursing herself for her weakness, she unlocked the door and swung it open.

Dark eyes, full of remorse met hers. Coarse stubble—at least two days' worth—peppered his jaw and chin. A coffee stain spread down his rumpled t-shirt, dirt clung to his jeans, and his black hair hung wild about him. He looked terrible.... yet so incredibly wonderful that she stepped aside to let him enter. "Are you okay?"

"No." He raked back his hair and walked to Bonnet's cell while she locked the door.

Concerned that he'd been attacked again, she followed him.

"You read another letter?" He gestured toward the folder in her hand.

She set it down on a barrel. "Yes."

He gave a half-smile and nodded. "Listen, Lexie. I've been a real jerk."

She certainly couldn't argue with that. Still, she waited, studying him for any sign of sincerity. She felt like she knew him well enough to tell, but then again, he'd fooled her once.

Even so, the man who was always so well put together, both in appearance and attitude, stood there looking like he was homeless and had lost all hope.

"I found the tureen." He swallowed. "In the bay window seat."

Ah. Ellie, of course. Lexie couldn't help but smile. Anger soon replaced her joy. She placed a hand on her hip. "Well, you better hurry to our apartment and arrest a three-year old girl!"

He frowned. "I deserved that."

"You actually thought I stole it. Admit it."

His sad eyes met hers. "Honestly, I didn't know what to think. I knew money meant a great deal to you, and you admired that tureen so much."

She withheld an unladylike growl. "And you thought so little of me, *knew* me so little, that you thought I would do such a horrible thing? Betray you like that?" She fisted hands at her sides until her fingers ached. "How could you? After all we've meant to each other."

Barret lowered his chin. "Like I said, I'm a jerk."

His admission, along with the remorse in his eyes, softened Lexie's anger. She leaned back onto a barrel. "You hurt me, Barret."

"I'm so sorry, Sunshine. I never meant to. I hope you can forgive me." Looking up, he took a step toward her. "I got hurt too. I thought you'd betrayed me. My heart nearly broke when I learned you hocked the bracelet I gave you."

His heart broke? "You told me it was mine, to do with as I wished. I didn't know there were conditions."

"That's fair." He rubbed his chin and took another step toward her. "I meant it as a gift of my love for you."

Love? She huffed. "Love thinks no evil, bears all things, believes all things, hopes all things, endures all things."

He smiled. "You've read the Bible?"

She crossed arms over her chest. "My mother quoted it a lot toward the end." Still, love or no love, Barret had meant the bracelet as a special gift to show his love, and she'd tossed it away.

He flattened his lips. "Did you really give the money to the women's shelter? Sorry, but I have to know."

The rage that had nearly abated fired up again. "Still don't trust me?" She stood and pointed toward the door. "I think you should leave, Barret. I have work to do. And you can cancel your bodyguards. I don't want your help anymore."

Why had Barret gone and said such a dumb thing? Right when he sensed Lexie's fury diminishing, when he sensed she might accept his apology. Stupid, stupid man!

She stood there, lips pursed, eyes sharp, gesturing toward the door as if she couldn't stand the sight of him.

Barret didn't blame her. But he couldn't move. He didn't want to leave. He feared if he did, she'd never listen to him again. "I shouldn't have said that. It was your money to spend."

Her forehead wrinkled. "Do you think I spent it on myself?" She blew out a sigh. "You really don't know me. The shelter was short on food and clothing, and some of the staff had been forced to take salary cuts."

A wave of shame struck Barret. Hard. A slap of reality that suddenly woke him from a deceptive dream he'd been living his entire life. He should have known. This wonderful woman cared more for others than anyone he'd ever met. His "I'm sorry" sounded pathetic, even to his own ears.

"Whatever, Barret." She picked up a broom. "Please leave."

"You going to chase me out with a broom?" He grinned, attempting to lighten the mood.

It worked. A tiny smile lifted her lips before she responded. "If I have to."

"Listen, Lexie. Like I said, I'm a jerk. Can you just give me a couple of minutes to explain and apologize? Then if you still want me to leave, I will."

Brushing a strand of hair from her face, she studied him, pondering his fate with eyes that suddenly grew moist.

It was then that Barret saw the true depth of pain he had caused her. This was not a woman who opened her heart easily to anyone, let alone a man. Yet she had taken a chance with him. And he had let her down like everyone else. Now he wanted more than anything to take her in his arms, wipe away her tears, and heal her heart with his love. But he knew she wouldn't receive him. Not yet.

And that broke his heart most of all.

She leaned on her broom. "Go ahead. I'll listen. But I've got work to do."

Barret would take what he could get. Drawing a deep breath, he began talking, using his words to sort out the brew of confusion churning in his gut. "I was raised a certain way. My parents were strict and religious. I can't think of a Sunday or Wednesday that we weren't in church."

Lexie began sweeping the floor, and he wondered if she was even listening. Still, he continued. "They loved us kids and never denied us any luxury or privilege. My father was strict, but I always knew he only wanted the best for me. He taught me to live a moral, honorable life as the Bible says. No lying, cheating, stealing, sleeping around, no drinking to excess, no cussing, no tattoos."

He said that last thing to see if she was listening, and sure enough, she glanced his way. "No wonder they hated me."

He wanted to deny it, but he couldn't. They might not actually hate her, but his father sure behaved as if he did. Which brought Barret back to his... whatever this was... confession?

"Since I was a child, I have respected my parents, been proud of them, felt blessed to be their son. I always thought they were such good Christians. Look at my father. He's an elder at our church, good friends with the pastor, an honorable member of Charleston society and a well-respected judge. But what I didn't realize about him—and about my mom—was that they aren't good people at all. Honestly, I'm starting to wonder if they are even Christians—if they are truly saved." Barret leaned against the brick wall, no longer speaking directly to Lexie, but more to himself. "I wonder if I even am."

He heard movement and Lexie appeared before him, staring up at him curiously. "Why would you say such a thing?"

Barret shook his head. "Because I actually *did* read the Bible for myself. Long ago, but the entire thing. And I see nothing in my parent's behavior that indicates they know God at all."

Lexie frowned and went back to sweeping. "They are a lot better than my family. You're being too hard on them."

Barret could hardly believe his ears. His parents had been nothing but cruel to her, and here she was defending them. Amazing. Maybe they hadn't committed crimes, maybe they'd followed all of God's commandments, but for what purpose? To appear righteous? To be admired? To gain a ticket to heaven? *Or* because they loved God? Which was the only reason that mattered. He'd always believed God had blessed his family because of their faithfulness, but it suddenly dawned on him that God had blessed them *despite* their wayward hearts.

"You have more love in your heart for others, Lexie, than they ever had. Good deeds mean nothing to God unless they spring from our love for Him, from our relationship with Jesus."

Halting, Lexie leaned on the handle of her broom and glanced his way. "Maybe you should have been a preacher, not a professor," she teased with a smile. "But aren't you Christians supposed to follow a bunch of rules? I thought that's what it was about. Being good and following God."

"No. That's just it. It's not about being good enough or doing good enough. It's about having a relationship with Jesus. Once that relationship starts to grow, good deeds follow out of a changed heart. The church, at least most churches, have it backwards." Excitement rumbled through Barret as things he'd read in Scripture began to make sense. "That's why I doubt my parents know Jesus. They have no love in their heart. They do their good deeds before men to be recognized and admired. All this time…" Barret rubbed the back of his neck and took up a pace. "And me too." He halted and faced Lexie who stared at him bewildered. "How much of the good I've done has only been for myself in the end?"

"Don't be silly. You're a good man, Barret."

"I doubted you, Lexie, even though my heart said differently. I doubted you just like my father because you don't go to church, and you have tattoos and a criminal past, and sometimes you cuss. But you have the biggest heart of anyone I've known." He wanted to tell her to give her heart to Jesus, but sensed she was too overwhelmed to receive it at the moment.

He approached her. "Thank you."

"For what?"

"Without you coming into my life, I never would have seen this. I never would have seen I was just as fake a Christian as my parents." He closed his eyes and prayed silently, not caring what she thought. *Thank you, Jesus for this woman and for revealing this to me. I repent and submit wholeheartedly to you as my Lord and King from here on out.*

"You're praying?" She snickered, set aside the broom, and went to retrieve the dustpan.

Opening his eyes, he smiled. "The start of a long and wonderful relationship."

"Well, I'm not sure what all that was about, Barret, but I don't seem to be angry anymore." She returned and stared at him, her eyes shifting between his. "Actually, I've never seen you so humble. And there's a light in your eyes that wasn't there before."

Barret could only smile. "Does that mean you forgive me?"

She shrugged, knelt to sweep the dirt into the pan. "I can see how your upbringing caused you to doubt me. Heck, I probably would have doubted me too if I were in your shoes. So, I guess so."

A thrill surged through Barret and he reached out to embrace her.

"Not so quick, Professor." Rising, she slanted her lips. "It's going to take some time to trust you again. I still think we are too different, especially about all this religious stuff."

Nodding, Barret backed off. At least she had left the possibility open. "I can wait."

Lexie replaced the broom and pan in the janitor's closet and shut the door. Either she was completely insane or this man had secretly slipped a love potion into one of her drinks. She opted for the first reason since bad decisions seemed to be her family's specialty. Still, she could not deny that he'd delivered his apology—though given more like a sermon—with humility and remorse and like a man who'd had a true epiphany.

"So, tell me what the letter said." He gestured to the folder on the barrel where she'd left it.

"Bonnet got caught, and while he was right here in this very dungeon"—she glanced toward his cell—"he hoped some other pirate... Moody, I think, would come to his rescue. But I know that didn't happen, so I guess Moody was captured too."

"Worley. It ended up being a Captain Worley," Barret offered. "But yes. So how many more letters? We've got to be near the end."

"Just three." Lexie's heart suddenly felt like a brick. Three letters and her relationship with Bonnet would end. It already felt like she was losing a best friend.

"No hint of where he put the treasure?"

She shook her head. "You can look over the letter if you like, just in case he left a clue." She was beginning to wonder if he left Melody any hint at all. The poor woman had never found the treasure. But if there was no treasure and there were no clues, why was someone willing to kill to get their hands on these letters? Lexie rubbed her temples. Nothing made sense anymore.

Move the letters.

She opened her eyes to find Barret had picked up the folder and was glancing at the letter. "What did you say?"

He looked up. "Nothing."

She was hearing things. "I need to collect the trash and then I'm done." Moving past him, she quickly went upstairs to empty the garbage cans into one big sack, then started down again to dump the cans in the dungeon.

Move the letters.

The words came strong, short, and commanding. Yet Barret remained engrossed in reading the last letter.

Lexie must not be getting enough sleep.

The clock struck 6:00. Quitting time. Gathering the garbage, she traded the bags for the letter from Barret. "Do you mind tossing these into the dumpster? I'll meet you outside."

CHAPTER THIRTY-FOUR

*B*arret studied the syllabus he'd just put together for an Early Colonial History class he was teaching in the fall. One more small change… he clicked the mouse and highlighted the word he needed to delete. Gone. Now, to send it to his boss, the history department head, for review.

His phone buzzed. Hoping it was Lexie, he grabbed it and saw Adam's name across the screen.

"Yeah, Adam. What's up?"

"You better get over to Lexie's apartment."

"Why?" Barret was already on his feet, his stomach clenching.

"She's okay. But the museum was broken into last night."

Grabbing his keys, Barret dashed out the door and down the stairs to the faculty parking lot, phone still pressed to his ear. "But not her apartment?"

"No. She's fine, but they tried to break in there too. Your bodyguard was able to chase them off."

After clicking the fob to unlock his car, Barret leapt in the seat and fired it up, even as relief loosened the tightness in his chest.

"She's just a little shook up. Thought you should know."

"Thanks, bud. Appreciate it." Barret pressed the red button and tossed his phone onto the passenger seat as he swerved out of the parking lot. The museum broken into? He and Lexie had just been there a few hours ago. He glanced at the car clock. 9:00 a.m. Poor girl probably hadn't gotten any sleep yet either.

The trip was a blur of morning traffic, red lights, and extreme frustration. By the time he pulled into the parking lot, he felt like slugging someone. Not the best attitude and one that quickly dissipated when he charged through the open door of her apartment—if you could call the tiny, cluttered room that—and saw her face. Exhaustion coupled with fear tugged on her otherwise lovely features as she sat on the only chair in the room, the bodyguard Barret had hired standing beside her.

"Are you all right?" Barret sat on the table across from her and took her hands. He wanted to pull her into his arms but wasn't sure she was ready for that.

She nodded and bit her lip.

"What happened?" Barret asked the bodyguard.

The man was tall, brawny and had that military look about him. "About an hour after she got home, I saw two guys trying to get in her apartment. I called out to them and started up the stairs, but they took off faster than greased lightning."

"What did they look like?"

"One guy was pretty big, the other kinda skinny. One had red hair, but I never saw their faces. I told all that to the police."

Barret nodded, not wanting to relinquish his hold on Lexie's hands.

The bodyguard headed toward the door. "Thought I should stay with her till you got here, Mr. Johnson. I'll return to my post outside."

"Thank you." Barret waited until he heard the door close before facing Lexie again.

"If you hadn't hired that bodyguard," she began, her eyes pools of angst, "I don't want to think what would have happened to me."

Barret smiled and lifted her hands for a kiss. "I'll never let anything happen to you."

She pulled her hands from his. "You can't promise that." She sank back into the chair and sighed. "They broke into the museum."

Barret swallowed. "I heard." Now that he knew Lexie was okay, terror made another appearance. *The letters!* "Did they...did they...?"

"No." She smiled—a sly, cat-like smile. "I moved them."

"From your locker?"

"Yup. While you were emptying the trash, I took them and hid them under the hay bail in Bonnet's cell."

It was no laughing matter, but Barret couldn't help but chuckle. "You did what?"

She grew serious. "I heard something, Barret. A voice in my head, but not in my head. It said, *move the letters*. So I did!"

Shock tumbled through Barret. "It was God. He knew they were going to break in. Wow." He scratched his chin and smiled. "God spoke to you, Lexie!"

⚓

Why would God speak to *her*? She'd never spoken much to Him, never read His Bible, never went to church. She was a criminal from a family of criminals in search of pirate treasure. She had no desire to know God or be holy, especially not if it meant being like Barret's self-righteous family.

Yet...she could not deny the voice within her, the command, which if she had not obeyed would have left her with none of Bonnet's letters.

"I don't know whether God spoke to me or not," she said, ignoring the delight on Barret's face. "Or if it was just instinct or intuition, but all they broke into was my locker. Can you believe it?"

"They didn't take anything else?"

She shook her head.

"If that doesn't convince you that there's a God who cares about you, Lexie, I don't know what will." Barret's eyes sparkled with an excitement she dare not entertain.

"Whatever the reason. The letters are safe for now."

Taking her hands in his again, Barret leaned forward on his knees. He'd come to her rescue yet again. He'd been at work, had important things to do, yet here he was within minutes of the attempted break-in. Adam must have called him, told him she was fine. Still, he had come. Now, he stared at her with those mahogany eyes, so deep and full of love, and she wondered if she could trust him with her heart again. She wanted to, especially the way he was looking at her now—like she was worth more than the treasure they were seeking. But…she couldn't.

"I'll let you get some sleep. You're safe now, Lexie. The guard will stay outside all day and then walk you to work." He lifted his hand and rubbed his thumb over her cheek, gently, sensuously.

Her insides melted.

Then rising, he glanced around the room—cringed slightly, no doubt at the size and condition—then made his way to the door. Opening it, he glanced back and winked at her. "See you in the morning at the museum?"

She nodded.

"Lock the door." He raised a brow and left.

November 9, 1718, Charles Town, Guard House Dungeon

Dearest Melody,

I have been informed that I am to be brought to trial on the morrow before the vice admiralty court on charges of piracy. I beg you, my love, not to be present. I do not wish you to see me chained and bound and in such a state as I find myself. I plan on giving my best defense, regardless of the prevailing suspicion that Judge Nicolas Trott was born devoid of a heart. Pray, do not make it more difficult for me with your presence. I only ask that you appeal to the Almighty for a shred of His mercy.

I long to see your face, my dearest. Please come to see me, if you can. If you cannot, I would love a letter from you…anything to brighten these endless gloomy days.

Yours forever,
Stede

November 10, 1718, Charles Town, The Home of Garrett Vanvelsin

Bonnet, chained at the ankles and wrists, stood before a row of desks brought together to form a judges' table in the home of Garrett Vanvelsin, the town's shoemaker, where a makeshift courtroom had been assembled. The infamous Judge Nicholas Trott sat at the center, examining papers before him as the clerk of arraigns read the list of crimes against Bonnet. A powdered wig of curls framed the man's sagging face and fell upon his fine blue damask coat. He adjusted the white cravat layered upon his throat so tight, Bonnet wondered how he could breathe. Perhaps he didn't have to. No doubt demons had no need of fresh air.

On either side of him sat ten assistant judges, an attorney general and an assistant attorney-general. Twenty-three citizens of Charles Town sat behind Bonnet, none of whom he recognized as friends, while behind them only a few spectators could fit in the small room.

"…for feloniously and piratically taking the sloop *Francis*, with her goods…" the man droned on and Bonnet shifted his feet, his chains grating over the wooden floor. "…and the sloop *Fortune*, with her goods."

Finally, Judge Trott glanced up, his cold glare spearing Bonnet. "How do you plead, sir?"

Bonnet returned a steady gaze. "Not guilty, my Lord."

Moans and gasps tumbled through the crowd. Judge Trott frowned.

Bonnet continued. "My pleading not guilty is because I may have something to offer in my defense, and therefore I hope none of the bench will take it amiss."

Nicolas Trott gave an incredulous snort and waved a boney hand for the prosecution to begin.

Bonnet didn't know whether to be relieved or afraid when Ignatius Pell was brought before the judges. His former bosun recounted to the jury the events leading up to the plunder of Captain Manwareing's vessel, *Francis*. 'Twas accurate to Bonnet's remembrance, but the tale did him no credit.

However, when the court allowed Bonnet to question Pell, he decided his best course of action would be to convince judge and jury that he'd received a pardon and hence, was on his way to receive papers for privateering. "Don't you believe in your conscience, that when we left Topsail Inlet, it was to go to St. Thomas?" he asked Pell.

Pell nodded. "Indeed, Cap'n. That were what you—"

"We have already heard these lies, Bonnet!" Judge Trott barked. "Your crew testified you deceived them under the pretense of going to St. Thomas."

Bonnet swallowed down his rising fury and offered the judge a smile. "I am sorry that they should take the opportunity of my absence to accuse me of that which I was free from." If only Bonnet still had the pardon, but saint's blood!, he'd lost it when he'd been captured.

"Humph." Judge Trott frowned—an expression which seemed most comfortable on his face.

"It were the truth," Pell continued, offering Bonnet a look of sympathy. "An' besides, it were not even Bonnet in charge. He were captain in name only, I swears on me mother's grave."

The judges eyes narrowed. "What's this? Are you trying to convince me that this man"—he scowled at Bonnet—"was not commander in chief?"

"He went by that name, but the quartermaster, Robert Tucker, had more power than he."

Bonnet offered Pell a look of gratitude.

The judge seemed unconvinced as the next witness was called, Captain Manwareing, who, thanks be to God, also appeared to harbor some fondness for Bonnet. After all, Bonnet had done no harm to his person and had taken care to treat him as a gentleman. But when Bonnet asked him, "Did you ever hear me order anything out of the sloop?" Manwareing replied that Bonnet had taken everything he had in the world and left his wife and children wanting for bread in New England.

Bonnet fisted his hands as Manwareing was excused. The man's testimony had done more harm than good, but Bonnet had one last hope. "If it please the court," he addressed Trott, "I wish to call upon James King." The young man was the only trustworthy witness who could testify that Bonnet had, indeed, received a commission to sail to St. Thomas for a privateering license.

James nervously shifted his stance before the row of judges, scrunching his hat in his hands. "Aye, sirs, I 'eard that Captain Bonnet had received such a commission, but only from another pirate aboard 'is ship."

Judge Trott scowled and waved the man away. Then, leaning over the table, he pointed a finger at Bonnet. "If this be all the evidence you have, I do not see this will be of much use to you. I grow weary of this nonsense. What are your last words of defense?"

A slow burning terror, that had begun with Pell's testimony, now completely consumed Bonnet, stealing all hope and leaving nothing but death behind. Still, he composed himself, raised his chin, and gave the best defense he could.

"May it please your honours, and the rest of the gentlemen, though I must confess myself a sinner, and the greatest of sinners, yet I am not guilty of what I am charged with. As for what the boatswain says, relating to several vessels, I am altogether free; for I never gave my consent to any such actions, for I often told them, if they did not leave off committing such robberies, I would leave the sloop; and desired them to put me on shore. And as for Capt. Manwareing, I assure your honours it was contrary to my inclination. And when I cleared my vessel at North Carolina, it was for St. Thomas, and I had no other end or design in view but to go there for a commission. But when we came to sea and saw a vessel, the quartermaster and some of the rest held a consultation to take it, but I opposed it and told them again I would leave the sloop and let them go where they pleased. For as the young man said, I had my clearance for St. Thomas."

Grumbling and whispers spread amongst the crowd, and Bonnet was moved to another room while the jury deliberated. It took them but minutes to determine his fate, and soon he stood yet again before the Judge, knowing already what the verdict would be.

"Guilty as charged."

Despondency made Bonnet its captive all through the long night. It wrapped its hopeless claws around him, squeezing so hard he could barely breath, barely think at all. He still had one more charge to face on the next day's trial, but he had no defense other than the one he'd already given. He couldn't even bring himself to write Melody. No doubt she had heard the verdict, but Bonnet had no hope to offer her.

Hence, when he found himself standing before Judge Trott the next day, he retracted his previous plea for the seizure of the *Fortune* and instead pled guilty.

"Very well." Judge Trott stared at him as if he were a filthy rodent caught in a trap. Indeed, he proceeded with a long discourse, severely berating Bonnet for his crimes.

"Being a gentleman that has had the advantage of a liberal education," he continued, "and being generally esteemed a man of letters, I believe it will be needless for me to explain to you the nature of repentance and faith in Christ, they being so fully and so often mentioned in the Scriptures that you cannot but know them."

Bonnet had heard Trott was deeply religious, but he found this appeal to faith strange in light of Trott's upcoming judgment. Why did the man care about Bonnet's eternal soul?

Trott huffed and shook his head. "This court's punishment, which I shall soon pronounce, pales in comparison to God's punishment for murderers. Does it not say in Revelation 'for murderers have their part in the lake which burneth with fire and brimstone, which is the second death'?"

An odd look over came the judge's otherwise cold eyes. "So that if you now will sincerely turn to Jesus, though late, even at the eleventh hour, he will receive you."

Bonnet shifted uncomfortably as an odd sensation pricked his despair.

Judge Trott's eyes turned to steel again. "You, Stede Bonnet, shall go from hence to the place from whence you came, and from thence to the place of execution, where you shall be hanged by the neck until you are dead. And the God of infinite mercy be merciful to your soul."

CHAPTER THIRTY-FIVE

A phone rang—*Lexie*'s phone with its familiar tune. Why was it so far away, so muddled, like it was at the bottom of the sea? Ignoring it, she returned to the horrid reoccurring nightmare she'd been having—the death march of Stede Bonnet. Over and over the macabre scene played out in her mind—Bonnet in shackles, head low, being led through the streets of Charleston, citizens booing him, tossing food and garbage at him; then the scaffold, the rope around his neck, the charges read, the crank pulled. Melody in the audience falling in a heap, sobbing uncontrollably.

Then the scene started over again. Each time a piece of Lexie's heart chipped away. Each time, she reached out for him, wanting desperately to save him. Each time, he remained out of her reach. And each time, she cried a little more.

The phone rang again. She should answer it, shouldn't she? She searched for a reason why as she clawed her way out of her nightmare and into the light of day. Her eyes popped open. She jerked to a sitting position and glanced around. Her bedroom at the apartment. Rubbing her eyes, she looked at the clock. 3:00 p.m. She had an hour left before she had to get up for work.

Her phone continued to ring.

Reaching for it, she pressed the green button. "Hello."

"Miss Cain?"

"Yes."

"This is Mrs. Anderson from the museum."

Her boss? Shaking her head to clear the cobwebs, Lexie gathered her wits. "Hello, Mrs. Anderson."

"I need for you to come see me before you start your shift. 5:00?"

"Okay."

"I'll see you then." *Click.*

No "goodbye," no "sorry I woke you," and no indication of what this was about.

Though Lexie could guess. In fact, as she now stood before Mrs. Anderson's desk in the small office of the museum, she knew exactly what it was about by the tight expression on the already uptight lady.

"You heard we had a break-in two days ago?"

Lexie nodded.

"The police tell me that only your personal locker was damaged. Nothing else stolen."

Lexie swallowed. "Yes, ma'am."

She raised one plucked and well-formed eyebrow. "Do you have an explanation? Are you keeping contraband in your locker?"

Lexie shrank back. "No, ma'am. I would never."

Mrs. Anderson folded her fingers together on the desk. "You've been a good employee, Miss Cain, but I cannot have someone here who will endanger this museum and its contents. Next time who knows what they will take."

Lexie's stomach dropped to the floor.

"Therefore, I'm going to have to let you go. You can work tonight, but please come by tomorrow to return the keys and get your last paycheck. That will be all."

Lexie, feather duster in hand, stood before Bonnet's cell and stared at her ancestor. Now more than ever she felt a kinship with him. He was about to be executed, and she was about to be unemployed. Not that one could compare the two, but she honestly felt as though a piece of her would be hanged alongside Bonnet. Especially since she could no longer spend her morning hours with him here.

"I wish I could have saved you." She forced back a tear. How ridiculous that she felt so strongly about someone who had lived and died three hundred years ago.

A rap sounded on the back door, and wiping the moisture from her eyes, she went to allow Barret inside.

"What's wrong, Sunshine?" He gave her a concerned look as he closed and locked the door. "You look sad."

She wouldn't tell him about Bonnet. "I got fired." Shrugging, she continued her dusting.

"Oh, no. I'm so sorry." He grabbed her hand, stopping her from her work, and pulled her into his arms.

She should push away from him. She should not allow his strong arms to encircle her with comfort as they were doing now. She shouldn't. But she couldn't help it. She needed someone to care, even if she couldn't trust him completely.

Leaning her head on his shoulder, she embraced him in return, absorbing his strength. "This is my last night here." A tear slipped from her eye and slid down her cheek.

Barret nudged her back, gripped her arms, and looked at her with care—genuine? She hoped so with all her heart. "Don't worry about the money. I can help out until you get back on your feet." He wiped her tear away with his thumb.

Angry—though why she couldn't say—she pushed from him. "I want no charity. I'll find something else." The last thing she wanted was to depend on this man's generosity again. The last time she'd done so, she'd been accused of thievery! Still, she couldn't help the fear that threatened to strangle her at being homeless again. What if she couldn't find work in time? What if she let Tracy and Ellie down, and they were all evicted from their apartment? She began dusting again but felt his stare following her around the room.

"It's okay to let people in, Lexie, to let people care and help you."

"Why?" Annoyed, she spun to face him. "So they can stab me in the back?"

He frowned and rubbed the back of his neck. "Everyone deserves a second chance."

She shifted her gaze to Bonnet. "Bonnet didn't get one."

"But you aren't Judge Trott." He chuckled. "A fact I thank God for every day. And therefore, I throw myself on the mercy of the court."

Lexie couldn't help but smile. Why did the man have to be so charming? "I fear, sir, the jury is still out."

Barret smiled. "Let me help you sweep and take out the garbage and then let's read another letter, okay?"

"Deal."

When the work was done, Lexie hopped over the iron chain separating tourists from Bonnet's cell, then reached under a block of hay beneath the figure of a pirate and pulled out the folder.

Barret smiled. "Interesting place to hide them. Aren't you afraid someone will find them?"

She hopped back over the chain, smiling. "No one cleans this cell but me."

November 25, 1718, Charles Town, Guard House Dungeon

Dear Melody,

Where are you, my love? 'Tis been fifteen days since my trial and no word from you has arrived, nor any indication that you have received my correspondences. I can only assume you are as disgusted with me as I am with myself. You have by now heard the testimonies of my barbaric escapades whilst captain of the Revenge and later Royal James. But you must believe me, dearest, the intent of my heart, of which I wrote to you heretofore, has always been sincere. I meant no harm to anyone. I only wished to procure a future for us and then to receive a pardon and sail to St. Thomas. As God is my witness, 'twas a company of ill-bred, uneducated and cruel barbarians, the leader of which was one Robert Tucker, which did enact the cruelties of which I am charged.

I am despondent and now find myself alone in this God-forsaken pit of stench and agony. Yesterday, all nineteen of Captain Worley's crew were forcibly hauled from this dungeon to be hanged at White Point. I must tell you that many were so horribly wounded that I doubt they made the trip to the noose before expiring this world. And now I am alone, left with the stink of death in the air. Forgive me, precious one, for speaking thus to a lady.

I do not fear death, but 'tis the hereafter which tortures my soul, for surely I deserve the hottest hell fire for my actions.

Despite his cold-blooded heart, Judge Trott left me with much to consider in his last words to me.

In addition, I have written several letters of appeal to various persons of power in the city, in hopes that one of them may be able to aid my cause and reduce my sentence.

My love, I beg you to come visit me in my despair, for I can find no other reason to live, save to see your angelic face and know that you still hold me in your fondest affections.

Forever yours,
Stede

November 30, 1718, Charles Town, Guard House Dungeon

A rat scampered over the soiled brick floor in front of Bonnet, stopped to lift upon its hind feet, and stared at him as if he found his presence an oddity. No doubt the vermin who inhabited this pit had not been accustomed to so many visitors as they had seen these last months. In truth, the guard had informed Bonnet that Charles Town had hanged nigh forty-eight pirates in three weeks.

In ten days, it would become forty-nine.

Bonnet rubbed his neck as a chill traveled through him, tightening every nerve.

A door above creaked open, and footsteps padded on the treads of the ladder leading down to the dungeon. No doubt 'twas the guard with the noon meal of the usual foul porridge. Bonnet wasn't hungry. He doubted he ever would be again.

The footsteps halted before his cell door and without looking up, he gestured toward the ground. "Just set it over there, if you please."

"Stede…"

That voice, that sweet, celestial voice that put angels' songs to shame. He dared to hope, dared to even look up. But he did. And there she was…his Melody, a vision of beauty, wonder, and grace, clinging to the old, rusty bars that kept them apart.

"You got ten minutes," the guard announced, then walked away.

Bonnet blinked, hardly willing to believe his eyes. Rising, he inched toward her, fearful she would disappear, a mere apparition in his loneliness.

But then he wrapped his fingers around hers on the bars and felt their soft warmth, and he smiled. "You came."

"Of course. I tried many times before. I so desperately longed to see you." Her blue eyes searched his, brimming with all the love he remembered, and an overwhelming joy swept away all his despair. He could die right there and be happy. She still loved him! She had not forsaken him.

"My father keeps a strict eye on me." She glanced over at the guard standing by the ladder. "I've come here many times, Stede, but they would not allow me entrance."

Bonnet drew her hands through the bars and kissed them. Her sweet fragrance filled his lungs, chasing away all the stench of the dungeon. Just knowing she had tried to see him... "Why did they allow you to see me now?"

Her lips slanted. "I paid them. Quite well. But we haven't much time. I must tell you, Stede, that the letters of appeal you've written have not gone unnoticed, for they have been printed in all the Charles Town newspapers."

"Indeed? This is good news."

She gave a coy smile. "And of course the ladies of our fair city are quite overcome by your predicament. They have made several appeals to the governor on your behalf."

Hope dared to peer over the mound of despair in Bonnet's heart. "To what effect?"

"None as of yet." Pulling her hands back, she glanced down. "But it will surprise you to hear that Colonel Rhett is also on your side."

"Rhett?" The very man who had captured him. "Surely you are misinformed."

"Nay, my love. He has offered to use his own money and personally escort you to London so your case might be referred to his majesty."

Bonnet could make no sense of it. Taking up a pace, he raked a hand through his hair, afraid to entertain such a dream.

"There is hope," she broke the silence. "You must not give up, Stede."

Halting, he faced her, wishing more than anything he could break through the bars and hold her in his arms. "You are a treasure, Melody. I am unworthy of you."

She reached for him. "My heart has always been yours, Stede."

He brought her hands to his lips for another kiss when a tremble coursed through them. Tears spilled from her eyes down her creamy cheeks.

"What is it, precious? What has you so distraught?"

Swiping her tears away, she lowered her chin for a moment before facing him again. "I am with child, Stede."

Bonnet's world tilted. Air fled his lungs. Shock pinched every nerve. He glanced down at her belly, remembering that wonderful night … weeks ago. Joy bounded through him, laughing and dancing like flames of a fire, even while the pain of loss squelched every flicker.

"You are… you carry… my child?"

Smiling, she nodded and pressed a hand over her belly.

Desperation took over his joy. He must get out of here! He must gain his freedom. He would not have his child raised without— A sudden fear struck him. "What will your father do?"

A whimper escaped her lips as her chest rose and fell. She gripped the bars. "I cannot think of that now. I must wholly count on your soon release. I must, for I cannot fathom what I shall do otherwise."

Bonnet slammed his fist on the brick wall, ignoring the pain searing up his arm. Melody would be cast away, condemned, labeled a trollop. Her life would be ruined. He would not allow it. He must be free!

"Time's up," the guard announced.

"I'm so afraid, Stede. I don't know what to do." Her frightened eyes sped between his.

Reaching through the bars, he caressed her cheek. "I will get out of here. You will not bear this child—*our* child—without me."

"I beg you to make one final appeal to Governor Johnson. Surely, if he heard directly from you and could clearly see that you are a gentleman of distinction, he would halt this unfair and ludicrous sentence you have been given."

"I will. I will write him today, my love."

She blew him a kiss and then she was gone, leaving him once again in a pit of darkness and death.

Honoured Sir,

I have presumed on the confidence of your eminent goodness to throw myself, after this manner at your feet to implore you'll be graciously pleased to look upon me with tender bowels of pity and compassion; and believe me to be the most miserable man this day breathing; that the tears proceeding from my most sorrowful soul may soften your heart, and incline you to consider my dismal state, wholly, I must confess, unprepared to receive so soon the dreadful execution you have been pleased to appoint me; and therefore beseech you to think me an object of your mercy.

I once more beg for the Lord's sake, dear Sir, that as you are a Christian, you will be as charitable as to have mercy and compassion on my miserable soul, but too newly awakened from an habit of sin to entertain so confident hopes and assurances of its being received into the arms of blessed Jesus, as is necessary to reconcile me to so speedy a death.

I implore you to consider me with a Christian and charitable heart and determine mercifully of me that I may ever acknowledge and esteem you next to God, my Saviour, and oblige me ever to pray that our heavenly Father will also forgive your trespasses.

Now, the God of peace that brought again from the dead our Lord Jesus, that great shepherd of the sheep thru' the blood of the everlasting covenant make you perfect in every good work to do his will, working in you that *which is well pleasing in His sight through Jesus Christ to whom be glory forever and ever is the hearty prayer of your honour's.*

Most miserable, and afflicted servant Stede Bonnet.

CHAPTER THIRTY-SIX

*F*orcing back the unmanly moisture from his eyes, Barret studied Lexie as she set down the letter and glanced at the figure of Bonnet in the cell. Tears spilled down her cheeks, and she sniffed and wiped them away. "I'm sorry. I'm so embarrassed. Why am I crying?"

Barret loved that she had such a big heart. "If I were to admit it, I almost did too."

Lexie snapped her gaze to his in surprise.

"I probably know more about Bonnet than most people, but…" Barret sighed. "Reading his own words, hearing his own thoughts and feeling his emotions"—he shook his head—"it makes him real, makes him come alive. I can't imagine how you feel, being his relative."

She smiled. "Thanks for not making fun of me."

"Never."

Their eyes locked for a few precious moments, and in those moments he saw a closeness, a bond growing between them that he prayed would never be broken.

"It also appears that good old Bonnet may have turned to God in the end," Barret added. Of course, he'd read Bonnet's letter to the governor before, but for some reason, his references to Jesus and repentance struck a deeper chord this time. He'd always thought Bonnet was merely using any means at his disposal—even lying about a Christian faith—to soften the governor's heart, but his words to Melody that Trott had given him much to consider made Barret think otherwise—at least he hoped so.

"Yeah, maybe." Lexie didn't seem quite as enthused. She slipped the letter back into the folder.

"Many of Charleston's citizens wrote the governor on his behalf, especially the ladies." Barret wanted Lexie to know how beloved Bonnet had been. "Even Colonel Rhett offered to escort him to plead his case before the king."

Lexie blinked. "Whoa. That's amazing." She shook her head and smiled. "He must have been quite the charmer. Wait." She rose from her seat on the floor in front of Bonnet's cell and narrowed her eyes at Barret. "Governor *Johnson*. Is he a relative of yours?"

Darn it! He wanted to deny it, say that Johnson was a common name, but he couldn't lie. His family was very proud that their distant relative had once been governor. "Yes."

Lexie's lips folded together in a scowl. "So, he didn't grant Bonnet a pardon."

It wasn't a question, of course. They both knew the ending of the story. Barret remained silent, watching Lexie stiffen and her face grow red.

"He deserved a pardon," she said. "He never intended to hurt anyone. You know that!"

Barret stood and lifted a hand in an attempt to calm her down. "I don't know what Governor Johnson's motives were. He didn't know Bonnet as we do."

"But all those women writing to him. And even Colonel Rhett, a highly respected officer in Charleston. Yet he refused to listen!"

"I'm sorry, Lexie. I can't be held responsible for what he did."

"Oh no? Your father would probably do the same thing, and you know it. Self-righteous, merciless, judgmental..." Instead of calling him a bad word, she growled and turned to stare at Bonnet.

Barret blew out a sigh. Honestly, she was probably right. "But you know *I* wouldn't."

"Doesn't matter." She faced him, anger flaring in her eyes. "Get out."

"What?"

"I said, leave, please."

"Why?"

"Because right now I don't want to hang out with someone who did this to Bonnet. At least not now."

"That's not fa—"

"I know it doesn't make sense. I know you didn't do it. But your family did. I can't betray him." She gazed at Bonnet and wiped a tear from her eye. "I *won't* betray him."

Barret knew better than to argue with Lexie when she got like this. He felt her pain. He felt the same way about Bonnet. And he was starting to feel the same way about his father. Whether Governor Johnson made the right call or not, Barret represented that decision to Lexie. From the very moment they'd met, she'd fought against their relationship, stating they were too different.

Maybe she'd been right all along.

"Okay. I'll leave." He paused a second, desperately wanting her to face him—to see the sorrow in his eyes, to come to her senses, and beg him to stay. But she kept staring at Bonnet. "I'm sorry. For everything." He started to leave. Wait. If she meant it this time. If they weren't going to see each other again, then what about the letters? He turned around. "All I ask is that when you're done with the letters, you let me borrow them for my book."

He realized his mistake the moment he saw the look in her eyes...as if she could kill him on the spot. "Is that all you care about? Is that the only reason you are here? Get out!" Her shout fired across the high brick ceiling and speared straight into his heart.

Pain shot through him—the pain of loss, the pain of despair, shame, and a gut-wrenching realization that he couldn't live without this woman. Turning, he opened the door and left.

The museum door slammed. Lexie jumped as the *crash* echoed across the dungeon, an omen of her stupidity. Moving to the door, she locked it, then leaned her head against the thick wood. More tears poured down her cheeks. Her vision blurred. Had she not cried enough that night? She knew she was being unreasonable, but she didn't care. Barret's family had condemned Bonnet to die a horrid death. They had shown him no mercy, though in her opinion, he, out of all the pirates, had deserved it. At least a second chance.

How could she have ever fallen in love with someone who came from such a family? Love. Yes, she *did* love him.

But in the end, all he seemed to care about were the letters. *Stupid, stupid girl!*

And now, she would have to forget him, put him out of her thoughts *and* out of her heart. It would take time.

Finding the treasure would help. Especially since tomorrow she would have bigger problems than a broken heart. If she didn't find another job, she, Tracy, and Ellie, would be living on the streets.

She glanced down at the folder still in her hands, then up at the clock. 5:00 a.m. She had one hour left. Just one final hour alone in this dungeon before she turned in her keys and became just another tourist.

Moving to Bonnet's cell, she sat cross-legged on the floor and pulled out the last letter. She'd already glanced at it when she'd first found the letters, thinking that surely the clue to the treasure would be in Bonnet's final words to Melody. She'd not found any clue, and in fact, had found the letter confusing and the numbers at the end meaningless.

Still, she had to try. Maybe she needed to have read *all* the letters in order to decipher it. Yet fear clawed up her throat as she stared down at the letter. If she couldn't, or, even worse, if the letter contained no clue at all, then all hope was lost.

Wiping the moisture from her eyes, she glanced up at Bonnet. "Little help here, Bonnet?"

December 8, 1718, Charles Town, Guard House Dungeon

My most precious love,

You have by now received news that Governor Johnson has refused all requests to postpone, stay, or pardon the harsh sentence which has been put upon me. In two days hence, I shall be escorted to White Point as were my fellow pirates before me, where I shall meet my maker. I am told I will not be allowed further visitors. My love, I am in the gravest agony, even far above my impending death, that I shall not see you again this side of eternity.

Please do not grieve for me, my darling. My time alone in this dark, dismal place has afforded me many hours of reflection and dare I say, prayer.

At first the hours passed with much inward groaning and hopelessness, but then a voice spoke to me, one which I had oft heard before. That voice, calm, soothing, yet authoritative has been with me since birth, guiding, directing, and comforting. I heard it when the choice was laid before me by my father of marrying you and losing my inheritance or marrying Mary. I heard it when I built my Schooner *Revenge* and set out to pirating.

It spoke to me when Blackbeard himself first entered my cabin to request an alliance. Over and over, my love, this voice warned me, pleaded with me to walk this way, make this choice. Even after I received my pardon, forsook all killing, and set my sights on St. Thomas, that strong voice tugged upon my soul, instructing me to quit the trade and follow the leadings of my heart. I even made a vow to God that if He allowed me to see you one last time, I would quit the trade. I now realize that though the Almighty kept up His part of the bargain, I did not.

I have been given a copy of the Holy Scriptures, and I have consumed the Almighty's Words like a man long-starved on a deserted island. What did I find within them? But God's appeal to follow Him in all our ways for He does direct our paths, He does tell us "This is the way, walk ye in it."

I am undone, my love. My Father in Heaven wished to spare me all the pain I have brought upon myself. But I have been a stubborn fool, ignoring that voice, that wise voice, and instead pursuing my own way. Proverbs 14:12 reads, "There is a way which seemeth right unto a man, but the end thereof are the ways of death." And Proverbs 11:19, "As righteousness tendeth to life; so he that pursueth evil pursueth it to his own death."

Therefore, I and I alone have brought this sentence of death upon myself. Every time I ignored the Almighty and made my own decision, I tightened the noose around my neck. It may please you to know that I have hence fallen upon my knees, repented of all my sins, and received the grace and favor of our Lord Christ.

My sweetest darling, my biggest regret is making you a partaker of my depravity and thus also a partaker of the punishment due only me. I will never see my child born. Nor can I do anything to stop the scorn and ridicule you are soon to suffer for my sake. All I can do is provide for you and our child a living which will of a surety keep you comfortable all your days.

I send a coin with this first letter. Keep it close. It contains all my love for you, all my hopes for you, all I have left to give you. Please do not attend my execution. I could not bear it. I wish you to remember me strong and full of life, with naught but love in my eyes for you, my most cherished love.

I love you, my sweet Melody. I have always loved you, and I shall continue to love you onward into eternity. You are the most precious gift God has ever given me.

I beg you, dearest, to bend your knee to the Almighty, receive His offer of grace through our Lord Jesus, and follow that small voice wherever it leads. Then, we shall surely be united again in a far better place than this horrid world.

I close this letter and seal it with my tears, tears of love, tears of sorrow, and yet tears of joy that will never fade for that glorious day when I shall see your face again.

3 11 28 43 17 2 59 64 4 19 1 24

For all eternity,
Stede.

Setting the letter down, Lexie allowed all the tears welling in her eyes to fall freely down her cheeks and drip from her chin onto her jeans. She sat there crying like a foolish child for several minutes, crying for her broken heart, crying for Bonnet's tragic end, crying for the incredible love he and Melody shared, and finally crying for the horrible life Melody ended up living. A tragedy, far worse than any Shakespearean tragedy. With one exception. It cut way too close to home. These were *her* ancestors. Their blood flowed in her veins. Apparently other things flowed, like bad decisions and not listening to or even acknowledging God.

If there was a heaven, she was glad to hear that Bonnet might be there. If there was a God and He actually *did* direct His children, could that be the reason for all the struggles that had come upon her own family? The reason why so many of them had been imprisoned, homeless, or living in poverty? Had they each ignored God's warnings and leadings and instead followed their own path?

Batting her tears away, she stared at Bonnet. *He* had come to believe that. Was it merely the delusions of a man who knew he would soon die? Or was there something to this God of his? Of Barret's God? She suddenly wished she had not tossed him out so she could ask him. He would be so thrilled to hear of Bonnet's conversion, and she had denied him that pleasure.

Lexie had always believed that if there was a God, He surely didn't care about her or her family. Instead, to her, it seemed He'd cast a curse upon them. Yet... had she been wrong all this time? Words from the sermon she'd heard in Barret's church rose to haunt her—words about choosing the right way, the narrow way.

She didn't want to think about it now. Dropping her gaze back to the letter, the sentence that had made her heart soar now leapt off the aged parchment.

All I can do is provide for you and our child a living which will of a surety keep you comfortable all your days.

Bonnet must have told Melody where he'd hidden the treasure. She had not been allowed to see him after this letter, so the clue had to be within these words. But where?

One thing she had noticed was that Bonnet separated each paragraph with an empty line, which he had not done before in any of his other letters. Odd. And these numbers at the end. At first she'd thought they corresponded to letters of the alphabet, but that would be far too easy and some of them were higher than twenty-six. And what was this about the coin? Bonnet said it was all he had left to give Melody.

She glanced up at the pirate himself, frozen in the same despondent position as always. "Care to give me a clue? A hint? No?"

Blowing out an exasperated sigh, Lexie stared back at the letter. *God, if you're there, can you help? I need help.* She surprised herself with the silent prayer, remembering when God seemed to have answered an earlier one, or so Barret had said. Would God bother to hear her? To help? She was about to shake her head for being so foolish when the words, *count paragraphs and numbers* rose from deep within her. Not audible words, but clear, calm, and concise.

She must be hearing things. Still... why not? Twelve paragraphs, twelve numbers. Weird. Now what? Each number must correspond to a paragraph. Rising, Lexie went to her locker, grabbed a pen from her backpack, and then sat back down before Bonnet's cell. On a whim, she took the first number, 3, and found the third word in the first paragraph, *by.* What the heck does that mean? Okay. The eleventh word of the second paragraph was *alone,* the twenty-eighth word of the third paragraph was *calm. By alone calm.* Hmm. She continued with the other numbers and paragraphs until a sentence formed.

By alone calm killing words am lord living coin onward I never.

Lexie growled and stared at Bonnet. "Have you lost your mind? This is nonsense."

Impossible. She bit her lip and scanned the letter once again. Something else had stood out to her. But what? There.

I send a coin with this first letter.

This wasn't Bonnet's first letter to Melody. Why would he say that? First letter...*first letter*! Taking the pen again, she wrote out the first letter of each word in the sentence, then stared at the result, her heart thrashing in her chest and a huge smile growing on her lips.

Back Wall Coin

"You clever devil, you." Standing yet again, her gaze landed on the brick wall that made up the back of Bonnet's cell. The coin was the key. The thugs who were following her had stolen it, but Lexie remembered the engraving. "R-T 10-7"

Bonnet must have hidden a map to his treasure in the back wall of his cell. But behind which brick? Leaping over the chain, she resisted the urge to hug him and moved to the back.

"R must be right." Starting at the right side of the wall, she counted ten bricks across. Now what?

"T. What is T? Top!" Gazing up, she counted seven bricks from the top and landed on one particular old brick. That had to be it! That *must* be it. It was definitely high enough off the floor so as not to be disturbed by other prisoners who passed this way.

Excitement buzzed through her as she returned to her locker to get a knife she kept for protection, along with a flashlight. Then grabbing a stool, she dashed back to the wall, located the brick in question, and began chipping away at the mortar around it. It came out remarkably easy—far too easy. That could only mean one of two things—either the mortar had decayed due to age, or the brick had been removed before. She opted for the latter. Both nervous and excited, she used the knife to pry the brick loose. Finally, that glorious sound of stone moving on stone delighted her ears. Moving the brick aside, she flipped on her flashlight, and peered inside.

There lay an old piece of parchment rolled up like a scroll with a ribbon tied around it.

Breath seized in Lexie's throat. Her pulse raced until she felt dizzy. This was the last thing that Bonnet had touched! It seemed almost too sacred to move. How had it not decayed? She supposed a lack of oxygen in the wall would account for that. Odd that Bonnet must have believed Melody would have access to the dungeon. But why not? Once she figured out the code, she could have bribed the guards to allow her entrance if no prisoners were being held. She could have pretended to need a moment alone to mourn the loss of Bonnet.

Then why hadn't she?

Tentatively, Lexie reached into the hole and ever so gently removed the scroll. She stepped down from the stool as tears filled her eyes. The scroll blurred in her vision. She moved to sit beside Bonnet, untied the ribbon, and slowly opened it.

It was a map. A glorious, wonderful map! A land mass marked as *Cranes Island* stood between two thick blue lines. One of the lines had the words *Cape Fear* written on it. Another smaller blue line crossed the land, made a sharp turn, and directly inland from that point, Bonnet had drawn a row of trees with the shape of a turtle at the center. Before the turtle, he'd placed a bold **M**—for Melody?

Lexie smiled. She knew it! While anchored in Cape Fear River, Bonnet had taken the treasure from his ship and buried it! She had no idea what the turtle was, but she couldn't wait to find out.

Winding the map up again, she brought it to her nose and took a deep breath. A mixture of mold, age, and hope filled her lungs and she knelt before Bonnet. "I found it, Bonnet! I found it! I'm sorry Melody never did, but *I* found it. Thank you." Leaning forward, she kissed his cold wax cheek, wishing more than anything that her intimate gesture would restore him to life.

Still, he remained, looking more grief-stricken than ever.

After returning the brick to its spot and doing her best to shove the crumbs of mortar back in place, she had one last thing to do in the office upstairs before leaving. Afterward, she grabbed her backpack, paid her final respects to Bonnet, and headed out the door.

Regardless of how she'd treated Barret, a bodyguard waited for her and walked her home. She smiled and thanked him, then slipped the key into the lock and entered the apartment as quietly as she could. At this hour, Tracy and Ellie would still be asleep, and she hated to wake them.

They weren't asleep. At least Tracy wasn't. She rose from the daybed she and Ellie shared and stared at Lexie, her eyes red and puffy, and a look of sheer horror on her face.

Shutting the door, Lexie tossed her backpack on the table and rushed over to her. "What's wrong?"

"They…they… took her."

"Who?"

"Ellie. They kidnapped Ellie."

CHAPTER THIRTY-SEVEN

*L*exie's world collapsed. *Kidnapped... Ellie?* It couldn't be. She was so tired she must be hearing things. Yet, one glance around the room revealed no sweet, angelic girl with bouncing blond curls. No innocent child fast asleep or playing with toys. Still, the words refused to make sense.

"Why didn't you call me?"

"I did!" Tracy sobbed. "You didn't answer."

Lexie dug her phone from her back pocket, only then remembering she'd turned it off after Barret left. She hadn't been in the mood for his apology texts.

Tracy blinked and started to spiral down, and, tossing her phone on the table, Lexie caught her before she fell.

Terror sprinted through Lexie's mind, seeking answers as she led Tracy to sit on the couch. "Who? How?"

"An hour ago. After the guard left to walk you home."

"We're calling the police." Lexie grabbed her phone from the table when a loud "No!" charged through the room.

Tracy pressed a hand over her heaving chest. "No police. They said they would kill her!"

A metallic taste filled Lexie's mouth. "Who said?"

"The men who broke in through the window." Tracy sobbed, dropping her head into her hands.

Lexie shot a glance at the front window. The screen was gone, but the window was intact. They always kept the windows shut, especially at night.

"It's all my fault," Tracy continued. "The air conditioning broke last night, and we were so hot. All I did was open it a crack to get some fresh air."

Lexie sat on the table in front of Tracy and grabbed her shoulders. "What men? Who were they? Why did they take her?"

Bloodshot eyes met hers. "They gave me a message for you."

Lexie's blood turned to ice.

"They said to meet them in the Western Cemetery at St. Philip's at 8:00 a.m. and give them the letters." She began crying uncontrollable, her body convulsing with each sob. "Or… they would… kill Ellie."

An hour later with the folder of letters in one hand and her Taser in the other, Lexie stood, once again, among the large oak and maple trees at the Western Cemetery. Memories of Barret being stabbed at this very spot rose to prick her guilt at how mean she'd been to him. Regardless of whether his main interest was in Bonnet's letters, he had been nothing but kind to her, had even risked his life for her.

But she couldn't think of that now.

She hadn't meant to bring the map, but in the mayhem, she'd forgotten that she'd slipped it in her back pocket. But the men wouldn't know that. She repressed a smile. Bonnet's letters would be of no use to these creeps now. Even if they *could* figure out the code, which they didn't seem smart enough to do.

No one was here at this hour, which was what the scumbags had planned on. Though the morning was cool, sweat slid down her back. Fear—*real* fear crawled over her skin like a thousand snakes, hissing and biting, threatening to poison all of Lexie's plans. The letters, the map, the treasure, all her hopes and dreams…none of it mattered anymore.

Nothing but getting Ellie back safe.

Funny how a single event could change her perspective on everything she thought was important.

Cheerful birds hopped from branch to branch above her, chirping and teetering a happy mood so at odds with the dark cloud of doom hanging over Lexie. Minutes passed like hours. If ever there was a time to pray, it was now, yet the only words Lexie could muster were, "Please help me, God. Please."

Did He hear her? He certainly had answered her prayer in the dungeon. She doubted she could have figured out Bonnet's code without some divine help. *And thank you, by the way,* she added.

Leaves crunched, and she snapped her gaze to two men heading her way—one built like a bulldozer, the other tall and lanky, both of them wearing sinister scowls on their faces. She recognized them immediately—the fiends who had made her life the past few months a living nightmare. The men who had almost killed Barret.

The men who had the life of an innocent three-year-old girl in their hands.

She wanted to shoot them.

Instead, she forced down her fear and stared them both in the eyes. If she'd learned one thing on the streets it was to never to show fear. Ever. Or it was all over.

They halted before her. "Got the letters?" the big one said.

"Got the girl?" she countered.

The skinny one thumbed toward a car parked along the street. "She's in the car."

"Bring her to me, and I'll give you what you want."

The big one snorted. "You'll give us what we want anyway." He took a step toward her.

Lexie shoved her Taser toward him. "Maybe, but not without a fight and a scream so loud, everyone within two blocks will come running."

The man chuckled, exchanged a glance with his partner, and then gestured with his head toward the car.

The skinny man darted off and returned within minutes with Ellie.

"Lexie!" the little girl squealed and started for her, but the man grabbed her arm and yanked her back. "Lexie!" she sobbed.

"It's going to be all right, Ellie." Lexie attempted a calm, cheerful tone. "You're coming home with me."

"I want my mommy!" Ellie wailed.

Rage stiffened every muscle. "Torturing a little girl? Oh, how proud you must be."

The large man with a mop of red hair gestured toward the folder in her hands. "Hand it over."

"First, give Ellie to me."

The man thought for a moment, then gestured for his friend to release the little girl. She flew into Lexie's waiting arms. Her sweet scent of sunshine and innocence flooded Lexie's nose as she squeezed Ellie with all her might.

The lanky man yanked the folder from her hands.

Lexie picked up Ellie and held her close, staring at the thugs. "You have the letters, now go and leave us alone."

The lanky guy opened the folder and scanned the contents, checking the date on each letter, no doubt, to make sure they were all there. Sniffing, he ran his sleeve beneath his nose. "Yeah, there's eighteen."

Lexie swallowed. How did they know that? How did they even know about the treasure? It made no sense. But at the moment, Lexie couldn't care less. She just wanted to get as far from them as possible.

"Check her pockets to make sure."

Lexie's throat closed. No way. She backed away. "A deal's a deal. Just go!"

But the man was on her within a second. She tried to set Ellie down so she could push him back, but the little girl's grip was as tight as a noose.

"Ah!" the man chuckled and held the scroll in the air. "What have we here?"

Horrified, Lexie could only watch as the men unrolled it, their expressions flashing with sinister joy.

The large man grinned at her. "You were going to keep this from us, eh?"

"You said you only wanted the letters."

Snorting, he grabbed her arm, dragging her and Ellie to the car.

She struggled against his grip. She jerked and yanked and groaned until pain spiked up her arm and across her shoulders. Ellie began to cry. "You have the letters and the map. What do you need us for?"

The skinny man blew out a sigh. "For all we know, this is a trick." He held up the scroll. "We know your boyfriend is a historian. He could have forged a fake map. So, we'll take you along just to make sure the map is real."

Gripping his macchiato, Barret stared out the window of his office. He was supposed to be writing lesson plans for the four classes he was teaching in the fall—classes that began in just two weeks—but every time he tried, instead of words on the computer, all he saw was the pain and anger in Lexie's eyes.

The last thing he'd wanted was to cause her pain, but how could he be held responsible for something a great, great ancestor had done? Yet her words kept clanging in his ears.

Your father would probably do the same thing and you know it

She was right, of course. Judge Gregory Johnson—the man he'd admired and wanted to emulate since childhood—would have condemned Bonnet to the noose as well. As he had done to so many criminals who'd been convicted in his court. He was known throughout the South Carolina justice system as *The Hammer,* a judge who gave the harshest sentence possible. Criminals and defense lawyers alike trembled in his courtroom.

Barret had always been proud of that fact—that his father put all those who chose the path of darkness behind bars where they couldn't hurt anyone else. But what if that person had a change of heart? What if a group of respected citizens stood up for him? What if the most honored member of society begged to appeal to a higher court for mercy? Shouldn't a judge take all things into consideration? Yes, people must pay for their crimes, but where did mercy come in? Perhaps if Bonnet had received a lighter sentence, Melody would not have ended up disowned and destitute. And Lexie's family history would have taken a different path. This "curse" she spoke of never would have happened.

And then she would never have come to Charleston.

And he never would have met her.

Now he was being selfish.

Even with the pain currently etching across his heart, he was a better man for having met her. Even if they never had a relationship again, she had shown him a different world, a different way of looking at things. A world of mercy and grace and kindness toward those in need. Not a world where one just threw money at problems to satisfy a ten percent tithing rule, but a world where one rolled up their sleeves and got dirty with those living in the gutter. A world where tattoos and piercings, a criminal past, and a disreputable heritage had nothing to do with the size of one's heart.

"Lord, if I never see her again, thank you for bringing her into my life." Just saying the words out loud caused a lump to form in his throat. He took a sip of coffee to wash it down, but even his favorite drink left a bitter taste in his mouth.

His phone rang. It wasn't Lexie. He'd programmed her ring tone to *Brighter than Sunshine* by Aqualung. It continued to ring. Expelling a huge sigh, he turned, set down his coffee, and answered it.

"Barret!" a woman's voice screamed.

It took Barret a moment to recognize it. "Tracy?"

"They took Ellie, and now Lexie's gone after them and I wasn't supposed to tell you, but I haven't heard from them and I'm going crazy. I don't know what to do. They will—"

"Calm down. Calm down. Slowly now." Barret could barely make out her words, they spilled from her mouth so fast. Yet the ones he could understand turned his blood to ice.

"Who took Ellie?"

Heavy breaths sounded. "Those guys after Lexie."

"Okay. And where is Lexie?"

"She went to give them the letters and get Ellie back."

Heart seizing, Barret grabbed his keys off the desk and dashed out the door, down the hall, and descended the steps to the faculty parking lot, phone still pressed to his ear. "Where?"

"She hasn't come back, Barret," Tracy sobbed.

"I need you to focus, Tracy. Now, tell me where." Barret pressed the fob, unlocked his car, and hopped in.

"The…the Western Cemetery at St. Philip's."

"Okay. I'm heading there now." Barret squealed out of the parking lot.

"I'm here, but they aren't here… They aren't here, Barret…" she wailed.

"You are at the cemetery?"

"Yes, when she didn't come back, I came here looking for them." Her voice trembled.

"Okay. Stay there, I'm coming to get you." Hanging up, he tossed the phone onto the passenger seat and raced through the busy streets. Why did emergencies always happen at rush hour? Whoops, he ran a red light. Glancing over his shoulder, he thanked God he hadn't hit anyone.

Sheer terror threatened to overtake his senses, but he couldn't let it. He had to remain in control. For Lexie's sake. Why had she been so stupid? She should have known better than to meet those hoodlums by herself! Even if she was angry at him, why hadn't she called?

Nearly a half-hour later—much too long—Barret skidded into a parking spot beside the cemetery, hopped out, and rushed up to Tracy. She wasn't hard to find. She sat on the ground, curled over, bawling. At the sound of his approach, she raised weepy eyes to his, and the look of desperation and despair within them nearly sent him to his knees.

Extending his hand, he helped her stand and then took her in his arms. "We'll find them. I promise."

She trembled then took a step back and held out a piece of paper.

"What's this?" Barret unfolded it. A map. A copy of an old map. Bonnet's map? His breath caught. Had she found it?

"She gave it to me," Tracy said. "Told me to give it to you if she and Ellie didn't return."

She *had* found it! Despite the circumstances, Barret was proud of her. That pride instantly turned to anger. Foolish woman! She should have called him right away.

"Okay. Let me make sure you get home all right." He ushered Tracy toward the street where he assumed she'd parked. Only then did he spot Lexie's car. His stomach sank.

Tracy faced him. "I'm fine, Barret. I can get home by myself. Just please..."—she took his hands in hers as tears filled her eyes—"Please find them and bring them home safe."

He nodded. "You have my word."

Yet, as Barret watched her drive away, he had no idea how he would keep that promise.

CHAPTER THIRTY-EIGHT

*L*exie realized two things in the long day's journey to North Carolina. One, these men were not very smart, as was usually the case with criminals, and two, she was more frightened than she'd ever been. Not even when her friend had been shot or Lexie had been locked up in juvenile hall, or she'd held her mother as she gasped her last breath had she been this scared. It was Ellie, the little girl shivering in her arms. Lexie deserved what she was getting, but not this sweet, innocent girl, whom Lexie had begun to love as if she were her own.

Tied up in the back seat of an old Honda, Lexie and Ellie had huddled together during the long drive to Wilmington. They'd only been permitted two sips of water and one bathroom break, and even that, Lexie had to beg for. Ellie was a brave little girl. More so than Lexie would have expected. Barely a whimper emerged from her mouth the entire trip. Only once did she ask where they were going and who these men were.

A booming, "Silence!" from the lanky man in front had sent a tremble through the girl.

Once in town, they had made several stops, which only dragged out the harrowing ordeal. But now, as night draped a thick curtain of black over the sky, the men shoved them into a small motorboat they'd rented.

Lexie had studied the map enough to know they were now crossing Cape Fear River, the same river where Bonnet had hidden his sloop during the hurricane season all those years ago. Oddly, as the men started up the motor and the gentle lap of waves accompanied the hum, she felt a strange connection to her ancestor—as if somehow he was watching and smiling down on her, proud that she'd found the map.

A chilled wind whipped around them, sending a shiver through Lexie, and filling her nose with the scent of fish, plant life, and swampy moisture. She swung her bound hands over

Ellie and drew her close, shielding her with her arms to keep her warm.

"Where are we going, Lexie?" the little girl whimpered.

"A boat ride. Isn't it fun, my little angel?" Lexie kissed the top of her head. "Just relax. We are going home soon."

The one called Bones—for she'd heard their names as they'd conversed during the trip—cast a scowl at her over his shoulder, visible in the lantern light he held.

She knew they had a ways to go. From what she remembered, they would have to go around the tip of the island, then up Brunswick River to Alligator Creek, which was nearly halfway up Eagle Island—or what Bonnet would have called Cranes Island. She only knew the names because she'd been so curious, she'd checked a current map of the area before she'd left the museum. She'd also made a copy of the old map. Just in case.

"So, how did you guys know about Bonnet's treasure?" She raised her voice above the motor, unsure why she even bothered to ask. Regardless, she'd always heard that when taken hostage, it was best to connect with your captors, make them like you, or at the very least, look at you as a fellow human being. That way, maybe they wouldn't kill you in the end.

She gulped.

Scott, the large one, who was sitting behind her, manning the motor, uttered a, "None of your business."

"Ah, why not tell her?" Bones grinned, then wiped his sleeve beneath his pointy nose. "It won't matter none." He glanced at her. "We knew your dad."

Lexie blinked. "In prison?"

"Yeah. He was in the cell next to ours. And he told us all about your mom's letters from this famous pirate and how there was rumored to be a fortune in treasure buried somewhere close."

Lexie fingered her earring. Of course. Made sense now. Despite being remarried and despite the fact that her dad had beat her mother—repeatedly—Lexie's mom had visited him often, especially after she got "saved." She'd wanted to convert him, to save his soul. Like that would ever happen. Still, she must have told him about her ancestry search and how she'd come by Bonnet's letters.

"Once the old lady died," Bones added, "we kept an eye on you. Then when you went to Charleston, we figured you'd found the letters."

The tiny boat leapt over a wave, sending cold droplets over Lexie. Ellie whimpered. Lexie held her tight and kept silent the rest of the way. Above them, a host of stars twinkled across the expanse of the sky, along with a quarter moon that seemed to be smiling at them. But that couldn't be. Was God looking down on her? Caring for her? Protecting her?

God, if you can hear me, if you answer any of my prayers, please answer this one. Please rescue us. Please save Ellie and get her back home to Tracy.

A gust of wind slapped her face in answer as they cruised around the tip of the island. Another ten minutes and Scott slowed the motor while Bones held up the lantern toward shore, shifting his gaze between the land and the map in his hand.

"There's the creek!" he shouted back at Scott, and the big man turned the motor, angling the boat up the small path of water.

Despite her dire situation, Lexie's heart leapt. They were *so* close! Bonnet, himself, had rowed up this same creek with his treasure. Now all they needed to do was find the landmark—a row of tall trees with something shaped like a turtle in the middle. It had to be a rock or boulder or some structure Bonnet had made. Would the trees still be standing after all these years? This part of the island looked completely uninhabited, no doubt due to the marshy soil, but could she trust that things had been left undisturbed? Surely, the structure would remain, and that's all that mattered. The M on the map—which probably stood for Melody—marked the spot right before it. And that must be where the treasure was buried.

Moving the boat close to shore, Scott sent Bones onto the land with his lantern, while they followed along in the water.

Soon, the creek made a sharp turn to the right, just like the map indicated.

"Gotta be close now!" Scott said.

"Over here!" Bones's shout echoed like a trumpet through the night sky.

Scott leapt from the boat, pulled it ashore, grabbed some shovels, and yanked Lexie and Ellie from the craft.

"This better be the treasure, missy, or it'll be the last thing you and this brat ever see." His foul breath blew over her as he dragged them toward the light from Bones's lantern.

Lexie shuddered, trying to calm the terror convulsing through her. Ellie began to cry.

"Keep the brat quiet!" Bones yelled over his shoulder as they approached. Then facing forward, he held his lantern high. Light spread over a boulder that really did look like a turtle. Only one tree remained to the right of the rock, but it was a small and green.

Scott shoved them both to the ground. Pain etched up Lexie's back. "Shh, Ellie. Shh. It will be okay." She kissed the little girl's forehead and peered into the surrounding darkness. From what she could tell, the landscape was mostly underbrush, dotted here and there with trees and bushes.

She glanced back toward where they'd left the boat. While the men were distracted with digging, maybe she could make a run for it. But how could she get Ellie in the boat and start the motor with her hands tied? *God?* She gazed into the black sky. Was He even listening?

"This is it!" Scott tossed a shovel to Bones and both men began to dig at the base of the boulder, greed dripping from their grins.

Lexie was most likely going to die right here on the island where her ancestor Bonnet had buried his treasure. She might even be covered by the very dirt upon which his feet had stepped, close to the place he had hidden all his hopes for a future with Melody. Maybe it was fitting. Her thoughts drifted to his last letter.

Bonnet had read the Bible and realized that God had repeatedly been trying to get his attention, to direct and guide him down the right path. He had recounted to Melody all the times God had whispered in his ear to go this way or that, but Bonnet had stubbornly gone his own way. He hadn't blamed God. He hadn't even blamed Blackbeard. Nor did he blame some family curse. Bonnet only blamed himself. And he had knelt before the throne of a mighty, yet loving God, and had begged forgiveness.

The sound of dirt crunching beneath shovel blades joined with the lap of waves and the mournful call of a distant night bird. Ellie, thumb in her mouth, fell limp in Lexie's arms. Good. It was better she was asleep.

As Lexie watched the men dig for the treasure she had once thought would save her life and remove her family's curse, she began to wonder if that was true at all. Would wealth change any of the decisions her family had made, any of the decisions her ancestors had made? Hadn't they all made their own choices to commit crimes, to steal and lie and hurt others in the hope of gaining some form of happiness? Had God whispered to them, leading them to Him, leading them down a better path, but, like Bonnet, they had not listened?

Barret had said God was a gentleman, that He never forced His will on His creation, but rather He loved, wooed, enticed, and tried to lead. It was up to the individual to answer His call, to follow Him and His ways.

There was no curse on her family!

She shook her head as an odd warmth flooded her, despite the chill of the night. Every one of her relatives, starting with Bonnet and Melody, had made their own choices, gone their own way, and had paid the consequences. How sad that must make God. How hard He tried to help His children choose the path of life, only to watch them wallow in the misery and despair of their own choices.

Barret. She blew out a sigh. She'd been cruel to him. All her life she'd been judged based on her family's history of crime, poverty, and imprisonment. Yet wasn't that exactly what she'd done to Barret? Judged him for what his distant relative had done? She needed to apologize.

If she got out of here alive.

Scott's shovel struck something solid, and he let out a whoop.

Oddly, Lexie no longer cared about the treasure. Instead, she bowed her head and prayed. *I'm so sorry for everything, Lord. I've been an idiot. Please forgive me. Please keep talking to me and help me to hear you. I want to follow you from here on out. I give you my life. If I am to die, then please bring me home. If you let me live, I promise to live for you. Oh, and please save Ellie!*

⚓

Barret vacillated between being more terrified than he'd ever been to being more angry than he'd ever been. The four-hour drive to Wilmington passed so slowly it seemed they were circling the globe. Once there, he and Adam stopped at a hardware store for supplies, then drove to one of the marinas on Cape Fear River, where the rented a boat and tossed in the shovels, blankets, first aid kit, and bottles of water they'd purchased. They also had two guns. Just in case. They had no idea what they were walking into or, rather, *sailing* into.

Thank God for Adam. Barret could not have asked for a better friend. Once Barret explained the situation, the man hadn't hesitated to accompany him, hadn't hesitated to agree to not alert his fellow officers. Hadn't hesitated to charge head-first into a situation that could get them both killed.

Now as they cruised Cape Fear in their small boat, Barret started to fear he'd dragged his friend into too much danger. The man had a wife, after all, and a child on the way. They had no idea how many men or weapons these people had. But this was Lexie and Ellie! Barret needed all the help he could get.

He glanced up at the black sky. A cloud drifted over the quarter moon, hiding it momentarily. *Lord, we could use some help here. Please help us rescue Lexie and Ellie. Please. And don't let anyone get hurt.*

Well, maybe the bad guys. He smiled.

Holding a flashlight, he glanced at the map and directed Adam, who handled the motor, up into Brunswick River and then finally Alligator Creek. If they were still here, they should see their lights soon.

A flash appeared in the distance. Barret's nerves stiffened. It had to be them. He glanced over his shoulder at Adam and the policeman's nod told Barret he'd seen it too.

Voices soon rose, riding upon the marshy wind. A shout, followed by laughter.

They came upon another boat hoisted upon the sand.

Switching off his flashlight, Barret leapt from the craft and helped Adam drag it beside the other one. He spotted Lexie's folder of Bonnet's letters lying on the thwarts. He nodded toward Adam, indicating they were in the right place. Should he grab them? No, they would only slow him down. Heart crashing against his ribs, Barret drew his gun, and Adam did the same as they crept toward the light.

The villains came into view. A lantern etched light and shadow across their faces, making them look sinister as they hunched around an old chest. Three yards to their left, Lexie sat on the ground, her hands bound, and Ellie in her lap.

Every ounce of Barret longed to run and take them in his arms, but instead, he and Adam dove behind a bush and surveyed the scene. Both the villains had guns stuffed in their belts. Not good. The last thing Barret wanted was a gun fight that might get Lexie or Ellie hurt.

The largest of the two men took his shovel and slammed it against an old iron lock on the chest. *CLANK*! He did it again. And again. And the third time, the lock fell.

Ellie let out a whimper.

So there *was* treasure, after all. "What is your plan?" he whispered to Adam.

CHAPTER THIRTY-NINE

Whatever was in Bonnet's chest, it must be valuable, for the looks of greed and joy on the creeps' faces said it all. Odd that Lexie suddenly couldn't bring herself to care. Sure, it would be nice to have money for a change, to not worry about bills, but at the moment she just wanted to get out of this alive.

Rustling drew her gaze in the direction of the creek. Leaves parted and Barret emerged from the darkness like a hero-of-old coming to her rescue. She must be dreaming. Rubbing her eyes, she looked at him again. He wore a black t-shirt and jeans and a smile on his face that both confused and delighted her.

She wanted to scream for him to run, to get as far away from there as he could before it was too late! But the scumbags noticed him. Scott had his gun in hand before he even rose to his feet.

"Ah, the professor boyfriend." He chuckled. "Not sure how you found us, but I give you credit."

Drawing his gun, Bones also stood, uttering a foul curse.

Barret lifted both hands. "I don't want any trouble. I'm just here for the girls. Hand them over, and we'll be on our way. There's no need for anyone to get hurt." His voice was calm and commanding, and not a speck of fear tightened his handsome features.

"Barret!" Ellie squirmed to be free of Lexie's grip.

He turned to the little girl and smiled. "Stay there, little one." Then facing the men, he added. "What do you say, gentlemen?"

"Gentlemen!" Bones snorted. "You think we're dumb? You seen our faces. I'm sure you know who we are by now."

Scott peered into the darkness around them, no doubt suddenly realizing Barret may have brought the police.

"I'm alone," Barret said. "Just let the ladies go."

"Keep your gun on him." Scott shoved his weapon into his belt and approached Barret, then patted down his legs and turned him around. He pulled a gun stuffed in the back of Barret's jeans and held it up. "Shame on you, Professor."

"Get over there." Bones gestured with his gun, and Barret inched toward Lexie.

Her heart sank. What was he thinking? Rushing in here without a plan? Facing two crazy armed men with a single gun? Yet she couldn't help but admire his courage *and* she couldn't help but love him for his knight-in-shining-armor attempt to rescue her.

But now they were all going to die.

Bones grabbed a rope to tie Barret up with, but before he could wrap it around his wrists, Barret swung a leg out and knocked him off his feet.

"I'll shoot you where you stand!" Scott shouted.

Lexie held her breath and covered Ellie's eyes as Barret grabbed Bones by the shirt, lifted him from the ground, and then used him as a shield.

A shot fired.

Bones fell limp in Barret's arms, and he tossed the man to the ground.

"Come on!" Grabbing Lexie's hand, he pulled her up and yanked her and Ellie across the clearing, diving into the darkness before Scott could recover from killing his friend and fire again.

Crack! The shot whizzed past Lexie's ear like a mad bee. She ducked, covering Ellie with her arms.

Ellie screamed.

More shots rang behind them.

The scent of Barret's cologne along with his warm breath showered over Lexie as he stopped and knelt beside her. He winced and a slight groan escaped his lips. "Follow me."

At that moment, she'd follow him anywhere.

He hauled Ellie into his arms, took Lexie's hand, and tore across the brush-strewn ground toward the creek. Shots peppered the air behind them.

Who was Scott firing at?

The water came into view, along with two boats, and Barret led her to a thick bush a few yards down shore. "Here, you and Ellie hide until I come get you."

Only then did she see the blood dripping down his arm. "You're hit!"

"Do as I say!"

"Barret!" Ellie screamed. "Don't go."

"I'll be right back. Be a brave pirate now, okay?"

The little girl nodded and stuck her thumb back in her mouth as Lexie drew her close.

Barret's footsteps thundered away. More shouts rang. Shots cracked. Footsteps thudded.

Scott dashed into view toward the boat. Though it was dark, she knew it was him for the sheer size of the shadow.

A gunshot boomed behind him. Wood cracked. Scott tumbled to the ground. The bulk of his body shoved the boat. It released its grip on the sand and began to drift away.

Only then did Lexie realize that Bonnet's letters were lying inside. "Stay here, Ellie. I'll be right back." She set the little girl down and charged toward the boat, still within a few feet of shore. Scott remained unmoving on the ground.

Barret appeared out of the darkness, holding a lantern. "What are you doin—?"

A hand gripped her from behind, tightening around her throat. She gasped for air as the metallic scent of blood stung her nostrils. *Bones.* Something sharp pierced her neck.

"Get in your boat, Professor and sail away, or I'll kill her on the spot."

Barret stared at the man, his expression unreadable. "Aren't you forgetting my friend?"

His friend? Adam. He must mean Adam. That had been the reason for all the shots.

Bones pressed the blade. "Naw. I knocked him out with a rock while he was looking at the treasure." Bones chuckled. "He's dead."

Dead? Lexie wanted to cry. So much sorrow, so much loss! For what? This stupid treasure! It was *all* her fault.

Shock, along with excruciating pain, crossed Barret's expression. Still he remained, shifting his gaze between her and Bones.

"I want my mommy," Ellie whimpered.

Desperate, Lexie struggled to be free. Moisture soaked into her shirt from behind. *Bones' blood?*

A flicker, a spark of hope appeared in Barret's eyes. He glanced back at the drifting boat, farther away now, but still within reach. Oddly, it sat lower in the water. Wait. A gurgling sound trickled over the sand. The boat was sinking. One of the gunshots must have hit it.

Barret saw it too. If those letters got wet, they'd be ruined. They meant everything to him. He could easily save them and leave as Bones had ordered.

Lexie wouldn't blame him, for all the trouble she'd caused.

He swung his gaze back to Bones. "No deal. Release her now, or you'll end up like your friend."

What? Lexie tried to speak, to tell him to leave, to save himself, but no words squeezed past the tight grip Bones had on her throat. Instead, she shook her head, pleading with her eyes for him to do as the man said.

Leaves crunched. Bones stiffened behind her.

Instantly he released her. Breath rushed in and out of her lungs as she backed away, holding her throat.

Adam held a gun to Bones' back.

Barret charged the villain and slugged him in the gut. "That's for threatening a lady and a child."

Lexie could hardly believe her eyes. Was it truly over? Were they finally safe? She blinked. Barret had chosen her over the letters! He'd seen Adam sneaking up behind her. He'd known she would be safe. Yet still he remained. Just in case.

Ellie dashed up to her and Lexie swallowed her up in her arms. "You're safe now, Ellie." She hugged her tight. And before she knew it, Barret's arms wrapped around them both, cocooning them in his warmth and strength.

"You came," was all she managed to say.

Barret brushed hair from her face and gazed down at her. "Of course."

A moan brought Lexie's gaze to Adam. "Are you okay?" Handing Ellie to Barret, she moved to check Adam's wound.

Still holding his gun on Bones, he dabbed the blood matted in his light hair. "I have a pretty thick head." He chuckled. "But, yeah. I'm feeling a little dizzy."

He started to wobble, and Barret set Ellie down and reached toward his friend. "Here, give me that." He took the weapon and gestured for Bones to move next to a still-unconscious Scott.

Adam nodded toward Barret's bleeding arm. "I'm calling for help." Lowering to sit on the ground, he flipped open his phone and called the local police.

While they waited, Barret tied up Scott—who was still alive—and Bones and put gags in their mouths. No need to hear any more of their stupid threats.

Lexie found the first aid kit in their boat and, using her limited knowledge of nursing, did her best to tend to both Barret's and Adam's wounds. She even dressed Scott's injury, a non-lethal hit through his shoulder. His head must have hit the boat pretty hard on his way down for him to be out so long.

During all of this, Ellie refused to release Barret. But Lexie couldn't blame her.

The first hint of dawn peered over the horizon in a line of crimson and apricot, and soon the police arrived. They hauled the villains onto their boat and took everyone's statements. Then as the medical professionals were working on Barret and Adam, Lexie snuck away to see Bonnet's treasure. She surprised herself that she hadn't even thought about it until that moment.

With Ellie in her arms, she approached the open chest and peered inside. Rays of morning sun glinted off the contents, causing her to blink. Gold and silver coins, golden engraved chalices, silverware, pearls, rubies, jeweled necklaces, engraved plates, tapestries…a fortune! A *vast* fortune. She ran her fingers over the chest—the chest that Bonnet had touched, that he'd carried and buried in this spot hundreds of years ago. Tears filled her eyes. Not at the treasure, but at the love he had for Melody…at all the hope he had for their future contained in this chest.

"Pretty! Jewelry!" Ellie pointed and squirmed to get down. Lexie complied and allowed the little girl to pick up a jeweled necklace.

"He must have taken it from Blackbeard." Barret's voice brought her gaze up to see him walking toward her, a bandage wrapped around his arm, his black hair askew, and looking more like a pirate than ever. "Adam told me what was in it." Halting, he stared at the contents. Shock widened his eyes. "Whoa. Yeah, had to be Blackbeard's. I don't think Bonnet ever took such booty himself."

"Booty?" She laughed. "Now you even talk like a pirate."

Ellie smiled up at Barret. "Ye may be gettin' wet!"

They both laughed as the little girl moved a short distance away to play with her necklace.

Shadows circled Barret's eyes and a spot of blood spread on his bandage, but otherwise he looked as handsome as ever. She still could not believe he'd…emotion clouded her vision, and she lowered her chin.

Wind tossed a strand of hair into her face, and she brushed it aside. "You gave up the letters for me."

He looked confused. "Did you think I wouldn't?"

"I guess I did wonder."

"I'm sorry if I ever made you think they were more important than you." He ran a thumb down her jaw and cupped her chin, bringing her gaze back up to his. "You are everything to me, Lexie."

She searched his eyes, finding only love within them. Her own eyes moistened. "I was mean to you, and I'm sorry. I had no right to be mad at you for what your ancestor did."

"It doesn't matter anymore." He drew her close and pressed her head against his chest. "I was so worried, Lexie. I couldn't bear to lose you." His arms, thick and muscled, barricaded her in his love, and she'd never felt safer than she did that moment.

"I hope you never do," she whispered into his shirt, not meaning for him to hear.

Barret pushed her back, smiling. "Did you mean that?"

She was about to answer yes when Ellie pushed between them. "Can we go home now?"

Barret scooped her up in his arms. "That's a great idea. You know, you have been a very brave girl today."

Ellie nodded, her curls bouncing in the breeze. "As brave as a pirate?"

"Braver!" He tapped her on the nose

Lexie stared back at the fortune. "I guess I'm rich."

"Not so fast." Adam limped up to them, a bloody bandage wrapped around his head. "Not according to North Carolina law—some act in 1906 which prohibits anyone who is not authorized from digging up and removing artifacts. I'm sorry, Lexie." He gave her a look of true remorse. "You can't keep any of this."

1 month later

Barret and Lexie stood arm in arm at White Point Gardens in Charleston before the memorial marking the spot where Stede Bonnet was hanged.

She read it out loud.

"𝕹ear this spot in the autumn of 1718
𝕾tede 𝕭onnet, notorious gentleman
𝕻irate and twenty nine of his men
𝕮aptured by 𝕮olonel 𝖂illiam 𝕽hett
𝕸et their just desserts after a trial

And charge, famous in American History
By Chief Justice Nicholas Trott.
Later nineteen of Richard Worley's crew
Captured by Governor Robert Johnson,
Were also found guilty and hanged
All were buried off White Point Gardens
In the marsh beyond low water mark"

They stood silent for a moment. Lexie glanced around the park that looked out upon the entrance to Charleston Harbor. Massive Oak trees, draped in Spanish moss, spread across manicured lawns dotted with various memorials and statues to heroes long since gone. Bonnet's was just a slab of concrete. Even so, she was surprised to find even that. For a pirate.

"Why didn't you bring me here before?" she asked Barret.

He rubbed his chin. "I didn't want to upset you. You were getting so attached to him."

"I was, wasn't I?" She should feel shame, but she didn't. "I still am, I guess."

"He touched me too."

A breeze swept over them, bringing the scent of the sea and freedom.

She glanced over her shoulder. "At least his last view would have been of the sea he loved."

Barret nodded, sorrow in his eyes. "What ever happened to Melody? Did your mother find out?"

"All she discovered was that when Melody's father found out she was pregnant with Bonnet's child, he disowned her and kicked her out of his home."

Barret sighed. "Cruel."

"Apparently, he told everyone in town, and she was shunned and spurned by most of the citizens, which is probably why she was never able to return to the Guard House dungeon to look for the map."

Moments passed. The lap of waves washed over Lexie, bringing with them a deep sense of sorrow for her distant relative, a longing to have helped her. "She ended up moving to Virginia where as far as we know, she lived out her days in poverty and disgrace. She named her son Stede. Did you know that?"

Barret smiled. "I didn't. Fitting." He glanced back at the monument. "Well, I guess only the government is going to benefit from Bonnet's treasure."

Lexie chuckled. "Serves me right, I guess. I always felt like I was chasing an elusive dream."

"But they gave you some money for the find."

"Yes, enough to buy a house for Tracy, Ellie, and me and open up my own women's shelter." Excitement buzzed through Lexie. She'd already found the property and was currently filing paperwork for the required permits. Once they went through, she would set things up and open her doors for any and all homeless and battered women and their children. If she had her way, there would never be another hungry woman or child in this city.

Barret drew her close. "I'm so proud of you, Lexie. You could have done anything with that money, but you choose to help others."

"It's going to be so great, Barret! A fun, happy place with lots of food and comfy beds and a playroom for the kids. And a garden." She smiled. "And I'm going to teach them all about Jesus and tell that though they may not have a good earthly father, they have a heavenly Father who loves them. And if they listen to His voice, He will guide them."

Barret scratched the stubble on his jaw, shaking his head. "It still surprises me to hear you talk like that. But I couldn't be more thrilled." He brought out the cross from beneath his shirt and rubbed it between his thumbs.

Lexie turned toward the sea, drawing in a deep breath of the salty scent. "It was Bonnet who showed me the light. His last words opened my eyes to the truth."

"Amazing that a man who lived three hundred years ago could help save someone today."

She nodded. "I came looking for monetary treasure, but instead I found the greatest treasure of all—a treasure that is timeless, that lasts for all eternity."

They were silent for a moment, both staring at the sea. "But your book, Barret?" She faced him. "The letters are lost. You must be devastated."

He shrugged. "Not really. Seems strange, but… I guess I was seeking after my own treasure in the form of worldly accolades. And I owe you for opening my eyes to what a self-righteous jerk I was. Along with my family."

"You?" She gave him a teasing smile.

He laughed. "Like you, I found a far better treasure." His smile faded as he suddenly seemed nervous. Shifting his stance, he fished for something in his pocket. Before she knew it, he was on his knees before her.

Her heart stopped beating.

"Lexie Cain, my sunshine, will you marry me?" He held out a ring—a simple gold band with a tiny diamond placed in the center.

Her breath escaped her. She didn't know what to say. Everything within her wanted to say Yes, Yes! But… "What about your family. They hate me!"

Barret gave a slanted grin. "My family is not asking you to marry them." He held up the ring for her to take. "They'll come around. We will pray for them."

Taking a moment, Lexie stared over the choppy waters of the bay, relishing in the warm breeze dancing through her hair. God, is this your will? She had decided she would not make any major decisions without consulting her new Father. She waited… waited… and there it was. Not a voice, not a shout, not a vision, but a gentle smile of approval flooding her spirit.

She faced Barret. "Yes! Yes, yes!"

Barret released a sigh of relief as she took the ring.

"Wait." Lexie examined the simple band. "Is this all you can afford?" she teased.

His brows arched. "No doubt if I got anything more expensive, you'd pawn it and give the money to some homeless woman."

She laughed. "It's perfect. I love it." Slipping it on her finger, she fell against him and welcomed his strong embrace. He lowered his lips to hers, and her world once again exploded in an ecstasy that went far beyond the physical, deep into her soul, where she felt an eternal bond develop between them. A bond that could not be broken by trials or age or even death, a bond that held a promise of love, laughter, and children, all gifts from a Creator who loved them—if they would but follow Him.

Withdrawing, she attempted to settle her whirling senses and leaned her head against his chest. Her glance landed once again on Bonnet's memorial. "I hope his last minutes weren't too horrible."

"History tells us is that he said nothing when given a chance, but that he seemed to be muttering as if he were terrified."

"Hmm. I wonder." Though the thought upset her, it didn't seem to fit the man who wrote that final letter to Melody. "I hope I see him again in eternity."

"I'm sure we will." Flinging an arm around her, Barret drew her close and together they walked down the stone path.

"I love you, Lexie Cain."

"I love you too, Professor Pirate. Forever and a day."

Bonnet stood in the wooden cart that had carried him from the dungeon, out the city's gate, and along the outer wall to the marshes of White Point. A crowd of people had followed behind, many of them shouting their support and sympathies. A few cursed. Most he ignored. Someone, perhaps a lady, had pushed a bouquet of flowers into his manacled hands. He gripped them tightly as the preacher began a lengthy prayer.

Above him, a noose hung from the crossbeam of a simple, square-framed wooden gallows. That noose was now placed around his neck and tightened.

He glanced over the scene, seeing everything... but none of it at all. As if he were in a dream, a terrible yet wonderful dream.

A representative of the Admiralty stood at the foot of the gallows carrying a silver oar, a mob stood behind him, murmuring and staring at Bonnet with horror. Over their bonnets and hats, the glistening white foam-capped waves spread across the harbor all the way to the sea. Wind coming off that magnificent sea blew over him, tossing his hair behind him, and filling him with memories of freedom, grand adventures... and overwhelming regrets.

Oddly, Bonnet felt no fear. He had expected to be terrified out of his wits. Instead, his thoughts drifted to the past year and a half of his short life. Memories passed like visions in his mind. His nagging wife, the death of Allamby, his son—the two things that had set him off on his foolish journey. He thought of what a bad pirate captain he'd been and smiled. Then a vision of Blackbeard appeared in all his frightening glory. Bonnet should blame him for his current predicament. The fiend had betrayed him more than once. Yet, in the darkness of the dungeon Bonnet had forgiven his old friend Edward. He had forgiven them all. Even Robert Tucker. He thought of the pardon he'd kept in his pocket and how he should have obeyed the voice of God and gone straight to St. Thomas.

He should have obeyed the voice of God all along.

He sought for Melody and was grateful to not see her face among the crowd. Melody. What would become of her now? He had failed her. He had failed himself.

But he had made peace with God. He had been forgiven and cleansed. In truth, he felt freer now with this noose about his neck than he ever had.

"Lord," he muttered. "Please take care of Melody and my child. Please have mercy."

The priest ended his prayer.

"Do you have any final words?" the official asked Bonnet.

But Bonnet had nothing to say. Not to these people. Instead, he stared out over the water and continued his prayer. "God Almighty, into your hands I place my spirit."

Someone pushed him from behind. His legs flailed, seeking solid ground.

The noose tightened.

He couldn't breathe.

The noise of the crowd faded.

He opened his eyes one last time. A bright light appeared on the horizon, growing larger and larger until it consumed his vision. From within it, a hand reached out to him.

And smiling, Bonnet grabbed it.

Author's Historical Note

It may interest the reader to know that Stede Bonnet was a real pirate. He was born in 1688 on the island of Barbados to Edward and Sarah Bonnet and grew up in a world of wealth and privilege where he received the best gentleman's education. In 1708, with the death of his parents, Bonnet inherited a vast estate of over 400 acres of sugarcane fields, and thus took his place among the Barbados aristocracy.

Bonnet married Mary Allamby in 1709, and with the marriage came additional acreage and fortune. The couple had their first child, a son, Allamby in 1712, but the child did not survive his first year. Though three more children followed, Bonnet never seemed able to overcome the death of his first son. History also informs us that Mary was a nagging wife, and Bonnet was quite unhappy with the union.

It is at this point in time that my novel picks up his story. I made every attempt to relay Bonnet's piratical adventures as accurately as possible, including all his weaknesses, strengths, failures, and successes. His concern for his fellow man and his interest in trading for goods rather than steal them are all sentiments attributed to him by history. He was, indeed, beloved by many of Charles Town's citizens, and he did, in fact, escape in women's attire. Also, the ships that he captured, the battles in which he was defeated, and his association with Blackbeard are all true events which occurred in his life.

Where I strayed from the facts, of course, was in his love affair with Melody, the letters between them, his visit to see her in Charles Town, and all thoughts and feelings Bonnet experienced. It is impossible to know the precise sense of a man from history books, but I did my best to convey Bonnet as he must have been. Did he have a lover and did she live in Charles Town? Did he bury any of his ill-gotten booty? We will never know, but it makes for a wonderful story.

I attempted to portray his trial as accurately as possible by including Bonnet's actual words in his responses to Judge Trott. I also used the judge's own words in his final sentencing of Bonnet. Bonnet's letter to Governor Johnson is a matter of record, and though I only placed a portion of it in this novel, you may visit my website to read it in its entirety.

Yet the real question lies in whether Bonnet repented of his evil deeds and fell on his knees before our merciful Savior. Based on what we read from history, I like to think he did. I pray he did, for during the process of writing this novel, I admit to becoming quite fond of him. Let us all hope to see him one day in eternity. Oh, the tales he will tell!

About the Author

AWARD WINNING AND BEST-SELLING AUTHOR, MARYLU TYNDALL dreamt of pirates and sea-faring adventures during her childhood days on Florida's Coast. With more than twenty-nine books published, she makes no excuses for the deep spiritual themes embedded within her romantic adventures. Her hope is that readers will not only be entertained but will be brought closer to the Creator who loves them beyond measure. In a culture that accepts the occult, wizards, zombies, and vampires without batting an eye, MaryLu hopes to show the awesome present and powerful acts of God in a dying world. A Christy award nominee, MaryLu makes her home with her husband, six children, four grandchildren, and several stray cats on the California coast.

One of the nicest ways to say "thank you" to an author and help them be able to continue writing is to leave a favorable review on Amazon! Goodreads, Barnes and Noble, Kobo, Itunes (And elsewhere, too!) I would appreciate it if you would take a moment to do so. Thanks so much!

Comments? Questions? I love hearing from my readers, so feel free to contact me via my website:

https://www.marylutyndall.com

Or email me at: marylu_tyndall@yahoo.com

Follow me on:

BLOG: http://crossandcutlass.blogspot.com/
PINTEREST: http://www.pinterest.com/mltyndall/
BookBub: https://www.bookbub.com/authors/marylu-tyndall
Instagram: https://www.instagram.com/marylu_tyndall/

To hear news about special prices and new releases sign up for my newsletter on my website Or follow me on Bookbub or Amazon!

https://crossandcutlass.blogspot.com/
https://www.bookbub.com/authors/marylu-tyndall
https://www.amazon.com/MaryLu-Tyndall/e/B002BOG7JG?

Other Books by MaryLu Tyndall

THE REDEMPTION

THE RELIANCE

THE RESTITUTION

THE RANSOM

THE RECKONING

THE RECKLESS

THE FALCON AND THE SPARROW

THE RED SIREN

THE BLUE ENCHANTRESS

THE RAVEN SAINT

SURRENDER THE SEA

SURRENDER THE NIGHT

SURRENDER THE DAWN

FORSAKEN DREAMS

ELUSIVE HOPE

ABANDONED MEMORIES

VEIL OF PEARLS

PEARLS FROM THE SEA DEVOTIONAL

TEARS OF THE SEA

WESTWARD CHRISTMAS BRIDES

WHEN ANGELS CRY

WHEN ANGELS BATTLE

WHEN ANGELS REJOICE

LIBERTY BRIDE

WRITING FROM THE TRENCHES

SHE WALKS IN POWER

SHE WALKS IN LOVE

SHE WALKS IN MAJESTY